THE LAST STRAW

Once again, Denise was totally helpless. And, once again, she was overwhelmed by an intense masochistic pleasure. She felt the wide skirt and petticoating of the maid's uniform being raised, then Helen's hands were yanking down the ultra frilly panties.

'Your efforts at removing my tights were admirable, Denise. But I'm afraid there's still the question of the earlier naughtiness. So, it's going to be two dozen whacks of my favourite ivory-handled hairbrush.'

As this appalling news sunk in, Denise felt Helen's hands pull the frilled edges of the basque tightly between her buttocks, thus exposing the naked skin of her two ample, shapely and soon to be rosy-red buttocks. Denise squealed helplessly into the fat, tight gag and wiggled her lovely, exposed backside with fear.

'You make such a lovely damsel in distress, Denise,' Helen teased, taking up the hairbrush from the dressing table and returning to her prone she-husband. 'But it's no good pretending to be frightened. I know you're loving every minute of this. I know it's what you've always wanted. And now you're going to get it. Day in, day out for the rest of your life, my sweet: total subjugation through permanent feminisation.'

THE LAST STRAW

Christina Shelly

Nexus

This book is a work of fiction.
In real life, make sure you practise safe sex.

Sections of this book have previously appeared in *Tales of the Maid*, published by the Fantasy Fiction Group.

First published in 2001 by
Nexus
Thames Wharf Studios
Rainville Road
London W6 9HA

Copyright © Christina Shelly 2001

The right of Christina Shelly to be identified as the Author of this Work has been asserted by her in accordance with the Copyright, Designs and Patents Act 1988.

www.nexus-books.co.uk

Typeset by TW Typesetting, Plymouth, Devon

Printed and bound by
Clays Ltd, St Ives PLC

ISBN 0 352 33643 9

All characters in this publication are fictitious and any resemblance to real persons, living or dead, is purely coincidental.

This book is sold subject to the condition that it shall not, by way of trade or otherwise, be lent, resold, hired out or otherwise circulated without the publisher's prior written consent in any form of binding or cover other than that in which it is published and without a similar condition including this condition being imposed on the subsequent purchaser.

Part One
The Hidden Self

One

Denis watched Helen, his beautiful, sad-eyed wife prepare for work. Sitting nervously on the edge of the large bed that dominated their bedroom, he beheld her with a mixture of despair and desire. There had been yet another argument, this time during lunch, and the last fifteen minutes had passed in painful silence. The argument had been tediously familiar, tired ground worn down another few inches. An argument about money and work. An argument about him. Weak, pathetic Denis: unemployed for two years now following a nervous breakdown; a pale, frail, vaguely feminine man who, at thirty, was perhaps unemployable; an intense neurotic whose anxieties and fears had left him virtually housebound. Yet even in the closed environment of the house he was useless.

'I can't take much more of this,' Helen said, her first words since the bitter exchange over vegetable soup and French bread.

He nodded weakly, relieved that at least she was talking again. His sad, pale blue eyes met her own dark brown orbs of fierce contempt through the full-length wardrobe mirror she faced while combing her lovely, coal-black hair.

'I know, I'm sorry,' he mumbled.

She sighed wearily. 'You're always sorry. But nothing ever happens. You still just sit there all day, biting your fingernails and doing nothing. No cleaning, no cooking, no effort. Just worry, anxiety, inertia. I can't take it any more. I can't work *and* be the perfect housewife. Particularly with my job. You should understand that by now, Denis. You have to help!'

He nodded again, knowing this would change nothing, knowing this was merely the prelude to another wasted day watching rubbish television and eating junk food. He nodded and felt the stark truth of his utter humiliation before the woman he loved, a humiliation he appeared powerless to overcome. He stared helplessly at Helen and realised he was on the verge of throwing his marriage away. But it seemed he could do nothing: he was frozen by a strange, dark fear and a remorseless self-pity.

Helen, near to tears, threw down the hairbrush and moved to the large mahogany dressing table to fix her make-up. She was dressed in only a white silk bra, matching panties and black, seamed tights. He swallowed hard and tried somewhat hypocritically to resist the inevitable arousal this lovely spectacle inspired. Guilt and desire indulged in a brief tug of war that left guilt rolling in the mud and Denis with a violent erection.

His wife, his wonderful wife, just two weeks past her twenty-fourth birthday. His junior by six years. A tall, slim, athletic brunette with a shapely and carefully trained figure, the highlights of which were a pair of exquisitely ample breasts and the longest, sexiest legs imaginable, legs now wrapped in the scented embrace of the sheer black nylon tights and beautifully accentuated by their impressively straight seams.

He watched hungrily as she crossed her legs impatiently and began applying a little blusher to the golden flesh of her perfect cheeks. His eyes were drawn to the strips of darker nylon that covered her cherry-red toenails. Briefly, he recalled the sensual feel of this second skin against her warm thighs. Nylon on flesh: the interaction of artifice and nature. He also remembered clandestine trips to this room during so many bored, lacklustre afternoons, afternoons in which he had found himself exploring her private drawers, caressing the soft nylons, the electric silks, the tingling satins, to find in the tactile experience of her most intimate garments a substitute for her body, the body denied him for nearly six weeks.

'No work, no sex,' she had said to him, the first sign that his helpless laziness was a real threat to their marriage. A practical response from practical woman from a particularly practical family. And so the terrible tension that had built up between them had been heightened by a deeper, more physical frustration. And his own response had been to withdraw deeper into the inert world of petty neurosis that now so completely dominated his life.

He watched. He could only watch. Watch and remember, watch and indulge an increasingly fetishistic sexuality, a substitute sexuality. Yet he was vaguely aware that in this fetishism there was something more than the recent sting of sexual denial. In some way he felt that fetishism had always been in him, a part of his sexuality, but denied, repressed, sublimated in the joys of a superbly physical partner.

'And it's not just me, Denis,' his wife continued. 'It's Mummy, too.'

Denis felt himself physically shrink at the mention of Helen's mother. Her terrible mother: a beautiful but grimly threatening sword that hung so eagerly over his head. The woman who seemed to have bought shares in their marriage and had tried to manage it ever since they stepped out of the register office. The woman whose considerable personal fortune, inherited from a long-dead, older husband, had purchased the house they lived in and paid the larger bills that Helen's small National Health Service salary could not meet. The woman who had effectively replaced Denis as the breadwinner, who had taken over the role of financial manager with a disturbing enthusiasm, and who made no secret of her contempt for Denis.

'She won't put up with this much longer,' Helen said, tears filling her beautiful eyes. 'You know how she feels about you. You know she wants me to divorce you. Either that or –'

'Or what?' he snapped, gripped by a sudden, rare anger.

Once again he found himself staring at her reflection as she faced his, her eyes glistening with a deep-rooted annoyance, her cherry lips quivering, her lovely face red with shame and bitterness. We are miles apart, he thought, unable to touch, unable to face each other except through the mediation of a mirror.

'Or what?' he repeated.

There was no reply. Helen wiped her eyes and rose from the seat. He stared at her perfect back as she rushed to the wardrobe and pulled out her blue nurse's uniform. Helen Mann, his lovely wife, a senior ward sister. She hurriedly stepped into the uniform, zipping up the back with a single impatient gesture, and then slipped on her sensible black leather shoes. In less than a minute, she had pinned back her thick, black hair, grabbed her overcoat and rushed from the room. As she did so, he pulled himself off the bed and followed her out on to the landing, shouting that same question 'Or what?' over and over. Reaching the bottom of the stairs, she turned to face him, tears pouring down her cheeks.

'I tried, Denis, I really bloody tried with you. But there's nothing I can do now. You've brought this on yourself. You've got nobody else to blame. Remember that!'

With this, she swept her handbag from the hall table and rushed out of the front door, slamming it loudly and leaving him staring into a familiar but now slightly altered abyss.

He descended the stairs wearily, walked into the living room and found himself staring at his pathetic reflection in the blank screen of the television set. He felt tears well up in his own sad, defeated eyes. He tried not to listen to the sound of Helen's car pulling out of the driveway. It was just after 1.30 p.m.: she would be out until at least eleven, maybe later. Until then he had only his dark, oppressive thoughts and the television to keep him company.

He had been active once: active, forceful and ambitious. An executive director, no less. A well-paid, driven individual. A man with a future. A future made brighter by the lovely Helen, whom he had met at a party thrown by an important client nearly three years ago and married six months later. But with money and a future came responsibility, and with responsibility came pressure. And pressure had a tendency to increase. And as it did, his responses became unsound. Never an overtly aggressive man, always uncomfortable with the cheap machismo of office life, he had begun to feel even more uncomfortable wielding a power that seemed to bring so much discomfort to those around him. His job was to make all the difficult decisions and thus all the enemies. The company was under tremendous financial pressure. People were 'let go', lives ruined. And it had been his job to do the ruining. And, eventually, he managed to ruin his own life, collapsing in his office from what the doctor referred to as 'physical and mental exhaustion caused by severe stress.' He had a month off work. A month became two, then three, then six. Then, knowing he could never face the office again, he resigned, determined to find a more meaningful job. But there had never really been any determination. Six months became a year. The world was suddenly a threatening, aggressive, vast place. And he was nothing: a creature who had crawled into its shell with no intention of coming out, who found even a trip to the local supermarket an ordeal of loud voices, angry eyes, pressing bodies; of threat and despair.

At first Helen had been wonderful: caring, sympathetic, a professional helper doing her bit to relieve another's suffering. After the breakdown, she had encouraged him to resign, to seek a new life. She often worked extra hours at the hospital and he had agreed to help out more at home until he found something else, something less stressful. But even her patience had been stretched and eventually snapped by the enthusiasm with which he had rolled up into a ball and blocked out the world. And as her understanding had disintegrated, the presence of Helen's mother became increasingly apparent. Samantha, as beautiful in her way as her daughter, another tall, statuesque brunette, a woman who had never liked Denis. His mental collapse had confirmed all her jibes about his weakness, his inability to cope and, worst of all, his effeminacy.

Now, facing this grim, blank screen, he felt the familiar knot of humiliation as Samantha's acidic comments were recalled. She had even begun to call him 'Denise', to tease him about his 'utter failure as a man', and to suggest the possibility of 'a change of gender'. The last time she had visited, she unleashed a series of brutal remarks about buying him a dress! But Helen had intervened and Samantha retreated. Yet in this humiliation there had been something else, something less unpleasant, something he still refused to think about. But even as he fought this ambivalent emotion, he found himself remembering the lovely Samantha, her long black hair, her body in superb condition for her 44 years. He remembered her in this very room less than a fortnight ago, in a trim blue suit, black sweater, black hose and high heels, her long legs crossed as she reclined in the leather armchair. He remembered trying to avoid staring at her impressive form, particularly her legs and the gleaming patent leather stilettos to which they led.

'A nice pink number, I think,' she had teased, her eyes filled with contempt. 'Yes. Very *you*. Pink with plenty of frills. Short as well, so we can see those shapely legs of yours. White tights for those legs. White tights and red high heels.'

He tried to cast the strange feelings inspired by this memory out of his mind. He walked to the living-room window and stared out at the world he so deeply feared. Almost the first thing he saw was the lovely Wendy – Wendy Parsons, the eighteen-year-old only daughter of Mrs Adele Parsons, their attractive if somewhat haughty next-door neighbour, a cool-eyed widow who had recently arrived in the close after returning from a long period in the United States, and whose contempt for Denis now matched that of Samantha's. Yet Wendy, in her beautiful, fresh, almost naive manner, had only a mildly curious, polite smile for the unfortunate Denis Mann, her gorgeous eyes forgiving, understanding, helplessly girlish. And now, as usual, his eyes drank her up with greedy, gulping looks of desire. She was simply stunning, a tall, athletic blonde brought up since her early teens in America and now with a very American outlook. A champion swimmer, whose firm, subtle body was today encased in a tight black sweater, a very short, pleated tartan skirt, very sheer black tights and a pair of provocatively high-heeled shoes. A young woman returning to her sixth-form college after lunch at home.

He watched as she disappeared out of the close, then found himself staring into the oblivion of his frustrations and inertia. He took up the TV remote control, pointed it at the empty square of green glass and pressed the 'on' button. At the exact moment the ugly face of a well-known comedian filled the screen, the doorbell rang.

He sighed, flicked off the TV and walked sluggishly out into the hallway. The bell rang again, longer, impatiently. He mumbled an angry 'all right, I'm coming'. As he approached the door he could make out the figure of a woman through the frosted glass, a vaguely familiar figure. He opened the door. Before him was Samantha, a dark smile lighting up her beautiful face, a large leather travel bag at her side. He gasped in surprise.

'You look shocked, Denise,' she sneered, strolling past him into the house, a fog of powerful perfume engulfing his reddening face.

Taken off guard, he could only close the door and follow her into the living room, a sense of deep unease spreading over him.

'Well,' she exclaimed, turning to face her son-in-law while placing the large bag on the carpet, 'doing nothing, I see. How unusual.'

'What do you want?' he snapped back, trying to sound contemptuous, but only managing worried and uncertain. Her lovely brown eyes lit up, the cruel smile broadened. He found it difficult to hold her fierce, merciless gaze. 'A little chat to begin with,' she replied.

He was angered by his utter sense of helplessness before this beautiful woman, an anger made worse by the physical attraction that stirred within him every time she appeared.

She lowered herself on to the sofa next to his well-worn armchair, adjusting her short skirt around her knees, her eyes never leaving his. She was dressed in a short, tight but perfectly tailored red suit with a crisp white blouse, plus black hose and heeled shoes. His eyes wandered over this gorgeous display and rested on the shoes, stunning black patent-leather stilettos with five-inch heels, sado-erotic footwear for the dominant female. She crossed her legs, causing the skirt to ride up her marvellous thighs. He swallowed hard, but didn't move an inch. He was a rabbit trapped in the hypnotic powers of this woman's exquisite, sex snake form, a particularly frustrated rabbit.

'Like the shoes?' she teased, stretching out her lovely, nylon-sheathed legs. 'They do great things for my legs. Don't you agree?'

His gulping, high-pitched 'yes' broadened her bitter smile.

'Sit down, Denise. I really do need to talk to you.'

He moved towards the armchair, but she gestured for him to sit by her, on the sofa. He obeyed, never taking his eyes off her legs, riddled with desire and the fear of facing those splendid eyes. Suddenly they were inches apart, her sweet perfume washing over him, the rosy smell of her hair teasing his nostrils. He was overwhelmed by an intense sexual arousal, and no amount of fear or distrust could save him now.

'You know how I feel about you,' she continued. 'And I know how you feel about me. There's no getting away from the fact that we don't get on. But that doesn't change the fact that you're my son-in-law, that you're married to my daughter, and that your current behaviour is making both her and myself very unhappy. You've turned poor Helen's life into a nightmare, Denise. You've ruined her whole existence with your silly anxieties. We've tried to help you, but you seem to be beyond normal help. You just don't seem to be up to the role required of you; you can't behave like a man. So maybe we have to stop treating you like one.'

His eyes finally met hers. 'What on earth do you mean?'

'Look. If it weren't for me, you'd be out on your backside. I pay the mortgage, the bills. I keep you in trousers, trousers I don't think you deserve, or, *more accurately*, feel comfortable with. I've put up with you because Helen says she loves you. Well, now Helen has finally seen sense. This morning she phoned and told me to go ahead with a little plan, a plan we should have implemented ages ago, a plan designed to shake you up a bit, to give you a role that you'll feel more comfortable with, and which will hopefully result in you behaving more like an active human being.'

'Look, never mind the lecture, just tell me the bad news. You want me out. And now Helen's finally had enough and she agrees. OK. I understand. But where can I go, you just –'

'No, no. We don't want you out. We want you *in*. In skirts, to be precise.'

The last sentence took a few seconds to sink in. 'In skirts! What the –'

The slap to his face was hard and fast. Stunned, amazed, he felt a burning spread over his right cheek and tears fill his startled eyes.

'Shut up, Denise!' Samantha snapped. 'I'm talking. You're listening. Do you understand?'

The ironic tone had gone, replaced by a cool, brutal authority. He was speechless, yet outraged, appalled. But still he could only nod, rubbing his cheek, trying not to cry.

'If you can't behave like a man, then it's time you started to behave like the sissy you seem to be, a particularly submissive and extremely girlish type of sissy. Put simply, we've decided to feminise you. A complete transformation. And if you don't agree, then you are indeed welcome to leave. But as you will have nothing except what I've bought for you, including your now redundant underpants, I think this latter option may prove difficult.'

'You can't be serious!' he blubbered, feeling the tears begin to trickle from his eyes and the humiliation burn into him like an inescapable, all consuming fire.

'Of course I am! Deadly serious. I've watched you, Denise. Watched you roll up into a ball of self-pity and surrender to the void of fear and neurosis. And I know what your problem is: you can't stand being a man, you can't live with the pressures that rest so uneasily on most of your sex. Deep down, you want to be a more feminine being. You want to be controlled, dominated, overwhelmed. You want to be a slave, to have all decisions taken for you. And they will be – *completely*. You'll become Helen's personal housemaid and general servant. On the surface utterly unrecognisable as a man, but beneath your panties still biologically male.'

There were no words left to protest with. He suddenly knew he was doomed to whatever fate Samantha had dreamed up for him. To leave, to walk out on Helen and face the real world, with all its awful threats, was too much to ask. His only option was no option at all: tearful acceptance. So he burst into tears.

'You cry very convincingly,' Samantha continued, her voice full of teasing sarcasm. 'Just like a little girl. Can I assume from this typically pathetic outburst that you assent to your new role?'

Amazed at himself, wiping the flood of tears from his burning cheeks, he nodded.

'Right. Let's get on with it. Helen will try to be back by eleven. That gives us eight hours to get you dolled up and the house spotlessly clean. On your feet and follow me.'

He obeyed her without hesitation, amazed by the ease with which he was accepting this bizarre turn of events. Yes, it was all too simple. Secretly, he knew why. Samantha smiled: he could see she was pleased, even surprised, by his speedy capitulation. She grabbed the leather bag and led him out of the lounge, up the stairs and into the main bedroom. He followed her shakily, unable to keep his tear-stained eyes off her shapely, black nylon-sheathed calves and thighs, his sex rock hard and leading him almost as surely as his beautiful mother-in-law to a strange, new life.

Two

Once in the bedroom, Samantha put the bag on the floor and faced him. 'First things first. From now on you call me Mummy. No other form of address will be acceptable. Helen will be addressed *at all times* as either Mistress Helen or Mistress. And you, of course, will be Denise. Understand?'

He nodded, on the surface quite appalled, but deeper down there was something else, a much more ambivalent feeling. Samantha stepped forward and slapped him again.

'When I ask you a question, Denise, I expect an answer! Now, *do you understand?*'

'Yes.'

'Yes *what?*'

'Yes, Mummy,' he mumbled, feeling his face burn the darkest crimson imaginable. He was so embarrassed, so utterly humiliated, yet far too frightened to resist.

She nodded, satisfied. 'Now the names are sorted out, it's time for you to undress.'

His hesitation inspired another hard slap. '*Get on with it!*' Samantha shouted.

So he undressed, struggling out of his jumper, nervously unbuttoning his shirt to reveal his particularly unimpressive chest, peeling off the shirt and placing it, together with the jumper, on the bed.

'And the trousers,' Samantha insisted, '*and* the underpants. *Everything!*'

Her words cut into him. The tears returned. Sobbing helplessly, he unbuckled his belt and unzipped the grey slacks. As they dropped around his ankles, he begged the room to swallow him. But worse was to come: after stepping out of the trousers and feebly removing his socks, he was faced with the appalling prospect of his underpants.

Samantha's beautiful, dark brown eyes bored into him as he fiddled with the elastic waistband.

'*And* the underpants, Denise. *Now!*'

With one swift, desperate tug, he obeyed, pulling the underpants down over his shaking knees and virtually staggering out of them. Then he faced her, hands instinctively covering his genitals, utterly defeated, his face a deep cherry-red. She laughed, her lovely eyes full of sadistic malice. She leaned forward and unzipped the leather bag. From inside, she took a pink toiletries bag. She then ordered him to follow her into the bathroom.

Her heels clicked viciously against the tiled floor of the bathroom, percussive whip cracks that sent new flinches of fear and worry through Denis's exposed body. She placed the bulging toiletries bag in the wash basin situated beneath the mirrored medicine cabinet. From the bag she retrieved a silver razor and a can of shaving cream.

'Luckily, you're not very hairy,' she sneered. 'But even the slightest speck of body hair is unsightly on a young lady.'

She shook the can vigorously. 'Hands behind your back and feet apart,' she snapped, approaching him, the can aimed revolverlike at his chest. 'Don't move an inch.'

He obeyed and cringed as a jet of thick white foam struck his chest and upper stomach. Samantha used her free hand to rub the foam into a thick lather spreading from his neck down to the tips of his pubic hair. Then, to his horror, she proceeded to squirt a fresh dollop over his entire pubic region. Smiling cruelly, she repeated the energetic massage around his genitals, covering his pubic hair and thighs in a thick, white slick of foam. Eyes closed tightly, he fought a losing battle against the inevitable arousal her hands inspired, an arousal which soon resulted in a blatant visual testament.

'Well,' she jeered, 'at least that part of you is working.'

Within a few minutes, she had covered his torso, arms and legs in the foam. He was shrouded in a soft, damp suit of white lather, and, thanks to her teasing application, very excited. Suddenly, all thought of humiliation had disappeared, as had the tears of despair. In their place was desire, desire fuelled by the strangest, darkest thoughts about this beautiful woman. His eyes travelled over the generous curves of her body, paying particular attention to the exquisitely streamlined shape of her breasts as they pressed against the tight material of the jacket and the splendidly erotic lines of her legs sealed in the sensual embrace of sheer black nylon.

Samantha ran the razor across his chest, leaving a trail of pale, perfectly smooth skin. Using the shower to rinse the razor, she set to work with expert precision, quickly removing the hair on his chest and stomach. His arms followed. Then, inevitably, his pubic region. He gasped with a tantalising mixture of fear and excitement as she quickly whipped off the thick, black hair around his genitals and thighs, then stripped the finer, lighter hair from the rest of his legs.

Within thirty minutes of walking into the bathroom, Samantha managed to remove every visible hair on his body, leaving him feeling more naked and vulnerable than at any other point in his adult life. His skin tingled fiercely yet not unpleasantly. It was as if he had been sealed in a stocking of the finest silk imaginable. He looked down at his body and was amazed. What he saw was the body of a baby, a grown mutant baby, a man plunged into a helpless babified state by a beautiful, dominant and utterly merciless woman.

Samantha, this dark angel who had now taken over his life, stood back and admired her handiwork, a satisfied smile on her face. As he studied his smooth, vaguely feminine body, she returned to the washbasin and produced a bar of pink soap.

'Use this to give yourself a thorough wash,' she commanded. 'And use Helen's shampoo to do your hair. You've got fifteen minutes.'

With this sharp command, she walked out of the bathroom. As the sharp click of her heels echoed around him, he walked to the shower. Once satisfied the water was predictably warm, he stepped under the mild, refreshing spray and allowed it to soak his freshly shaven body. The physical experience of warm water on smooth skin was quite startling. It was like feeling for the first time, as if his sense of touch had suddenly been returned to a long denied level of intensity. Initially this was unsettling, but gradually the soft caress of water against his pink, exposed skin became rather pleasant. He found himself soaping his body with a new curiosity, examining each shaven section and pondering how just the removal of a few pieces of hair could make a male body seem so distinctly feminine.

He washed himself thoroughly, as ordered. The scent of the soap was a delicate rose and his body was quickly engulfed in this sweet, girlish aroma, an aroma that remained strong even after he had rinsed himself with an equal precision and set to work washing his thick, blond hair with his wife's shampoo.

By the time Samantha returned, Denise had stepped from the shower and was drying himself. His mother-in-law's entrance was announced by the now familiar click of heels, but as he stood with his back to her on the edge of a cloud of damp steam, he didn't actually see her enter the room.

'Good!' she snapped. 'You're showing a bit of initiative – who would have thought it was possible.'

He turned and a helpless gasp of astonishment escaped his lips, for she had removed the jacket and dress and was now standing before him in a stunning black satin panelled basque, black stockings and high heels, her marvellous figure displayed in all its mature but undeniably shapely glory. Her eyes burned with a black comic cruelty and her wicked smile broadened as his own eyes widened with shock and desire.

'Is there anything wrong, Denise?' she teased. 'I thought I'd slip out of those rather stuffy clothes. I'm sure you don't mind. After all, we're just two girls together.'

He nodded, dumbstruck, his arousal once again embarrassingly obvious. She marched past him to the washbasin and took a tin of talcum powder and a slender bottle of body spray from the toiletries bag. She quickly covered his already scented body in the pungent powder and then added to this a cloud of the powerfully scented feminine spray, concentrating on his armpits, chest and genitals. Soaped, powdered, perfumed, he struggled against the overwhelming odours of femininity and the fierce excitement inspired by the intimate presence of Samantha's luscious, semi-clad form.

She insisted he dry his hair more thoroughly. He obeyed with evident ill temper. When finally satisfied, she led him from the bathroom back to the bedroom. Here, the first thing he noticed was that the leather bag had disappeared and in its place on the bed was a startling array of feminine undergarments, together with a beautiful pink dress. The dress was incredibly intricate. Made from satin, it had a high, white lace-frilled neck, long, lace-frilled sleeves and, around its short hem, layers of thick lace petticoating. A dress for a little girl, a deliberately babyish but also incredibly sexy garment made for only one purpose: his humiliating feminisation.

He found himself staring at the lovely, delicate dress with something approaching desire. Yet not just a desire born out of an attraction to a sexually arousing garment: deep down he knew this was a desire *to wear* the garment, a sudden, shocking need that was quickly cast out of his mind by what remained of his masculine identity, a defence mechanism created by years of careful, but not entirely successful socialisation.

Denise was intensely aware of Samantha watching his reaction to the dress.

'Gorgeous, isn't it?' she said quietly, casually.

'Yes,' he murmured in reply. 'Very.'

'It'll look great on you.'

These words clawed him back from the brink: his eyes widened in humiliated disbelief and he stepped away from the bed.

'There's no point in resisting it, Denise. I know you can't wait to put it on.'

'That's not true!' he exclaimed. 'You know I've got no choice!'

She laughed bitterly, stepped closer to the bed and took up a white pantie-girdle, an ornately decorated, thick elastane panelled undergarment with a very high waist. 'Put this on first – it will cover your so-called manhood.'

His eyes filled with a mixture of anger and uncertainty. His face beetroot red with embarrassment, he took the garment from her and stared at it in total disbelief.

'Come on!' she snapped. 'I haven't got all day – there's work to be done!'

So he stepped into the soft, thick pantie-girdle, pulled it up his smooth legs and over his shapely thighs. After a few minutes of wiggling (which clearly amused Samantha), he managed to pull the undergarment up over his genitals and position its sturdy, rubber-reinforced waist section around his stomach. The girdle was a perfect fit, gripping his waist snugly and completely enveloping his genitals and lower torso in taut, smooth elastane. He stared down at this fetishistic smothering and sighed with defeat, his face coated with a film of humiliation.

'It's you, Denise,' Samantha joked. 'Now stand still while I add the corset.'

He watched with some trepidation as his lovely tormentress took up a black, lace-trimmed garment from the bed and held it before him. It was a mini-corset made from satin and leather, with a series of silver hooks and eyes sewn into its curved back panels. Samantha made him raise his arms above his head and then wrapped the corset around his waist. He gasped as she pulled the two ends together in the middle of his back, forcing the air from his lungs and pushing his already insignificant stomach even further inward. This had the effect of exaggerating the width of his chest and forcing him to stand more upright. Suddenly the lazy slouch which had characterised his helpless submission to fear and anxiety was gone. He stood tall, braced and stiffened, a new 'man'.

'Now that's much better,' Samantha exclaimed. 'A vast improvement in your posture. I should have done this months ago.'

He felt the combined restraining power of the girdle and the corset overwhelm his weak, under-exercised body and tried once again to repress a sense of disturbing excitement. Samantha's accusations spun in his mind as the arousal caused by this restraint increased. Perhaps she's right, he thought.

'I chose the tights especially: the most feminine pair I could find.'

She was holding a pair of white, patterned tights before him now, gossamer thin, yet firm enough to hold an intricate design of beautiful white roses. Tights designed to add to the theme of this dressing, the theme she had teased him with on more than one occasion, and which had been much more than hinted at during the preparations for this transformation: the sissy girl, the ultra-feminine, dainty, yet appallingly sexy adult baby boy-girl; a strange mixture of submissiveness and sweet, helpless femininity.

He took the tights from her. He took them and was immediately returned to those lonely afternoons spent secretly dipping into Helen's clothing drawers, caressing pair after pair of sheer black nylon hose and remembering how wonderful they had felt against her warm, firm, willing skin. A sickening, ecstatic fetishism, a fetishism he thought was rooted in his wife's absence, but now –

'Sit on the bed if you find it difficult. Roll them up and slip in one foot at a time, then draw the tights up your legs. Quickly, Denise – don't just stand there like a half-wit!'

He sat on the bed, feeling the corset and pantie-girdle tighten around his body as his backside sank into the soft mattress and silky sheets, a far from unpleasant sensation. He rolled the delicate legs of the tights into two soft, white nylon bowls and placed a foot in each one. Then he nervously drew the tights over his feet and ankles, one leg at a time. The feel of the sheer, ultra-soft fabric against his freshly shaven skin was almost overwhelming. He fought an audible gasp of pleasure as he guided the hose up over his shins and knees; he was plunged into an erotic realm of feminine softness and beauty and could not believe the intensity of the arousal this film of delicate, gentle nylon inspired. As he drew the tights over his thighs, he felt his sex strain desperately against its pantie-girdle imprisonment. Any doubts he might have had about his reaction to this feminisation disintegrated under the startling pleasure imparted by the heavenly caress of this gorgeous fabric.

'It's rather – nice,' he mumbled.

Samantha laughed. 'Yes, no doubt. But it's rather nice, *what*?'

He looked up at her as he stretched the tights over his upper thighs and pantie- girdled torso. 'It's rather nice, Mummy,' he said hesitantly, yet without resistance, without the embarrassment this word, this confession of utter submission, had previously inspired.

He positioned the tights around his waist and rose from the bed to examine his legs in more detail. The tights were a perfect fit. They also revealed the surprisingly shapely lines of his long legs to perfection.

'Well,' Samantha teased, 'you seem to have a very feminine pair of legs. Most women would envy you.'

He blushed, but, to his amazement, it was more out of pride than embarrassment. He ran his hands over the sheer fabric enveloping his shaven skin. It felt wonderful! There was no escaping this simple fact.

'And I thought this was going to be difficult,' Samantha said, taking a pair of spectacularly frilly lace and silk knickers from the bed. 'But I should have realised, Denise: you're a born she-male. This is *you*, what *you* really are. You've just been waiting for the right person, and it seems *I'm* the right person.'

She handed him the knickers. Without command or instruction, he drew them over his beautifully hosed legs and positioned them around his waist expertly. There followed a moment of exquisite hesitation as Samantha knelt down and took from beneath the bed a pair of gleaming, red patent-leather court shoes with mountainous five-inch heels and a lovely diamond butterfly positioned on each sharply pointed leather toe.

'The pièce de résistance as far as those splendid legs are concerned, I think.'

She placed the shoes at his feet. He stared at them in utter wonderment. How often had he watched Helen slip into heeled shoes and admired the erotically enhancing effect on her own superb legs? And, maybe not so subconsciously, how often had he secretly envied her the pleasure of this enhancement?

He stepped forward and, with a feminine tentativeness, placed his right foot into the corresponding shoe. The second followed quickly. Like everything else Samantha had prepared, the shoes were a perfect fit. He felt exquisitely elevated, made obviously taller, but also more graceful, more of himself and the world, more complete. Yet this was his first time in heels and his untrained balance produced a few precarious wobbles. He gasped, reached out instinctively for support. Samantha grabbed his arms and steadied him.

'Just relax,' she whispered. 'Find your centre of gravity and calm down. Let the shoes become part of you.'

He followed her advice and tried to dispel the natural trepidation the heels produced. It was difficult, but he felt that was part of the pleasure. A look of fearful concentration lighting up his face, he took a tentative step forward. Then another. Then he was walking in the heels, or rather carefully mincing, as the shoes seemed to demand. Samantha watched each step, a smile on her full, red lips, a knowing sparkle in her golden brown eyes. And as he minced before her, he found himself becoming even more aroused by the idea of parading in such a carefully feminised state before this beautiful, dominant woman. Now Denis realised how intensely attracted he was to Samantha, how he had always been attracted to her, even during the darkest moments of mockery and contempt. And with this realisation came a strangely unreal guilt, a feeling of betrayal, an automatic response, a programmed reaction. Yet he felt it wasn't so bad to desire this woman, his mother-in-law, and that this desire was itself part of her plan for him, therefore surely acceptable to his equally beautiful wife!

Once he had demonstrated an ability to walk in the heels, Samantha led him to Helen's dressing table.

He stared at his reflection, especially at his naked, shaven chest and the corset which so effectively imprisoned his stomach.

'First, we'll need to fix your hair,' Samantha said, her voice cooler, more businesslike.

Taking one of Helen's hairbrushes from the table, she worked quickly, with a combination of grace and speed, needing only a few minutes to transform his hair into a carefully shaped ornament of blonde curls that highlighted the naturally feminine curves of his face.

'Not perfect, by any means,' she said, 'but it'll do until we can get you to a good hairdresser.'

He found her self-criticism harsh, and was about to tell her so when she produced a pot of foundation cream and poured a little of the light tan liquid on to her elegant fingers. 'Now, keep very still while I apply this.'

She covered the whole of his face and upper neck in the lightly scented cream, her fingers cool, careful, gentle. He watched the few masculine lines of his facial structure disappear. His face was softened, toned down, made even more effeminate. Soon he could see what she was seeing: the beginnings of a rather pretty girl.

After the foundation cream came the wonderful experience of Samantha applying a blood-red lipstick to his lips. As she guided the soft red tip of the stick over these once embarrassingly feminine lips, her own face was only an inch or so from his. He fought the urge to reach out and touch her.

The lipstick was followed by a peach eyeshadow, black eyebrow and eyelash highlighter and the slightest touch of peach blusher. Then Samantha stood back to study her work and Denis found himself facing someone else: an attractive woman.

Samantha's initial smile of satisfaction seemed to have changed to a smile of surprise. She was taken aback by the success of this crucial part of Denis's feminisation. But not as much as Denis! For him, this lovely creature was a fundamental challenge to his already badly dented sense of masculinity. Suddenly, the thing deep within him, the thing that had always secretly worried and, at some unconscious level, excited him, was fully exposed; the thing that Samantha had seen so clearly in his breakdown and subsequent descent into utter neurotic apathy: the woman in him.

'You look very convincing,' Samantha whispered. 'I'm very impressed. This is far more –'

Her voice trailed off. She told him to get up and come back to the bedside. He carefully raised himself to his high-heeled feet, grabbed one last look at 'his' new face, and then carefully minced over to the bed.

He found it difficult to walk in the heels without swinging his hips. His steps were short, dainty, as Samantha had instructed, but they were also helplessly provocative. At first this made him feel vaguely ridiculous, but then he thought of the pretty face in the mirror, the she-male he had so easily become, and embarrassment faded into a strange pleasure in his own natural femininity.

He stood before his mistress, his mother-in-law, his 'Mummy', his head lowered in a fetching imitation of feminine modesty, his penis straining against the tight layers of nylon, satin and elastane, a rock-hard manifestation of a distinctly ambivalent masculinity.

Samantha took up the splendid pink satin dress. She held it out before him, displaying it, revealing pearl button fastenings that stretched from the bottom of the full skirt right up the very tip of the high, lace befrilled neck. She held the dress out and smiled encouragingly. He swallowed hard, gripped by fear and apprehension, heart pounding, and then stepped into it, willingly plunging himself into the inescapable embrace of true femininity. As Samantha drew the dress over his scented, powdered, corseted body, Denis was truly lost and Denise was most certainly found.

Samantha carefully positioned the dress around his girlish form and began to button up the back. The dress was a perfect fit, its bodice section grasping his already corseted waist snugly and adding another layer of restriction. The layers of petticoating sewn into the skirt made it impossible for him to see either his hosed legs or the high heels.

When the dress was secured, Samantha took a large, lace-trimmed pinafore of white silk from the bed. This she carefully slid over his head and around his waist, tying it in place with a fat bow at the base of his spine. Then she stepped back to take further stock of her creation, her smile now almost envious. Then she was back by the bed, taking up a long length of pink silk ribbon. This she wrapped beneath his long, curled hair and drew up to just above his forehead, securing it with another large bow at the front of his hair.

'Gorgeous,' she whispered, her voice thick with what could only be described as arousal.

She took his hand and led him to the wardrobe mirror, the same mirror that, only a few hours before, his wife had stood before. Now 'he' was presented to himself. Revealed. Denise, in all *her* glory, unveiled to Denis.

He could say nothing, he couldn't even move. His breathing was constricted, his heart hammering with surprise and pride, his hosed legs weak. Before him was a truly beautiful, ultra-feminine girl, a pretty, sexy, baby maid, a sensuous blonde she-male indistinguishable from a real girl. A startling transformation. He was so aroused by the sight that he nearly passed out. Denise. Sweet Denise. So innocent in the intricate pink dress, yet also so erotic. Her long, shapely legs superbly complemented by the lovely patterned tights and dainty high heels, her expertly painted face framed by the pretty pink ribbon, her slender body perfectly enhanced by the tight folds of the wonderful dress.

'I can't believe it,' he mumbled, transfixed by this beautiful image, this feminine creature who had suddenly been revealed to the world.

'No. I've never truly realised just how feminine you are,' Samantha whispered.

Her words echoed in his head. He felt as if every drop of his masculinity had evaporated in the intense heat of a powerfully luminous feminine persona. My self is trickling away, he found himself thinking. But there was no fear, no horror. For this was the loss of a hated self, a despised, weak, helpless, anxious self that had left him a nervous wreck, useless to himself, to his wife, to life. Now, out of the initial inertia of amazement, he felt a new energy begin to flow within him, *her* energy, *her* vitality, the power that he had spent all his masculine energy trying to suppress.

'I feel alive. I feel awake. For the first time in ages.'

'Yes!' she replied. 'That's exactly it. Rebirth. But this is only the beginning, Denise: there's still a great deal of work to be done.'

He turned to her, smiled a sweet, sexy smile and nodded. 'Yes. I understand, Mummy.'

Three

Samantha took his hand and led him from the bedroom. 'We've got six hours. I want this entire place spotless in four. You'll start downstairs and work up. The kitchen, the living room, the dining room. Then upstairs: your bedroom, the spare bedroom, the bathroom, the toilet. That means washing up, polishing, floor cleaning, dusting. An ordeal by fire, Denise.'

He minced on to the landing behind her. This catalogue of chores was frightening, but the thought of sweating over the domestic duties he had so systematically ignored for the last two years while dressed in this highly appropriate baby maid's costume was also intensely exciting.

This new, feminine self appeared distinctly submissive, and it was surely the thought of being *forced* to carry out these tasks by the lovely Samantha, rather than the tasks themselves, that excited him. Indeed, as he somewhat unsteadily followed her down to the kitchen, a wildly delicious sense of absolute subjection washed over him. He was lost in an exquisite ballet of sweetly rustling satin and lace-edged petticoating, each movement emphasised by the tight embrace of the corset and pantie-girdle, by the gentle, yet firm caress of the nylon tights, by the sexy mincing demanded by the heels, and by an all pervasive sense of his own essential femininity.

Once in the kitchen, Samantha turned to him. 'I'm sure you know where all the cleaning implements are, given Helen's unsuccessful efforts to make you look after the house. I'll keep an eye on you, but I expect you to be able to do a satisfactory job without my supervision. I'll inspect each room as you complete it. If I'm not happy, you'll receive a sound spanking. If I have to spank you more than once, there'll be no dinner and, when you've finished, you'll spend the rest of the evening bound, gagged and locked in the spare-room wardrobe.'

Her threats were delivered with a teasing irony, as if she knew he would love to be spanked by her, and even more to be bound and gagged in this exquisite costume by such a beautiful, all powerful woman. Yes, he knew that, never mind how hard he tried and how good a job he did, he would be spanked and, eventually, tied up; and this increased the terrible sense of feminine arousal that was sending quivers of submissive delight through every muscle in his sissified body.

And so, under her initially watchful eye, he began the long list of domestic tasks, starting in the kitchen with the relatively simple problem of the washing-up, then proceeding on to washing and cleaning the cooker, the sink and, finally, the tiled floor.

At first, his long untested domestic abilities resulted in a noisy, clumsy simulation of a serving girl at work, but as he became more accustomed to the subtleties of moving in this lovely excess of ultra-femininity, his actions became more fluid, more graceful. And by the time he bent down to begin cleaning the floor, mop in hand, pink rubber gloves pulled tightly over his hands, he was a rather convincing maidservant.

He worked hard at ensuring each task was performed with maximum efficiency, yet at the same time he was constantly aware of Samantha's watchful eyes and of the need to make every movement sweetly feminine. As he laboured, he delighted in the rustle of the dress, the constrictive embrace of the corset, the slight, feminine walk demanded by the clicking heels and the soft kiss of sheer white nylon against the straining muscles of his silky smooth and very shapely legs.

As he followed the washing of the floor with a careful, systematic polishing, he noticed Samantha leave the room.

Alone, he was tempted to adopt a more masculine manner to speed things up a little, but this practical consideration was considerably outweighed by the pleasure of his new graceful, feminine pace and the erotic possibilities it provided. He was enjoying his femininity too much suddenly to revert to the brutish efforts of a male self from which he felt increasingly alienated.

By the time Samantha returned, he had cleaned the kitchen thoroughly. The room was spotless and Denis, or rather *Denise*, was already quite worn out. Although the pleasure of working in such exquisite attire provided an obvious erotic entertainment, the practical problems of labouring in the clothing had become quite apparent. He was feeling extremely hot and the constrictive nature of the undergarments had begun to make his already laboured breathing difficult. But he stood to a steady, high-heeled attention as Samantha inspected every inch of the kitchen, and he tried not to show any of the weakness that had led to his feminisation.

It was with the strangest sense of disappointment that he received her verdict.

'Perfect,' she purred, facing him with a cool, yet impressed smile. 'I'm quite amazed.'

And so it continued. After the kitchen, the living room. More dusting and polishing, plus the careful tidying and ordering of objects and vacuuming. Then the living room, then the hallway. And not a word of complaint from Samantha – just her slightly surprised smile and maybe a new sense of regard for this sissy she had named Denise. And without the expected words of criticism and the threatened physical result, he began to wonder if the erotic undertone of her original threat was imagined. But then came the stairs, and her inspection of his now quite exhausted efforts to vacuum them clean. On the third step she discovered a tiny piece of cotton thread.

'What's this?' she snapped, holding the microscopic strand before his perfectly made-up but obviously tired face.

'I –'

'You what?'

'I don't know, Mummy.'

She grabbed him by the ear. He squealed and instinctively tried to pull free, but she was already hauling him up the stairs towards the spare room, his feet fighting desperately to keep him upright in the sexy, yet now once again precarious heels.

They rushed into the spare room. It was as it always was: a small single bed on one side, the large, unused spare wardrobe on the other. Yet now there was also a white chair in the centre of the room, and upon it one of Helen's ivory-handled hairbrushes.

Samantha picked up the hairbrush with her free hand and sat down, pulling Denise with her. The poor, now sobbing she-male was hauled over his mother-in-law's long, black-stockinged legs. In an explosion of pink satin he was laid flat on his stomach across her lap, his right arm pulled up painfully behind his back and the dress and petticoats pulled back to reveal his befrilled and very shapely backside. Denise faced the floor, felt the heat of Samantha's body against his, moaned girlishly as Samantha tightened her grip on his arm. He knew she was also excited by this somewhat mock punishment, a punishment that was, in the context of the masochistic heart of his new feminine self, a reward.

Samantha delivered six hard, resounding whacks to his backside. Despite the thick layering of the pantie-girdle and the frilly knickers, the whacks stung terribly and his feminine cries of pain were genuine. And the louder he cried for mercy, the harder the whacks became, as he knew they must, as the rules of this erotic game demanded.

Once soundly spanked, he was pulled to his heeled feet. Tears of pain filled his pretty blue eyes and his pantied buttocks burned fiercely. But this was a burning that soon turned into a far from unpleasant warmth, a warmth that spread across his buttocks and down between his legs, then to his most intimate regions.

'Now, get out there and make sure there isn't another silly error, otherwise it'll be a double dose on your behind and the cupboard.'

Samantha's words were delivered with a splendid authoritarian enthusiasm. She was the perfect dominant mistress. Beholding her tall, perfect form in the ultra-sexy basque, black stockings and splendid high heels, her gorgeous, generous breasts fighting their tight restraint, he could feel only total sexual worship. He nodded politely, whispered a hoarse, 'Yes, Mummy', and returned to his cleaning duties.

The upstairs took maybe two hours. By the time he had finished the final room, the now ominous spare room, he had managed to avoid a second spanking, but he was utterly exhausted. His ankles ached, his back ached, sweat soaked his body beneath the dress (which had now become extremely uncomfortable). He could feel the corset and pantie-girdle bite deep into his boiling skin, and the make-up on his face felt like a slowly baking layer of hot mud.

It was now dark outside. As Samantha inspected his final efforts, he felt his stomach begin to rumble and his balance fail through tiredness. He hadn't eaten since early in the afternoon and in the last eight hours he had been subject to physical and mental pressures not felt for over two years.

Samantha was saying something. She had discovered a spot of dust by one of the legs of the bed. His eyes widened in genuine horror as she marched towards him, her dust-coated finger held out before him accusingly. Suddenly this erotic game was becoming a major effort of will.

'Nearly, but not quite, Denise,' she said, her voice filled more with teasing sarcasm than anger, her dark eyes glowing with sadistic triumph.

He sagged visibly before the evidence of his failing. Yes, he had wanted to suffer her threatened second punishment, but that was before two hours of hard labour in the bedrooms, bathroom and toilet. The whole of the upstairs of the house was now spotless, as clean as it had ever been. And the effort involved had left even his new masochism severely dampened.

'Now, strip off that dress and the petticoating immediately!' she snapped.

He obeyed tiredly, receiving a hard slap to the face for his cumbersome efforts, a slap that left his left cheek stinging and humiliation momentarily replaced with genuine male anger. But in a few awkward seconds, he stood before her in the intricate, restrictive underwear, swaying in the heels, fearfully awaiting the threatened punishment, the dress and petticoats laid out neatly on the bed.

'Stand to attention!' she shouted, slapping his right cheek again. 'I'll be back in a few minutes, and I expect to see you standing exactly as you are now.'

With this she left the room. Exhausted, confused by the new feelings that were flooding over his delicately feminised body, he stood tall and rigid in his sexy underwear and heels, awaiting Samantha's return with a tortuous mixture of fear and desire.

Samantha returned only a few moments later carrying a small pile of underwear and a roll of silver bondage tape. She placed these items on the bed, and took a slender white nylon stocking from the pile.

'Put your arms behind your back, with your wrists crossed.'

He obeyed and his wrists were quickly and tightly tied behind his back with the stocking. Another stocking was used to secure his elbows, a particularly painful binding which forced his chest to stick out provocatively. Thus secured, Samantha told him to open his painted mouth as wide as he could manage, took a pair of white panties from the pile and then held them teasingly before his fascinated she-male eyes.

'These are Helen's,' Samantha informed him, 'from the dirty washing basket. Something to remind you of her.'

Then she forced the soiled panties deep into his mouth and made him close it tightly shut. She tore a strip of thick bondage tape from the roll and, with a beautiful, teasing smile, pressed it tightly over his curving, feminine lips.

Helen's most intimate scents filled his mouth; the sense of humiliation was absolute: feminised, bound and pantie-gagged; at the mercy of this beautiful, wicked woman, whose dark eyes were now filled with the fire of a most perverse passion.

Samantha moved closer, grabbed him by his girdled waist and pulled him back towards the chair. She sat down, taking up the hairbrush as she did so, and then, with frightening ease, stretched him over her warm, sensual lap. She administered twelve hard, stinging slaps to his backside. He squealed uselessly into the gag as the pain shot through his most tender regions. The well-gagged squeals became increasingly high-pitched and girlish, and by stroke number ten his heeled feet were wiggling with a distinctly feminine desperation and his cries were little more than baby-girl sobs of outrage and extreme discomfort. It was almost as if Samantha was beating the last vestiges of masculinity from his psyche.

Huge tears trickled down his red face as, following this stern punishment, he was pulled back to his feet. Tottering dangerously, he was led to the wardrobe. Samantha threw open the doors and forced him inside. He moaned pathetically but did not resist as he was plunged into total darkness. He felt more stocking bonds being applied at his hosed ankles and knees. He sensed another stocking being tied to the one binding his wrists. Then his arms were being pulled up behind his back, forcing his head and chest forward and bending his body into an 'r' shape. It soon became apparent that Samantha had attached a second stocking to his wrists and then secured the free end to the hanging bar which crossed the interior of the wardrobe. This had caused his backside to jut out helplessly and left him balancing painfully on the beautiful red heels.

'I suggest you try to keep as still as possible,' Samantha teased. 'If you lose your balance, I'll have a lot of explaining to do.'

The doors were closed and locked. He was left in an awful, total blackness, the only sounds the pathetic, feminine whimpers that managed to escape his tightly gagged mouth.

In the darkness he was pure sensation. Isolated from sound and vision, he was nothing but physical feeling and need. The feeling of red-hot buttocks, of the heat of the beating and its familiar journey down into his genitals, of the soft, mouth-filling pantie gag and its intimately sweet taste mingled with the smell of sweat rising from his own tired body. The feeling of helplessness: bound so tightly, so inescapably, sadistically positioned in such a way that even the slightest movement would tighten his bonds and force his arms even further upward. A feeling of anxiety came with the knowledge that his exhausted body could at any moment just give up and collapse. And, of course, with this came the feeling of desire, a dark revelling in this tortuous and inescapable imprisonment, in this total subjugation at the hands of the beautiful Samantha. Pain and a strange, fierce pleasure.

His imprisonment felt eternal and by the time Samantha eventually opened the doors, he was numb with pain and hunger. Yet the strongest feeling was still desire. His erection now appeared permanent, his sense of feminine submissiveness at its boiling height. As she released him from the cupboard, he squealed thankfully into the gag and wiggled his pantie-girdled buttocks in sweet, girlish gratitude.

Samantha untied his feet and knees after releasing his arms from the bar and then carefully helped him out of the wardrobe. With his arms still tightly bound behind him and the gag still firmly sealed in place, he appeared the perfect damsel in distress. And he was, despite the obvious discomfort of the punishment, clearly enjoying every moment.

'You're beginning to stink quite badly,' she scolded. 'Very unladylike. When I've untied you, I want you to strip and follow me to the bathroom. However, under no circumstances remove the gag – unless you want to go back into the wardrobe.'

He stood as still as his tiredness and hunger would allow while she freed his arms and legs. Then, his mouth still taped firmly shut, he removed the layers of feminine underclothing, gasping into the gag with relief as each section of boiling skin was exposed to the relatively cool air of the room.

In a matter of a few minutes he was naked, his continuing excitement obvious, and following Samantha to the bathroom.

His eyes feasted on her beautiful rear during the few seconds it took to get to the bathroom. Such a splendid, perfectly formed backside, so superbly complemented by the tight, elegantly shaped basque. Such a marvellous pair of legs, long, exquisitely curved, and so effectively displayed by the sheer black nylon stockings, their long seams dead straight, running in lines of erotic longitude down to her gleaming high heels.

In the bathroom, the tape was torn painfully free of his mouth and the pantie gag removed. He was then put under a steaming shower and told to wash himself thoroughly with scented soap while Samantha changed.

Once washed, he stepped from the shower, grabbed a towel and began to dry himself. Samantha returned as he was finishing his hair, now dressed once again in the smart, sexy business suit.

Without a word, she took him by the hand and led him back to the main bedroom. Here a whole new collection of delightfully feminine clothing was laid out on the bed, clothing of an even more intricate nature than his previous costume.

'You'll have to look your best for Helen, Denise. She deserves it.'

So another wondrous, highly exciting dressing began. First, a black, satin-panelled basque, frilled with thick red lace and decorated with a pattern of red silk flowers. A perfect fit, of course, that constricted his smooth torso wonderfully. The basque was fitted with long, black elastane suspenders which announced the beautifully seamed black nylon stockings Samantha then presented to him. Following her previous instruction, he carefully rolled each stocking up into a ball and slipped it over the relevant leg. The stockings were much finer than the tights, and the sensation they produced against his hairless legs was even more exciting.

To Samantha's obvious delight, he had very little difficulty attaching the stockings to the suspenders (memories of undressing the lovely Helen in happier, sexier times were still strong in his mind). Over the stockings went a pair of black, ultra frilly, silk knickers. A new, thicker mini-corset of black leather was added to his already restrained waist. Then, a gleaming pair of black patent-leather stilettos were produced, shoes with incredible six-inch heels. As Samantha helped Denise into them, the most exquisite mixture of pleasure and trepidation washed over him, a mixture that produced a charming look of girlish apprehension in his beautiful blue eyes. But, having spent a day in high heels, he found walking in these new shoes a relatively straightforward process.

He returned to the dressing table to have his hair expertly restyled and bound with a beautiful white silk ribbon, which was tied in the fattest, sweetest bow imaginable. The careful making up was repeated, but now the lipstick was a bloody cherry-red and the eyeshadow a light blue. Also, his chewed fingernails were carefully covered with long false nails and then expertly painted so that they matched exactly his glistening lips. Once again, he found himself marvelling at this new self and helplessly squirming with pleasure in his lovely feminine undies.

Samantha, satisfied he was suitably painted and combed, applied more powerful scents and sprays to his neck, underarms and chest and added two lovely, clip-on diamond stud earrings to his girlish ears. She then helped him up from the dressing table and led him back to the bed. Here he beheld the final item in this second glorious feminisation. Held aloft by a grinning Samantha was a second maid's dress, but this one was of the most expensive and sheerest black silk, its neck, sleeves and hem beautifully trimmed with French lace, its long sleeves puffed, its skirt extra short and fitted with a deep white sea of frou-frou petticoating.

With Samantha's assistance, he stepped into the heavenly, unbelievably soft and forgiving dress. Like the sister dress, it had a pearl button-up back and was a perfect, snugly tight fit. The petticoating, however, was far more elaborate and bellowed out beneath him like a sudden, frozen explosion of lace snow.

Placed before the long, elegant mirror, he was revealed as a supreme fantasy. A stunning blonde, she-male maid, her long, shapely legs sheathed in the finest black silk, her slender waist covered in the figure-hugging dress, her pretty blue eyes filled with an amazed desire, her blood-red lips curved into a sexy, yet modest smile, her gorgeous hair tied in place with the lovely, dainty ribbon.

Satisfied that her work was complete, Samantha led Denise out of the room, back down the stairs and into the living room. The digital clock on the video recorder read 10.55 p.m.: Helen would be home any minute.

'I think we've got a little time to put the finishing touches to Helen's surprise,' Samantha said.

Denise nodded prettily, never taking her splendid blue eyes off the gorgeous dominatrix.

'A truly effective and submissive maidservant must be able to curtsy before her mistress.'

Under Samantha's instructions, Denise began to attempt a suitably servile curtsy. He took up the hems of the thick petticoating and the heavenly dress to reveal his sexy, elegantly patterned stocking tops, then performed a sweet, delicate and very deep curtsy. Unfortunately the high heels quickly got the better of him and he very nearly lost his balance. Samantha quickly helped him to find a suitable centre of gravity. And after three or four attempts, Denise was performing exquisitely precise and delightfully girlish curtsies.

Then there was a truly heart-stopping sound: a key being turned in the front door – the return of Helen.

Denise's eyes filled with a mixture of nervous fear and secret pleasure. He stared helplessly at Samantha. His mother-in-law smiled reassuringly and told him to stay calm, to let the feminine take control, to surrender herself completely to the powerful force that had been awakened within him.

The door opened, Helen entered the foyer, the door closed. She was hanging her coat in the hall and sighing wearily. Denise's heart was pounding, he was a doe-eyed fawn captured by a beautiful black cat, he was a sweet, helpless she-male about to be revealed to the love of *her* life.

Helen walked into the living room. The first person her eyes fell upon was Samantha.

'Mummy,' she said, surprised, her eyes already turning to Denise, 'what are you –'

Helen beheld Denis and her mouth dropped open in amazement, her eyes widened in utter astonishment, she almost staggered under the weight of the shock. Denise, his heart in his mouth, his black-stockinged legs shaking with a particularly feminine fear, executed a perfect and utterly submissive curtsy, uttering the word 'Mistress' proudly as he did so.

'Meet Denise,' Samantha announced, 'your new maid and general she-male slave.'

Poor Helen, her eyes never leaving Denise, quickly sat down before she fell over.

'I can't believe – you – you actually did it. Good lord. It's amazing – really amazing! He's so convincing!'

The words, fractured, disconnected, revealed the simple truth of Samantha's genius and the true feminine nature of Denise, the startling creature Denis had now become.

'I never really thought you'd go this far,' she continued. 'I'm lost for words.'

A furious pride gripped Denise. Samantha smiled broadly.

'He's perfect,' *her* mother-in-law explained. 'His movements, his mannerisms, his instincts. I knew it all along. And he loves it, Helen. Just look at him – he's as horny as a bitch on heat. It turns him on. And it's not just the outfit. He's deeply masochistic. He wants to be controlled, feminised, utterly dominated. And now he's yours. He'll clean, cook, wash and serve in *any* way you want. He'll do anything you want, Helen. *Anything.*'

Helen looked at Denise with something approaching genuine elation. A gorgeous smile suddenly filled her lovely face, a smile that broadened as Samantha described the endless possibilities opened up by this spectacular transformation.

Then Helen stood up, walking towards Denise, her eyes burning into her new slave, her body suddenly firm, upright, completely under control. She faced her slave. She slipped a hand under Denise's chin, tilted her head up carefully, examining, feasting her eyes on this beautiful she-male who had once been her husband.

'Anything?' she whispered. 'You'll do anything for me?'

Denise could only confess the truth with a nervous smile, 'Yes, Mistress. *Anything*.'

Samantha then announced it was time for her to leave. Denise watched in amazed silence as Helen said goodbye, embracing her mother, tears in her eyes, pure gratitude in her voice.

'I can't thank you enough, mummy. I never thought this day would come.'

Samantha smiled modestly. 'We've still got a way to go. I'll be back tomorrow. It'll be interesting to see the results of your first day together. I've bought her a couple of uniforms and accessories, but you'll need more – as we've discussed. Remember, this is only the beginning. Katherine and the Last Straw Society will want her ready to begin work in six months. She'll spend the next week here. Then, we'll move on to the House.'

They embraced again – a long, loving hug of joy.

As her mother left, Samantha's strange words teasing Denise's she-male imagination, Helen turned towards her new slave and with a wicked smile, purred, 'Well then, Denise, let's see what you're made of.'

Four

Perhaps she – for pretty Denise can now only be 'she' – had been asleep for just a few, blissfully painless moments. But maybe Denise had merely fainted, overcome by the sea of sweat and discomfort she had spent so many hours enduring. Yet now it was daylight: the dawn sun was bleeding through the curtains into the spare room. It was daylight and there were sounds, the sounds that had awoken her. Yes, the door was being unlocked! She squealed into the fat gag and fought her tight, cruel bonds, begging for release.

Then the door was opened and an electric light filled the room. Then a cold, ironic laugh – Helen's laugh. Denise squealed again and tried to look up from the bed, but the hog-tie made it very difficult to see much beyond the frilled edge of the quilt. Yet she could imagine the sight that had moved Helen to laughter: Denise dressed in one of her wife's more outrageous baby-doll nightgowns, a pink see-through affair with layers of deep lace frills; Denise with her hands and feet bound with black stockings and pulled tightly together by a black leather belt, a thick strip of silver masking tape covering her mouth, her cherry-red, bulging cheeks betraying the pair of soiled black nylon tights Helen had used to firmly gag her new slave some eight hours before. Denise, then, in tight and very humiliating bondage.

Helen's hosed legs entered Denise's field of vision. Denise squealed louder and struggled with a girlish desperation against the taut, unyielding bonds.

'My, my, you are a sight, Denise! A quite delicious sight!'

Helen knelt down by the bed, her beautiful face inches from Denise, and she tickled her beautiful, distressed she-husband under her cherry-red chin. 'I hope you slept well, petal. Sorry for nodding off like that. I *was* coming back to untie you, but I'm afraid you wore me out – I was asleep as soon as my head touched the pillow!'

Denise snorted angrily. Helen laughed at this useless display of contempt.

'That,' she snapped, 'will cost you a very sound spanking.'

Denise immediately fell silent. Her buttocks still burned from the numerous spankings inflicted during their 'love' making the night before, spankings which, despite their fury, had left the she-male with an erection that now appeared permanent.

'But perhaps you'd enjoy the spanking. So maybe I'll just have to think up something a little less to your perverse tastes.' Helen stood up. 'Perhaps I should leave you here for another hour, while I have breakfast. Maybe you'll have calmed down by then.'

Denise shook her head with a panic-stricken desperation. The resulting cruel laughter brought more terror, but then Helen began to untie the bonds. Denise signalled her gratitude with more little girl squeals and a few helplessly sexy wriggles.

'Calm down!' Helen snapped, stroking Denise's pert backside threateningly. 'There's no point in struggling: I can do whatever I want. And you know it.'

It took a few frustrating minutes to untie the tight knots that held the belt in place, but it was eventually removed and Denise, with a one-girl chorus of pained moans, was able to straighten her tormented body. It was a much easier matter to remove the stockings binding her arms and legs, but when ordered to rise from the bed, it quickly became clear that Denise would require a little time to unlock limbs stiff from a protracted bondage ordeal.

Helen helped the shaken she-pet to her feet. Tears of pain began to well up in her face as the life flooded back into her tormented body. A brief flicker of concern passed over Helen's face, but it quickly passed: in five minutes, Denise was upright, her breathing heavy but regular through the gag and her complexion changing from deep red to a more healthy pink.

'I want you to go to the bathroom,' Helen ordered, satisfied there was no permanent damage. 'You will shower, shave your body thoroughly and then apply the powders and perfumes provided. Then report back to me in my bedroom, so I can dress you. After lunch, we'll go into town. We need to get rid of all your useless male clothes. You'll also need a suitable hairdo. I'll arrange an appointment while you shower. Mummy will be coming to dinner tonight, and I want to make sure you're fully prepared for her visit. Do you understand?'

Denise was both amazed and horrified by her wife's announcement. The thought of being taken out of the house dressed as a woman was utterly terrifying. Yet behind this terror there was a powerful arousal inspired by the thought of Samantha: just the mention of her name was enough to create a deep excitement, an excitement that was becoming all too apparent via the unsightly bulge which was now poking through her sweet baby-doll nightgown.

Helen could not resist mocking Denise's helpless masochistic desire, a desire made even more amusing by the fact that, before securing her she-husband the night before, she had forced a sheer white nylon stocking over Denise's sex and then tied it tightly in place with a pink ribbon. The sight of Denise in a nightie, her hair still held in place by a thick white ribbon, and her now rigid sex sheathed in a pretty white stocking, was enough to raise a particularly wide and cruel smile.

'Do you understand, Denise?' she repeated with a somewhat false anger.

Denise, blushing furiously, made a brief, sweet curtsy before her wife-mistress.

'Good. Now put on your shoes and get on with it.'

Denise, still a little shaky, climbed into the gleaming black high heels from the night before. After a few seconds recalling the fine art of feminine balance, she minced sexily from the room, her prissy yet graceful steps indicating that she had remembered to ensure every delicate, feminine movement was made to please her mistress.

Once in the bathroom, Denise quickly undressed and set about removing the gag, which had tormented her for the past eight hours. Peeling the thick tape from her lips was a particularly uncomfortable process, but the eagerness to free her mouth was far greater than the fear of a little pain. She pulled Helen's now soaking tights from her mouth with a loud gasp of relief, then dashed to the sink and took a long drink of water. Her thirst quenched, she cleaned her teeth, then gathered up the nightie and placed it in the dirty washing basket before turning on the shower and gratefully submerging herself beneath a powerful jet of hot, steaming water.

As the aching slowly faded from her body, Denise found herself recalling the events of the previous day with a mixture of amazement and pleasure. Suddenly, Denis was no more: the tedious, neurotic life of male self-pity was over. A new self was being forged in soft feminine clothing, a pretty, submissive she-male. Suddenly, her wife was happy, energetic and, in her now marvellously dominant way, loving. How easily Helen had taken to her role as mistress; nearly as easily as she, sweet Denise, had taken to the role of transvestite slave.

As she applied scented soap to her still smooth body, she recalled Helen's speedy transformation into a steely-eyed dominatrix. The damp mist filling the shower seemed to part like psychic curtains and then Denise was back in the living room ten hours before.

As soon as Samantha left, Denise presented herself as demurely and sweetly as possible and awaited her instructions. Helen was still a little taken aback by the authenticity of Denise's transformation, but she seemed determined to take control.

'You make a very beautiful woman,' she said.

Denise blushed and smiled helplessly. 'Thank you, Mistress.'

'But there's a difference between making and being. Do you understand? You can indicate assent by a short curtsy.'

Denise curtsied in reply, bringing a smile to Helen's lovely face.

'Good. But you'll talk only when I give you permission. For talking without permission, you'll spend the rest of the night after the meal gagged. Now, you can prepare my supper.'

Denise curtsied once again and minced into the kitchen, her high heels clicking loudly on the kitchen tiles, her backside wriggling brazenly through the gleaming, tight black satin of the lovely uniform.

Fifteen minutes later, Denise served Helen from a tray containing a plate of scrambled eggs and toast, plus a cup of tea. As Denise placed the tray on her mistress's lap, Helen curtly ordered her slave to keep her knees together and her lovely hosed legs as straight as possible when bending forward. Denise obeyed, carefully adjusting her position, and revelling in this ritual of enforced femininity.

Once Helen was served and satisfied, Denise was allowed to bring her own supper from the kitchen, moving between the living room and the kitchen in a sexy symphony of rustling stockings, petticoats and satin, all accompanied by the percussive clicking of the high heels.

Eventually, she stood before Helen, the tray held before her.

'Kneel.'

Denise found herself, much to Helen's amusement, struggling to kneel in the precariously high heels with a fully laden tray in her hands. By the time she finally managed to lower herself, she was sweating with effort, her ankles aching terribly, the corset biting deep into her sides.

'Place the tray on the floor.'

Again, Denise obeyed without question, her stockinged legs now forced tightly together, her shapely ankles touching.

'Take up the plate and eat. I want to see careful, suitably feminine gestures and petite portions. Remember, you're a pretty she-male now, and you must act and think like one at all times.'

Denise obeyed, performing a delicate ritual of consumption for her mistress, who watched every move carefully while consuming her own meal.

As Denise ate, her eyes wandered over Helen's tight blue and white uniform and gorgeous, black-hosed legs. When they had first met, Denise had confessed her secret fetish for women in uniform. Memories of watching *Carry On Nurse* as a child had haunted her sexual imagination throughout her teens and early adulthood. She still found one scene, in which an extremely pretty nurse was stripped, bound and gagged, intensely erotic. She had managed to tape the film during the early days of her 'illness', and had subsequently spent many lonely, desperate hours watching it repeatedly. Now, as she knelt before her exquisite wife in this intricately feminised state, she saw this was simply a fantasy of identification. Her desire then (and now) was to be that lovely helpless nurse struggling in all her bound splendour.

The outcome of this sweet reminiscence was, of course, an even more furious erection. By the time she finished the meal, she was in a state of intense arousal, her eyes following Helen's shapely, nylon-sheathed thighs up to the edge of her uniform dress, the she-male's mind filled with dreams of the perverse pleasures that lay ahead.

'I think it's time we went upstairs,' Helen then announced. 'Put the dishes in the sink – you can wash them in the morning.'

As gracefully as possible, Denise rose to her high-heeled feet, took up the trays and carefully carried them to the kitchen. When she returned, she found Helen standing, her lovely eyes watching every comely, feminine movement of her new she-husband. It was obvious she was enjoying every second of Denise's sissy subjugation.

'Follow me upstairs,' she ordered.

Denise followed her as she had followed her gorgeous mother-in-law earlier, a feeling of ecstatic anticipation coursing through her perfumed, delicately clothed form, hoping that two years of frustration and emptiness were about to be spectacularly cast aside. She was filled with a lovely, girlish mixture of fear and desire: she was a virgin she-male about to be taken by her stunning, loving mistress.

As they climbed the stairs, her wide eyes were helplessly drawn to the straight, teasing seams of Helen's tights and to the wondrous promise of her wife's graceful, erotic stride. Then they were in the bedroom facing each other, Denise's heart pounding furiously. She could hardly breathe. It was like the first time they had made love. Helen had taken her then, taken control, dominated, as always whenever they made love. Denise had been a real virgin, her wife a much more experienced woman. It had been their greatest moment together. Until –

'Remove my uniform and put it on the dresser chair,' she ordered, turning her back on Denise to allow easy access to the zip that traversed the curving line of her perfect spine.

Hands shaking, breathing heavy, Denise obeyed, pulling the zip fastener down her wife-mistress's back and revealing a flawless ocean of tanned skin dissected horizontally by the slender white strap of her bra, then the sheer, dark fabric of her tights and the shaded white of her panties.

Denise carefully eased the uniform dress over her wife-mistress's broad but shapely shoulders and gently pulled it over her gorgeous body until it was gathered around her hosed ankles. Helen then casually stepped out of the uniform to reveal her splendid form in all its glory, a divine vision of pure womanhood that forced Denise's already furiously excited sex to climb another inch up her basque-imprisoned stomach.

As ordered, Denise hung the uniform over the leather-backed chair by the dressing table and then minced back to her mistress. Helen stepped out of her shoes and sat down on the bed, crossing her shapely legs as she did so.

'Now take my tights off. And be careful: if you ladder them, I'll spank you until your backside catches fire.'

She uncrossed her lovely legs and stretched them out before her she-husband. Instinctively, and with surprising ease, Denise found herself kneeling before Helen and very carefully slipping her hands under the waistline of the tights. She then gently pulled them over Helen's lovely hips, slipped them gingerly under her splendid backside (which, in a brief gesture of co-operation, Helen raised slightly) and began to guide them fearfully down her beautiful thighs. Beads of sweat trickled from Denise's forehead and into her lovely, blue eyes. It was as if she were a bomb disposal expert involved in a life or death struggle with a particularly suspect device.

Soon she had the tights over Helen's ankles and gently pulled them free of her feet. Her bare, tanned legs were presented to Denise, the limbs of a perfectly sculpted classical goddess, and the tights were now in the she-male's sweat-soaked hands, their scented, warm softness a startling manifestation of Helen's physical beauty.

'Give me the tights,' Helen ordered.

Denise obeyed and watched helplessly as Helen carefully examined the tights, smiled and rolled them into a surprisingly compact ball, the exterior of which was their damp gusset section.

'Now open your mouth as wide as possible.'

No sooner did she obey than her stunning wife-mistress forced the tights deep into her mouth. Yet again, she was to be gagged with Helen's most intimate underwear, yet again Helen's sweet bodily odours filled Denise's mouth.

'Close your mouth over the tights, lips together.'

Denise just about managed this and the effort made the fat hose-gag even more uncomfortable. Yet her discomfort was, of course, utterly irrelevant. She could only try to hold back the signs of her obvious pain and watch with widening baby girl's eyes as Helen took a familiar roll of bondage tape from the bedside table, tore a long strip from it and then sealed her soft, girlish lips shut, winding the tape around the back of *her* head and once more over the lips in one tough, determined gesture. Her cheeks bulged like a beautiful trumpet player's, her eyes widened even further with feminine fear, and a helpless, high-pitched squeal of protest managed, somehow, to escape the gag.

Helen, in only a white bra and matching panties, then rose to her feet and pulled Denise to her high-heeled feet with surprising ease. She then virtually dragged her she-husband to the dressing table, took a pair of stockings from a drawer and used them to tie Denise's wrists and elbows tightly behind her back. Denise was then forced back to the bed in a succession of desperately dainty, high-heeled minces and thrown face down over the soft, white silk-sheeted mattress. Helen then took two pillows from the top of the bed and slid them under Denise's stomach, forcing her befrilled, petticoated buttocks up into the air. What felt like a third stocking was then used to secure her dangling ankles.

Once again, Denise was totally helpless. And, once again, she was overwhelmed by an intense masochistic pleasure. She felt the wide skirt and petticoating of the maid's uniform being raised, then Helen's hands were yanking down the ultra-frilly panties.

'Your efforts at removing my tights were admirable, Denise. But I'm afraid there's still the question of the earlier naughtiness with that wilful little girl's mouth of yours. So, it's going to be two dozen whacks of my favourite ivory-handled hairbrush.'

As this appalling news sunk in, Denise felt Helen's hands pull the frilled edges of the basque tightly between her buttocks, thus exposing the naked skin of her two ample, shapely and soon to be rosy-red buttocks. Denise squealed helplessly into the fat, tight gag and wiggled her lovely, exposed backside with fear.

'You make such a lovely damsel in distress, Denise,' Helen teased, taking up the hairbrush from the dressing table and slowly returning to her prone she-husband. 'But it's no good pretending to be frightened. I know you're loving every minute of this. I know this is what you've always wanted. And now you're going to get it. Day in, day out for the rest of your life, my sweet: total subjugation through permanent feminisation.'

The first whack sent a bolt of pure pain shooting through her body. A hard, cruel strike – much harder than

Samantha's almost playful slaps earlier. She wanted to scream, but her cry of protest was easily reduced by the pungent black nylon ball filling her mouth to a muffled, feminine squeal of severe discomfort. After four whacks, the tears were welling up in her big blue eyes. Her girlish wiggles were futile, yet they were also quite genuine efforts to escape the extremely unpleasant blows, and her sexy, pert behind was already turning a deep red.

And so it went on, a true ordeal that left tears pouring from her eyes and her body ridden by a series of girlish spasms of supreme distress.

By the time Helen completed the punishment, poor Denise was reduced to a pretty bundle of pure pain. However, by the time her ankles were untied and her underwear straightened, the fire burning in her tender flesh was already transforming into that very different kind of heat experienced during the punishments delivered by Samantha, a heat that quickly spread between her legs and up into her stiff sex.

Denise was then pulled back on to her high-heeled feet and Helen wiped the tears from her eyes with a scented handkerchief.

'Let that be a warning to you, my naughty pet: I'm not to be ignored.'

Denise nodded warily, trying to hide the fact that the severe spanking was now having a most agreeable after-effect, an effect heightened considerably as Helen proceeded to release her slave's arms and commanded her to undress.

'I want you to strip completely, Denise. And I want it done in a suitably feminine manner.'

Helen helped Denise unbutton the beautiful maid's dress then watched as the lovely she-male stepped out of it and placed it carefully on the bed. The dress was followed by the ultra-frilly knickers and the wonderfully high heels. After these gorgeous items came the fine, sexy stockings, eased down her perfect, silky legs and over her girlish feet via a series of sweet, feminine movements. She then carefully folded the stockings and placed them on top of the dress. The corset followed, relief filling her pretty blue eyes as she temporarily escaped its tight embrace. She then managed to unzip the lovely basque and add it to the pile of dainty feminine attire on the bed.

Now Denise was naked, her sex rigid, her arms at her side, her furious desire a halo of fire surrounding her smooth, helplessly feminine she-male form.

Helen, her eyes taking in every inch of her she-husband's nakedness, her smile broadening, picked up the clothing from the bed and placed it on the dresser.

'Lie on your back on the bed, arms above your head, legs together.'

Denise obeyed, the cool silk sheets caressing her boiling buttocks and sending a shiver of pleasure through her body. Helen then climbed on top of her, straddling her like a horse and binding her wrists together with another stocking. She used yet another to tie her wrists to the headrest. She then swivelled round on Denise's silky smooth chest and repeated the process with her she-husband's slender, feminine ankles, leaving her tightly secured and utterly helpless: bound, gagged, stretched tight on this rack of love.

Helen then resumed her original position facing Denise, her legs stretched wide just below her slave's stiff sex. Before Denise's amazed, wildly excited eyes, Helen then teasingly unclipped her bra and let it casually fall away to reveal her splendid breasts. Denise squealed hungrily into her inescapable hose gag as Helen began to caress her breasts and tease her helpless she-husband.

'You'd love to have these in your mouth, wouldn't you?'

Denise nodded furiously.

'Well, that's rather difficult at the moment. You'll just have to make do with my tights. Are you enjoying your gag?'

Denise again found herself nodding, her eyes nearly popping out of her carefully feminised head.

'Yes, of course you are. You're loving it all. Being bound, gagged, dressed up. Being my sweet little pet, my she-male, my slave. You even enjoyed the spanking. Well there'll be plenty more spankings and I'm sure I can find loads of amusing little items to gag you with in the dirty washing basket. I'm sure mummy has plenty of pretty mouth stoppers as well. And then there's the girls at work – an endless supply of soiled panties and tights to keep you quiet.'

Sex sweat soaked her body, moans of helpless ascent to Helen's teasing suggestions forced their way through the thick bondage tape.

'And your clothes? Yes, you really love your lovely, sexy girl's outfits. And that's all you'll have to wear from now on. From tomorrow, you will be kept permanently as Denise. There'll be a little explaining to do: I intend to make sure everybody knows the truth. There'll be no silly tales about a visiting friend or a husband who walked out on me. Everybody will be told that you've decided to become a girl. Denis is now Denise. I want everyone in the whole world to know my husband is a beautiful transvestite.'

Her teasing words drove poor Denise mad, but there was no escape in the brutal relief of orgasm. Helen appeared determined to have her moment of supreme triumph and control, a moment that culminated in a violent tossing aside of the bra, a removal of her now very wet panties and a violent ripping free of Denise's tape gag. This was followed by the speedy removal of the soaking tights from her she-husband's bulging mouth before she climbed on to Denise's smooth, sweat-soaked chest, spread her legs wide and carefully lowered herself on to her she-husband's face.

'I think you know what to do, Denise. And, remember, this is the only exercise that sluttish little tongue of yours is likely to get for a while.'

And so Denise obeyed, using her tongue to pleasure Helen, slipping it into her wife-mistress's soaking sex and carefully bringing her to a loud, angry orgasm within a few heated minutes. But once was nowhere near enough: over the next hour, Denise was forced to pleasure her wife orally at least ten times, her own desires drowned in a sea of pungent female sex juice. This oral pleasuring was mixed with more hard, enthusiastic spankings, which only served to arouse the masochistic she-male even more intensely. And once Helen's sex was adequately pleasured, she demanded that her backside receive 'a good tongue cleaning', a demand poor Denise met without question, demonstrating her love and subservience through this most demeaning of acts.

Eventually, Helen collapsed at her she-husband's side, her heart pounding, her eyes lit by a glowing fire of satisfied desire. Between gasping breaths she announced this was easily the most pleasure Denise had ever given her, and she made it clear that this level of performance would now be required at all times.

After a pause, Helen rose from the bed and walked somewhat unsteadily to the wardrobe. She returned with a lovely pink baby-doll nightdress, a delicately teasing affair that she had not worn for many lonely, sad months. She placed it at the foot of the bed, then took a white stocking and a length of pink ribbon from the dressing table. Then she began lovingly to caress Denise's semi-flaccid sex back to a suitably impressive state of arousal.

'Of course, you want to come, my little baby girl. But what you want and what a naughty she-male needs are two very different things.'

Helen climbed back on to the bed. Denise was now fully, angrily erect, and she offered no protest as her wife-mistress proceeded to replace the hose and tape gag. Helen then returned her attentions to Denise's furiously excited sex. Gripping the stiff, red shaft with one hand, she took the soft, very sheer white nylon stocking and carefully slid it over Denise's engorged member, inspiring babyish, tightly gagged squeals of helpless pleasure. And once the stocking was pulled taut over Denise's rigid sex and inflamed balls, it was a simple matter to secure it tightly in place with the ribbon.

'There,' she whispered, 'all ready for bed.'

Helen untied Denise and pulled the pretty she-male to her now very weary feet. Denise was then ordered back into the high heels and told to stand to attention.

'Hands above your head.'

She did as Helen ordered. The lovely pink night dress was then quickly lowered over her arms and body. Yet again, it was a perfect fit.

'Shopping for you will be easy,' Helen teased, admiring the baby doll and the lovely sissy it contained.

Denise blushed and fought a moan of masochistic pleasure, her mouth taped tightly shut, the tights a pungent, soaking ball held firmly in her she-male mouth, her sex secured in a lovely prison of soft white nylon, her shapely, ultra-feminine legs so sexily displayed by the gleaming high heels. The baby doll added a wondrous, befrilled and beautifully fitting final touch of girlish innocence to this spectacle of transvestite servitude.

'I could eat you whole, my pretty pet,' Helen whispered, taking two of the black stockings from the bed and rebinding Denise's arms tightly behind her back at the wrists and elbows. 'But I definitely think it's time you were put to bed.'

Helen then led her somewhat unsteady she-husband from the room, down the landing and back into the spare room. Here, Denise was ordered out of the heels and placed face down on the small, single bed. Her ankles were retied with another stocking and then, in a moment of inspired cruelty, Helen decided that a few minutes of 'body discipline' would be amusing. So, using an old belt, she tied poor Denise's shapely ankles and wrists together in a tight and extremely uncomfortable hog-tie. Denise squealed painfully as she was bent into a taut 'U' shape. Helen laughed and told her to be quiet or she'd be left like this all night.

'I'm going to shower and change for bed,' she said. 'I'll pop back in a little while and release the belt. I expect to find you suitably demure when I return.'

But she didn't return. After closing the curtains and turning out the lights, she patted Denise on her shapely, befrilled backside and left the room, locking the door behind her. Then poor Denise was alone: bound, gagged, unable to move an inch, a lovely she-male damsel in distress forced to spend a particularly uncomfortable and frustrating night in a state of severe restraint, her only company the intimate taste of her wife's most personal regions soaking through the soft, sexy tights into her mouth.

And now, as she recalled her night of discomfort in the shower so many hours later, she couldn't deny the pleasure the memories brought her, a pleasure which ensured her sex was still standing to a firm, unyielding attention as the gentle water tickled and caressed, and which inspired more erotic thoughts about her distinctly feminine future.

Five

After the shower, Denise minced back into the bedroom and stood to attention before her gorgeous wife-mistress. She was naked except for the high heels, her hands submissively at her side, her body carefully reshaven, powdered and perfumed, her hair combed into a feminine sculpture of lovely blonde locks.

'You're learning very quickly,' Helen said. 'But that doesn't really surprise me: you're merely following your natural feminine instincts.'

Denise performed a small, sweet curtsy to express her agreement and Helen smiled broadly.

'As you can see,' she continued, gesturing towards the bed, 'while you were in the bathroom, I gave some thought to what you're going to wear today.'

On the bed was a collection of beautiful feminine attire, all of which clearly belonged to Helen. Denise minced forward to examine the clothing, her sex already beginning to display signs of a deeper interest. Neatly laid out on the bed were a white silk blouse, a silver grey miniskirt, a matching jacket, a familiar white pantie-girdle, the mini-corset from the night before, a pair of silver-grey tights and a pair of white cotton panties frilled with the obligatory white lace.

'I thought the simple, sexy look for a Saturday afternoon's shopping.'

Denise nodded, now fully aroused.

'Take off your shoes and get dressed. Start with the pantie-girdle and the corset. And remember: I want to see feminine care and gentleness, yet also precision.'

Denise curtsied her understanding. She picked up the girdle and carefully stepped into it. The foundation garment's tight, all encompassing caress still excited her: the sense of soft but inescapable constriction was utterly delightful, and Denise sighed with pleasure.

The mini-corset was already clipped shut and reduced to a much tighter fit. She hauled it over her girdled hips with a sharp intake of breath and manoeuvred it into position around her waist.

'I've tightened the corset by two inches,' Helen said. 'There are three more inches of reduction left. I expect you to be able to bear the maximum reduction by the end of next week: a slender waist is essential for a sissy.'

With the corset so restrictive, donning the tights was an uncomfortable but still very sensual experience. She was forced to sit on the bed to guide the sheer nylon hose over her long, smooth legs. The feel of the cool, soft nylon against her freshly shaven legs was wonderful, and all thoughts of the restraining corset faded as she pulled the tights over her knees, up over her thighs and then, after standing, positioned them around her waist. The feel of sheer nylon and the superb visual enhancement of her already shapely legs were easily the most erotic facets of her cross-dressing experience so far. It was the tights that made her *feel* physically feminine.

After the tights, she slipped the elegant blouse over her bare shoulders and gasped with pleasure as the soft, gentle breeze of silk brushed against her shaven chest and arms. She fumbled slightly with the pearl buttons, but eventually secured them right up to the very high neck. And it was only as she reached the last button that she noticed the two strands of matching silk ribbon that hung from each side of the neck of the blouse. Helen then stepped forward and tied these strands in a large, perfectly feminine bow.

Then Helen watched as Denise gracefully slipped into the pretty, lace-frilled panties and smiled her approval. 'Simply gorgeous,' she teased. 'Now the skirt.'

Denise took up the skirt and stepped into it. She drew it over her hosed legs, her fingers brushing against soft, electric nylon as she did so, and positioned it around her waist, carefully tucking the blouse into the skirt.

The skirt was very short, barely covering her upper thighs. It made her feel intensely vulnerable (and thus terribly sexy!). Helen then told her to step back into the high heels. Denise obeyed and found herself tottering girlishly in a skirt that left very little to the imagination, facing her beautiful wife-mistress in a state of utter feminine subjugation and intense excitement.

'Excellent,' Helen whispered to herself, helping her she-male slave into the matching jacket.

Denise was then led to the dressing table. The tights rustled sexily against her shapely thighs and the skirt swayed teasingly against her backside as she minced forward. She was lowered on to the dresser chair and, once again, found herself facing a strange, half-recognised reflection. But this recognition was quickly lost in a layer of expensive and expertly applied make-up. Foundation cream, silver eyeshadow, a thick, cherry-red lipstick were the ingredients of this stage of the transformation. Then Helen undertook a careful restyling of Denise's hair into a more 'fifties' style and added clip-on stud earrings to her slave's petite ears. And, as if this wasn't enough, Denise was then fitted with long, dark false eyelashes and, to her amazement, a set of lipstick-matching cherry-red nails.

'Perfect,' Helen announced, as Denise beheld her reflection with a sense of thrilling unease.

'This is really incredible,' her wife-mistress continued. 'Your bone structure, your lips, even your ears. I can't imagine why I never noticed it before, why it took Mummy to bring it to my attention. You really are quite beautiful, Denise.'

Denise could only agree, marvelling again at her fully feminised reflection and realising that she would never return to the lie that was Denis: this was the person – the identity – she had always secretly craved.

Helen turned Denise to face her. The lovely she-male sat straight-backed, her hosed legs tightly together, her elegant hands resting in her lap.

'Stand up.'

Denise obeyed, feeling an intoxicating sense of feminine poise as she carefully balanced herself on the gleaming high heels.

'You've a very firm centre of gravity. That's very important in these shoes. But your steps are still too long – there's still the sense you're about to break out into a manly stride. That must go. And the best way to get rid of it is to hobble you while you're in the house. I'll use a stocking for now, but we'll have to get something more appropriate later on.'

Denise watched, still enthralled by the perfection of her feminisation, as her gorgeous wife-mistress took one of the black stockings used to tie her earlier and bound her nylon-sheathed ankles together, leaving only three or four inches slack between her legs to enable the smallest, daintiest of steps.

On Helen's command, Denise attempted to walk forward. The best she could manage was a delicate mini-mince, a series of baby girl steps that created a constant and quite helpless wiggle of her hips and backside, and which brought peels of cruel laughter from Helen.

'Wonderful!' she taunted. 'Now you look more like a true she-pet. And that's how I want you to walk *all* the time, with or without heels, until it becomes natural.'

Denise curtsied her acceptance. Helen smiled triumphantly. 'Arms at your side!' she continued, 'hands out at a ninety-degree angle to those fabulous legs. Think baby-doll, think sissy boy in panties.'

Denise thought all these things and more. She walked around her beautiful wife-mistress filled with an overwhelming pride, the same pride she had felt when Samantha praised her.

'Now,' Helen said, 'I want you to go downstairs and prepare a light lunch. A soup, some bread, et cetera. I'll shower and get dressed. When we've eaten, you'll help me get your old male clothes together.'

Denise wiggle-minced from the room in a state of ecstasy. Every movement in the gorgeous, sexy clothes filled her with a helpless pleasure. She was being totally overwhelmed by femininity and she loved every pretty, sexy second of it.

Negotiating the stairs proved somewhat testing with the stocking hobble. The descent took nearly five painful minutes, but she eventually managed to make her dainty way down the stairway, through the living room and into the kitchen. And once in the kitchen, she prepared two cans of tomato soup and two thick slices of buttered, wholemeal bread, a lovely she-male domestic going about her maid's tasks.

She made a point of warming the soup as slowly as possible, trying to time her presentation of the meal with Helen's appearance. Her efforts were amply rewarded: as she laid a bowl of the steaming soup on the dining table, the living-room door opened and Helen entered. Denise turned and curtsied deeply before her mistress, feeling the skimpy little skirt rise up her long, silver-grey nylon-sheathed thighs to reveal a teasing glimpse of lace-frilled panties. As she curtsied, her eyes never left Helen's beautiful form; for Helen was wearing a tight black sweater, a short red tartan miniskirt, very sheer black tights and high heels. She had also bound her gorgeous hair into a very prim and stern bun held in place with a lovely pearl hair grip. She looked stunning, a spectacularly dark contrast to Denise's shimmering blonde.

They ate at the table in relative silence, Helen watching Denise's careful, ultra-feminine gestures and giving the odd whisper of advice.

After lunch, Helen led Denise back to the bedroom, forcing her lovely she-husband to mince desperately in the stocking hobble and heels with a succession of playfully sadistic 'hurry ups' and light slaps on her shapely, wiggling backside.

In the bedroom, Denise was ordered to remove every item of Denis's clothing from the wardrobe and drawers. The clothing was loaded into two large suitcases, and in half an hour, an entire wardrobe of predictably drab male clothing was sorted and packed, a previous life wiped out in a ballet of dainty wiggles and pantie-revealing bends as Denise moved gracefully between the wardrobe and the cases, a process supervised by Helen, who sat cross-legged on the bed, her own tartan miniskirt hitched up statuesque, black-hosed legs to reveal a teasing hint of her underwear.

Denise then carried the cases to the car with some difficulty. Walking out into the broad daylight in her lovely attire was a shocking, yet also exciting experience. Suddenly there was the immediate reality of the world beyond the house, the world that Denis had avoided so carefully for two years. The sense of utter exposure was both terrifying and deeply arousing. As she struggled towards the car in the sexy miniskirt, her ankles so clearly hobbled, her backside wiggling helplessly, she had the most intense sense yet of her utter feminine subjugation and its inescapable, permanent nature. She could feel a million eyes bore into her sexy form and hear an even greater number of amazed gasps. But there was no one in the street – Denise's debut was witnessed only by Helen.

Helen opened the boot of the car. The cases were placed inside, then the boot was slammed and locked. Helen guided Denise to the passenger door. Before she opened the door, Helen knelt down and untied the stocking hobble. Then Denise was quickly placed in the front passenger seat and told to secure her seat belt. As she climbed into the seat, the grey skirt rose up her lovely hosed legs to reveal the full glory of her sexy, lace-frilled white panties. Denise blushed furiously, fought to straighten her slight skirt, and then, following a struggle caused by the long, cherry-red nails, secured the seat belt across her expertly feminised upper body.

Denise sat in thrilled silence as Helen locked the front door of the house and then climbed into the car beside her.

'I managed to get an appointment with Anita while you were in the shower,' Helen said, 'but it's not until after four. So we've got the whole afternoon to get rid of the clothes. I've told Anita all about your decision to become a she-male, so there'll be no misunderstandings. She was fascinated, of course, but more than willing to fit you in.'

Denise fought a look of fear and embarrassment as Helen started the car.

Six

Soon the car was heading into the heart of the city. Denise faced straight ahead, terrified of looking at the streets that passed and the vehicles moving in the opposite direction. She was overwhelmed by a hypersensitivity to herself and the busy, noisy world around her, a hypersensitivity bordering on panic. It was as if a veil of male misunderstanding had been removed from the world and she was confronting reality for the first time. But at the heart of this enlightenment was fear, a fear rooted in her old self – the fear of discovery. She was terrified of being exposed, revealed; of being identified as a lovely she-male by the crowds of men and women who now surrounded her, of suffering an appalling exposure, a humiliation far beyond anything Samantha and Helen could conceive.

Then the car had stopped. They were outside a small, slightly rundown shop on a quiet side street.

'We're here,' said Helen, turning to Denise. ' Get out and unload the cases.'

The fear and panic increased. Her heart felt like a balloon about to burst. Her lovely she-male mouth parted to voice terror, even a refusal to move. But then Helen was angrily releasing her she-husband's seat belt and whispering fiercely into her ear.

'Pull yourself together, you silly little girl! If you don't do what I tell you immediately, I'll throw you out and leave you. You can go and be a man somewhere else. Here, with me, you're a girl, the girl you were always meant to be. It's your choice.'

These cruel words had an immediate effect. Despite her panic, Denise opened the car door and gingerly stepped out into the street, revealing her long, grey-hosed legs to two passing men and immediately inspiring a rowdy chorus of wolf whistles. Then she was standing in the middle of the street: unrecognisable as a man, no longer a man. A beautiful, sexy woman.

Denise tottered to the rear of the car, her heels striking the pavement with loud percussive clicks that seemed to announce the truth of her new identity to the world. She pulled the cases from the boot and struggled forward behind Helen as they entered the shop.

The shop was empty except for a very pretty teenage girl standing by a long counter. She greeted the two lovely women with a beautiful smile.

'May I help you, ladies?'

She was no more than eighteen, a beautiful, brown-eyed brunette, with long, thick hair and the body of an angel, a body displayed perfectly by a short pinafore-style black dress, a white sweater, black tights and modest black court shoes.

'Yes,' Helen replied. 'My husband's had enough of these clothes, so we'd like to donate them. There's quite a lot, and, as you can see, he, or rather she, won't be needing them again any more.'

It was this last brutal sentence, delivered with a nod towards Denise, that told the terrible truth. The girl's eyes turned towards Dense and widened in amazement.

'You mean, this is your –'

'Was,' Helen interrupted. 'I prefer to see him as her now, more of a wife really.'

The girl drank up every inch of Denise with her big brown eyes. Denise blushed furiously and stared down at her delicately hosed and high-heeled feet, a feeling of complete humiliation tormenting every thought and gesture.

The girl smiled, then laughed loudly. 'He's a transvestite!'

'Yes,' Helen replied, joining in the laughter. 'Most definitely.'

'But he's so –'

'So real? Yes, I was surprised as well. But at least we've found one thing she's good at.'

Trying to control her amusement, the girl told Denise to place the cases on the counter. This she managed to do, but only by making a number of rather rough male gestures as she levered the cases up with her nylon-sheathed knees.

Helen sighed angrily. 'Please, Denise, grace, ease, *ultra-femininity*.'

The girl laughed again and Denise tried desperately to hide a rising tide of distinctly male anger.

'We still have a way to go with her, but with a little perseverance and a very firm hand, I'm sure she'll soon be a perfect sissy. However, I really do think she needs to learn that public displays of her bad old ways are totally unacceptable.'

'Absolutely!' the girl replied, her lovely smile and gorgeous eyes filled with cruel amusement.

'Do you have somewhere private where we can teach Denise the error of her ways?'

Poor Denise could hardly believe her pretty little ears, and was horrified when the girl took Helen to the back of the shop and they disappeared together through a curtained doorway. Pearls of laughter followed, then the curtain was pushed aside and Helen ordered Denise to join them.

Denise minced forward to the doorway. She was then led by Helen into a large storeroom filled with an amazing variety of cast-off clothing, all of it female. The beautiful teenage girl stood in the centre of the room by a tall wooden chair, a table-tennis bat in one hand, a large rubber ball in the other. A look of sheer sadistic glee filled her lovely face.

'Mary thinks a sound spanking is in order, Denise, and I agree,' Helen announced, grabbing the she-male's arms and forcing them behind her back.

Before she could protest, her wrists were tied tightly together with a length of silk ribbon. A second ribbon was used to secure her dainty, hosed ankles. Then she was made to hop over to the chair, a feat accompanied by the whip crack of female laughter. As she fought to maintain her balance, Mary quickly gagged her with the rubber ball. Helen then tied the ball in place with a white nylon stocking.

Once secured, Denise was hauled over the hard wooden chair. Hands unseen hitched up her skirt and her pantied behind was carefully positioned for the punishment.

'Mary suggested twelve of the best, Denise, and I think it's only fitting that she gets the pleasure of administering your punishment.'

The bat struck poor Denise's helpless bottom with a force that was both shocking and painful. Denise squealed angrily into the ball gag as the second and third blows quickly followed. Tears quickly welled up in her pretty blue eyes and a hand suddenly pressed hard into her back, holding her firmly in place as the spanking seemed to increase in ferocity. Humiliation, pain and anger merged into a futile outrage: there was nothing the lovely she-male could do but accept her punishment.

'She squeals like a little baby!' Mary exclaimed. 'Perhaps you should put her in nappies rather than skirts. If you do, I'd love to babysit.'

'Good idea!' Helen replied, her own voice tinged with excitement.

Then it was over. As tears streamed down her face, her tender, pert buttocks once again on fire, Denise was pulled back to her feet. She expected to be untied, but instead Helen took Mary aside and made sure Denise could hear every word of the conversation that followed.

'It's just after one, now. I need to get some things in town. I was planning to take Denise with me, but it might be quicker if I left her with you and came back about quarter to four. I'm sure you can find somewhere quiet to put her.'

Mary smiled and nodded eagerly. 'Oh, I'd love to look after her! Take as long as you want.'

Helen thanked Mary, kissed poor Denise playfully on a red, gag-inflated cheek and left through the curtained doorway.

Denise stared fearfully at her new mistress, her poor bottom stinging terribly. She was amazed Helen had changed the plan so quickly and left her in the hands of this complete stranger. Unless this was all part of the plan!

Mary smiled thoughtfully at Denise. 'You really are a very sexy little thing. How on earth did you ever pass as a man?'

Denise's eyes widened as Mary moved towards her and she instinctively shuffled back towards the chair.

'Stand still!' Mary snapped, grabbing Denise by the shoulder. 'If you're going to be a girl, then you need to learn self-control and correct posture. The best place for this is the basement. I'll untie your ankles, otherwise you'll have to hop down a flight of very steep stairs.'

Denise's ankles were duly untied and then Mary led her to a large trap door by the curtained doorway. As Mary bent down to raise it, Denise was treated to a vision of her pinafore dress riding up very shapely thighs to reveal dark stocking tops and red garters. The pain of the spanking was slowly being cured by the medicine of an unmistakably male desire!

Mary pulled the trap door open to reveal a dimly lit wooden stairway disappearing into a murky half-light. She then positioned herself behind Denise and helped the tottering she-male climb down on to the first step.

They descended into a large, cool, concrete chamber filled with huge linen baskets. The plastered walls had been painted a bright white. A weak, electric light revealed a small door at the far end of the chamber which could only be reached by following a slender corridor between the baskets. Mary guided Denise through this corridor, the she-male's heels echoing loudly against the concrete, her steps still short and delicate, her breathing heavy through the rubber-ball gag.

When they reached the door, Mary opened it with a key taken from a pocket in her dress. She entered the room beyond it and flicked on a light that revealed row upon row of dresses hanging from racks built into three walls. On the floor beneath the dresses were hundreds of pairs of shoes, and in wooden boxes in the middle of the room were what appeared to be countless pairs of panties, bras, girdles – all kinds of lingerie. One particularly large box was filled with nothing but tights, another with stockings.

Denise was led into this strange room and made to stand by one of the racks. She found her pretty eyes wandering helplessly over the vast variety of clothing. Yet despite this variety, there was an almost obsessive order. She also noticed that the clothes were spotless, some even appeared brand new.

While Denise considered this abundance of feminine attire, Mary took a handful of stockings from one of the boxes. 'Right, let's get you nice and comfortable, babikins,' she teased, creating a parting between the dresses and shuffling Denise into it. The poor she-male could only moan in horror and amazement as Mary proceeded to bind her ankles, lower and upper knees and thighs with the stockings. She then added to this bondage sculpture by securing Denise's arms below and above her elbows and at her shoulders, pulling them into one taut, pained limb in the process. Another stocking was used to secure her already bound wrists to the stocking binding her upper knees, forcing her to stretch backward painfully. Next came the final touch of humiliating excess: a pair of large pink bloomers. These were quickly stretched over Denise's head and tied in place around her neck with yet another stocking, the crotch area positioned deliberately to cover the whole of the she-male's face and plunging her into a pink-tinted darkness.

With Denise thus totally immobilised, Mary pushed the two separated rows of clothing together around the helpless she-male, burying her alive in a sea of scented feminine fabrics.

'The pressure of the dresses should keep you upright. After a few hours of this, I'm sure you'll have a much better idea of feminine posture.'

These were Mary's last teasing, sadistic words. Denise heard her walk across the room and flick off the light, turning pink-tinged darkness into total blackness. The door was then shut and locked.

Pretty Denise was left tightly bound and gagged in the centre of a rack of dresses, a servile sex object hung up for storage purposes while her mistress went shopping for more tools to assist in her intricate and inescapably permanent feminisation.

Alone, helpless, unable to move an inch or say a word, she was truly confronted with her new self. Here, in this dark tomb, she found herself staring into the true face of her startling transformation; a beautiful face; a face she desired intensely. Even here, in this far from comfortable, intricately restrained state, she was in a kind of ecstasy. She was completely captivated by her enforced femininity and by the demand for complete obedience it represented. As she strained against the layers of taut, unyielding bondage, as she moaned helplessly into the tight gag, she knew this was something she craved terribly. And Helen knew, and Samantha knew, and even the lovely, wicked Mary knew.

Two hours passed, two terrible yet wonderful hours; two hours in which lovely Denise came to realise that the spankings, the bondage and the humiliation were essential to her transformation into a beautiful, deeply masochistic she-male. And the longer she waited for the return of her beloved mistress, the harder and more desperate her tightly sealed sex became. By the time the door was opened and the light turned back on, Denise was in a state of aching, mad need.

Voices followed the return of the pink light. Helen's, Mary's. Mocking voices, beautifully teasing voices.

Mary's voice: 'I thought a suitably precise storage was in order, to teach her the meaning of feminine suffering and patience.'

The sound of the women's laughter grew louder, closer. Then the dresses were parted and Denise was revealed.

'My, you have gone to town on her!' Helen exclaimed. 'She looks even sexier for it. She seems to glow in bondage. It's natural for her to be tied and gagged. And she loves every second of it.'

Denise's legs were untied. She was then made to totter clumsily out into the centre of the room, still unable to see through the bloomers.

'You must come and visit, Mary. Regularly. You've obviously got a very powerful imagination.'

The stocking binding the bloomers was removed and the spectacular piece of pink underwear was pulled from her head. Helen and Mary stood before her smiling, appraising, both obviously aroused.

'Well,' Helen said, 'it's nearly time for her appointment with the hairdressers. I think we need to untie her, adjust her make-up and get going.'

Mary untied the rest of Denise and removed the gag with a mock gasp of disgust.

She then gently guided the sexy she-male from the room, up the stairway and back into the shop. Here, Helen applied a fresh layer of make-up, redesigning her eye shadow and liner, painting her lips an even darker shade of red, and carefully restyling her hair. Perfume was sprayed in the necessary areas and her clothes carefully straightened. Despite her ordeal, Denise soon looked quite beautiful.

Mary was left with a disturbingly long kiss from Helen and an open invitation to visit Denise. Denise was made to curtsy deeply before this pretty, devilish girl and then led from the shop to the waiting car. Once inside the vehicle, Helen checked that her she-husband was tightly belted in and as they pulled into the traffic she began to speak.

'I've bought you a special little present for tonight, my pet, and I can't wait for you to try it on.'

Denise nodded and smiled as sweetly as possible.

'You may thank me, Denise.'

'Thank you, Mistress. Thank you very much.'

Helen smiled and patted Denise on her shapely, hosed knees. 'You're adapting quickly. Which is very good. Although we're going to have to do some work on that voice. I can't have a pretty little she-husband who talks like a bricklayer!'

Helen parked in the city centre and they made their way towards the hairdressing salon, which was located on the main high street. Denise, following Helen's instructions carefully, was soon mincing with a charming daintiness across the car park and through the crowded Saturday afternoon streets, her heels echoing like gun shots against concrete walkways and pavements. As she took short, quick steps and wiggled her barely covered backside, she once again felt a thousand eyes drill into her. She was a stunner, a helpless object of both male and female fascination, and there was nothing she could do but enjoy the admiring stares of men and the envious glances of women.

The salon was packed. Mirrored walls were lined with brilliant white sinks. Facing each sink was a large, leather-backed chair containing a woman mummified in a pink protective gown, her head inside a dryer or being worked on by one of the army of pretty female assistants. As Helen and Denise entered, virtually every head turned to face them, each pair of eyes filled with a curiosity that betrayed the manager's indiscretion concerning the she-male. Titters and knowing looks confirmed this.

'Helen! Lovely to see you again!'

A woman emerged from the waiting customers, her eyes filled with excitement. This was Anita, the manager, a long-time friend of Helen, an ex-nurse who had become disgusted by the poor pay and long hours. Denise had never really met her. But then Denise had never really met any of Helen's friends.

Anita was older than Helen. In her late thirties, yet she was still quite beautiful. Tall, full-figured, she was dressed in a tight red dress, white hose and red high-heeled pumps, her thick, gleaming blonde hair spilling over her shoulders, her pale blue eyes fixed firmly on the lovely Denise.

'And this is?'

'Yes,' Helen said, smiling broadly, 'this is Denise.'

'He . . . she's gorgeous! How incredible, how absolutely incredible!'

Denise blushed and tried to avoid Anita's intense gaze. But every woman was staring at her: she was a lovely she-male magnet attracting every disturbed, envious, amused pair of eyes.

'I'd like Denise to have one of your specials. What I'm really looking for is something intensely delicate and very,

very feminine, even a little girlish. Yes: girlish and sexy at the same time.'

'I see it . . . yes, I definitely see what you're getting at,' Anita replied, appraising Denise, examining every inch of her with fascination.

'Good. I still need to get one or two things in town, so I'll pop back in about an hour. If she misbehaves in any way, feel free to punish her. I suggest you make sure she's kept secured, as well. She has a tendency to fidget.'

Helen left Denise with a beautiful, teasing smile. The lovely she-male, now gripped by a sickening panic, was led by Anita to the only empty chair in the salon. More giggles and whispers surrounded her as she was helped into the chair by one of the young female assistants. Another assistant stepped forward with a pink plastic coverall. The coverall was slipped over her head and positioned so that it obscured the whole of her upper body, a bright pink plastic cocoon holding the lovely Denise in a helpless and highly exciting stasis. Anita then took a length of cording from a plastic box by the sink and used it to bind the she-male's shapely ankles tightly together.

Helped by the two girls, one a lean, blue-eyed redhead, the other a plump brunette, Anita personally dressed Denise's hair. Denise, fascinated once again by her beautiful, girlish reflection, stared into the mirror and watched Anita transform her into an even lovelier image of perfect femininity. On either side of Denise were older and certainly less attractive women. They also watched, but not with fascination: their eyes betrayed a jealousy of this impostor, this usurper, whose existence questioned the whole nature of the carefully defined gender barriers within which their identities had been formed.

As she styled Denise's hair, Anita chattered continually, asking her assistants for scissors, styling creams, sprays, and engaging her she-male customer in a decidedly one-way conversation. Denise smiled weakly, still intensely embarrassed by the spectacle she and Anita seemed to be creating, and listened with some difficulty to Anita's machine-gun discourse, trying not to let her eyes linger on the blonde's considerable chest, which was so brazenly displayed by the tight red dress, and which was now pressing repeatedly against Denise's face and neck.

'I suppose a lot of women would be appalled if their husbands said they wanted to dress up as girls. I can't understand why. I think it's marvellous that you should want to express your feminine side in such – detail. I suppose it helps if you can get away with it, and you can certainly do that, Den– Denise. You're absolutely gorgeous.'

Denise smiled and uttered a slightly pathetic 'Thank you'. Through the mirror, she watched the two assistants exchange knowing looks. Their smiles said so much more than the high-speed babble of the buxom Anita.

It took a good hour for Anita to produce an acceptable hairstyle, an hour of chatter, gossip and banal comment. But despite the vacuity of her discourse, her skill as a hairdresser was unquestionable. By the end, Denise was facing an image of startling, radiant femininity from an age when female beauty was far less questionable. Her spectacular blonde locks had been sculpted into a work of retro-art, a classic fifties hairstyle reminiscent of Marilyn Monroe. A sea of carefully shaped blonde waves washed over Denise's delicate, naturally feminine head and face, a silver halo framing her pale blue eyes and delightfully full cherry-red lips, the perfect topping for this particularly delicious she-cake.

And then the final touch: a pretty red ribbon made of beautifully sheer silk was tied in a tight, fat bow over her equally silky hair.

Denise stared at her reflection in disbelief, her mind overwhelmed by the reality of her reflection. How can this be me, she asked herself; how can I have become this beautiful woman? And amongst the other customers, there was an equal bafflement, expressed as stunned silence and a wintry collection of icy looks which hid a deeper, warmer envy. All except one look, one proud, yet slightly ironic look from the eyes of the lovely Helen. She had entered the salon as Anita stepped back to admire her masterpiece and was now standing directly behind Denise, who was smiling helplessly, happily – amazed and thankful – eyes of gratitude and love aimed through the mirror at her beautiful wife-mistress.

'You've done a predictably expert job, Anita. Just what I was looking for.'

Surprisingly, Anita brushed aside the compliment. 'It was easy,' she said, suddenly awkward in her tight sexy dress and high heels. 'He – she's a natural beauty. All I had to do was bring out what was already there – reveal the hidden self, as it were.'

'The hidden self,' Helen repeated, her splendid brown eyes once again boring into Denise like a hungry she-wolf beholding her helpless prey.

The assistants removed the coverall. Denise's ankles were untied and she was helped to her feet. No form of payment was made, just another genuine thank-you and a kiss between girlfriends. Then Helen led Denise through a corridor of jealous stares and back out on to the street, the afternoon light fading, the streets now lit by the pale orange of electric street lamps.

As they had left the salon, Helen gave Denise two bags of shopping to carry and, despite this, she minced along beside her wife-mistress with surprising ease. Suddenly, even in the midst of such a public display, she felt perfectly at ease with her ultra-femininity, and the hungry male glances and comments were taken as obvious compliments on her womanly beauty, her authenticity, her true feminine image. For the first time in months, she was at one with herself.

Seven

They had driven back to the house in silence, Denise revelling in her delicate femininity and trying to make sense of the strange events of the afternoon. She was intensely aroused and found herself returning to the bizarre adventure with the gorgeous, wicked Mary. Helen's open invitation rang in her tormented memory, as did her wife-mistress's promise that even more unusual forms of feminisation were to follow.

Denise minced from the car carrying the two plastic bags. The poor she-male was almost crying with anticipatory pleasure as Helen opened the front door and led her into the living room. Following Helen's instructions, Denise then placed the bags on the sofa.

'Stand to attention, my pet, and put your hands behind your back. Come on – legs together! Ankles touching!'

Denise obeyed eagerly, now desperate to see what was hidden in the bags.

'I know you want to see what I've bought you, but we'll have to wait. Mummy is coming to dinner and you will be the centre of attention. You'll need to take a shower and reshave. I want you silky smooth, powdered and perfumed in thirty minutes. Then we can think about dressing you up.'

Denise's poor girlish heart leaped into her mouth at the mention of the wondrous Samantha. A pretty mixture of fear and desire filled her eyes.

'And I expect you to be on your very best behaviour. Do you understand?'

Denise nodded and curtsied.

Denise was then led back to the main bedroom and told to undress. Helen watched as her she-husband elegantly stripped, placing her lovely, modest clothes on the bed, her eyes girlishly downcast, a sweet blush igniting her lovely cheeks.

Within a few minutes, Denise stood in the pantie-girdle and mini-corset, her fierce, helpless erection clearly visible through the tight elastane material of the girdle. Helen helped her out of the corset and then ordered her to remove the pantie-girdle. As she did so, her highly excited sex was exposed to Helen's amused eyes.

'We really will have to do something about that,' she teased.

Blushing even more furiously, Denise placed the girdle on the bed and slipped back into the high heels. She then minced under Helen's watchful gaze into the bathroom.

The gorgeous she-male showered and reshaved from head to toe, using one of Helen's shower caps to protect her startling blonde locks. After carefully drying herself, she applied a luxurious variety of powders and perfumes to her delicate, smooth body, then returned to the spare room, or rather, as it was to be now, *her* room. Helen had placed on the bed a whole new outfit for the evening ahead – the outfit that had filled the two plastic bags. Before her was an elegant, intricately decorated basque, a pair of very sheer, black nylon tights with sexy, pencil-thin seams, a pair of white silk panties, what appeared to be a velvet choker and a pair of long, white glacé gloves.

Helen entered the room as the she-male beheld the new attire. 'Something rather sexy for Mummy, I think. As you're going to be our maid for the night, I thought this would be the most appropriate blend of submission and sensuality.'

Denise slipped off the high heels and eagerly stepped into the lovely silk panties, their cool, gentle caress against her freshly shaven skin almost too pleasurable. And after the panties came the sexy but demanding tights. It took a while for Denise to ensure that the seams were straight enough for her wife-mistress and her hesitation earned her a rather sharp slap on her pretty, now finely hosed backside. Denise was quickly overwhelmed by the highly erotic effect of the tights on her smooth, scented and perfectly shaped legs, an effect made all too apparent by the rigid pole pressing against her hosed stomach.

The basque was a full-bodied affair. Denise was required to step into it, pull it over her body, then allow Helen to pull it firmly into place over her tights and lower torso. It was then secured by means of a zip running the length of the she-male's elegant back. It was almost tighter than the mini-corset, the satin panels hugging her stomach with an intensely erotic force. This spectacular black and red creation was covered in a lace rose pattern and the reinforced bra cups that pressed against her disappointingly flat chest were thickly frilled with dainty black lace.

Once the basque was secured, the long, brilliant white gloves were carefully rolled over Denise's slender arms. To her delight, the gloves reached up her shoulders and felt like soft satin snow falling on her freshly shaven skin. She found herself studying her arms in helpless fascination and carefully flexing her fingers in their sexy glacé prisons.

Then Helen secured the pretty velvet choker around her she-husband's pale, thin neck; an addition that brought a sigh of pleasure and a more friendly pat on Denise's shapely bottom.

'You look delicious, Denise. Mummy will be so pleased with you.'

Denise smiled sweetly and curtsied her thanks.

'Now,' Helen added, 'the final touch!'

From beneath the bed, she then retrieved the amazing stilettos of the night before, two perfect sculptures of elegant black patent leather, each with a cruel, ultra-high heel.

Denise stepped into the shoes without instruction: suddenly, the heels were so natural, so utterly *her*. And how simple it was for this sweet transvestite beauty to follow her wife-mistress from her room, down the corridor and into the main bedroom, each step a careful, pretty mince producing the sexiest of wiggles and the most delightful she-male smile.

In the main bedroom, Denise found herself once again before the dressing-table mirror.

'Eventually you'll learn all the necessary make-up skills,' Helen purred, taking up a large pink powder puff. 'I expect you to be able to do most of this yourself by the end of next week.'

Denise nodded eagerly, looking forward to the pleasures of applying her own make-up. But for now, she could only watch as Helen worked her magic with foundation, blusher, highlighter, eye shadow, lipstick, lip gloss and the beautiful ivory-handled hairbrush.

In less than fifteen minutes, the transformation was complete. Another white silk ribbon held her delightfully thick and wavy hair in place, and a powerful French perfume covered her neck and shoulders.

Helen helped Denise to her feet for inspection. The seams of her tights were straightened, the basque carefully adjusted at her chest, and the gloves pulled tight just beneath her shoulders. Satisfied, Helen motioned her splendid she-husband over to the large bed. It was only now that Denise noticed the strange halter-like device placed upon it. Further inspection revealed a set of leather shackles joined by a silver chain: an intricate hobbling device!

'This will help teach you an appropriately feminine walk. After a week of wearing the hobbler, a dainty mince will come quite naturally.'

Denise watched in astonishment as Helen proceeded to fix the hobbler to her hosed legs. She was then required to walk up and down before her wife-mistress. The short length of silver chain restricted the movement of her legs to a tiny, little girl totter, which was significantly exaggerated by the high heels. She displayed herself before Helen with an intense pride and enthusiasm, eager to please her queen with the tiniest and daintiest of steps. She was in a state of submissive bliss as her high heels carried her across the soft white carpet of the bedroom. This was all so easy for Denise: she was a genius at femininity!

* * *

It was after six by the time Helen and Denise entered the living room. The house was still spotless from the thorough cleaning of the day before, but Helen insisted that Denise quickly dust and polish the living room while she began to prepare dinner for Samantha.

Denise went about her household chores with a graceful ease, each movement elegantly feminine and punctuated by the percussive clicks of heels and the clinking of the hobbler's silver chains against her hosed ankles.

By 7.00 p.m., the meal was simmering and Denise was preparing the dining table. She was told to set only two places: her own evening meal was a glass of slimming drink and an apple, both quickly consumed in the kitchen after the table was set.

Then it was 8.00 p.m. Helen checked Denise's hair and make-up one more time and ensured that her seams were straight. She then led the gorgeous she-male from the kitchen and told her to stand by the dining table, arms at her side, hands raised upward slightly, legs tightly together.

And this was how Denise remained for thirty awful minutes of helpless apprehension and anticipation, watching the living-room clock move slowly towards 8.30, the appointed time for Samantha's arrival. At 8.25, Helen returned to the living-room. Denise released a helpless gasp at the sight of her beautiful wife-mistress, for she had changed from her earlier, slightly girlish attire into a stunning black evening dress, its plummeting cleavage revealing her ample, tanned bosom, its short hem proudly displaying her long, black-hosed legs, a display beautifully accentuated by another pair of very high-heeled, black patent-leather court shoes. Around her neck was a choker of silver pearls. Her thick, black hair was freed from the earlier bun and now fell with deceptive indifference over her bronzed shoulders. Her lips were painted a bloody cherry-red, and a light blue eye shadow set off her startling brown eyes to perfection.

Then the doorbell rang. The awful, heart-stopping doorbell. For a moment Denise and Helen found themselves staring with equal trepidation into each other's lovely eyes. Denise's poor girlish heart pounded with helpless excitement as Helen went to open the door. Then the sound of Samantha's voice complimenting her daughter on her evening attire. Denise fought terror and furious arousal. She swayed in her own ultra-high heels and her sex felt like a rod of hot metal pressed against her stomach.

Samantha entered the room first, producing an immediate and very deep curtsy from Denise.

'She looks so sweet, Helen,' the gorgeous dominatrix announced, consuming quivering Denise with cruel eyes. 'You've done a marvellous job.'

Helen followed her mother into the living-room, blushing, laughing, unsure whether to be proud or contemptuous.

Samantha was dressed in a tight black sweater and figure-hugging black leather trousers, plus very high heels. Her hair had been swept into a loose bun held in place by a diamond clip, and her fierce brown eyes still possessed that perverse passion, that need to dominate and control everything and everybody, and especially the lovely, timid Denise.

The sleek, perfectly streamlined outfit made Samantha look like a beautiful, dark-eyed panther. She walked up to Denise, her smile deadly, and slipped a long, flawless hand under her chin, gently bringing the lovely she-male's head up to expose her fear and desire filled eyes.

'Have you missed me, Denise?'

Denise swallowed hard, Samantha's powerful musk perfume filling her flaring nostrils. 'Yes, Mummy. Very much.'

Her smile broadened. 'Good. But Helen's been taking very good care of you, hasn't she?'

'Yes, Mummy.'

'Yes, I can see she has. And you look so much better for it, my sweet baby girl.'

Poor Denise was now quite giddy with arousal. Her gaze strayed helplessly from Samantha's gleaming eyes to her superb, perfectly outlined and tightly restrained bosom.

'Yes – and you obviously feel better,' she teased. 'Helen tells me you're a fast learner. Particularly when it comes to walking like the sexy little she-pet you most surely are. So let's see you walk – parade for me.'

Denise curtsied her compliance and began to walk up and down the room in front of the two beautiful women.

Denise took an intense pride in her tiny steps, wriggling her backside with great effect and holding her pretty head high. The hobbler caressed her ankles and calves, but each sweet, high-heeled movement was well within the strict limits set by the training device. She could hear Helen whispering to her mother and hoped her words were complimentary. Samantha appeared fascinated and excited by the spectacle of Denise, and her beautiful smile widened as Helen continued her hushed monologue.

'Very good, Denise. Now come over to Mummy and stand to attention.'

Denise obeyed without a second's hesitation, mincing eagerly to Samantha's side and regaining her taut, subservient posture.

'Helen and I are very pleased with you,' Samantha purred. 'There's obviously work to be done over the coming weeks and months to ensure that your transformation is total and irreversible, but your natural femininity bodes very well for the future. Helen will oversee your initial progress, but our plans for you require a fundamental physical and mental alteration, and this can only be carried out under very special conditions. As these are only available at my home, we've decided that, at the end of next week, you will be brought there and placed under my complete control for a period of six months. You will receive training in all aspects of femininity and submission. Eventually, if you perform well, you will be allowed to act as my personal maid. Both Helen and I, and my colleagues at the house, are in favour of a strict regime which will involve constant work and severe punishment for any failure to perform your duties as required. If you succeed in meeting our requirements, you will be returned to Helen and allowed to act as her maid on a permanent basis.'

Denise curtsied her understanding, trying hard to avoid a helpless gasp of excitement: the thought of being placed once again in Samantha's deliciously firm hands filled her with an aroused anticipation of further wicked humiliations and erotic adventures.

'We still need to do something about your voice and breasts,' Samantha continued. 'There's also the question of permanently removing all that nasty body hair. Helen can deal with the hair. We'll sort the rest at the house.'

Helen and Samantha seated themselves on the sofa and Denise was sent to the kitchen to fetch a specially chilled bottle of Chablis and two glasses. Despite her excitement and nervousness, she managed to hand the glasses to her mistresses and fill them without spilling a drop of the golden liquid. She then stood to attention with the bottle by her side as the women talked.

'Katherine is keen to meet our little wonder,' Samantha said, crossing her long, leather-sheathed legs. 'Actually, it was she who suggested you pay that little visit to Mary.'

'Mary was wonderful!' Helen interrupted. 'And so imaginative. She even suggested putting Denise in nappies.'

Samantha laughed. 'An excellent idea. I'm sure she'd look perfectly divine in baby clothes.'

As this bizarre conversation continued, Denise saw a picture emerging, a picture which partly explained her earlier ordeal. By 'Katherine' Denise knew Samantha was referring to her close friend Katherine Shelly, the wealthy and famous entrepreneur, the woman who had been alluded to the day before in the context of something called 'The Last Straw Society'. Denise, as Denis, had known Katherine Shelly reasonably well. Denis had worked as a public relations consultant and his portfolio had included Shelly Cosmetics for nearly three years. Indeed, it was at one of Katherine's parties that Denis had originally met Helen and, subsequently, Samantha. Katherine was another beautiful, wilful woman, a woman Denis had found very attractive, but her notorious lesbianism had prevented any attempts on his part to develop this attraction. And Mary was Katherine's daughter. Yes, it made sense: Katherine had two teenage children: a daughter and a son.

'And Christina? We shouldn't forget her!' Helen added. 'After all, if it wasn't for Christina –'

Samantha smiled. 'Yes. Christina is really the key to all this. The prototype, as it were.'

'I was amazed when you told me. I didn't think that sort of thing happened.'

'It does. And it will happen much more.'

This part of the conversation only added to the confusion surrounding the events of the afternoon. Christina was referred to as Mary's 'unfortunate sister' and a 'daughter to be proud of' in amused, ironic tones. Yet Denise knew Katherine Shelly had only the one daughter. A little bit had been given, a little bit had been taken away. But Denise had heard enough to understand that there was much more to her splendid feminisation than had initially been apparent.

The evening progressed like a dark, erotic dream, with Denise continuing to serve wine to Samantha and Helen. The women consumed the entire, expensive bottle very quickly and were soon in the early stages of inebriation. This inspired them to tease Denise more overtly. Constant compliments on her delicate femininity and exquisite figure were intercut with threatened punishments and planned humiliations. And the more cruel the plans, the more aroused the women became and the more aroused lovely Denise became. When Helen described her she-husband's bondage ordeal at the hands of Mary, Samantha became particularly excited.

'Yes! Just like I told you. She loves it – being tied up and gagged – being utterly helpless. She's a total masochist.'

'Absolutely. She was so turned on, I thought she was going to burst.'

'I've brought along a few special items to make sure she doesn't.'

Samantha then climbed to her high-heeled feet and left the room. Helen turned her beautiful eyes on Denise.

'This is more than you deserve, my pet. I just hopeful you're grateful.'

Denise curtsied her gratitude, her eyes filled with desire and helpless curiosity. Samantha came back into the room carrying a sports bag and dropped it at Denise's lovely legs. She extracted from it what appeared to be a large rubber ball attached to two thick lengths of leather strapping.

'A ball gag, petal. A nice fat ball gag for that sweet little mouth of yours,' Samantha teased, dangling the gag before Denise's wide eyes. 'I know you'd prefer my panties, but they're reserved for special occasions. I've decided you'll be required to wear a gag in my presence at all times, unless of course you are required to speak. You must come to see language as a privilege, Denise, a privilege bestowed by Helen and myself for good behaviour. And as your voice is still so unpleasantly masculine, and is unlikely to improve until I can arrange for a set of special injections, it's best if Helen and I can be saved any but the most necessary sounds from that particular orifice. Now open wide.'

Denise obeyed, watching in amazed horror and arousal as Samantha pushed the large, red rubber ball deep into her mouth, her soft, full, cherry-red lips quickly forming a delightful bow of desire around its inescapable diameter. The ball was then buckled firmly in place at the base of her neck using the black leather straps.

The gag forced her tongue flat against the floor of her mouth and made any sound impossible. It also pressed angrily against her rouged cheeks and made breathing through her nose an initial strain.

'Now isn't that better?' Samantha teased. 'It certainly makes you look almost unbearably sexy – a real damsel in distress. And believe you me, there's some distress to come!'

Denise was then made to serve Helen's carefully prepared meal gagged and hobbled (Samantha having shortened the slack on the hobble chains by two inches). At first, her breathing was quite laboured and Samantha scolded her for making 'unladylike' noises while serving the delicious prawn cocktail starter (a scolding which resulted in a hard slap on her pert backside from Helen). After a few minutes, however, the lovely she-male was able to control her breathing and continue her duties in the dainty manner demanded by her mistresses.

And so it went on: the teasing, the slaps, the drinking and eating. The two lovely women worked their way through two more bottles of Chablis, plus a spectacular three-course meal. By ten p.m., they were both very drunk and also very turned on. And poor Denise was exhausted and starving. Yet she was also intensely aroused: there seemed to be no humiliation or cruel jibe that would not add to the masochistic pleasure this ritual inspired.

Just after ten o'clock, Helen handed Denise a lovely white, lace-frilled pinafore and the she-male was sent to the kitchen to work her way through the vast pile of washing-up. It took her nearly an hour to wash and dry every plate, glass, dish and saucepan, and eventually she found herself swaying wearily before the sink, her previous enthusiasm now severely dampened.

She tottered back into the living-room just before eleven o'clock to find that Samantha had changed into the most startling of costumes. Her poor she-male eyes nearly popped out of her pretty little head as she beheld her stunning mother-in-law standing in the middle of the room clad in a black leather basque, black seamed stockings and shoulder-length black rubber gloves, her glorious legs now graced by a pair of gleaming black patent-leather, Victorian ankle boots. And in her gloved hands was a fierce-looking ivory-handled riding crop.

Helen stood behind her mother, still dressed in the sexy evening wear. The room was filled with a powerful static sex energy that made the hairs on the back of Denise's long neck stand on end. She curtsied deeply and awaited her fate.

'Helen has tried to talk me out of thrashing you, Denise, and, reluctantly, I have agreed,' Samantha announced. 'However, if you fail to follow my instructions exactly, I can promise that sexy little bottom of yours will feel the kiss of this crop. Now step forward.'

Denise obeyed instantly, watching in grim fascination as Helen took two lengths of black rubberised cording from the sports bag and stepped behind her she-husband. The she-male's glacé-sheathed arms were then tied tightly behind her back at the wrists and elbows, forcing her unimpressive but eager chest forward and causing her to sway precariously in the high heels.

Samantha then landed a light but still painful cut of the crop to her slave's hosed thighs. 'Upstairs with you, my pretty sissy petal. And be quick about it!'

Spurred into action by the crop, Denise tottered desperately forward, Samantha following behind. More 'encouragement' was provided by the crop as they went out into the hallway and up the stairs to the main bedroom. The lovely she-male eventually wiggle-minced into the bedroom on her heeled and hosed feet, gasping into her gag, desperately trying to avoid losing her balance.

'By the bed, babikins, and stand to attention!' Samantha snapped, her voice betraying the intense pleasure this ritual was inspiring.

Denise obeyed, tears of exhaustion beginning to trickle from her lovely blue eyes.

At the bed, she found herself confronting a truly bizarre spectacle. The bed clothing had been removed completely and replaced with a white rubber sheet. A series of large silver buckles had been fitted to the sides of the mattress. On top of the rubberised mattress was what appeared to be a long, pink rubber bag, three pink phallus-like objects of different sizes (one of which was attached to two lengths of pink leather strapping), a very large pink rubber sheath and numerous lengths of thicker pink leather strapping. She also noticed that a jar of clear gel had been placed on the bedside table.

Samantha put the crop down on the bed and set about untying the she-male's arms. Denise found herself wondering why she had been bound in the first place.

'Now I want you to strip, Denise. And quickly!'

Lost in a whirlpool of confusion, exhaustion and desire, she began to remove the long, sexy gloves, peeling them from her silky arms with a delicate feminine care that was now quite instinctive. Samantha, her amazing body still a powerful visual magnet for her she-male 'son'-in-law, unzipped the basque tightly imprisoning Denise's slender frame and helped slip it from her body, whispering her plans with wine-stained breath as she did so.

'You're about to embark on a true adventure, Denise, an adventure that will require a firm and unyielding inner discipline, the discipline of that marvellous femininity we have discovered sleeping in the ruins of Denis. Helen, my colleagues and myself intend to create a perfect she-male, a beautiful, submissive and intensely feminine creature whose true sex will shatter every prejudice and preconception concerning the nature of gender. Your training will involve learning many new skills: make-up, hair care, feminine dress sense; domestic skills such as cooking, ironing, sewing; physical skills – how to walk, to talk, and how to please women.'

Denise wiggled out of the pantie-girdle, then she carefully unrolled the tights and removed the pearl choker. Then there were only the panties, skimpy, befrilled white nylon through which her burning, rock hard erection strained angrily.

'We're also going to have keep this under the strictest control,' Samantha continued, suddenly grabbing the panties and pulling them down in one violent tug to reveal the full, furious tumescence of Denise's paradoxical manhood.

Poor Denise moaned into her fat, utterly inescapable gag, intensely aroused by this forced striptease, the smell and sight of Samantha almost too much to bear.

'Now, bend over, legs apart, fingers touching the floor.'

Baffled by this instruction, she hesitated, earning a swift cut from the crop to her naked backside. She squealed into the gag and instantly assumed the required position, spreading her legs wide and thus parting her buttocks. She watched out of the corner of her lovely eyes as Samantha then took up the jar of gel, daubed a large blob on to one rubber-gloved hand and disappeared behind the prone slave.

'The heart of you will be complete subservience, my pet. The symbols of this subservience will be legion, and this is possibly the most intimate: the anal plug. You will wear a rubber phallus in your backside until your training is complete. It will teach you humility and assist your feminine walk. We will start off with a relatively small plug, but larger ones will be inserted on a regular basis. It will be removed only on permission of your mistresses.'

Then a cool, sticky finger was probing her helplessly twitching anus. The pressure was increased. Denise squealed into her gag, surprised by the pleasure she was feeling. Within seconds, her back passage had been thoroughly lubricated and relaxed. Yet when, after a delirious pause to display the short rubber phallus before the she-male's wide, baby-blue eyes, Samantha slowly slid the wicked device into her slave's rear, there was a helpless tightening. But Samantha continued to gently but firmly guide the phallus into Denise's back massage, and the deeper it progressed, the more apparent the pleasure of its entry became. Poor Denise was soon moaning into her fat gag, her fierce erection pressing against her smooth stomach, her eyes filled with a new and intoxicating pleasure.

'Are you enjoying yourself, my pretty baby?' Samantha teased.

'Mmmmmmpppphhhhh!!!!!!!' came Denise's high-pitched, desperately aroused reply.

Then it was home, slotted tightly and deeply into position. Denise was made to stand upright, her buttocks closing around the plug and sealing it firmly in place. A most unusual and intensely pleasurable sensation followed. She could feel the slick, intimate probe caress the walls of her back passage with each movement. Then she was led closer to the bed and the caress became an erotic toying that produced a further series of excited moans. But Samantha was no longer interested in her behind. Suddenly she grabbed Denise's sex and pleasure was replaced by fear.

'Now to the naughtiest part of you,' she whispered, dark eyes lit by cruel passion, her gorgeous, basque-imprisoned chest heaving with an obvious arousal. 'If we don't keep it under control, it's going to pop up at the most inconvenient points in your training. So we need a suitably disciplining device. And this, I believe, is it.'

From the bed she took the strange pink sheath. On closer inspection, the sheath was revealed to be a particularly cunning penis restrainer, a device made from rubber with a thin silken cord attached to the open end. The truth of the restrainer, however, was inside, for its interior had been lined with teasing black silk.

Poor Denise's eyes widened with fear and desire as the cruel logic of the restrainer became apparent.

'Yes, awful, isn't it,' Samantha teased. 'But very necessary. It's designed to make you aware of your desire and its subjugation, not to punish you for it. A full erection is such a common, unconsidered thing for most males. But for a she-male slave girl, it is a privilege given only by her mistresses. You will therefore be restrained at all times except when you need to carry out natural functions (for which, of course, you will need special permission), or when you're being awarded physical release. The restrainer will not allow full erection, so there's no danger of nasty little accidents in your panties, but it will make you very aroused. The silk is the finest money can buy. As you walk it will constantly caress and tease your sex and thus keep you continually excited, but, at the same time, the actual level of erection will be restricted. You will never be able to achieve enough of an erection to come, despite a constant desire to do so. In a way it will be the ultimate masochistic delight: pleasure experienced instantaneously with its denial. You will come to associate desire and domination even more intimately, and therefore become even more submissive. An intricate little philosophy of control which I'm sure you'll appreciate more and more as time goes by. Now stand still.'

Denise could only watch in horror and arousal as Samantha slipped the restrainer over her erect sex. The soft, cool inner surface immediately began to caress the tender flesh of her sex and quickly gave notice of its appallingly frustrating capabilities. Moans of pleasure were also moans of furious frustration. Samantha stretched the restrainer taut at the base of Denise's penis, then wound the cord around her testicles, securing it with a tight knot via a small slit cut into the opposite side of the cruel device. In the process a full erection was forced into a straining, angry 'nearly there' state which was constantly being kissed and cuddled by soft black silk, adding a new level to her already intense sexual arousal.

Satisfied that the restrainer was adequately secured, Samantha then took up the strange pink rubber bag and placed it at Denise's feet.

'Step into it, Denise.'

The lovely she-male obeyed and watched in amazement as Samantha proceeded to draw the bag up over her long, silky legs. Eventually it was stretched against her thighs like a taut layer of new skin. Yet Samantha kept pulling, and in a few seconds she had drawn it over her thighs, her imprisoned and angry sex and up to her waist. Denise was then made to place her arms tight against her sides so that they too could be imprisoned in the bag as it was drawn over her stomach and chest and, eventually, positioned tightly around her long, pale neck. This left the sexy she-male helplessly sealed in an inescapable rubber cocoon and transformed into a strange sex snake.

'A body glove,' Samantha announced. 'An extremely efficient restraining device for the overactive she-male.'

Now poor Denise couldn't move a muscle – she was completely restrained and very tightly gagged, a helpless sex toy lost in a wildly masochistic ecstasy.

Then, after clearing away the remaining collection of bizarre and increasingly sinister items, Samantha gently laid Denise on her back on the bed.

The poor, overexcited she-male felt like the most helpless baby, and her wide, sexy eyes betrayed the pleasure this infantile state inspired, a pleasure made even more severe when Samantha took up one of the lengths of thick leather strapping and stretched it tightly over her heaving, rubberised chest, securing each end to the silver buckles built into the sides of the rubberised mattress. She then repeated this process with the other straps at Denise's stomach, thighs, knees and ankles, ensuring an even more complete form of immobilisation. And once satisfied her slave couldn't move an inch, she took up the largest of the three dildoes, the one attached to two lengths of thick pink leather strapping. Poor Denise could only watch in astonished helplessness as Samantha then proceeded to fit the curved base of the dildo over the fat ball gag filling her pretty mouth and tie it tightly in place at the back of her neck. This left the bizarre sight of sweet Denise secured to the bed, sealed in rubber with a huge, nine-inch dildo rising from her gagged mouth! The spectacle was made even more bizarre when Samantha went on to secure Denise's head to the bed with further lengths of strapping at her neck and forehead. This left the unfortunate she-male beauty unable to do anything but stare fearfully at the ceiling. Then came the final indignity: the third dildo, slightly smaller than the one secured to her mouth, was fitted over her tightly restrained genital region.

'Objectification,' said Samantha, her voice a haunting message from some unseen part of the room. 'One of the essential parts of becoming a true she-male. You must learn that you are nothing but a serving and pleasure object, my sweet. Your own pleasure is irrelevant: you are here to please your mistresses. And tonight you will, by becoming a simple, rubber sex toy for Helen and I to play with.'

As she spoke, Denise heard the sound of unclippings, unrollings, the kicking off of shoes: Samantha was undressing! Then there was the sound of the door opening and a helpless, cruel laugh that so obviously belonged to Helen.

'Mummy, you're so – imaginative!' she exclaimed.

'Yes. But this is nothing compared with what I have in mind for the coming weeks!'

And so poor Denise could only lie utterly still, staring upward and filled with a terrified arousal. It was clear she was to be used as nothing more than a human dildo, her own pleasure denied by the wicked restrainer which now refused the possibility of any true relief. In a few seconds, Samantha would lower herself on to Denise's mouth and Helen on to her mocking, replacement sex. And all the lovely, utterly helpless and furiously frustrated she-male slave girl would be able to do was squeal uselessly into her fat, inescapable gag. Yet even in this supreme moment of torture and humiliation, there was a terrible, dark excitement and an even clearer realisation of her deeply masochistic feminine self, the real, molten heart of Denise. And with this realisation, even in this most subjugated of moments, there was a genuine elation.

Part Two
Babikins and Christina

Eight

Seven days had passed since Denise's spectacular introduction to femininity at the stern hands of her beautiful mother-in-law, Samantha. Seven long, hard days, during which her wife-mistress Helen had completed the first phase of Denise's transformation into a sexy, ultra-submissive maidservant. A period during which Helen had also completed her own transformation from a tired, defeated wife into a gorgeous dominatrix. With Samantha's guidance, and to Denise's amazement, Helen had established absolute power over her pretty she-husband through the development of a previously unseen side of her personality, at the heart of which was the sudden manifestation of a startling physical presence. And the stronger Helen's new self had become, the more servile, passive and intensely feminine Denise wished to appear.

Since the strange and perverse events of the previous Saturday night, Denise had undergone further physical transformation, an intense period of maid training, equally rigorous instruction in feminine deportment, dress and behaviour, and constant discipline. The masochistic, sissy she-male that Samantha had so confidently predicted lay at the heart of the neurotic, lazy and disturbed man once known as Denis had blossomed into a beautiful vision of feminine submission.

By the end of the first week Denise had become a shapely strawberry blonde of medium height, her thick, glistening hair carefully styled in the manner of a fifties film star and held in place with a very wide, white satin ribbon. Her full, helplessly pouting lips were painted a deep cherry red and her baby-blue eyes were teased by long black eyelashes, eyes sweetly emphasised by pale blue eyeshadow and gently curving eyebrows. Her girlish ears were pierced, each sporting a lovely diamond stud earring. Her cheeks were rouged a subtle peach and often darkened into crimson thanks to the many delightful humiliations she was forced to undergo by her gorgeous wife-mistress. Her body was encased in a tight, figure-hugging maid's dress of expensive pink satin, the purest paradigm of absolute surrender, its long, puffed sleeves, high neck and very short hem frilled with a delicate white lace. Over the dress was a gorgeous white silk pinafore, also trimmed with lace, and tied at the back in the fattest and most feminine bow imaginable. Over slim, feminine hands were pulled gleaming white glacé gloves held in place with intricate rows of pearl buttons. Layers of frou-frou petticoating bellowed out from beneath the short skirt of the stunning dress to reveal long, perfectly shaped legs sheathed in sheer white nylon stockings held in place by white and pink lace-trimmed garters. The delicate lace frills of her delightful white silk panties were just visible through the sexy mist of petticoating, and her small, dainty feet were imprisoned in pink, patent-leather, Cuban-heeled court shoes.

Yet beneath this picture was an even more erotic image. A soft, silky smooth body, utterly hairless thanks to the daily application of a very powerful hair removal cream. The slightest sign of breasts, mere rosebuds waiting to blossom, which hardly justified the lovely lace-trimmed, satin brassiere that Denise had become adept at securing each morning. Breasts fed by twice-daily injections of powerful hormones provided by Samantha and administered by Helen. Baby breasts which would soon grow into a magnificent 44-inch bosom. A rapidly shrinking waist made possible by the constant presence of a boned, red and black satin-panelled corset, tied tightly in place with long white laces by Helen; untied only twice a day at Denise's bathing times, and then retied just that little bit tighter to ensure a continued progression toward a perfectly feminine waist of merely twenty inches. And then the intimate nether regions of our sexy she-male. Firstly, her sex, still so distinctly male, but kept permanently imprisoned in the sheath of pink rubber lined with constantly teasing black silk, and again only removed by Helen twice a day to ensure natural bodily needs were regularly addressed. Secondly, her pert, always womanly buttocks, between which was secured a ribbed dildo of pink rubber designed to ensure that every high-heeled step brought intense and inescapable anal pleasure. And all of this held firmly in place by a white, elastane-panelled pantie-girdle, over which were positioned dainty white silk panties.

As this teasing, intricately designed beauty, Denise had quickly learned that her role was to serve her wife-mistress in any way she saw fit without question. In just seven days, she had demonstrated a very impressive willingness to learn and perform her various duties with an intricately feminine grace and control, but also with a real enthusiasm. Helen had made it clear to Denise that this was the greatest miracle: the way in which feminisation had given her once slothful, weakling husband the will to live, to act, to become part of the world again. And Helen encouraged this new simpering, servile femininity through various carefully chosen rewards, all of which involved stern punishment and relentless humiliation. For with Denise's enthusiasm had come a very powerful masochism. Not only did she love to serve, but she loved to be forced to serve.

So, inspired by the hardest of spankings, the tightest bondage and the most inescapably silencing of gags, Denise had begun to learn to cook, to dress, to sew, to clean, to iron, to wash; she had learned the mysteries of make-up, the simple grace of feminine movement in the highest of heels, how to sit and how to stand, how to turn each breath into an erotic tease designed to torment the eyes of men and inflame the jealous hearts of women. In the rare moments when not tightly gagged, she had begun to speak in a higher, more girlish voice. She had even learned to shop within a budget through two intensely embarrassing and very exciting visits to the local supermarket fully dressed in feminine attire. A beautiful, efficient, willing servant, who no one could mistake for a male; Helen's gorgeous, utterly obedient and very frustrated she-husband maid.

Yes, frustrated. For since her imprisonment in feminine attire, Denise had been quite deliberately denied any form of sexual release. She had been restrained at all times except when supervised by Helen, and now the poor she-male felt like a sexual pressure cooker constantly on the verge of explosive overheating. Yet, paradoxically, the more she was denied release, the more she enjoyed her erotic subjugation, the more she wanted the lovely Helen to completely control her every feminine thought and movement.

Denise's masochistic need and sexual frustration had been quite deliberately enhanced by Helen's choice of dress. Every day her wife-mistress wore the sexiest, most provocative and teasing clothing, much of it new, all of it designed to drive Denise wild with desire. The tightest sweaters, the shortest skirts, her long legs enveloped in the sheerest black hose and given final beautiful emphasis by stiletto-heeled shoes. Clothing which Denise was forced each night to pick from Helen's bedroom floor and to wash and iron; to worship as icons of Helen, her new goddess.

Despite Denise's forced abstinence, Helen sought to take full advantage of the sexual pleasures offered by her she-male slave. Each evening, after a hard day's slavery, Denise found herself on her knees, hands and feet tightly bound, her head between Helen's long, powerful legs, her tongue deep inside her wife-mistress's sex. Her aim: to bring Helen to repeated and very noisy orgasm. On one or two occasions, poor Denise was gagged with Helen's freshly soaked panties and then her stuffed mouth was fitted with the deeply perverse dildo that Samantha had so memorably introduced the week before.

Denise had also been denied any form of intimate social contact with Helen. Like Samantha, Helen favoured her slave's enforced silence. Denise spent each day tightly gagged, either with pairs of Helen's soiled panties or the fat ball-gag. When not required for her domestic or sexual duties, she was confined to her room, the old spare room, now converted into a very pretty little girl's boudoir. The conversion, carried out earlier in the week, had been a particularly humiliating experience. Over two days, the highly embarrassed she-male had been forced to serve tea and biscuits to the two young men who had painted the room a lovely shade of baby pink, fitted a thick, fluffy white carpet and then delivered a particularly ornate white dressing table, matching wardrobe and a new single bed (complete with pink silk encased pillows and pink satin covers). And, as promised, Helen had made it quite clear to these two grinning youths that the room was for her transvestite she-husband, who had then duly been presented to them in her beautiful black maid's dress and matching sissy attire. The poor she-male had been made to curtsy before the amazed, clearly disturbed men. Perhaps they had expected a grotesque drag queen. Instead they found themselves confronted by beautiful, utterly convincing Denise, and in their eyes there was no mockery or hatred, but rather an obviously distressed and confused desire. And, to her horror, Denise had found their response highly exciting! Suddenly, embarrassment had turned to arousal and there she had been, serving the tea and biscuits with a teasing care, making sure to bend sweetly before the two startled men, to show her black stockinged legs to full advantage and even expose the sexiest glimpse of her ultra-frilled white knickers. And all the time Denise had noticed Helen watching her performance very carefully, her mysterious smile betraying very deep and strange motives.

But now the seven days were over. It was late Friday afternoon and Helen's special leave had come to an end. Tonight she would be returning to the nightshift at the local hospital, where she worked as a staff nurse. Today the initial phase of Denise's training was complete. Tonight the next phase would begin. At around 5 p.m., Samantha would arrive to take Denise to her luxurious country home to begin the next stage of the feminisation, and Helen was now preparing her delectable she-pet for this new and no doubt deeply perverse adventure.

Denise stood before her wife-mistress, her she-male heart pounding with fear and helpless arousal. The prospect of being placed under the absolute control of Samantha for the next six months filled her increasingly girlish mind with a highly erotic mixture of dark foreboding and masochistic excitement. She had not seen Samantha since the bizarre events of the previous Saturday, but her presence had been behind every step Helen had taken to establish her authority. And every night there had been the long, detailed phone calls, the strange discussions regarding Denise and her feminine future, calls overheard by Denise as she carried out her relentless round of domestic duties, and which had increased the enigma of Samantha and the mystery of her plans. This mystery had deepened that very afternoon by the delivery of a costume especially provided especially by Samantha for Denise's journey to her home, a costume Denise was now modelling nervously for the amusement of her wife-mistress.

The cruel idea behind the costume was obvious: to move Denise's transformation on to a new level of exquisite humiliation by turning the lovely she-male into a baby girl. A beautiful, white satin dress was at the kinky core of this concept, a dress covered in elegant and very intricate white lace flowers, a dress heavily frilled at the very high, pearl-buttoned neck, the long, puffed sleeves and the very short skirt. Yet although the skirt was short, it was also very wide, and a thick, multi-layered pink and white lace petticoat exploded out from beneath its bellowing edges to reveal Denise's gorgeous legs, gift-wrapped in sheer, seamed stockings of white silk, into which were sewn a charming design of tiny teddy bears. On the she-male's dainty feet were the most delightful white, silk-lined, stiletto-heeled ankle boots, each with a complex web of pink silk ribbon lacing and a large silver butterfly buckle.

Yet this was only the beginning of a particularly infantile spectacle. For over each of Denise's hands had been secured a pretty, fingerless white silk mitten tied in place at the wrist with a fat white silk bow. What could not be seen, however, was that beneath the mittens, each of the gorgeous she-male's hands had been forced into a taut fist and bound in place by a skin-tight, pink rubber sheath which rendered them totally immobile. And if this reduction to utter helplessness was not enough, a large, ornate white silk and satin baby's bonnet had been placed over her lovely head and tied in place at her dimpled chin with another very fat white silk bow. Yet even this gorgeous symbol of babyish submission was not the end of poor Denise's humiliations, for forced between her pink lips was a fat dummy gag fitted with a huge oval teat that filled the poor she-male's mouth completely, a dummy gag tied in place at the base of her neck by two pink ribbons which stretched tightly over her bulging, pink-rouged cheeks and were connected to the slightly curved front plate pulled firmly against the curves of her mouth.

Beneath this teasing mass of babified delight was an even more embarrassing collection of childish garments. The standard rubber restrainer has been replaced by sheer black nylon sheath, referred to by Helen as 'Mummy's sex stocking'. Stretched taut over Denise's rampant penis and swollen testicles, its fundamental purpose was to rub relentlessly against the aroused surface of her extremely frustrated and angry sex and to reveal any 'naughty outbursts' that might result from the endless excitement it created, outbursts that 'Mummy' intended to punish severely. To ensure that this new, cruel device was kept tightly in place, a red silk ribbon had been tied around her scrotum and secured in a tiny bow. To add to Denise's helpless arousal, and thus to increase the likelihood of 'outbursts', a thicker, longer dildo had been carefully secured between her shapely buttocks. Over these perverse mechanisms of restraint and teasing excitement had been secured a very large, very soft and very embarrassing white nappy, which was held firmly in place by two large silver safety pins. Over the nappy had been positioned a pair of extra large, pink rubber baby pants, complete with a teddy bear motif and delicate latex-frilled edging. And finally, there was the inescapable presence of the corset, tightened an extra inch by Helen's expert hands only that morning.

An image of startling, babyish beauty. A masterpiece of humiliation and bondage. The doorway to the creation of a new mind, the mind of an ultra-feminine she-male whose sole desires in life were to be as pretty as possible and to serve her mistresses without question. An image that brought a wide smile of triumph and amusement to Helen's face and which clearly stimulated the deeply masochistic Denise.

'Mummy's little angel,' Helen teased, walking around her she-husband, inspecting every sensual angle.

Poor Denise could only moan into her dummy gag and try her very hardest to stand upright, legs tightly together, immobilised hands crossed in the lap of her incredible baby girl's dress, her eyes wide with a terrible sexual hunger as they tried to follow the beautiful form of her wife-mistress around the living room.

'Mummy will be along in about two hours, but I want you to be ready for her a little beforehand, so that you can get used to your new costume. I also want you to be utterly immobilised while we wait for her, to give you time to contemplate what has happened in the last few days and to consider what is to come. So, I'm going to tie you up in the garden while I have tea with Mrs Parsons and Wendy.'

Helen laughed loudly as Denise's baby blue eyes instantly widened in terror. A pathetic squeal of horror seeped from the fat dummy gag and her full cheeks flushed angrily.

'There's nothing to be worried about, Denise. I've told them both all about your new state. About how much you want to be treated like a pretty little girl and maidservant. They've even seen you in the supermarket. They were *very* impressed. Especially Wendy. And I know how much you like Wendy.'

Denise could only plead helplessly with her gorgeous wife-mistress through sad doe eyes, memories of the beautiful Wendy filling her mind with a confused mixture of fundamental male desire and terror at her impending humiliation.

Smiling broadly, Helen led Denise out into the garden by a helpless, mittened hand, the lovely she-male taking what had now become instinctively tiny, mincing steps in the elegant high-heeled boots, her pert buttocks swaying enticingly through the thick nappy and pretty rubber pants, her eyes drawn to Helen's long, black-hosed legs, legs that were today set alight by a black leather miniskirt, black patent-leather stilettos and a beautiful, virtually transparent white silk blouse. The she-male's nylon restrained sex, now so long without release, strained angrily against its delicate, sheer prison. Denise could not remember one conscious second during the last seven days when she had not been fully erect.

The large garden was already prepared for the planned entertainment. A white rubber mat was laid out on the grass by the patio, close to a wooden table and four wooden chairs. Denise noticed numerous lengths of pink silk ribbon on the table and watched anxiously as Helen picked them up and led her to the rubber sheet. She then carefully helped Denise to sit on the mat and used the ribbons to bind the sexy she-male's arms tightly behind her back at the wrists and elbows. Following this, Denise's legs were also drawn tightly together and bound at the booted ankles and at her sweetly hosed knees. Helen insisted that Denise place her legs flat out on the sheet to ensure a gloriously full view of her stocking tops and rubber pants, thus also making it very clear to anyone coming into the garden that the unfortunate beauty was very tightly nappied.

Leaving Denise in this exposed position, Helen returned to the house. It was a surprisingly hot early spring afternoon and the layers of infantile clothing quickly became very uncomfortable. By the time Helen returned, poor Denise was already boiling hot and, thanks to the dummy gag, desperate for refreshment. Helen was carrying a silver tray laden with china cups, a china teapot and, to Denise's horror, a very large, pink teated baby's bottle. As she placed the tray on the garden table, the front doorbell rang.

Helen smiled cruelly at Denise and went back into the house. The babified she-male could only sit helplessly and await her impending, utterly humiliating exposure, her sense of shame mixed with the most intense sexual excitement. Her rigid sex fought desperately to escape its sheer nylon prison, even though her heart was beating rapidly with fear and embarrassment. Then there was the sound of laughter, of merry female voices, a symphony of doom for this she-male in distress.

Helen led Mrs Parsons and her teenage daughter into the garden, her manner frighteningly relaxed, her tone almost indifferent.

'Of course, if it wasn't for Mummy, he'd still be sitting around the house driving me insane. But thanks to her, things have definitely changed for the better.'

And then they were before her, a broadly smiling Helen, a dumbstruck Mrs Parsons, and a highly amused Wendy.

'Oh, she's absolutely gorgeous!' Wendy announced in her broad, American accent. 'Your own little baby girl. You're so lucky!'

Wendy's words, obviously meant to tease and mock, cut into Denise. Suddenly, shame was all she knew. Desire faded, reality flooded her mind. Momentarily she was he again, she was Denis, ridiculously feminised, humiliated, pathetic. But then Wendy was crouching down beside the lovely she-male, her beautiful blue eyes filled with cruel intent and perverse pleasure. A truly stunning young woman, her long blonde hair bound in a sexy ponytail, her full lips painted a light peach, a tight red sweater very effectively displaying her substantial, firm breasts, her long legs sheathed in black hose and quite deliberately exposed by a very short, red tartan miniskirt that rode up over her thighs as she moved closer to her babified prey. A smell of sweet vanilla mixed with lemon filled the she-male's nostrils as Wendy leaned forward and playfully tickled Denise under the chin.

'Who's a pretty little baby?' she teased, her red panties clearly visible through the sheer fabric of her hose, her breasts now only a few teasing inches from Denise's face.

Humiliation and reality were suddenly forgotten. Now there was only the force of desire. The delicate, highly feminine she-male had returned, and she could only signal her pleasure at this sublime torment by moaning through her inescapably tight dummy gag.

'I think he's enjoying the attention,' Mrs Parsons joked, her original shock now transformed into contemptuous amusement.

'Not *he*,' Helen stressed, showing Mrs Parsons to the table. 'Denise is very much a *she*. In every way bar one, in fact.'

The women laughed as they sat down. Mrs Parsons, a few years older than Samantha, was still very attractive. Like her daughter, she was a striking blonde, but her hair was cut shorter, in a rather masculine manner. She was dressed in a light blue suit, white hose and white court shoes with surprisingly high heels. Around her long, slender neck she wore a band of white pearls. Like her daughter, she was very tall, and despite the fact she was now in her mid-forties, her figure appeared trim and shapely.

As Helen poured Mrs Parsons a cup of tea, the older woman turned to face Denise, slowly crossing her long legs, a look of fascination on her flawless face.

'She is really most remarkable, Helen.'

'It was really all Mummy's doing. She introduced me to the idea. Although it wasn't really her idea in the first place. Some friends suggested it originally.'

'Friends?'

Despite Wendy's close and very personal proximity, Denise found herself straining to listen to the conversation, which appeared to be another piece in the jigsaw puzzle that was Samantha and her mysterious plans.

'Yes. Katherine Shelly, in particular.'

'Shelly? *The* Katherine Shelly?'

'Yes. The owner of Shelly Cosmetics.'

'Your mother keeps very rich company.'

Helen smiled. 'They've been friends for ages. Mummy has a lot of contacts in the fashion world. Her old job – she was a model for a while.'

'But Katherine Shelly is a very powerful lady.'

'So Mummy tells me. And she seems to be using her power politically. She's even formed her own society. She's called it 'The Last Straw Society'. Very radical, extremely feminist. But not –'

'Not skin-headed lesbians in boiler suits?'

'Exactly.'

'And Denise is part of that?'

'Apparently. I'm not being told that much about it, to be honest. All I know is Katherine Shelly's son was the prototype and Denise is mark two.'

At this point Wendy jumped to her feet and returned to the table.

'I love her!' she exclaimed, sitting down by the two older women. 'She's so cute! I could play with her all day.'

'I'm sure they'll be plenty of opportunities,' Helen said, taking up the large baby's bottle. 'You can feed her if you like.'

Denise could only watch in horrified disbelief as Wendy's beautiful mouth broke into an even wider, sexier smile and she took the bottle from Helen before rushing back to the captive, babified she-male. She quickly untied the ribbons holding the dummy gag in place (filling Denise's face with her tightly constrained, very ample bosom as she did so) and then pulled it from the she-male's parched mouth with a highly amusing 'pop'. Yet before Denise could utter a syllable of protest, Wendy shoved the fat teat of the baby's bottle into her sexy, she-male mouth.

'All you have to do is suck, babikins. Mummy will do the rest.'

And, to her surprise, Denise was soon sucking quite furiously, the cool, sugared milk the bottle contained a very instant and much needed cure for her terrible thirst.

Even in the heat of this humiliating feeding, Denise could still overhear the conversation between Helen and Mrs Parsons.

'And how far does this transformation go?' Mrs Parsons asked. 'You said she was still physically a male. Will that change? Will she be fully transformed into a girl?'

Denise couldn't help biting particularly hard against the rubber teat at the mention of her potential emasculation!

'Mummy is adamant there will be no sex change other than basic body alteration and breast growth. She has certain plans for Denise that are apparently at the heart of the Last Straw philosophy. It's not about turning men into women. It's about turning them into servile, sissified she-males. She also seems to feel that Denise has certain bisexual tendencies that can be exploited.'

Although relieved by the news that she was to remain physically male, the mention of 'bisexual' tendencies brought a new and very black fear to her helpless, girlish heart. Earlier, as Helen had prepared Denise for Samantha, she had taken great pleasure in slipping the larger dildo into her she-husband's well-greased anus. As she had done so, poor Denise had released a very obvious moan of pleasure.

'You like this, don't you?' Helen had teased. 'And I'd bet you'd like it more if it was a real cock. Perhaps we should find you a man. I'm sure there are plenty of hunky blokes who'd like to take charge of such a sexy bundle of fun.'

Denise had remained silent, appalled by such a suggestion. But even more worrying had been the slightest hint of excitement that lurked at the back of her mind, an excitement first experienced during her strange encounter with the two young workmen.

Further furtive listening was suddenly made impossible as Wendy slipped her free hand beneath the sea of sweet baby petticoats. Denise nearly choked on the bottle as Wendy pressed a teasing hand against her plastic pantied, nappied and tightly stockinged sex.

'Oh yes,' she whispered, 'baby would love to have a big, firm master, wouldn't she? And I'd like to be there to watch him take you.'

Poor, pathetic, sissified Denise was only seconds away from exploding into the sex stocking, her eyes glued in rabbitlike fascination to Wendy's gorgeous bosom. Then the doorbell rang again.

'That'll be Mummy,' said Helen, rising from her chair and going back into the house.

Wendy pulled the teat from Denise's lips and quickly replaced the fat dummy gag, making sure to tie it tightly in place with the two ribbons. She then climbed to her feet and demurely straightened her short tartan skirt, Denise's hungry eyes feeding on her long, hosed legs. Patting Denise on her bonneted head with a wicked smile, Wendy then returned to the table as Helen led Samantha into the garden.

Helen introduced Samantha to Mrs Parsons and her lovely daughter, while Denise stared in a desperate, eroticised awe at her superb mother-in-law, an awe that was reproduced in the gazes of Wendy and her own prim, proper and very beautiful mother. For Samantha had dressed to kill. In the middle of this surreal Sunday afternoon gathering, she was a truly astounding manifestation. Her thick, jet hair fell about her strong, broad shoulders in glossy waves. Her full, blood-red lips were moulded into a smile of aloof curiosity and amusement, a smile that promised only the kiss of unforgiving control. Around her deceptively slender neck was tied a black velvet choker with a beautiful emerald centrepiece. Then there was her suit: a startling black leather suit, which consisted of a very tight jacket opened to reveal the teasing crevice between her superb breasts and a matching micro miniskirt designed to display her splendid legs to their staggering utmost, legs sheathed in the finest black silk hose and visible to the shapely top of her firm, strong thighs, legs perfectly accentuated by a pair of stiletto-heeled, black patent-leather court shoes. This was the uniform of absolute female domination, and Samantha was the archetypal dominatrix.

'I see you've all met baby Denise,' she joked, following the introductions. 'Good work, Helen. I'm sure Katherine will be very impressed.'

'I think she's so sweet!' Wendy enthusiastically announced. 'I can't believe she was ever a man.'

Samantha laughed scornfully and approached the tethered bundle of feminised childishness that was Denise.

'Well, whatever the person once called Denis was, he certainly wasn't a *man*. But *she* has all the makings of a rather good sissy maid, with a little bit of training.'

Towering over the bound, babified she-male, Samantha appeared a true divinity. Denise could only stare up at her with large, childish blue eyes that betrayed desire and helpless, terror-streaked excitement.

The mention of Katherine Shelly hinted at the deeper levels of humiliation and subjugation to come, and as Samantha carefully knelt down to take a closer look at her sissified captive, Denise felt only intense arousal at the prospect of falling into the perverse hands of these two powerful women.

'You look very excited, babikins,' Samantha teased, an invisible cloud of rose-scented perfume washing over her pretty, imprisoned charge. 'Are you enjoying your nappy and your big fat dummy gag?'

Denise, of course, could only nod in helpless ascent, her eyes feeding on the supreme beauty of Samantha.

'Good. We'll soon have you fully transformed. A few weeks with me and you'll be the prettiest, sissiest little she-male imaginable. Christina will be very jealous, of course, but I think she'll also be very happy. You'll make a lovely playmate for her, in more ways than one.'

Samantha rose to her feet and returned to the table, taking a seat as Helen poured afternoon tea.

Mrs Parsons was very interested in discovering more about the Last Straw Society, but Samantha quickly cut her off.

'I think you really need to talk to Katherine. I'm sure she'll be more than willing to discuss our little group with you. I'll ask Helen to arrange a meeting. You should bring Wendy as well. We encourage younger members. They are surprisingly eager to practise what we preach.'

'Is it true Katherine Shelly has feminised her son?' Wendy asked, her gorgeous eyes filled with a quite wicked glee.

Samantha smiled patiently at the lovely Wendy, her eyes tinted by more than admiration for this young woman's beauty and enthusiasm. 'Yes. Christina is the original model on which Denise is based and will be developed. She is a little younger than Denise, and possessed a very distinct feminine beauty before her mother decided to transform her. Denise, however, has both physical beauty and a willingness to achieve. However, thanks to her mother and, most importantly, her sister, she has learned to accept her role and is now an excellent personal maidservant to both women. She has been trained to please in every way without question and come to desire her feminine subjection. But the poor little thing has been rather lonely, and I'm confident that she and Denise will become the very best of friends.'

Denise listened to Samantha's every word. The mystery of Christina was finally solved: she was Katherine Shelly's son, or rather *was* Katherine Shelly's son! The phrase 'the model on which Denise is based and will be developed' hung in her sissy mind like a flashing neon arrow pointing to a future of inescapable femininity.

'I'd love to meet Christina,' Wendy said, turning her sensual, teasing eyes on Denise. 'And her sister – she sounds like fun.'

'Mary is a very powerful personality. And she has been instrumental in moulding Christina's own personality. The silly sissy was obviously very upset when her younger sister was more or less put in charge of her feminisation, but now she is Mary's utterly devoted servant. And I'm sure Mary would love to meet you, Wendy – as would Christina.'

Shortly after this, Samantha brought the conversation to an end by rising to her high-heeled feet and announcing her intention to return home with Denise.

'I'm glad we've met,' she said to Mrs Parsons and her daughter. 'It's always good to meet like minds. And I'm sure we'll meet again. But now it's time to get babikins here home and tucked up in bed.'

Samantha then produced a chain leash and white leather collar from a pocket in her jacket. Handing it to Helen, she said, 'If you'd do the honours, dear.'

The other women watched as Helen proceeded to untie Denise's ankles and knees, then carefully helped the lovely, babified she-male to her feet, her arms still tightly bound behind her. Once this precarious balancing act had been achieved, Helen secured the collar around the frilled high neck of the spectacular baby dress and led a helplessly mincing Denise back to the patio.

'She has the sweetest little walk,' Wendy observed. 'And she's such a tease – the way she wiggles her bottom!'

Helen laughed. 'She has a gift for it, I'm afraid. A proper little miss.'

'She'll drive boys wild with desire. Will she have breasts?'

'She's already on a cocktail of hormones designed to ensure rapid breast growth without the usual shrinkage downstairs.'

'Will she have big breasts? I'd love to think she'll have a pair of real, ultra-sensitive melons!'

The women laughed loudly at this amusingly crude intervention.

'Christina has responded particularly well to the hormone treatment,' Samantha said. 'We've managed to get her up to forty particularly impressive inches, and expect at least the same response with Denise.'

Denise's eyes widened in astonishment at the thought of her future bosom. Samantha then took up the leash and led Denise back into the house, the other women following behind.

'Forty inches!' Wendy exclaimed. 'That'll teach her a thing or two about being a woman!'

Nine

The car cruised through the countryside. It was early evening now. Besides Samantha, there appeared to be no one else in the vehicle. However, locked in the boot there was a particularly dainty and well-secured package: the lovely Denise, now blindfolded, very tightly bound and very securely gagged. She lay face down on a white silk sheet, her arms still pinned behind her by the ribbons, her ankles tightly resecured and tied with a length of rope to her wrists. Positioned in this strict, uncomfortable hog-tie in this cramped, dark space, the dummy gag still filling her mouth, Denise was about to be delivered to a most bizarre destination.

The sexy she-male had been placed in this inescapable bondage a few minutes earlier by Samantha, an act witnessed with much amusement by Wendy, Mrs Parsons and Helen in the driveway. There had been no goodbye between Helen and Denise, just the briefest exchange of glances before the blindfold was tied in place by Samantha. In Denise's eyes had been the familiar fear tinged excitement, in Helen's little more than cool amusement. Denise knew that her wife-mistress would return to work safe in the knowledge her she-husband was in very good hands and that soon she would have a perfect sissy maid eager to obey her every command.

With only the rhythm of the car for company, Denise reviewed the last few hours and her forthcoming adventure. It was now clear that her feminisation was part of a much larger plan revolving around the mysterious Last

Straw Society and Katherine Shelly, a woman who Denise, as her former male self, had once known well. It was also clear that Mary, the wicked beauty at the clothing store, was Katherine's daughter, and that her brother, Katherine's son, was not locked away in a sanatorium, but living as a fully feminised maidservant, a maidservant whose experiences were now being replicated and extended in the creation of Denise.

Then there was the undeniable reality of the self-discovery at the heart of Denise. Whatever had happened or would happen, Denise could not deny the pleasure that was flowing through her tethered body, the strangely life-affirming joy that the revelation of her masochistic femininity had brought her. Even now, in the tightest of bondage, dressed in baby clothes and nappies, a fat dummy forced between her girlish lips, Denise could not deny she was a willing victim, an eager sissy. She knew she would never escape her complicity in her servitude. And perhaps it was this willing enslavement that was at the heart of Samantha's plan: having exposed the molten feminine core of Denis, she was now making Denise the perfect slave by fulfilling Denise's deepest, darkest and most secret desires.

It took about an hour to reach Samantha's large, secluded country home, an imposing Georgian mansion that had once been the residence of her husband, a now deceased aristocrat. That Samantha should be a widow had always seemed appropriate to Denise. Before her, all men were inadequate and weak, and it was almost as if her husband had simply been removed. Following his death, Samantha had quickly incorporated her inheritance into a total fortune worth over five million pounds. That Helen had insisted on her own life independent of such wealth had surely been an early sign of her strong psychological connection to her mother and the limited future of Denis.

After a bumpy ride down what Denise took to be the deceptively overgrown track that led from the main road to the house, the car drew to a halt. Denise, now numbed by her inescapable bonds, released a pathetic moan of discomfort as the boot opened. Cool, country-scented air filled the boot and then strong hands were releasing the sexy she-male from the cruel hog-tie.

'Take her to the nursery. Katherine and Mary will join us there.'

Samantha's voice, but not Samantha's hands. These hands were strong, yet careful. The rope was removed, the ribbons binding her ankles were united, but her arms remained tethered and the dummy gag was left firmly in place, as was the blindfold. As her legs were freed, the hands moved hungrily over her stockinged legs. There was interest here – *desire*.

She was helped from the car on to the gravel driveway. The leash was reattached to the collar and she was gently pulled forward.

'Let me lead you.' A soft voice, the voice of a young woman. An unfamiliar voice.

The leash was taken up and Denise minced forward.

'You're very pretty.' The voice again. A voice filled with obvious excitement.

Then Denise was led up steps, into what she took to be the main hallway. Suddenly a symphony of clicking heels filled her ears. Heels striking marble in what she remembered to be a very large foyer. The volume diminished: they were now walking down a corridor. Then more steps; but this time down rather than up. Denise whimpered fearfully into her gag as the mysterious guide slid a hand beneath her petticoats and on to her plastic-pantied behind.

'It's OK. I've got you.'

By the time they reached the next level, Denise was violently erect, yet also troubled. There was something about this soft, girlish voice, something too right, too perfect – like the voice of a Frenchwoman speaking a precise, faultless English.

Then there was the sound of a door opening and Denise was led forward. After a few dainty steps, she was brought to a halt and turned around. Then the hands were at her head, removing the blindfold. Then light. Powerful, momentarily blinding. And from the light emerged a vision, a truly glorious vision that Denise would never forget.

Standing before her was a tall, very beautiful woman. Maybe in her early twenties. A woman dressed in a spectacularly sexy French maid's costume, which consisted of a gorgeous black satin dress, frilled at the high sleeves, plunging neckline and very short skirt with red lace, and a gleaming white silk pinafore, also frilled with white lace and tied in two massive bows at the rear of her neck and the centre of her back. Beneath the dress was a mass of billowing frou-frou petticoating, which raised the short skirt to reveal two very long, extremely shapely legs sheathed in sheer, seamed black silk stockings held in place by red, lace-trimmed garters; legs that led teasingly downward to feet imprisoned in a pair of impossibly high, stiletto-heeled, open-toed mules, each decorated with a dainty pom-pom of red feathers. A tall, yet very buxom brunette, whose long black hair was tied in an intricate pony tail by a white silk ribbon, a ponytail which had been positioned to run around her slender neck and over her very substantial and provocatively displayed chest. A woman with a tiny, obviously corseted waist (which served to accentuate her substantial bosom). A woman with the largest, darkest brown eyes Denise had ever seen, and with the most perfect cherry-red lips painted into a sweet, tempting bow. Around her long, slender neck was a simple red velvet choker. Large, pearl earrings hung from her small, delicate ears. And on top of her lovely mass of hair was a sexy, white lace maid's cap decorated with red silk flowers.

She was a vision of sissified feminine perfection. And Denise knew, as she had suspected a few minutes earlier, that this was Christina. But never mind how much she struggled to see this stunning beauty as particularly well-feminised male, she could not help but be immediately and intensely attracted to her. And it was obvious that the feeling was mutual, for in Christina's lovely eyes was pure desire, a very powerful sexual excitement that filled the room with an erotic static electricity. Yet with Denise's attraction came a painful shame. The memory of the pleasure she took in teasing the workmen came flooding back, as did Helen's wicked threats to find her a male lover. Helen, beautiful, imperious Helen, her wife, her mistress; the woman she was to serve as the most willing of slaves. Helen, the woman she betrayed as her sex strained against its teasing nylon prison before this stunning she-male maid.

'Mummy said you were gorgeous, Denise,' Christina purred. 'And she was right. But when Mistress Samantha has finished with you, you'll be just even more delicious.'

Then, as if taking her queue from Christina, Samantha entered the room, followed by Katherine Shelly and her daughter, Mary.

Christina immediately lowered her head and curtsied deeply. The women ignored her and surrounded Denise, whose guilt suddenly evaporated into fear and desire.

'I hope she fulfils your expectations, Kathy,' Samantha said, stepping forward and tipping Denise's chin upward with an elegant index finger, forcing the she-male to look at Katherine and her daughter.

Katherine was dressed in a blue silk trouser suit and predictably high heels, her black hair cut short. She was older than Samantha, yet still very beautiful. With the voluptuous figure of a woman perhaps ten years younger, she had the haughty bearing of someone who had come to expect obedience without question. Mary was dressed in a simple white sweater, a very short red leather skirt, white nylon hose and white high heels, her long black hair tied in a ponytail similar to Christina's. She seemed about the same age as her she-male sister, although Denise knew her to be no more than eighteen, and therefore two years younger than Christina.

'She's wonderful,' Mary said. 'Even better than when you first introduced her.'

'Yes. You've done an excellent job, Sam,' Katherine added, her voice strong, confident. 'Denise appears the ideal subject.'

'I hope so,' Samantha replied, a slight deference in her voice. 'But she'll have to try very hard to live up to Christina.'

The beautiful maid blushed and curtsied appreciatively.

'We'll see. I'm sure Christina will do all she can to help Denise find her true self. Won't you, Chrissie?'

Another sexy curtsy. 'Yes, Mummy. Of course. In any way you wish.'

'Do you like Denise?'

'She's lovely, Mummy.'

Christina's intense, highly aroused eyes seemed to feed on Denise as she replied and Denise felt an intense humiliation wash over her.

'I'm glad,' Katherine continued. 'because you'll have a very significant role in her training. I believe you've progressed enough to be able to provide Denise with a full introduction to her new status. However, if I find out you've failed to meet the highest standards in her training, you'll be punished severely.'

'Thank you, Mummy.'

'You may feed her now. Then put her to bed. And milk her thoroughly before leaving. I expect you to be available to serve dinner at seven.'

'Yes, Mummy,' Christina replied, a broad, excited smile now lighting up her beautiful face and another deep curtsy announcing the departure of the three women.

Once the three mistresses had left, Denise found herself taking in her surroundings with some considerable unease. She was in a large, windowless room decorated in the manner of a baby's nursery. The walls were painted a very light pink and decorated with pictures of smiling teddy bears. The thick carpeting was also pink, as was the very high ceiling. The only normal furniture was a large white dressing table and a red leather-backed stool. A long, white panelled wardrobe was built into an entire side of one wall and, to her horror, a very large baby's cot was positioned in the centre of the room. By the cot there was an equally large baby's high chair and a small plastic table.

'Now then, babikins,' Christina beamed, 'let's get you ready for supper.'

Before Denise could protest, Christina slipped a hand under her baby petticoats and gently led the bewildered she-male to the high chair. Denise felt a deeply ambiguous anger wash over her as Christina's hand eagerly explored her tightly plastic-pantied bottom. Being so tightly bound and dummy-gagged, all she could do was moan helplessly.

Once by the chair, the younger she-male slid back the pink tabletop attachment and untied the ribbons binding Denise's wrists and elbows.

'Up into the chair, Denise. There's a good baby.'

With Christina's eager assistance, Denise climbed awkwardly into the chair.

'Arms out in front of you,' Christina whispered.

Denise obeyed with a gagged whimper of despair, watching fearfully as the lovely maid used specially fitted leather shackles to secure her tightly mittened hands to the arms of the high chair. She then repeated the process with Denise's ankles using similar shackles attached to the chair's front legs.

'There – that will stop you falling out,' Christina whispered, replacing the table top and locking Denise securely in place.

Christina then took a large pink plastic bib from the dressing table and tied it around Denise's befrilled neck. On the bib, in large rose-coloured letters, were the words 'Baby Denise'.

'Now, just relax and I'll bring supper.'

Denise could only watch in confused horror and excitement as Christina then minced out of the room, her long legs set alight by the teasing seams of the ultra-sheer, black silk stockings.

She was gone maybe five minutes, and in this time Denise pondered developments with an increasing trepidation. She was in the hands of a much younger she-male who clearly found her sexually attractive. What was even more worrying was that Denise herself was utterly unable to resist her advances and, without a doubt, was more than a little attracted to Christina. Helen and Wendy's teasing words concerning her bisexuality rang in her increasingly feminine mind like bells of doom.

Christina returned with a silver tray holding a single white china bowl and two large baby bottles filled with white liquid. A smile lit up Christina's beautiful face as she placed the tray on the tabletop before Denise.

'I think I need to slip out of this dress – I don't want to spoil my best uniform before dinner. Mummy would give me such a terrible spanking, and I'm sure Mistress Mary would think up some awful punishment.'

Denise watched in amazement as Christina then proceeded to remove the elaborate pinafore, placing it over the railings of the cot, and then carefully unzipped the elegant maid's dress. Denise's sense of doom was now almost overwhelming, and when Christina revealed her gorgeous, sex-bomb figure sealed in a beautiful, black and red panelled basque, she knew she was in the grip of a most ambivalent and inescapable desire.

The basque's main and very successful function was to display Christina's large and extremely shapely bosom. Poor Denise could not take her eyes off Christina's incredible and very erotic feminine form, and even failed to notice as the gorgeous she-male removed her dummy gag and then untied and removed the ornate bonnet.

'Your hair is wonderful!' she exclaimed, bringing Denise out of her sex trance, even though Christina's startling chest was now only inches from her very flushed face.

Christina was clearly aware of the effect she was having on her babified captive. 'Does baby like Chrisse's undies? I put this on especially when Mummy told me you were coming to stay. Mistress Mary bought it for me last Christmas. It does wonders for my chest. Mummy says you'll have an even bigger bosom by the time the hormone treatment has been completed. Apparently Mistress Samantha is very keen for you to have the biggest titties possible. Of course, I'm very jealous. But I'm looking on the bright side – more for me to play with!'

Before Denise could get a word out of her newly freed mouth, Christina had taken up a spoonful of the thick baby food that filled the bowl and forced it between her lips.

'Mistress Bridget invented this stuff when I was first put into nappies. It's an apple and cinnamon flavoured meal that provides all the basic proteins and vitamins. Three square meals a day as part of a very strict diet. This and Mummy's special milk are more than enough to keep a growing sissy going.'

The soft, sweet food tasted far from unpleasant, and Denise, suddenly realising that she was starving, found herself eating it without complaint, wondering as she did so who Mistress Bridget might be.

As she ate, her eyes continued to wander desperately and guiltily over Christina's impressive body. Despite her substantial chest, her waist was tiny, no doubt the product of very severe corset training. The basque was very tight and designed to disappear between rather than cover her very firm, pert buttocks, thus exposing them in a most erotic manner. The front had obviously been designed with Christina's rather unique anatomy in mind, for it was much wider between the legs, and a surprisingly large, rectangular bulge rising to the edge of her perfectly flat stomach clearly betrayed her true sex. However, this betrayal was quite deliberate: the basque had been designed to accentuate rather than hide Christina's status as a very sexy she-male.

As Christina spooned the food into Denise's mouth, her free hand slipped beneath the table and then under the full petticoating of Denise's elaborate baby-girl outfit. A moan of surprise escaped Denise's full mouth as Christina began to gently rub her hand against the plastic pants.

'You really are too lovely, Denise. I'm sure I won't be able to control myself much longer. But I think you'd like it if I lost control.'

Then their eyes met. Try as she might, Denise could not hide the fact that she was excited by Christina's intimate caresses. Yet even as her pretty eyes betrayed her arousal, she shook her head angrily. But the more outraged Denise became, the more gentle Christina's smile became and the harder she stroked her lovely captive through the plastic panties.

'Mummy said you would resist at first. But I can see you're just pretending, babikins; just trying to hide your true feelings.'

After the food, Denise was forced to drink the two bottles of sweet milk, encouraged by Christina to swallow every last drop. Then, eventually, and to her great relief, she was released from the chair. But this was only the beginning. For once freed, the dummy gag was quickly replaced and she was led out of the nursery into a large bathroom directly across the hall. And all the time her eyes were pinned helplessly to Christina's superb legs and backside, both of which were displayed with deliberate provocation by the basque, seamed stockings and heels, and given a helplessly erotic intensity by a graceful, mincing walk.

'My room is next door,' Christina said. 'Mistress Samantha had this bathroom installed especially for her live-in maid. I understand she was originally a real girl, but I have been performing the role on and off for the past six months. However, the house is too big for one maid. That's why Mummy and Mistress Samantha want us to share the role as soon as you're ready. Eventually, you'll be returned to Mistress Helen and a replacement will be found, but Mistress Samantha is quite adamant you will remain a regular visitor.'

The bathroom contained a bath/shower, a toilet and an elegant Victorian-style basin positioned before a large rectangular mirror. All the fittings and the floor were styled in a pretty pink, white-streaked marble which served to enhance the general aura of erotic femininity.

As Denise examined these new surroundings, Christina began to remove her various items of intricate baby clothing. Denise then realised that Christina was stripping her naked and her pretty baby-blue eyes widened with a deliciously feminine fear. Christina, noticing this, laughed softly.

'Don't be afraid, babikins. I'm going to give you a nice, thorough wash and get you into your night clothes. Then we'll put you to bed. You must be tired after such a hectic day. And if you behave yourself, I'll give you a very special treat.'

Denise could only moan fearfully into her dummy gag, realising that her only option was to surrender to the younger she-male's plans.

Christina helped her out of the spectacular baby dress, then the petticoating, then her training bra and then her extra tight corset. She carefully unlaced and removed the pretty ankle boots, and helped her charge step out of the delicate, babyish stockings. And each act in this undressing was accompanied by a shockingly sexual electric charge. Despite Denise's efforts, she was soon even more deeply aroused, and by the time Christina began to slowly slip the plastic panties down her long, silky legs, both she-males were helplessly excited. And this highly erotic situation was made much worse when, having removed the panties, Christina began to unfasten and unwrap the nappy.

'Hold still, babikins,' Christina teased, unfolding the large white towelling with an expert ease, her tightly restrained breasts rubbing against Denise's smooth stomach as she leaned forward to pull the nappy free. And as she did so, poor Denise's violently erect sex suddenly popped out like a long concealed jack-in-the-box, its furious tumescence restrained only by the sheer black nylon stocking sheath.

'My!' Christina exclaimed, her eyes wide with delight. 'You are a big girl! I'm surprised you haven't burst through the nappy.'

Denise turned the brightest shade of crimson and watched helplessly as Christina then slipped a long, elegant hand over Denise's angry, stockinged erection. The lovely she-male could only cry into her tight gag with an agonised mixture of outrage and pleasure and fight the now almost inescapable urge to orgasm.

'Naughty, naughty,' Christina teased, gently masturbating her overwhelmed playmate. 'I can see a few very unfortunate stains on this stocking. I'll have to tell Mistress Mary. A sissy must exercise absolute control at all times. Now, take a deep breath, because I'm going to take the stocking off.'

The sensations created by Christina gently teasing the soft nylon stocking from Denise's molten sex were appalling. Tears of frustration, desire, humiliation and fear trickled down the lovely she-male's rouged cheeks; any second she would come, cruel restraint resulting in a furious explosion, an eruption that would undoubtedly earn her some strange, perverse punishment at the hands of Samantha or Katherine Shelly or even Katherine's wicked daughter. But then the stocking was free and the hands were no longer torturing her. Then, in a state of sex shock and still tightly dummy-gagged, she was guided into the shower, Christina's hands about her waist and buttocks.

In the shower, Christina slipped a semi-transparent plastic cap over Denise's gorgeous blonde hair and instructed her to wash thoroughly with a large white sponge and a bar of pink, perfumed soap. Denise obeyed, never taking her eyes from Christina, who stood at the edge of the shower bombarding her captive with admiring looks, the younger she-male's eyes particularly interested in one particularly prominent piece of Denise's anatomy.

Once she was suitably showered, Christina dried, powdered and perfumed Denise, her every move a subtle and deeply embarrassing caress, which was made worse by the continuing and very fierce erection. Denise's make-up had been washed away by the shower and Christina was clearly very interested in the natural beauty that been revealed.

'Mummy insisted I have plastic surgery to make my face as feminine as possible. In your case, Denise, I think you're quite gorgeous enough already. I'm very jealous, and very turned on. What fun we're going to have!'

Naked and suitably horrified by these words, Denise was then returned to the nursery, where she watched in helpless fascination as Christina proceeded to take from the wardrobe a very long and very beautiful pink silk nightdress frilled at the sleeves and neck with inches of thick white lace.

'I couldn't help noticing the anal plug,' Christina said, holding the gorgeous nightdress before Denise. 'It looks very big. Mummy told me to leave it in place as a new size was only added this morning. I was plugged, but Mummy gave me to an older transvestite for nearly six months, as well. Daphne – her name was Daphne – taught me how to please men in every way imaginable. I didn't like it at first, but Daphne was rather good at showing me the advantages and, well, let's just say that I grew to like being taken from the rear rather a lot. But don't worry, Mistress Samantha feels I'm the only teacher *you'll* need.'

Denise's eyes widened in genuine horror as Christina revealed the brief tale of her own violation. She felt the plug filling her backside move deeper as her buttocks clenched in fear and apprehension.

Christina placed the beautiful nightdress over the cot next to her own dress and returned to the wardrobe, quickly producing a very large, fluffy white nappy, another pair of pink plastic panties, a pair of pink stockings and what appeared to be a pair of pink satin booties.

'Now, I want you to lie down on the carpet, sweetness – so I can put you into a fresh nappy.'

Assisted by Christina, Denise hesitantly obeyed, soon finding herself on her back and staring up at Christina's startling form, her sex standing to a furious, helpless attention. Then Christina was kneeling by her pretty, fearful captive, her eyes filled with a fierce sexual hunger.

'I think I'd better give you your little treat now, as you'll be all nappied up by the time we get you into the cot.'

With this, and to Denise's utter amazement, the beautiful, busty she-male leaned forward and gently took Denise's rigid, straining sex in her mouth. Denise squealed angrily into the gag, suddenly acutely aware that she was being molested by another she-male, by a biological male whose startling feminine beauty hid a fundamental physical truth. The terrible shame Denise felt multiplied a hundred times and it was this shame more than any real anger that made her try to push Christina away. But Christina was very strong and easily held her dainty charge down. And then the struggles weakened, Christina's expert sucking and tongue tickling bringing an almost immediate pleasure. The frustrations of the past week overwhelmed her already fragile moral sense and very soon there was no need for restraint. Then she exploded, squealing with blind sex fury into the fat dummy gag, her body bucking and bouncing uncontrollably under Christina. The stored sexual energy of seven days erupted into Christina's more than willing mouth. The lovely she-male rose with Denise, pressed her hands against her struggling thighs and swallowed every last drop of Denise's volcanic, spurting come. And when the older she-male was spent, her beautiful eyes glazed over, her pretty eyelashes fluttering, Christina sat back and smiled broadly at her helpless, exhausted and very reluctant lover.

'You certainly enjoyed that, babikins!' she teased, her hand returning to gently caress Denise's now semi-flaccid sex.

Denise could only moan in exhausted amazement and struggle pathetically to resist the obvious outcome of Christina's fresh caresses.

'I just hope you give as good as you take.'

Denise's only response was a look of utter humiliation and self-hatred.

'I know you want more, babikins, but it's nearly seven o'clock and Mummy wants me to serve dinner.'

As Denise shook her head weakly, Christina quickly wrapped her in the large, exquisitely soft nappy and, using a huge silver safety pin, pinned it tightly in place. She then helped Denise to her somewhat unsteady feet and into her nightwear. The dazed she-male, once again filled with embarrassment and shame, and quite astonished by what had happened, was quickly guided into the pretty and very squeaky plastic panties, then led to the extra-large cot. Christina brought the stool from the dressing table and told her dazed charge to sit down. The younger she-male then helped Denise into the beautiful and very sheer pink nylon stockings. As they were rolled up her smooth, soft legs, Denise found herself helplessly surrendering to new waves of sexual pleasure. The stockings were self-supporting, needing neither garters nor suspenders, and Christina teased her quite mercilessly as she gently smoothed them over her ultra-feminine legs.

'You have the prettiest legs, Denise! And don't you just love the feel of the stockings? I can't imagine how I ever lived without the sexy kiss of sheer nylon and silk.'

Once the stockings were positioned, Christina slipped Denise's small, girlish feet into the dainty, pink satin booties, securing each white silk lace in a large, childish bow. Then came the gorgeous nightgown. Helped to her feet, Denise could only gasp into her fat gag as the beautiful garment was gently lowered over her head. It was as light as a feather and as sheer as the finest gossamer. The cool silk fabric seemed to tickle her shaven, smooth skin, to tease her with hidden, wickedly soft lips. It ran from a high, befrilled neck down the whole length of her body to the edges of her stockinged ankles. Sewn into the hem of the dress was what appeared to be a red silk ribbon with two delicately tapered ends that dangled from tiny slots at the front.

After smoothing the dress over Denise's sexy form, Christina resealed Denise's hands in the immobilising rubber sheaths and the fat, pink mittens. Then the lovely bonnet was tied tightly back in place.

'There we are, all ready for bed,' Christina purred, her eyes eating up the delicious spectacle of the babified sissy.

Denise was helped from the stool and brought to the edge of the cot. Christina removed her lovely maid's dress from the cot rail and placed it over the stool. She then unlocked the front, wooden panel to reveal a freshly made bed of white silk sheets and two very large matching pillows. Christina helped Denise on to the bed, placing her flat on her back. And it was only as she did this that Denise noticed the leather cuffs positioned halfway down the bed. Their function was obvious, and Christina was quick to lock Denise's mittened hands in them, causing a brief sense of panic to wash over the older she-male: now she was totally at Christina's mercy! But no further violation followed. Instead, Christina took up the two ends of the ribbon belt running around the hem of the nightdress and tied them in another fat bow, tightly binding Denise's ankles together. Once again, she was utterly helpless.

Satisfied that her charge was now sufficiently restrained, Christina rested her wonderful backside on the edge of the cot and gently stroked Denise's very hot and bothered brow. Denise's eyes immediately filled with fear and a moan of ambivalent resistance escaped her gag.

'You're a very lucky sissy, Denise. Mummy and Mistress Samantha are going to make you into a perfect she-male maidservant. That means you'll become the most feminine, dainty, submissive creature imaginable. And the greatest thing is we are to become very, very good friends, because I will train you. Mummy believes we should never be allowed to have any form of sexual contact with real girls. This is a key part of her philosophy. This is how she creates real sissies whose only function is to serve women in every way. To her, a woman's body is a holy temple. Man, men – well, they are absolutely inferior. A sissy, a true she-male slave, that is the only acceptable form of male. A fully feminised male who has the privilege of partaking in the beauty of women and is dedicated to serving them. But we're still males deep down and we still have our natural desires. She could have us altered, a proper sex change, but that would defeat the object – the control, the absolute domination of male desire. The channelling of that desire for female needs. As she-males, we are far more willing to serve because our desire is intact and it is their property. But we need release, we have to have a physical life. Without it, we would go mad; we'd be inefficient, sullen, even rebellious. So she has come up with the perfect answer: we satisfy our needs through each other. We become the perfect examples of the feminine archetype that men secretly wish women everywhere to be and in the process become helplessly desirable to one another.'

Denise was to be turned into a sissy she-male homosexual! She squealed angrily into her gag and shook her bonneted head violently. Christina's lovely eyes lit up with a cruel amusement.

'There's no point in resisting, silly. I fought it for ages. But then I saw this was the only way. And it's not so terrible. I'm a very good lover – as you've seen.'

As she laughed at Denise's increasingly futile protests, it became clear to the older she-male that they, Christina and Denise, were to become a living manifestation of

Katherine's cruel, perfect philosophy. She moaned desperately into the dummy gag and arched her back angrily as Christina's free hand then began to wander over the teasing fabric of the nightdress. Babified, bound, gagged, enveloped in a sea of pink silk, Denise was utterly helpless and, much more disturbingly, beset by a very real sexual arousal, an arousal she fought desperately, trying to recall images of her gorgeous wife, of her future life as Helen's perfect she-male maid.

'I'll be in at six tomorrow morning,' Christina said. 'You'll need to be carefully prepared to meet the mistresses.'

With this, and to Denise's massive relief, Christina then pulled up the side panel and locked it in place. As her field of vision was restricted by the bonnet, she could only listen to Christina slipping herself back into the dainty maid's dress. Then her new lover shouted out, 'Sleep tight, babikins!' and the room was plunged into darkness. Then she heard Christina shut and lock the nursery door.

Tied tightly in place, nappied and dummy-gagged, Denise stared into the blackness of her feminine soul to confront the strange and frightening events that had just thrown her into a pit of utter despair, a pit made darker and deeper by the fact that she was also aware of the perverse desires that had been unleashed inside her by this encounter with the gorgeous Christina, desires she was now fighting with an increasing sense of doubt. Teased and ravished by another she-male, with the promise of much more to come, Denise was ashamed and worried. But, despite this, there was a growing part of her that was filled with a desire for more. Christina's splendid, highly erotic image suddenly filled her mind. She was both horrified and excited by the prospect of the morning. Yet even as she struggled with these contradictory thoughts and feelings, she began to feel terribly tired, then exhausted, then unable to remain conscious. Within two minutes of the light being turned off, Denise was lost in a deep sleep, a sleep induced by two large bottles of milk laced with a strong sedative and a number of very powerful female hormones.

Ten

She returned from a dreamless, bottomless pit of sleep like a diver rising slowly from the depths of the ocean. Her mind enveloped in the confusing haze of semi-consciousness, she was briefly unaware of where she was or what had happened to her. Then, emerging like a developing photograph, there was the lovely face of Christina, her deep brown eyes filled with love, curiosity and desire.

'Wake up, babikins. It's six o'clock! You've been in the land of nod for eleven hours!'

These fresh, teasing words opened a black box of memories. The strange and highly erotic events of the previous night came flooding back. Denise moaned into her dummy gag with sleepy surprise and a first, confused desire. Within seconds her sex was rock hard and her mind possessed by a fierce, but shame-tinged need.

As Christina moved into sharp focus, Denise noticed that she was dressed in a striking red inversion of maid's costume she had worn yesterday. Where the previous dress had been a gorgeous creation of sheer black satin with red trimmings, this new dress was exactly the same design but coloured bright red with black trimmings! Also, she was wearing matching red seamed nylons and red leather stilettos (with *black* pom-pom feathers fixed to each toe). This all became much clearer as Christina stretched over her babified charge to release the leather shackles securing her in the cot, as did her black suspenders and the intricate black lace trimming which covered the lovely dress. Unlike yesterday, however, her gorgeous black hair had been bound into a very tight bun with a pretty diamond clasp and her dainty white lace maid's cap rested neatly upon it like a sexy snowflake.

As Denise beheld the wonderful spectacle of her she-male lover to be, Christina quickly freed her mittened hands and untied the bow binding her ankles through the material of the nightdress. To Denise's surprise and severe disquiet, she then quickly rolled the long pink dress up her pink stockinged legs and over the bulging plastic panties. The panties themselves were hauled down in one swift tug and Christina then carefully inspected the nappy. It was only at this point that Denise realised that during sleep she had thoroughly wet herself!

'Oh dear, babikins, you've had a little accident!' Christina exclaimed, a cruel smile lighting up her beautiful face.

Poor Denise blushed furiously, experiencing a new, even deeper sense of utter humiliation.

'Mistress Mary will need to know this when she inspects you. I'm afraid you must expect a very sound spanking.'

Denise was helped from the cot and quickly stripped down to her soaking nappy and mittens. Christina then led her from the nursery to the bathroom. Here, the nappy was removed and gingerly disposed of via a large dirty washing basket. The mittens followed, and Denise was soon under the shower washing herself from head to toe with a wide variety of feminine soaps and shampoos.

Christina led her from the fog of scented steam some fifteen minutes later. The gorgeous, younger she-male then carefully dried her sexy charge in a large and very thick pink towel and then returned her to the nursery. Here, Denise was placed on the stool before the dressing table. As she sat before the table's oval mirror, she beheld a ghost from the very recent past: Denise confronted Denis. A much younger, softer looking Denis, his blond hair in disarray, his body silky smooth, the sweet, sexy buds of she-male breasts a physical hint of the feminine future awaiting her.

Almost immediately, Christina began transforming the ghost of Denis back into sexy, sweet Baby Denise. The gorgeous younger she-male used an electric hairdryer to bring Denise's hair back under feminine control, eventually teasing it into lovely, little girl waves of soft blonde silk. Using a giant powder puff taken from the maze of feminine make-up items on the table, she bathed Denise in a fine mist of powerfully scented pink dust, dabbing the pad against her face, neck, shoulders and upper chest. Sitting up straight, arms at her side, Denise quickly found her eyes wandering from her own disturbing reflection towards Christina, watching with a deeply ambivalent fascination each careful feminine move, each charming, girlish gesture, listening to the sensual sounds of her rustling petticoats, the electric whispers of red-stockinged thighs. The beautifully sheer satin of the spectacular maid's dress rubbed against Denise's smooth, naked body and Christina's powerful French perfume tickled her baby-girl nostrils. Her sex remained rigid throughout, staring up at Denise like an inescapable confession of her absolute desire for this now permanent state of ultra-femininity.

Once suitably powdered, Christina gently guided Denise to her feet. At Christina's insistence, she soon stood firmly to attention, her hands clasped behind her back, her buttocks forced tightly together and pressing the anal plug even deeper into her expanding back passage. An inadvertent moan of pleasure followed and Christina then took an ornate blue bottle from the table and enveloped her charge's helplessly feminine body in a haze of a very strong, musk-scented perfume. The perfume instantly recalled Samantha: it was the fragrance her mother-in-law had worn the day before.

Powdered and scented, Denise watched with increasing excitement as Christina took from a drawer in the dressing table a sheer black nylon stocking. Retrieving the blue bottle, she then engulfed the stocking in a cloud of the musk perfume.

'A fresh, scented sex stocking will be positioned every day, babikins – so Mistress Mary can keep an eye on any naughty emissions. So take a deep breath, because I know how much you like the feel of sheer nylon on your cock'.

Poor Denise obeyed, closing her eyes tightly as Christina bunched up the stocking and slipped it carefully over the bulging head of her engorged sex. A delightfully girlish squeal of pleasure exploded from Denise's pretty mouth as the stocking was pulled tightly over her sex, positioned around her scrotum, and then tied securely in place with a red silk ribbon.

'Dear me ... you are a sensitive little thing! And so noisy. No wonder Mistress Samantha has insisted you be gagged at all times.'

The stocking was followed by a fresh, very thick, scented nappy, which was wrapped around Denise's waist, pulled tightly between her legs, then fixed in place with another huge safety pin. After this, Christina carefully selected a large bundle of underclothing from the wardrobe and placed each item carefully on the table by the cot.

With a knowing, teasing smile, she took up a lovely powder-blue satin and silk training bra and held it before Denise.

'Mummy suggested a powder-blue look for today, babikins. She wants you to be as pretty and sissified as possible, and so do I,' Christina purred, slipping the delicate straps of the bra over Denise's silky, slender arms and securing the ribbon-covered clasp at the centre of her surprisingly muscular yet shapely back.

The dainty bra contained Denise's darling budding breasts with ease, but even this mildest feeling of containment and support filled the beautiful she-male with a genuinely feminine joy.

The bra was followed by a delightful matching corset decorated with beautiful blue flowers, which Christina managed to pull even tighter than the day before, forcing more air from Denise's lungs and reducing her already slender waist at least another inch.

After the corset came the most exquisite pair of powder-blue, very sheer and delicately seamed stockings decorated with hundreds of tiny silver stars. Denise was put back on the stool and handed a stocking. With practised ease, she slid the sensuous, fetishistic object over her left foot and up a long, shining leg. Sighing with pleasure as the soft nylon caressed her baby smooth skin, she pulled the stocking into place around her left thigh, the darker, slightly elasticated and self-supporting top holding it firmly in place. She then carefully repeated this balletic manoeuvre with the second stocking, eventually smoothing the sheer nylon over her thighs with small, girlish hands, her eyes glued in fascination to the sparkling stars.

Returned to her feet, Denise was presented with a large pair of powder-blue plastic panties edged with inches of delicate white lacing. These the sissified she-male quickly but gracefully slipped up her gloriously stockinged legs and pulled tightly into position over the thick, restraining nappy.

As Denise adjusted the panties, Christina took from the wardrobe a truly spectacular pair of stiletto-heeled ankle-boots and presented them with a mock curtsy before her stunned she-male charge.

Each boot was covered in a gleaming skin of powder-blue silk; each had delicate sky-blue silk ribbon laces running through sparkling silver eyes; each pointed toe was topped by a lovely white feather pom-pom; and wrapped around each ankle was a band of tinny silver bells.

'Aren't they lovely!' Christina cooed, gently slipping the boots over Denise's stockinged feet and tying them firmly in place. 'Mummy is particular fond of the bells. She wants your every movement to be accompanied by a sweet, babyish tinkling. This way you will never be able to escape observation and control, and you'll be constantly reminded of your absolute servitude.'

Once the boots had been secured, Christina turned Denise back to the mirror and began to apply the final touches of make-up to her pretty face. Denise could only watch in awe as Christina added a mild cream foundation to her helplessly feminine face, the younger she-male's long, elegant fingers gliding over her soft skin with a silky, erotic ease. After the foundation came a delicate powder-blue eyeshadow, a gleaming cherry-red lipstick and a gentle peach rouge. Then, a touch of black eyeliner and the careful location of a lovely jet-black beauty spot at the left corner of her sensual mouth.

Reborn in the mirror, Denise was again helped to her feet and led back towards the wardrobe, each babyish wiggle mince accompanied by the sweet tinkle of the tiny bells. Made to stand to a graceful but firm attention, her hands clasped tightly behind her back, Denise could only watch with excited fascination as Christina took from within the wardrobe a truly amazing dress: a spectacular baby girl's dress of exquisite powder-blue silk, covered in a dazzling pattern of pale blue and white lace-edged roses, its wide, very short skirt supported by a magnificent sea of matching powder-blue lace petticoating, its high, pearl-buttoned neck and long, puffed sleeves also ringed with exquisite blue lace.

'This is one of Mummy's creations. It's simply marvellous. And you're really a very lucky little girl to be allowed to wear it,' Christina said.

The younger she-male then moved behind Denise, who instinctively raised her long arms above her head to allow Christina to lower the dress over her sissified body.

Then it was as if Denise has been submerged in the essence of babyish femininity, enveloped in the molten core of the masochistic need for absolute surrender that was at the heart of the personality Samantha had called to life. The dress was everything that had happened and would happen, a perfect symbol of her intricate feminisation. She could not help but moan with pleasure as it was gently guided over her feminised body and then secured in place with a long row of ornate white pearl buttons that ran from the base of the dress to the lace-frilled and very high neck, which gently tickled Denise's sweetly dimpled chin.

Once the dress was secured, Christina, her lovely dark eyes filled with a glowing admiration, took two powder-blue silk mittens from a drawer built into the lower section of the wardrobe. They were similar to the dainty pink mittens Helen had imprisoned Denise in yesterday, but even more elaborate. Sewn into them was the same intricate pattern of blue and white lace roses that so ornately covered the gorgeous dress. Like the pink mittens, a silk band (also powder-blue) ran through each sleeve, yet unlike their pink cousins, these mittens also had a band of the now familiar tiny silver bells attached just beyond the ribbon fastening. Before fixing the mittens to Denise's hands, however, Christina placed them on the table by the cot and produced two pale-blue rubber sheaths, each of which was stretched tautly over Denise's hands only when the she-male had been made to create two very tight fists. Thus, as yesterday, her hands were made useless, and over these sheathed stumps were stretched and tied the two belled, silk mittens.

'Mummy has insisted that you wear the mittens when not carrying out tasks involving your hands. As you will spend the morning being inspected by Mistress Mary, then meeting Mistress Samantha and Mummy, you will wear the mittens. This afternoon, the mittens will be replaced with our standard glacé serving gloves.'

Denise was returned to the dressing table and again made to sit before the large oval mirror. The image that confronted her was one of delightfully sweet little girl femininity. Christina, her own feelings made obvious by her fascinated gaze, could not fail to notice Denise's arousal.

'Yes, you really are utterly adorable, babikins. Mummy and Mistress Samantha will be so pleased! I must admit I'm having trouble keeping my hands off you. I'm not too sure how much longer I can hold out!'

Despite her continued embarrassment and shame, Denise found herself smiling a sweet, excited little girl's smile. She watched as Christina then proceeded to take a large pink-teated dummy fitted to a pale-blue plastic base from a drawer in the dressing table. Two lengths of pale blue ribbon were attached to eyes in each end of the base.

'A fresh dummy gag for you, petal. To keep you nice and quiet in all that sexy finery. I hope you like the special teat. Mary has had quite a few specially designed.'

It is only when Christina drew her attention to it that Denise noticed the teat. Unlike the dummy gag she currently wore, the new pacifier was fitted with a long, very fat and ribbed pink rubber phallus! Before she could utter a moan of protest, however, Christina quickly untied and removed the existing dummy and forced home its perverse replacement. Poor Denise squealed with outrage as the gag was rammed home and tied tightly in place. She tried to shake her head angrily, but Christina managed to hold her reasonably still and finish fitting the humiliating device.

'Please, Denise, there really is no point in fighting! I'm much stronger than you, and if you continue to resist me, you'll be spanked.'

Christina's tone was suddenly forceful, determined. Denise was appalled to be so helpless, so weak, so vulnerable before this beautiful, younger she-male.

Then Christina's tone changed. 'Get used to it, babikins – sucking cock is an art every sissy she-male maid must learn in this house.'

The phallus filled her mouth completely, pressing hard against the top and back of her mouth and making even the slightest squeak of protest impossible. Its length was matched shockingly by its breadth, and poor Denise found that her rouged cheeks were now bulging in an absurd and utterly humiliating manner, as if her mouth were filled with a very large pair of panties or even bloomers, or, and no doubt intentionally, as if she were a chubby-cheeked baby girl. Her sense of violation was absolute. And in this darkest moment of subjugation, she found herself suddenly determined to resist any plan designed to turn her into a homosexual sissy slave. Again she thought of Helen, of beautiful, imperial Helen. Surely *she* could not be party to this wicked plan – surely *she* would come and claim her she-husband!

As Denise considered her fate, Christina took a silver chain from the drawer that had held the gag. She knelt down by Denise's high-heeled feet and attached the chain to two small silver hooks built into the inside ankle of each elegant boot. Once more, the lovely she-male was to be tightly hobbled, the chain allowing only six inches for her to wiggle and mince within. Then came a final item from the wardrobe: a large, blue lace-trimmed baby's bonnet of the same delightful, flower-patterned silk from which the spectacular dress and mittens had been made. Startled and filled with a familiar fetishistic delight, Denise moaned her pleasure at the prospect of being imprisoned in this perfect symbol of absolute sissification. Fear was transformed into desire so easily – perhaps far too easily.

Lowering the bonnet on to her thick head of dazzling baby blonde hair, Christina whispered in a hoarse, aroused voice, 'I crown thee queen of the sissies!'

The younger she-male then tied the matching silk ribbons attached to the bonnet in a large bow at Denise's chin, surrounding her lovely head in a halo of baby-girl perfection. Denise's transformation was complete: once again she was the delightfully sissified, ultra-feminine she-male, sweet as Swiss chocolate, sexy as the wickedest erotic secret. Christina's eyes were filled with desire for this beautiful sex pet, her own silk gloved hands wandering over her charge's tightly restrained waist, over her fledgling chest, over the delicate lace edging of the sumptuous bonnet.

'I want you so terribly, babikins. This is such cruel temptation. But I must obey my mistresses. As must you. But we'll be together soon, my love. I promise.'

Poor Denise could only utter a well-muffled moan of confusion, the fat, penis-shaped dummy gag so effectively and humiliatingly filling her darling mouth, her own well-secured, tormented sex rock hard beneath layers of sensual nylon, thick nappy towelling and scented plastic panties, her eyes drinking deep both of her startling powder-blue reflection and, however reluctantly, of Christina's stunning form sealed in the fetishistic delights of the highly erotic maid's costume. Christina's beauty was undeniable, as was Denise's own intense desire for this spectacular feminisation. But still there was a real, fundamental resistance to the idea of becoming Christina's lover. It was the bridge too far, the final barrier between her and a complete and utterly irreversible surrender.

Denise was then helped back on to her high-heeled feet.

'First you will be inspected by Mistress Mary,' Christina announced, her tone now matter of fact, efficient. 'Then you will be fed and taken to meet Mummy and Mistress Samantha. After this, you will be handed back to Mistress Mary so that your training may begin in earnest. But now you need to be secured.'

Using two matching powder-blue silk ribbons, Christina then tied Denise's arms behind her back at the wrists and elbows, using gloriously fat bows rather than knots to secure the bindings. Then a familiar white leather collar was fitted around her powder-blue silk and lace-encased neck. A chain was attached to the collar and Christina quickly took up the slack, a wicked, hungry smile lighting up her gorgeous face. It was clear she enjoyed dominating Denise.

And so Denise was led in a state of highly excited, yet fearful anticipation, tightly bound, dummy-gagged and hobbled from the nursery by the beautiful Christina, her tiny, delicate and rapid steps creating the helplessly sexy wiggle that had now become all but instinct for the gorgeous, sissified she-male, a wonderful display accompanied by the dainty tinkle of the bells wrapped around her ankles and wrists. She was taken from the nursery, back down the long, dark corridor that seemed to run beneath the large house, and back up the steep concrete stairwell (a slow, careful process, overseen with intimate attention to her plastic-pantied bottom by a cooing Christina). Then they were in a much brighter, shorter corridor, their heels striking a highly polished wooden floor, the tiny bells echoing around them. This corridor led through to the entrance foyer area, a vast space flooded with early daylight. Now their ultra high heels were striking a beautiful white marble floor streaked with threads of gold.

Denise tried to comprehend the full size and glamour of the house through the restricted view allowed by the bonnet. As Denis, she had visited the house only a few times, always at night and always under rather stressful circumstances. Now, freed of the petty jealousy and fear that defined her previous male self, she was able to surrender wholeheartedly to the grandeur of Samantha's splendid home.

The hall was dominated by a beautiful winding staircase that led to the first floor. To the left of the staircase was a set of imposing double doors, which she knew led to the library. There was another corridor on the opposite side of the staircase, just beyond the library doors. This led down to the kitchen. Also on the right of the staircase, smaller, although still very elegant doors led respectively to the living room, the dining room and a large banqueting room used by Samantha for the many parties she hosted throughout the year. In the centre of the hallway was a large white marble statue of a beautiful naked woman, a striking and perfectly designed work in the classical style, whose model was very obviously Samantha. And this was no image of submissive femininity. This was a vision of spectacular female power, of physical control and certainty – a martial image of warrior womanhood. The statue reflected the vast array of paintings that lined the walls of this impressive house, each and every one a picture of a woman or women, many expensive masterpieces, others specially commissioned, all of powerful historical figures, of mythical goddesses, of supreme, dominant women.

A swift tug on the leash drew Denise's attention away from the splendour of the hallway, and she was led across the beautiful marble floor into the banqueting room, a large, rectangular space, now empty, its dark wooden floor bare except for an oval rug placed in the exact centre of the room. On the rug was a small coffee table and a simple, wooden chair. The walls were covered in more paintings, all on the same basic theme that was present throughout the rest of the house. The banqueting room, like the hallway, was filled with crisp morning sunlight, its source a set of French windows that stretched from one end of the room to the other. Windows without decoration or curtains, which looked out on to the vast, beautifully kept grounds of Samantha's impressive estate.

Sitting in the chair was Mary, beautiful and cruel, her lovely brown eyes beholding the two she-males with amusement and contempt. She was dressed in another short, tight leather skirt, this one jet black, with a very tight matching nylon sweater, the sheerest black hose and stiletto-heeled mules. Her gorgeous hair was once again bound in a deceptively girlish ponytail, the single hint that this startling dominatrix was only eighteen years old, a few years younger than Christina and a frightening fourteen years younger than Denise. But here, in this room, in this house, in this new world within which Denise had been imprisoned, she had absolute power; here in this room, she was easily the most senior, and her word was the Law. Both Christina and Denise acknowledged this with deep curtsies. Christina's curtsy was smooth, elegant, deliberately designed to reveal her dark red stocking tops and befrilled red panties. Denise's curtsy was awkward and quite desperate in her tight bondage.

Mary rose from the chair. 'Bring Denise to me.'

Christina obeyed with a further curtsy and a hoarsely whispered 'Yes, Mistress.' Denise was led on to the rug and brought before the tall, sexy girl, her bells ringing sweetly, her tiny high-heeled steps providing a dainty visual accompaniment.

Denise performed another awkward curtsy and stared with due deference at Mary's gleaming, black patent-leather shoes, trying unsuccessfully to avoid her superb, black nylon-sheathed legs.

'You look rather lovely, Denise,' Mary teased. 'Christina has done an excellent job. Do you like the way you look?'

Denise curtsied again and nodded.

'Do you like being a pathetic little sissy?'

Again a curtsy and a nod.

'Yes. You're a natural. Which is more than can be said for Christina. We had to try very hard with Christina. Do you know she's still a virgin? Well, strictly speaking. Never had a woman. Never will have one now. Prefers pretty little things like you. But that wasn't always the case. No: Christina used to have a lovely little girlfriend when she thought she was a boy. But I soon put a stop to all that silliness. After all, the poor girl was my best friend!'

As she delivered this cruel, bitter assault, Mary began to circle Denise and Christina, regarding them with cold, wolf-like eyes. Denise listened in horror to this dreadful teasing of Christina, whose own head now hung very low indeed.

'You must tell Denise all about Liz, Chrissie. Yes, I insist you tell her all about your feminisation. And we mustn't forget about Daphne. Daphne was Christina's second love, Denise. But Christina wasn't very happy about it at the time. Why? Aren't you dying to know why? Well, Daphne was a rather lovely she-male. A little older than you, Denise; maybe thirty-five or so. And very experienced. She was the plaything of one of Mummy's friends, and *very* kinky. Mummy actually gave Christina to Daphne as a birthday present – we even gift-wrapped her! Literally packed her off to Daphne's home for six months. For six months she was Daphne's sissy pet, a beautiful living doll who Daphne taught all the secret, naughty acts of she-male love. Turned her into quite an expert. And by the time she came home, all she could think about was Daphne and her special ways. Poor Liz couldn't get a look in then. Not that she wanted one, of course, once she discovered that her boyfriend was a dainty little sissy who preferred panties and hose to pants and trousers!'

Now Mary was standing directly in front of Denise, her powerful musk perfume washing over the frightened she-male like a scented mist of doom. Then, suddenly, a thought entered her head: here I am, thirty years old, terrified by an eighteen-year-old girl with a particularly vicious tongue. And this girl intends me to become the homosexual lover of another transvestite slave! But this thought, a throwback, a residue, faded quickly, as sweet, sexy, doe-eyed Denise returned, her heart pumping with helpless sissy fear before this particularly determined and youthful mistress.

'Has she *behaved* herself?'

A moment of hesitation from Christina earned her a very hard slap across the face. 'I said has she behaved herself!'

Christina curtsied deeply, dragged from her pit of humiliation. 'Sorry, Mistress. No – she wet her nappy during the night.'

Mary laughed. 'Look at me, Denise.'

Denise obeyed, forcing her baby-blue eyes to meet Mary's glowing brown orbs.

'How old are you? Thirty, did we say? A thirty-year-old she-male who wets herself. Pathetic. Disgusting. No wonder you're in nappies. If I had my way, you'd stay in them forever! But what else should I expect from such a silly, pretty little sissy.'

Mary regarded Denise with withering, terrifying contempt. Then she turned to Christina. 'Remove her panties and nappy and put her over the table.'

Christina obeyed instantly, stepping forward and quickly pulling up the layers of Denise's petticoating, dragging the plastic panties down around her booted and belled ankles and then unpinning and unwinding the fat, thick nappy. The instant she did this, Denise's large, violently erect, stocking-encased sex popped out once again and Mary's eyes widened in disbelief.

'Look at that, Christina!'

Mary stepped forward, pushed Christina roughly out of the way, and then, to Denise's horror, grabbed the tightly stockinged sex.

'You're a big little girl, aren't you! And Helen says putting you in nappies is the only thing that makes you stiff. I'm sure Christina has already had a taste of this particularly prime pork. Was it nice, Chrissie?'

'Yes, Mistress, it was lovely,' Christina whispered in response, her eyes now filled with tears, her cheeks red with a terrible embarrassment and an even more terrible desire, an embarrassment shared by a deeply blushing, appalled Denise.

'Well, I expect you to make absolutely sure this naughty thing is kept clean and tightly stockinged at all times. I will expect to see the previous day's stocking each morning. If there is the slightest stain, she will be locked in the dirty laundry basket for an hour with my jogging panties in her mouth and a tube of Ralgex smothered over this wayward tool.'

Mary released Denise's engorged sex and allowed Christina to bend the startled she-male over the coffee table. The younger she-male then carefully positioned Denise's exposed and extremely pert behind.

'A wet nappy gets you twelve strokes of my hairbrush, Denise. If it happens again, twelve strokes of the cane. I'll add four more each time you repeat this naughty act.'

The hairbrush, long, ivory-handled, was taken from the table by Christina and handed with another servile curtsy to her mistress.

'This brings back memories of the shop, Denise. But I think you'll find my enthusiasm has increased since our last encounter.'

And poor Denise could only agree as she received twelve hard, fast wacks of the hairbrush against her tender, sensitive, girlish backside, her cries drowned out by the fat penis-shaped dummy gag, huge tears soon welling up in her lovely blue eyes, her quickly reddening buttocks soon wobbling desperately and erotically under the repeated blows.

Then it was over. Or was it? Heels clicked. There was more movement behind her. Then a sharp pain in her enflamed left buttock.

'You will continue to receive the twice daily injections of hormones, my sweet.' One more painful injection accompanied Mary's teasing explanation. 'We've found sexual stimulation makes a very obedient and willing sissy, so regular doses should keep you suitably submissive.'

Following the injections, Denise was pulled to her hobbled, belled and heeled feet by Christina, the nappy and plastic panties were resecured, and she was once more standing before the sexy, sadistic Mary.

'Christina will take you to the kitchen for breakfast. Then you will be presented to Mummy, Samantha and Auntie Bridget. After this, we'll begin your training in earnest.'

Her buttocks stinging painfully, tears filling her lovely eyes, her erection firmer than ever in its teasing layers of feminine imprisonment, Denise was led from the room by Christina, across the foyer and down the second hallway. As she followed behind Christina, she could tell from the anger in her steps and the small, poorly hidden sniffles that the younger she-male was very upset. Mary had clearly touched a very raw nerve.

At the end of the hallway was another set of precarious steps. These led down to a large, once Victorian but now very modern kitchen. The array of gleaming, hi-tech kitchenware that Denise beheld was evidence both of wealth and volume: this was the kitchen for a house used to entertaining large numbers of people.

Christina led her mincing charge to a large table located in the far corner of the room. This, Denise presumed, was where the servants ate. As they approached the table, Denise noticed a familiar adult-size high chair standing behind the table. Then, to her surprise, a voice filled the room – a female voice.

'Chrissie! Is this her? Oh, she's absolutely gorgeous!'

Christina turned towards the voice, tugging Denise to a halt. Walking towards them from the other side of the kitchen was an attractive, matronly lady in her early fifties, her plump, but still rather shapely figure well displayed by a tight and surprisingly short black dress, her long, curvy legs sealed in sheer black hose, her feet imprisoned in high-heeled court shoes. Her hair, thick, black with streaks of grey, was bound in a tight bun with a silver clasp. Her friendly green eyes were filled with a surprising warmth and absolute fascination.

Christina curtsied deeply. 'Mistress Grace, I didn't expect you so early –'

'Don't worry about that, Chrissie. I came in to see Denise. Sam has told us so much about her. I'm afraid I just couldn't wait.'

Following Christina's example, Denise performed a deep, dainty curtsy before this impressive woman, her eyes directed with due modesty and deference at Mistress Grace's elegant shoes.

Grace smiled appreciatively at this servile gesture. 'I see she's been well trained. And what a beauty! I never expected this. She looks so utterly adorable in this outfit. Sam should keep her in nappies forever!'

'Mistress Mary is of a similar opinion, Mistress,' Christina replied.

'I'm sure Mary has her own no doubt bizarre reasons for saying that.'

'Mistress Grace acts as house manager and is also the Treasurer for the Last Straw Society,' Christina said, turning back to Denise.

It was clear to Denise that Christina was deeply attached to Grace. There seemed to be none of the coldness of the dominatrix that informed the behaviour of the other women in the house. Her friendly tone and warm smile recalled an affectionate aunt rather than an ardent feminist and hater of men. Denise wondered how she managed to interact successfully with the likes of Samantha and Mary.

Grace then stepped forward and took the sissified she-male's beribboned face in her hands. 'A real darling, Chrissie. Katherine chose well.'

Denise was mystified by this remark, given that Samantha had been the engineer of this intricate feminisation. But the compliment still managed to fill the lovely she-male with pride.

'I'll feed her, Chrissie. You get the bottle, I'll put her in the chair.'

Christina curtsied with the sweetest of smiles and minced over to main kitchen work area. As Christina prepared the bottle that was to be Denise's breakfast, Grace took up the leash and led the babified she-male to the high chair, her large green eyes eating up Denise's gloriously effeminate form.

There was no doubt that Grace had once been a very beautiful woman and was still very attractive. Her ample, very sexy figure was expertly displayed by the tight black dress, and as she untied Denise and helped her into the high chair, the babified she-male was treated to a face full of heaving bosom and, much to her surprise, hands that roved with a passionate curiosity amongst her pretty undergarments.

'Perhaps I could convince Sam to let me have you for a while. As part of your training. Yes, come and live with me for a few weeks, babikins. I'm sure I could make you very happy.'

Denise could only look at this attractive, teasing woman with aroused eyes and wonder about the many ways that Grace would find to make her happy.

Christina returned armed with another large baby's bottle and a wide smile. By now Denise had been locked and tied into the chair and was immobilised, her petticoating exploding out of the seat and exposing her delicate powder-blue stocking tops and plastic panties, an exposure that only served to increase Denise's deeply masochistic arousal.

Grace took the bottle from Christina. The dummy gag was removed and the large rubber teat of the bottle gently pushed between Denise's soft, curving lips. Almost instinctively, she began to suck on the hormone-laced, sugared milk.

She consumed the milk with a desperate enthusiasm, only realising how thirsty she was once the teat was firmly between her lips. As she fed, her eyes remained filled with the highly erotic spectacle of Grace.

Gradually the quality of Denise's already intense sexual arousal was changing. Where before she had been very much aware of her surroundings and very strange circumstances, now she seemed only truly aware of the absolute sexual moment, of the immediate thrill of her highly sexualised being. It was as if the world had been made sex, as if desire had entrapped and transformed this bizarre house and turned it into a giant generator of fierce, static sexual energy, an energy that now washed over Denise in waves of increasing size and power.

Every sense had been heightened, particularly the sense of touch. Every gorgeous, delicate, teasing feminine fabric which so erotically imprisoned her girlish body now seemed to be kissing and caressing every silky inch of her scented skin. It was as if she were being ravished by the sexy garments that enveloped her body! She was submerged in a gentle sea of tactile delight; and as she squirmed in her baby bondage, as Grace, with her beautiful green, highly aroused eyes and superb body, fed Denise the sweet formula, the lovely she-male experienced an epiphany of pure desire, a moment of dazzling insight into herself and its molten sexual core. She was sex. And sex, this intricate, masochistic, ritualised sex, was the very force of all life. Now her submission to this feminised condition, this state of complete sissification, was absolute and inescapable.

As she sucked hungrily on the soft rubber teat and the sweet milk trickled down her throat, as the anal plug teased and stretched the ultra-sensitive walls of her anus and the sheer nylon fabric of the stocking restrainer tormented her permanently engorged sex, she realised, if only momentarily, that her being had become the embodiment of slavery: a slave to her feminisation, a slave to all women – a slave to desire.

Then her eyes fell once again on Christina. The lovely, younger she-male was standing next to Grace, her own dark eyes filled with need and adoration, her large, perfectly shaped breasts rising and falling rapidly beneath the smooth, tightly fitting red satin of the elaborate maid's dress. Her beauty was undeniable, as was her erotic appeal. Poor Denise could not now deny that she was deeply attracted to the glorious younger she-male. Memories of Christina's lips brushing against her sex like silken rose petals, of her warm, sensual mouth holding the older she-male in the most intimate of embraces, filled her mind. The shame, the guilt, the fear of surrender, was overwhelmed by the powerful effects of the hormones. Yet even as she capitulated to this desire, her ultimate mistress, there remained a trace of doubt and perhaps the slightest of insights.

Grace finished the feeding and stepped back, clearly very excited.

'Perhaps we can take her to my room and play for a little while,' she mumbled, her eyes almost glazed over with arousal.

Christina, clearly equally stimulated, smiled, but gently shook her head. 'Mummy and Mistress Samantha wish to see her immediately after breakfast, Mistress.'

'Yes, of course. Well, maybe another time.'

Then Grace lent forward and kissed Denise on her forehead, her hand sliding once again beneath the sissy's petticoats. 'Yes, another time, babikins – another time *soon*.'

Before Denise could express her own enthusiasm for such a reunion, Christina had resecured the dummy gag and started to release her charge from the high chair. By the time Denise was standing, her arms tightly rebound behind her, the leash taken up by Christina, Grace had left the kitchen, her movements appearing unsteady, a woman temporarily unbalanced by sexual hunger.

'I'm sure you'll be seeing much more of Mistress Grace, babikins, and I can see the prospect excites you,' Christina said, tugging on the leash and leading Denise from the kitchen.

Soon they were climbing the beautiful, winding staircase and mincing in tiny, sissy steps down the long, brightly lit corridor that dominated the first floor of the house. Eventually they wiggled to halt before a particularly large door. Each movement during this brief journey had been a terrible, ecstatic torment. With her enforced little girl's walk, with her delicately stockinged thighs brushing gently together, with the babyish tinkling of the bells and the constant rubbing of the nylon restrainer and anal plug, poor, pretty Denise was now unable to stifle a constant, high-pitched moan of pleasure. With her lovely eyes filled with the startling spectacle of Christina's long, red-stockinged legs and the teasing wiggle the younger she-male so expertly demonstrated with each high-heeled step, there was now no resistance to the fierce sex heat burning her sissy body alive.

'The initial hormone rush will fade after about an hour,' Christina said, just before she knocked lightly on the door. 'If you weren't gagged, you'd be screaming in ecstasy.'

From behind the door came Samantha's stern, cool voice – a simple command to enter.

Christina pushed open the doors and led Denise inside. The older she-male, her body and mind afire with molten sexual need, wiggle-minced behind the lovely Christina into an ornate, Victorian-style anteroom which seemed to lead on to a large bedroom. A soft orange light filled the room, bathing cream-coloured walls in delicate shadows and revealing a vast array of framed pictures, mainly drawings, almost all erotic, almost all portraying the many varieties of lesbian love in graphic detail.

A large, black leather sofa dominated the centre of the room and sitting upon it was Samantha – beautiful, supreme Mistress Samantha. This morning she was dressed in a semi-transparent white silk blouse with gleaming silver pearl buttons, a short black and white check skirt, sheer black hose and spike-heeled court shoes of black patent leather. A lacy black bra was clearly visible through the blouse, as were the rising mounds of the large, creamy breasts the bra somewhat inadequately restrained. Her thick, dark hair cascaded over her broad shoulders like a river of black gold, and as she beheld Denise, her blood-red lips arched into a cruel, vaguely amused smile.

Denise was positioned directly before the sofa. Samantha rose from her seat like a sleek, deadly feline, her dark, predatory eyes pinned to the dainty, babified form of the lovely she-male. A bolt of white hot lightning flashed across her eyes as she beheld her prey, a viscous pleasure transformed into high voltage static electricity. If Denise had been foolish enough or able to touch her, the pretty sissy would have been fried to a pathetic sissy crisp.

This was Samantha's moment of ultimate satisfaction. As she stood before moaning, twisting Denise, well over six feet tall in her spiked heels, a true dominatrix towering over her she-male slave, she was surely the perfect vision of triumphant female power.

'You look very pretty, Denise,' Samantha almost whispered.

Instinctively, Denise curtsied her appreciation of the compliment.

'You've done very well, Christina.'

Christina curtsied her own appreciation and stepped back to allow Samantha to move closer.

'But I can see you're suffering, Denise. An inevitable effect, I'm afraid. An almost unbearable pleasure. But you should remember this is only the beginning. Soon you'll come to accept sexual arousal as a fundamental and very permanent part of your day-to-day existence. What seems terrible now will become second nature. It's just a question of developing a tolerance. And it's also a question of acceptance. The more you resist, the more it will hurt. And we know you're resisting. There's still part of you that is fighting your destiny, your true sissy nature; a residue masculinity that is terrified and appalled by the prospect of a final, absolute acquiescence to sissidom. And it should be afraid, because this acquiescence is its total destruction. But you will surrender, babikins. I can assure you of that.'

Denise struggled to listen: the permanent white noise of desire interfered with every word. The tormented she-male could only truly *see* Samantha, this gorgeous vision, could only consume her with hungry, desperate eyes and moan her savage, animal need into the unyielding dummy gag.

'Your training begins today,' Samantha continued. 'During the first month Mary and Christina will supervise the first stage of your transformation into the perfect she-male slave and maidservant. This preliminary phase of your training will help you perfect your feminine and domestic skills. During this phase you will remain babified. Once you have demonstrated an acceptable level of performance, you will be allowed the costume of a maid and will pass the following five months under my personal supervision. You will be my maidservant, to be used by me as I see fit. As my sissy slave, you will come to learn the true meaning of submission.

'During your stay with us, you will also be tutored by Christina in the intricacies of she-male sex. I am sure Christina has explained the philosophy of the Last Straw Society to you by now, so you know intimate, sexual contact between yourself and any female is strictly forbidden. However, Christina has been especially trained to provide all the sexual pleasure you could possibly want, and it is our intention that you will become lovers as quickly as possible.'

For a brief moment in the midst of the sex storm Denise was trapped within, there was a dark, outraged glint in her tormented eyes. Despite the madness possessing her, she could still understand the dreadful implications of these particular words.

Samantha smiled at this brief flash of rebellion. 'Yes, you're still angry, there's still resistance. That terrible residue is burning away inside you. But it won't last long – Christina will soon put it out.'

As Denise struggled with the grim reality of her fate, Katherine appeared in the bedroom doorway. She was dressed in a beautiful, dark blue silk trouser suit.

'It's the perfect sissy,' she teased, her eyes filled with a gleeful malice. 'You really have outdone yourself, Christina.'

Katherine strolled into the anteroom, her feet wrapped in fierce high-heeled pumps, and embraced Samantha, kissing her passionately on the mouth. She then turned to the two she-males.

'I don't think she's very happy about her fate, Kathy,' Samantha sneered, lowering herself back on to the sofa.

Katherine released a sarcastically polite smile. 'Well, she'll just have to learn nobody really cares about whether she's happy or not. Anyway, Christina will soon persuade her to accept the inevitable.'

Poor Denise could only stare in furiously aroused amazement at the spectacle of these two beautiful women discussing her transformation into a homosexual she-male. It was if she were trapped in a wildly surreal and highly erotic nightmare.

Samantha continued to detail their plans.

'At the end of the six-month training period, and on condition that you meet the required standards, you will be returned to Helen to act as her maid on a full-time basis. You will still have duties associated with the Last Straw Society, and will no doubt be a regular visitor to this house, but if you behave yourself, your permanent position will be as Helen's sissy slave.'

This was the light at the end of the tunnel: if she could survive for six months, she would be returned to Helen, to her wife-mistress, to the world of servitude she understood and so very much desired!

'But now you must begin your training,' Samantha continued. 'Christina will take you to Mary. She will get you started straight away. There will be a strict routine involving constant hard work. Given your performance so far, we are optimistic you will progress through the next month with few problems. However, you should know that the slightest failing will be severely punished. You will find Mary a particularly hard task mistress, I'm sure. But it will be for your own good in the long run.'

Samantha then returned her attention to Katherine. Christina took up the leash and the two she-males curtsied deeply. As the flames of sex hunger continued to torture Denise, Christina led her from the room, the laughter of the two stunning women echoing behind her as she was led into the hallway and back towards the stairs.

They had minced only a few feet when another door opened and a woman stepped into the corridor. Christina immediately executed a deep curtsy and Denise quickly followed suit. The woman was blonde, tall and very striking. Dressed in a pale blue suit, with a predictably short skirt, white hose and matching high-heeled shoes, she appeared more 'traditionally' feminine than Katherine and Samantha, but her cold, ice-blue eyes emitted a gaze of such brutal power that Denise felt herself physically quake as they fell upon her babified form.

'This is her?'

Sharp, hard words in a vaguely foreign accent.

'Yes, Mistress Bridget. This is Denise,' Christina replied, genuine fear vibrating in her sissy voice.

The woman suddenly moved closer to Denise, taking her dimpled chin in a long, elegant hand and tilting her face up towards the light.

Her eyes appraised Denise as if she were a scientific specimen.

'Katherine was right: a very good subject. I can do a lot with her. Have the injections begun?'

'Yes, Mistress. Mistress Mary administered the first this morning.'

'Good. The new serum should ensure growth in a few weeks. Then we'll operate.'

Denise fought to understand. Yet before the words could be given any real meaning, the cool blonde suddenly walked off, heading with a deceptively feminine walk towards Samantha's room.

'Mistress Bridget,' Christina explained. 'My step-aunt. Mummy's half-sister. A plastic surgeon and research scientist. She is responsible for the various hormone treatments. She will also perform implant surgery once your breasts have grown sufficiently.'

In the whirlpool of desire overwhelming Denise's mind and body, this new information was processed as incoherent fragments making only limited sense. But the cold eyes of the new Mistress remained clear and inescapable, a threatening, dark reality that inspired real fear. In Bridget's eyes there had been the icy heart of the sociopath, a being who saw others, or maybe certain types of others, as little more than objects to be used. It was in Bridget's eyes that Denise saw the true and absolute nature of her subjugation: she was to be little more than an automaton here, a pretty domestic functionary and sex slave. Little more than an inanimate object. As Christina led her towards the winding stairs, she felt as if she were about to dive headfirst into a bottomless whirlpool of self-annihilation.

Eleven

A few minutes later they were back in the kitchen. Mary was seated at the oval table reading a magazine. As the two sissies minced towards her, she rose from her chair. Denise and Christina curtsied.

'You will begin the first phase of your training immediately,' she snapped, addressing Denise with familiar contempt. 'During the next month, we will concentrate on basic domestic duties and your feminine skills – movement, general deportment, make-up, body care. You will also begin to learn how to meet your mistresses more intimate needs. Christina has been charged with ensuring that you receive a thorough introduction to she-male sexual techniques. This will allow you the necessary physical release and help prepare you for your eventual role within the Last Straw Society. You will remain babified throughout this first phase and will only be permitted to wear the clothing of an adult she-male when you have proven that you can perform your duties in the manner required by your mistresses.

'You will rise at 5.30 a.m. with Christina. She will be responsible for all your deportment, dress and make-up training. You will be presented to me at seven o'clock each morning for inspection and a behaviour report. I will be responsible for any formal punishments that may be required, but other mistresses may also punish you as and when they see fit. The morning will be dedicated to domestic training and household duties. You will be expected to learn all the basic domestic skills required of a personal maid, including cooking and needlecraft. In the afternoon, you will undertake movement and dance classes, together with related physical exercises designed to ensure the required feminine demeanour. I will personally supervise these sessions, with assistance from Chrissie. In the evenings, you will both serve your mistresses as required. Chrissie will train you in sexual technique for at least thirty minutes at the end of each day. We will expect you to be tucked up in your cot by no later than ten o'clock.'

Mary's words were delivered with indifference, her mind elsewhere, this introduction providing little of the perverse entertainment she seemed to relish. Denise understood most of what was said: while she was still in a state of considerable sexual arousal, a little reason seemed to have returned to her strange world of submission and ultra-feminisation.

'The method of your domestic training will be simple: you will assist Christina with her daily household duties. She will report to me on your progress at the end of each morning. If you are deemed to be unsatisfactory in any area, you will be punished at the subsequent morning inspection. Do you understand everything I have said to you so far?'

Denise curtsied her understanding, her eyes never leaving Mary's high-heeled feet.

'Good. As I have more important things to do, you can begin to help Christina straight away. I will expect to see you both back here at one precisely.'

Mary then walked from the kitchen, her heels filling the air with rapid, impatient clicks, and Denise was left trying to avoid Christina's beautiful, probing eyes.

'I have to do the ironing and clean the kitchen this morning, so we'll start with this simple task,' the younger she-male said. 'I understand Mistress Helen has already provided you with some domestic training, so this shouldn't be too difficult.'

As Christina spoke, she moved behind her sexy, babified charge and began to untie her arms. 'I'll free your arms so you can use your hands, but you'll remain hobbled and gagged at all times during the first month, except of course when we need your mouth for other things.'

An excited light flashed across her eyes as she uttered these final words and Denise stepped another inch closer to the abyss of ravishment that awaited her at the hands of this beautiful she-male.

Once Denise's arms were free, Christina removed the powder-blue satin mittens, together with the bracelet of tiny bells, then eased the rubber sheaths from her girlish hands. As her hands were freed, numbness turned into a dull tingling, then painful pins and needles, before normal feeling slowly returned. As Denise flexed her fingers, Christina produced a pair of beautiful powder-blue, glacé gloves from a pocket in her maid's pinafore.

'You will wear gloves whenever required to act as a maidservant. The mittens will be worn at all other times during this initial phase of your training.'

Despite Christina's matter of fact tone, it was clear that she truly enjoyed being Denise's tutor. As she slipped the soft, shiny gloves over Denise's hands, their eyes met and locked together. Denise felt her feminine heart jump and her stockinged legs weaken. She was staring into two beautiful, bottomless pits of dark, unyielding desire. Her sex stretched hungrily against its gentle nylon prison and she was unable to deny an intense attraction to the gorgeous she-male.

'How will I be able to resist you, babikins?' Christina whispered, her tightly pinafored chest rising and falling rapidly, her long, teasing tongue rolling slowly across her moist and very full cherry-red lips. 'I want tonight to come so very, very quickly.'

Denise, despite the relative calming of the sex heat, moaned into her fat dummy gag and, perhaps surprisingly, pulled her long, delicately hosed legs tightly together in order to clench her buttocks and force the anal plug an inch deeper, thus increasing the intensity of the addictive physical pleasure that now constantly tormented her.

Once the gloves had been fitted and the belled bracelets replaced, Christina took up the silver chain leash and led her charge across the kitchen to a small, previously obscured doorway. She led Denise through the doorway into a large, brightly lit but windowless room. By the far wall of the room was a bank of washing machines and two industrial-size dry-cleaning units. Beside the washing machines were two white plastic baskets filled with clothing. On the opposite side of the room were two ironing boards, with an electric iron resting on each.

'This is the laundry room,' Christina said. 'We'll be spending a lot of time here. Looking after the clothes of our mistresses and ourselves is one of our main domestic responsibilities. The baskets contain washed and dried clothing that need ironing and storing. I loaded both washing machines earlier this morning. Our main task now is to iron the dry clothing and dry the freshly washed clothing.'

And so, under Christina's careful tuition, Denise began her training as a maidservant to the beautiful, dominant women of the Last Straw Society. The next two hours were spent trying to concentrate on ironing the wide and inevitably erotic variety of clothing which belonged to the women who lived in the house. Although the sex heat torment had lessened, her deeply fetishistic sexuality was intensely stimulated by the sensual array of fabrics and materials that came under the iron. Lost in a world of exotic underwear, an apparently endless variety of elegant and very sexy skirts, blouses and dresses, her task was to ensure that each garment was ironed perfectly and then either hung on a mobile rack or folded and stored in another plastic basket at her high-heeled, belled feet.

With Christina working on the second basket, the two she-males laboured in a strange, erotically charged silence. The two ironing boards had been placed opposite each other, so Denise found herself constantly looking up at the younger she-male, a vision of submissive loveliness in her intricate maid's costume, her delicate ironing motions putting Denise's often awkward strokes to shame. And each time she did look up, she was confronted not just by the stunning beauty of Christina, but by the frank, hungry light that shone from her lovely brown eyes.

After completing the ironing, the two sissy maids prepared the clothing for delivery to the rooms of their mistresses and sorted the next batch of ironing collected from the two dryers. The ironed clothes were then delivered, and the two she-males were soon hard at work cleaning the kitchen.

Denise could see that the kitchen was absolutely spotless. It was obvious that Christina laboured long and hard in this room each day. It was also clear that the reason for cleaning was not actually to clean, but to provide ritualised, humiliating and continual work for the she-male housemaids. As they scrubbed, washed and polished each surface into a mirrorlike sheen, they were affirming their absolute submission in the act of slave labour. And this labour was made even more laborious and tiring by the tight corset, the dainty, figure-hugging dress, the sweet baby bonnet, the so high heels, the hobbling chain and the fat, unyielding and very phallic gag that filled Denise's soft, she-male mouth, a final and very cruel device of restriction which reduced her breathing to increasingly desperate and rapid gasps. And the harder they laboured, the more they sweated. Denise, in particular, was soon soaked in a film of warm, sticky sweat that made her intricate, tight clothing even more uncomfortable. This ensured that efficient labour was almost impossible and that error was inevitable. But this too was surely part of the ritual of submission: she was bound to make a mistake and thus bound to be punished.

And sure enough a glass slipped from her powder-blue, glacé gloved hands and smashed on to the gleaming kitchen floor. Christina patiently cleaned away the aftermath and then returned Denise to her cleaning duties, playfully patting her plastic-pantied bottom as she did so and warning her that Mistress Mary would have to be informed of the breakage.

By 1 p.m., the two she-males were hot, bothered and near to exhaustion. When Mary returned, Christina duly informed her of Denise's error and the beautiful younger mistress smiled at her wickedly: it was very obvious poor Denise would suffer the next morning.

After a brief lunch, fed to Denise by a smiling, cooing Christina, the two she-males returned to the nursery. Here, Christina slowly and teasingly stripped Denise naked, except for the fat dummy gag and the stocking restrainer. Denise squirmed with a terrible mixture of embarrassment and desire as the younger she-male carefully peeled away her sissy attire, whispering words of love and need as she did so. Then, to Denise's amazement, Christina also began to undress. With a quite wicked smile, she slipped out of the damp, somewhat wrinkled pinafore and dress, out of her shoes, stockings and, finally, out of the gloriously tight basque that imprisoned her sex-bomb figure. Poor Denise's already furious, sheer nylon-wrapped sex became almost incandescent with animal rage as Christina unclipped the silver hooks holding the basque firmly in place and pulled it from her marvellous body. Suddenly, Denise was facing a topless Christina, confronting a truly magnificent pair of very large and perfectly formed breasts, pale rose orbs of feminine delight that demanded slow, loving caresses and which totally entranced the older she-male. But the spell was suddenly broken when Denise's baby-blue eyes were pulled down to the undeniable symbol of Christina's true biological self. Perhaps the words large and perfectly formed could also be used for what she beheld: a very substantial, very stiff and tightly restrained penis, an impressive male sex imprisoned in a pink satin restrainer very similar to the one Denise had originally been imprisoned in by Samantha, a device designed specifically to arouse wildly while denying any final sexual release.

Denise turned a deep crimson, embarrassment competing with guilt and, to her horror, arousal. Amazed, yet also enveloped by a sense of utter despair, she discovered she was actually attracted to Christina's maleness! But no, this could not be: she was convinced this was a sick side-effect of the hormones that had been pumped into her. But then Christina's long, elegant hands were reaching out for her own violently erect sex and her equally long, blood-red fingernails were gently teasing the nylon-sheathed tip of her angry penis. Denise, initially outraged, backed away, squealing into her gag and shaking her head furiously.

'Please don't fight me, babikins. Please. All I want you to do is stroke me back. I can't do anything, really. Mummy won't take the restrainer off until this evening. Just the gentlest of touches now, though. *Please.*'

Denise saw the desperate, addict's hunger in Christina's lovely eyes, the utterly irresistible power of her need. This poor creature was as tormented as she.

Denise wasn't sure whether it was pity or desire, but something stronger than her fundamental fear and self-disgust made her step forward and take the satin-wrapped sex in her trembling hands and begin somewhat clumsily to stroke it. In response, Christina tilted her head far back, tossing her long, tidal wave of jet black hair over her broad shoulders as she did so, and released a long, desperate squeal of pleasure, her splendid breasts bouncing with joy. Then, almost instinctively, Denise placed a hand on one of these incredible breasts, impressed and deeply aroused by its silky softness and truly perfect design. Then her fingers were teasing a long, hard nipple and poor Christina was almost screaming her pleasure and frustration, able to experience what she had so clearly craved for a very long time, but now unable to fulfil its potentially spectacular promise.

In response to these erotic ministrations, Christina grasped Denise's stockinged sex and began to masturbate her charge through the ultra-sheer fabric. Denise moaned with an immediate and inescapable pleasure into her dummy gag, feeling the torments of the past few hours suddenly well up in her engorged sex. Then she ejaculated violently into the stocking, a thunderous sexual explosion that saw her knees buckle and an insane squeal of pleasure erupt from her stopped mouth. Suddenly she was on her knees, Christina by her side, thick white come trickling through the stocking on to the carpeted floor of the nursery, the room itself spinning, a sense of incredible relief flooding through her feminised body. But this relief was short-lived, and quickly transformed into a sense of failure and disgust. She had allowed herself to be masturbated to a furious orgasm by this desperate, clearly homosexual she-male, and she had, in the process, confessed her own desire; and now Christina's dark, enflamed eyes were beholding her with a look of pure sexual adoration.

'Oh dear, babikins,' she gasped, letting Denise's come flow freely over her hands as she continued to stroke the now semi-flaccid sex. 'If Mary found out about this, we'd both be severely punished.'

But there was no fear in her voice, only elation, triumph, even joy: Denise had returned her affections and demonstrated conclusively her own sexual feelings for the younger she-male.

'I think this should be our own little secret, don't you?'

Denise could only nod her agreement, suddenly terrified of the consequences of her lack of control, imagining the twisted punishment that Mary would no doubt invent for this most fundamental of transgressions.

Then Christina gently removed the soaking stocking, helped Denise to her feet and into the bathroom. A few minutes later they were sharing a steaming hot shower, Christina's sex still straining desperately against the waterproof satin restrainer, Denise once again violently erect and hungry for further kinky sexual release. But although Christina carefully soaped and sponged Denise's body, and Denise responded in kind (paying particular attention to Christina's lovely breasts), there was no further overt love-making. Christina seemed determined to keep the pleasures of this physical contact on a controlled level and move on to the next stage of this bizarre day.

Soon they were out of the shower. They dried each other with large, scented pink towels and applied powerfully scented powders and perfumes to their soft, feminine bodies, their eyes often locked tightly together and betraying a very mutual desire.

Back in the nursery, Denise was made to sit at the dressing table and instructed to restyle her hair and make-up while Christina returned to the apparently bottomless wardrobe to seek out a new and no doubt ultra-kinky costume for the afternoon. As Denise, still naked, carefully worked on her hair, she found herself staring at her breasts, or what at the moment passed for her breasts. Two small mounds indicated the first stage of the drug-induced growth that would soon flower into breasts even larger than Christina's. And, staring at these childish orbs, she found herself deeply envious of beautiful, buxom Christina. Her attraction was, she knew, quite fatal: it was only a matter of time until the younger she-male tried to take their currently rather tame love-making to its logical and frightening conclusion. Christina had already spoken of being 'taken from the rear', and Denise knew she fully intended to introduce her to the joys of anal sex at the first opportunity. But this was an opportunity that Denise, even in the throes of her current passion, could still not envisage. Indeed, as she began to apply foundation cream to her soft, pale cheeks, she resolved to keep their relationship at a distinctively non-penetrative level. But the question was: how?

Then Christina was behind her, staring longingly at her reflection, the younger she-male's own naked body filling the mirror. Christina appeared quite impatient and insisted on helping Denise quickly finish off her make-up, apparently satisfied with just a touch of peach lipstick, matching eye shadow and the gentlest hint of rouge.

Then Denise was pulled from the leather-backed stool and led back to the table in the centre of the room. On the table were what appeared to be two nylon body stockings, one red and one a familiar powder-blue. By the body stockings were two very skimpy pairs of matching silk panties, a single black nylon stocking and a red silk ribbon.

'We have fifteen minutes to get into these costumes and report to the gym.'

Her impatient voice was filled with genuine fear and Denise knew enough of this house to heed her exhortation.

Christina took up the single black stocking, quickly balled it up and, after the briefest, sexiest of glances between the two gorgeous she-males, she slid it slowly and teasingly over Denise's rigid sex, bringing yet another moan of helpless pleasure from her gagged mouth and a sexy wiggle of her pert bottom. Christina secured the stocking with the ribbon and then set about fitting her charge with her new costume.

First Christina took up the powder-blue panties and helped Denise step into them. The kiss of silk against her freshly washed and powdered body was pure sexual electricity and more aroused moaning followed as the younger she-male pulled them up her charge's long legs and over the once again tightly stockinged sex. And it was only as Christina fitted the panties over Denise's sex that the older she-male saw they were little more than a pouch designed to envelop and hold firm her last vestige of maleness. The edges of the panties were merely thin lengths of silk, as was the gusset section that slid under her legs and up between the cheeks of her buttocks, leaving her bare backside quite deliberately exposed to view.

The panties were followed by the body stocking, a feather-light piece of pure fetishism that she donned by stepping into the stretched open neck and then pulling or rather wiggling it up her lovely body and over her shoulders. To her surprise, the four limb sections of the stocking were designed to cover completely her hands and feet, the feet very much like any type of hose, with the darker, firmer nylon fabric around the toes and heels, and the hands two fingerless gloves which stretched tightly over each hand. Soon her entire form was tightly enveloped in sheer, powder-blue nylon.

While Denise gamely struggled with her own costume, Christina quickly donned her own cherry-red outfit and minced back to the wardrobe, returning as Denise somewhat awkwardly tried to adjust the G-string style panties through the soft fabric of the body stocking. In Christina's nylon-sheathed hands were two pairs of shoes. She placed one pair at Denise's feet and the older she-male's lovely, baby-blue eyes widened in amazement, for before her were a pair of white, patent-leather court shoes with incredibly long, very slender and very sharp heels.

'Seven inches,' Christina whispered, her own eyes filled with fear and wonder as she placed the other pair of shoes, made in the exact same style but from black patent leather, at her own feet. 'We wear these for deportment training. You'll find them very difficult to deal with at first, but that's the whole point: the shoes are all about balance and controlled movement.'

And so Denise stepped gingerly into these bizarre, cruel shoes, and found herself elevated most uncomfortably. At first she could only sway, as if balancing on a tight rope stretched across an abyss. Christina, clearly used to the shoes, slipped them on to her feet and then minced carefully over to Denise, taking her by a hosed hand and carefully guiding her forward. Denise found that she could only manage rather desperate and very tiny steps – this was the only way she could move forward with any momentum. Indeed, what the shoes reduced her to was an embarrassing shuffle come wiggle motion which made her hosed buttocks wobble absurdly and her hips gyrate like a physically handicapped go-go dancer. And as she tottered forward, her eyes fell on Christina, her own movements surer, but also severely restricted. Like Denise, Christina's totter forced a severe wobbling of her hose-sheathed buttocks, but, more importantly, it caused her large, nylon-restrained breasts to bounce up and down in a frantic, deeply humiliating and, for Denise at least, very arousing manner.

The two she-males tottered out into the long, dark corridor and back towards the steps that led into the main part of the house. Climbing the steps was even more difficult than when Denise had been blindfolded, bound and gagged, and by the time they had negotiated the steps and minced desperately back across the house and into a large, brightly light room located just beyond the kitchen, a room in which Mary stood waiting for them, Denise knew they were late and would be punished.

'Where have you been?' Mary snapped, her dark eyes filled with an obviously fake outrage which hid a very real and deeply sadistic delight. 'You should've been here five minutes ago!'

Christina curtsied quickly and tried to apologise, but was cut short by a single gesture from her sister. Denise, too, attempted to curtsy, but this just managed to undermine her balance completely and she began swaying precariously, her arms flapping, a squeal of fear seeping from the dummy gag. Luckily Christina managed to grab and steady her before she collapsed into a dainty heap on the floor.

'Both of you over the stools – *now!*'

A wave of sickening fear washed over Denise as Christina led her to two tall wooden stools placed in the centre of the room. As they tottered fearfully forwards, Denise began to take note of their surroundings. A very large room, a room with one whole wall that was a huge mirror. On the other side of the room were numerous exercise machines: a rowing machine, an electric treadmill, and a general workout bench designed to support a variety of physical exercises. They were in a gym dominated by the startling presence of Mary, a teenage dominatrix who was dressed to tease and terrorise, her earlier sexy schoolgirl look having been replaced with a skin-tight black leotard, a thick, metal-studded, black leather belt pulled tight around her slender waist and a pair of knee-length, stiletto-heeled, black leather boots. She wore elbow-length black rubber gloves and an ivory-handled riding crop was fixed to the studded belt. Her hair was tied in a tight bun, her lips painted blood red, and her eyes burned with twisted desire. She was the goddess of retribution, a grim, helplessly erotic vision of female power and control. And, of course, she was beautiful, her breasts rising and falling rapidly under the tight material of the leotard, her long, muscular legs perfectly complemented by the gleaming boots. Just to look at her was to know you were doomed, and as Christina helped her poor sissy charge lie face down over the first of the stools, Denise could feel the fear coursing through her gorgeous companion's body. They were to be punished together – they were to suffer together.

Denise found herself lying face down over the stool, her stomach resting against the black leather seat, her tightly hosed buttocks expertly exposed. Christina instructed her to grip the legs of the stool and to lower her head so that she was staring upside down through the underside of the stool at her own hosed legs and tightly imprisoned, still very stiff sex.

And then the world ended. A savage electric pain bit into her backside and sent a scream of shock and terrible pain hurtling into her dummy gag, a scream that emerged as a high pitched squeal of agony. Somehow, Mary had managed to sneak around the stools and deliver a blow from the crop without being seen. Then came the awful sound of another sharp whack against hosed buttocks and another very loud, girlish scream of pain, this time from Christina.

And so it went on. Twelve hard, unforgiving strokes of the crop delivered to each she-male, twelve strokes that left them trembling with pain and sobbing helplessly. Twelve strokes delivered with an expert touch that, despite their severity, did not even stretch the nylon material of the tight, glovelike body stockings.

When the punishment was complete, Mary ordered the two sobbing she-males to their feet and told them to face the mirror. They obeyed without a second's hesitation, struggling to their precariously high-heeled feet, Christina having to assist Denise and lead her to within a few feet of the long, mirrored wall.

Then they were facing their reflections, beholding their own carefully feminised forms and, behind them, the imposing, flushed, very excited and very exciting form of Mary.

Denise could not help but be impressed by the erotic effect of the tight body stocking on Christina's stunning figure. Her large, perfect breasts strained angrily against the nylon material as she sobbed pathetically, large tears of discomfort pouring down her cheeks. The poor creature was, like Denise, in terrible, burning pain and her breasts not only strained but bounced angrily as she wiggled her buttocks to try to cool the heat that was consuming them. Then, there was her sex. Her very large and very stiff sex, fighting both the cruel satin restrainer and the skimpy G-string that held it flat against her stomach; an impressive tool that Denise, despite her own pain and well-gagged sobbing, could only feel a disturbing attraction towards.

As she beheld Christina, she also beheld herself. Shorter than Christina, much thinner, vaguely ludicrous because of the dummy gag. And, even without Christina's startling chest, a much more feminine creature. Her own restrained sex quite large, yet the rest of her surprisingly shapely form slender, delicate, even petite; a form given final ultra-feminine life by the lovely powder-blue body stocking, the very high heels, the blue, tear-stained eyes and the carefully sculpted blonde hair. A different kind of beauty: the mould within which a gorgeous, dainty, and utterly submissive she-male was to be created.

'When you've both stopped admiring yourselves,' Mary suddenly intervened, 'I want you to bend over and touch your toes.'

Christina obeyed immediately, demonstrating a truly balletic grace as she carefully stretched forward, legs tightly together, and touched the gleaming patent-leather tips of her shoes, once again exposing her now crimson hued and sublime bottom to Mary's cruel gaze. Poor Denise, however, struggled desperately, firstly with her balance in the heels, and secondly with her lack of physical fitness. Not only could she not bend forward with anything like the poise and elegance of Christina, but she could barely bend her body forward at a ninety-degree angle, never mind touch her toes! Yet rather than punishment, Denise received only mocking words.

'Christina was even feebler than you when I started to train her, so I wouldn't worry too much, Denise. A month of these sessions and we'll have you fit and flexible. And, of course, utterly imbued with true feminine elegance in every movement.'

The rest of the afternoon passed with surprising speed. The pain gripping her buttocks was quickly forgotten as Mary, using Christina as her demonstration model, began to instruct Denise in basic movement. Nearly three hours of wiggling, stretching and mincing followed. Simple exercises designed to increase the femininity of each gesture, each step, each tilt of the head and flick of the wrist, were repeated over and over until they were instinctive gestures of an extremely dainty sissy. And every error, even the slightest slip, was punished with a flick of the crop across her buttocks and, to Denise's horror, across Christina's buttocks as well. As the two she-male beauties minced around the room, their sexes bouncing in the tight nylon restraint of the body stockings, Christina's breasts adding a splendidly erotic counterpart, Denise found herself, even when engulfed in a new film of exhausted sweat, highly aroused. To be so carefully trained and so utterly dominated by the gorgeous Mary, this athletic, cruel girl, was a tremendous turn-on. To perform for her, and to expose the very core of her feminine being in the process, was the most delicious act of sissy submission.

By the time they were dismissed from the gym, it was nearly five o'clock. The exhausted sissies minced back to the nursery, their buttocks stinging, the heat from the repeated cuts of the crop now flowing freely between their legs and into their tightly restrained, engorged sexes. Back in the nursery, they again undressed each other in a quiet dance of half-caresses and teasing, shy glances. Then Christina insisted that Denise bathe herself, fearing they might again get carried away.

'We have to be careful, babikins,' the lovely younger she-male whispered, slipping the stocking restrainer from her charge's red hot, iron shaft. 'Without self-control, we're doomed. If we cannot obey ourselves, we cannot obey our mistresses. This is a crucial lesson.'

Trying to avoid another violent orgasm, her eyes closed tightly shut, her dummy-gagged moans loud and delightfully high-pitched, Denise nodded desperately and, once freed of the stocking, minced naked into the bathroom, her sex staring up at her like a rigid monument to the essence of ambivalent she-male desire.

By the time she returned, carefully washed, powdered and scented, Christina had slipped into a very short, pink silk bathrobe and was collecting the pile of sweaty clothing from the floor. She came over to Denise and quickly removed the dummy gag, putting a silencing finger to her lips as she did so.

'Make your face up and wait for me. Dinner is at seven, and we must serve it. But I'll need to help you dress. And you *mustn't* say a word, my darling.'

Obeying Christina's words, Denise positioned herself before the dressing table and began to make up her smooth, girlish face, using her vivid she-male imagination to transform herself into the perfect image of submissive femininity.

By the time Christina returned from her own bathing, still wrapped in the pretty, tight robe, Denise had completed her face, using cherry-red lipstick, powder-blue eye shadow, a light foundation and a hint of peach-toned rouge.

Christina smiled gently at her charge and complimented her on her make-up, popping the dummy gag back into her mouth almost immediately and securing it tightly in place.

'You look lovely, of course,' Christina whispered, tying the gag in place with a teasing grin, her eyes filled with that frank and absolute desire which Denise was finding increasingly hard to resist.

Denise responded with a fierce blush and a helpless wiggle of pleasure that made her stiff, unstockinged sex brush against Christina's thigh. Christina laughed quietly and then took the rigid, red penis in her hands, delicately stroking its fat, angry head and the vein pulsing along its impressive shaft. Denise squealed her pleasure and, to her not so great surprise, pushed her sex deep into Christina's eager hands.

'I'll have to wrap this up again, sweetness. But I don't won't another explosion, so I'll have to tie you up.'

Denise's little-girl blue eyes widened with excitement at the mention of bondage. Christina returned to the dressing table, her own stiff sex clearly visible through the taught, pink silk robe, the curving globes of her gorgeous buttocks swaying provocatively against the material as she delicately minced forward.

Soon the older she-male was securing Denise's arms behind her back at the wrists and elbows with soft, white nylon stockings, thus pushing her chest and sex forward helplessly and exposing them for whatever teasing Christina had planned.

Denis moaned into the gag as the knots were tied and instinctively pressed her legs tightly together to force the plug deeper into her anus.

'You like being tied up, don't you, babikins?'

Denise could only moan her pleasure and nod weakly.

'Well, there'll be plenty of opportunities for you to be tied and gagged very tightly. I'll make sure of that. And so will the mistresses.'

Once Denise was adequately bound, Christina stepped back to admire the stunningly sexy damsel in distress she had created. Then, from a pocket in the bathrobe, she took another scented, very sheer black nylon stocking and slowly, teasingly, rolled it into a ball, her dark, sensual eyes filled with sex rays, her satin-restrained sex peeping from beneath the robe, her breasts rising and falling rapidly with a fierce she-male arousal. She pressed the stocking to her lips, kissed it, then stepped forward. Slowly, gently, with an agonising care, she rolled the stocking over Denise's boiling, rock-hard sex, never once letting her aroused, hungry eyes leave Denise's flushed face. Denise squealed with furious pleasure as Christina tormented her.

'I know we shouldn't do this, but I just love playing with you, my sexy petal. And you musn't come. Not this time. If you do, imagine the fun Mistress Mary will have!'

Denise's arms strained with a playful despair against her bonds, her pert backside wiggled in mock outrage. Any second she would explode into the stocking and love every violent second of her uncontrollable orgasm. But then Christina's hands were gone. The stocking was wrapped tightly around her sex and tied in place with a pink silk ribbon secured in a fat, sissy bow. A feeling of profound frustration flooded over her, she squealed angrily into her gag, watching Christina return to the wardrobe with sad, desperate eyes.

'I meant what I said, babikins,' the younger she-male teased, not even bothering to turn her head as she began to take the various elements of a new costume from wardrobe, bending over as she did so to expose her perfect backside to Denise's infuriated gaze.

Christina returned carrying a large pile of very odd-looking clothing. Denise squealed her need again and actually shook her stockinged sex at Christina in absolute sexual desperation. Christina laughed and placed the clothing on the table by the cot.

'There's no point getting all little missy with me, petal. No means *no*. We'll have plenty of time later on. Now we have to get you dressed up to serve dinner.'

Rather than beginning with the pile, Christina returned to the dressing table and took another very large, fresh nappy from a bottom drawer. After quickly scenting the nappy, she returned to Denise and fitted it tightly between her legs and around her waist with a sexy lover's smile, clipping it tightly in place with another very large silver safety pin. After the nappy came the first item of the strange clothing: a pair of powder-blue, latex rubber pants, trimmed with masses of white lace at the waist and legs.

'Mummy has specifically asked that you wear rubber tonight, babikins.' Denise gingerly stepped into the strange item of underwear. She was surprised by how thin and light the rubber material was and how easily it traversed her smooth legs and stretched over the large nappy. The panties covered the nappy like a film of powder-blue paint, reproducing the exact appearance of the thick, woollen towelling like a bizarre rubber mould. And as they mirrored the form of the nappy, they also seemed to contract in size and press the nappy even more tightly against Denise's delicately feminised body.

After the panties, came matching powder-blue rubber stockings. These were even thinner than the panties and again very easy to guide up her long, shapely legs. Denise was fascinated as the stockings instantly became a sheer, flawless second skin, fitting perfectly against the erotic contours of her lovely legs from the tips of her girlish toes to the tops of her smooth thighs. Easily self-supporting, the stockings left the gorgeous she-male with two shiny powder-blue legs and an even more intense erection.

'The stockings look wonderful on you, babikins,' Christina whispered, taking up a striking rubber corset from the pile of clothing and carefully wrapping it around her charge's torso.

The clinging nature of the rubber made it perfect for foundation wear and corsetry. Tied in place with silken cords running through silver eyes fixed to the rear panels, the corset could be pulled even tighter than its initial and very considerable restrictive grip. Denise felt the air pushed from her lungs and another inch was lost from her already very slender waist. Yet her response was to look lovingly at Christina and squirm with excitement in this spreading cocoon of sexy rubber.

After the corset, the pièce de résistance: a beautiful powder-blue baby-girl's dress also made from latex rubber and very similar in design to the elaborate outfit she had worn earlier. With white pearl button fastenings running from the white lace-frilled and very short skirt to the equally frilled and very high neck, Denise, with her arms held out, was able, at Christina's instruction, to step directly into the dress. A gasp of pure pleasure escaped her dummy-gagged mouth as the younger she-male pulled the dress around her charge's sexy she-male form and then quickly began to button it into position, sealing Denise in a taut body-glove and a new world of exquisite, fetishistic delight.

'Eventually, you'll be able to wear a special rubber bra with this outfit,' Christina said, smoothing the dress over her charge's petite form, 'but until you have a proper bosom, it's very difficult to make this work – padded bras tend to crush and look unrealistic.'

Denise nodded her understanding and watched in continuing awe as tight powder-blue rubber gloves were stretched over her hands and the lovely silk and satin bonnet from earlier in the day was brought out of the wardrobe and once again secured over her beautiful golden hair. Then the finishing touch: the return of the striking boots with their cruel and helplessly erotic stiletto heels and their gleaming skin of the finest powder-blue silk.

'You will help me serve dinner to the mistresses,' Christina explained, 'so your hands need to be free.'

Denise curtsied her understanding. Christina then carefully examined her charge, smiled and led her to the mirror by the wardrobe. Denise gasped into the teasing phallic dummy gag as she beheld her new, ultra-feminine image. A vision of rubberised perfection, a beautiful, doe-eyed rubber maid, her perfect she-male body encased in a sweet cocoon of powder-blue latex. Her pretty blue eyes widened with arousal and she released a moan of undeniable pleasure.

'Yes, you look absolutely marvellous, my sexy pet,' Christina whispered hoarsely, her tightly restrained sex now clearly exposed through the folds of the silk gown. 'The mistresses will be very pleased, I'm sure.'

Christina then retied Denise's hands and elbows behind her back with the stockings and perched her on the stool before the dressing-table mirror. She then returned to her own room to dress for dinner.

She returned maybe twenty minutes later, beautifully attired in the spectacular black maid's dress that Denise had first seen the day before, a vision of perfect feminine submission, whose every sexy movement filled the older she-male with a powerful, yet not wholly unquestioned desire.

Then they were mincing back down the corridor and through the house, and in a few minutes they were back in the large kitchen, curtsying sweetly before a broadly smiling Mistress Grace.

'A stunning vision!' she exclaimed, beholding the lovely Denise, her eyes feeding hungrily on this she-male beauty.

Dressed in a white silk blouse, a simple black, knee-length skirt, matching hose and heels, Mistress Grace was the perfect image of female authority. This outfit made Denise realise that she was, despite her obvious maturity, a much more shapely and attractive woman than had originally appeared to be the case.

'You both look gorgeous,' she added, her eyes falling lovingly on Christina, who quickly curtsied her appreciation of this carefully added compliment.

Then they were set to work. Mistress Grace had prepared most of the evening meal and it was now just a question of carefully serving it to all the mistresses.

The first course was a delicious vegetable soup. It was served in four ornate china bowls and placed on to a large silver tray by Christina. Denise was then instructed to take the tray to the dinning room. Taking the tray from the serving table was a genuinely terrifying experience. Although she had served meals to Helen every day during her initial training, this had always happened in familiar surroundings with a relatively small, lightly loaded tray. Now she found herself tottering on her high heels, constricted by the layers of tight latex rubber, her mouth filled with the phallic dummy gag, her vision restricted by the elegant bonnet. The tray was also heavy, and as she minced forward, she fought to prevent it tipping forward and spilling the contents.

Luckily, Christina quickly moved in front of her, carrying a second tray stacked with bread rolls. Smiling reassuringly at her charge, she led her across the hallway to the entrance of the dining room. Opening the door with a free hand, she turned to Denise.

'Don't worry, babikins. You're doing very well, and you look absolutely fantastic.'

As she followed Christina into the room, her heart thumping loudly in her pretty she-male head, she experienced a fear bordering on terror. Yet beneath this terror was the deepest and fiercest feeling of masochistic arousal. Even to herself it was now apparent that she was becoming the most perfectly programmed of she-male slaves.

The dining room was very large and beautifully decorated. In the centre of the room was a long rectangular table. At the far end of the table sat Katherine, Samantha, Mary and Bridget, the four beautiful mistresses holding an animated conversation. The two she-males tottered towards them. As they reached the mistresses, Christina curtsied deeply and placed the rolls on the table. Denise tried to do the same, but her curtsy was more a pathetic half-stagger which brought a loud laugh from Mary.

'I think you're going to need a lot more practice at curtsying with a tray, Denise,' Samantha said, her eyes filled with contempt. 'Something for you to concentrate on tomorrow, Mary.'

Mary nodded and smiled, her cruel eyes never leaving the older she-male. Denise knew she would suffer tomorrow afternoon.

'But she does look positively delightful,' Katherine added. 'The rubber really does show her off.'

The women laughed and Denise felt a wave of pleasurable embarrassment wash over her. She placed the tray down on the table and executed a perfect sissy curtsy of absolute obedience.

Christina and Denise proceeded to serve the soup as carefully and daintily as possible. Denise tried to make every gesture and movement a delicate act of feminine submission, fighting to remember the painfully taught lessons of the afternoon. As she served, Denise also tried to study her mistresses, listen to their conversation, watch how they interacted, in order to understand the dynamics of communication amongst these beautiful women.

It was obvious that Katherine was the leader of the gorgeous group. She sat at the head of the table, dressed in a red velvet trouser suit, a suit that matched her long, glistening fingernails and full, moist lips. Her manner was confident, her firm, calm voice dominating the conversation. The other women, despite their own obvious claims to the status of dominatrix, deferred to her. Katherine Shelly: the leader, the regal beauty at the head of this strange society. And as Denise served her supreme mistress, she realised that little had changed. As Denis, Denise had served Katherine with equal enthusiasm, so eager to win her favour and her company's prestigious account. Then it had been lies and hypocrisy, the male delusion of competition and aggression badly disguising the true nature of the so-called professional relationship: subservience to beauty and power, to the imperial presence of a truly dominant woman who knew what she wanted and exactly how to get it.

Denise found herself behaving in the most blatantly sissified manner before Mistress Katherine, performing each movement with an exaggerated feminine grace and daintiness. As she leaned forward to serve this gorgeous divinity, her latex-sheathed legs forced firmly together, her befrilled, rubberised bottom clearly and quite deliberately exposed, she felt not only the familiar electricity of masochistic surrender, but also a form of devotion, perhaps even love. But despite her desire, this was not sexual love. It was the love of a servant for her mistress, and it felt perfectly natural, an essential part of this new personality called Denise.

The discussion was about Christina and Denise.

'Mary tells me that Denise is a natural dancer,' Katherine said.

'She seems to possess an instinctive physical femininity,' Samantha replied. 'You chose very well, Katherine.'

The other women nodded their agreement. Even the icy Mistress Bridget seemed impressed.

'Yes, Kathy, she is perfect for reorientation surgery. I couldn't ask for a better subject. Her height and general physique are exactly right for the amendments we require.'

Katherine smiled modestly. 'I'm glad. But I'm still worried about her psychological reorientation. I suspect we'll face some resistance – ultimately.'

'Christina is already working miracles, Katherine,' Samantha said. 'And once we are through the first phase, I'm confident I can ensure her full transformation. Remember the trouble you had with Chrissie? It takes a little time, but she'll accept her role fully in the end.'

Denise listened to Samantha's words with fear and trepidation, trying not to let this discussion of her fate divert her attention from the task of serving her mistresses.

Of all the women, there was no doubt that Samantha remained the most beautiful and, to Denise, the most desirable. She could not help wondering if this was because she appeared the most extreme of the mistresses, in her attitude, in her tastes, in her very physical presence. Dressed in a tight black sweater and a short black leather skirt, her startling main of jet-black hair spilling freely over her broad shoulders, she projected an image of pure sexual power that none of the other mistresses seemed able to approach. Her dark, smouldering eyes, never leaving Denise as she performed her domestic duties, her large, firm, perfectly shaped breasts within inches of the she-male's sissified face as she leaned forward, Samantha had perfected the image of the gorgeous, merciless dominatrix. And Denise was to be her slave: at the end of phase one of this bizarre training regime, she was to be placed in the hands of Samantha, to act as her personal maidservant. And the thought of this impending enslavement was almost unbearably exciting.

Denise remained confused by the reference to the role that Katherine had played in her creation. To her it was Samantha and Helen who were the main 'conspirators'. How could Katherine have been involved? Then there was the ominous reference to reorientation surgery. It appeared that she was to undergo a much more extreme physical transformation than she had originally been led to believe.

The four women were soon joined by Mistress Grace, her smile soft and gentle, her eyes pinned like orbs of pale blue glue to the lovely Denise. Grace was extravagant in her praise for the older she-male and teased Denise relentlessly throughout the rest of the meal, her hands wandering over the slave's latexed legs and thighs as she bent forward to serve the food. Denise could only whimper a tightly gagged but helplessly excited response to these caresses, her eyes never leaving this lovely mistress's plump, shapely breasts as they strained against their exquisite prison of pure white silk.

Four courses were served over two hours. The two she-males spent the evening mincing back and forth to bring more food, more wine, more of everything from the rows of carefully laid-out dishes in the kitchen. There was no time for furtive glances or caresses between the two maidservants. Bonneted and tightly dummy-gagged as she was, it was very difficult for Denise to get a clear view of Christina, except for her stunning, nylon-sheathed legs, which seemed to be constantly before her eyes, teasing her still rock-hard sex with waves of strong yet ambivalent desire. Yes: ambivalent, an ambivalence that had been made worse by the thought of Helen. Her beautiful wife-mistress, the woman whom she ached to be with, to serve and to worship. The woman who, during that first incredible week, had made the deepest sexual mark on sweet Denise. Again, as her eyes traversed Christina's splendid legs and beheld the individual beauty of each of her mistresses, she was torn between two desires. In these women's hands she was to become a carefully trained, physically perfect she-male pet whose only sexual release would be with her own kind. And it was in Helen that she saw a possible escape from this fate. Once she was back in Helen's safe hands, surely things would be as she had originally imagined: mistress and spectacularly feminised slave, a mistress for whom she would endure any humiliation and perform every service without the slightest whimper of protest.

But even as she was thinking these desperate thoughts, Christina was suddenly behind her, in the kitchen, her hands running over her tightly rubberised behind, whispering words of love into her baby-girl ears.

'Only the washing-up to do now, babikins. Then we can retire. Mummy has told us to get an early night, and she has promised to remove my restrainer.'

But Denise did not resist, she did not struggle against these words. She felt Christina's long, sensual hands explore her rubber-covered behind and thighs and gasped with pleasure into the fat and very phallic dummy gag, its thick ridges pressing against her soft mouth as she arched her back with pleasure and forced her bottom into the younger she-male's more than willing hands.

They collected the plates and empty glasses and returned to the kitchen, the mistresses now discussing 'the new building'. As she wiggle-minced from the dining room, Denise remembered the building. Earlier in the day, during her punishment at breakfast time, she had found herself, however briefly, staring out of the large, French bay windows that poured light into so many rooms on the ground floor, and into the vast, ornate gardens. Towards the end of the gardens there was a large building site and emerging out of it a half-formed building surrounded by a skeleton of scaffolding. At the time she had wondered what this construction might be, but having spent the day so effectively gagged, she had been unable to pursue the matter with Christina.

Christina led her back to the kitchen and together they had set about washing, drying and storing a mountain of washing-up, their lovely uniforms protected by gleaming white rubber aprons. And as they worked, Christina congratulated Denise on her performance.

'You were wonderful, petal. The mistresses were so impressed! Mistress Mary will make you suffer tomorrow, but she'll make you suffer every day. But Mummy really does like you, and she so wants us to be together. And so do I. Now all we have to do is store the plates and it's bedtime.'

It was 9.30 by the kitchen clock when the two stunning she-males minced from the kitchen and back through the caverns of this old, odd house to their slave quarters. Christina was clearly in a state of extreme excitement: her dainty, perfectly feminine steps were quick, eager, even desperate, her lovely backside rocked almost ecstatically beneath its sexy umbrella of lace frou-frou petticoating, and her black stiletto heels sounded a sharp, rapid rhythm against the stone floors. Yes, this was the percussive music of desire, its vibrations sending teasing currents of need coursing over her beautiful, so expertly sissified body.

Once they were back in the nursery, Christina immediately set to undressing Denise, her eyes filled with a very powerful and fundamental sexual desire. Suddenly, it was if as poor Denise were being ravished. Christina's words of love had become growls of animal pleasure, Denise gagged whimpers were both whimpers of fear and pleasure.

'Tonight we'll begin to give each other a true, mutual pleasure, my love. Tonight you'll begin to learn the delights of she-male passion.'

Her words were hoarse, fast, raw; her movements no longer subtle or graceful. The sexual energy that had been so tightly secured during the day was now being given a rare opportunity for release.

Within a few chaotic minutes, Denise had been stripped down to her delicate, tight, very sheer stocking restrainer and the fat dummy gag. It was as if a whirlwind had ripped her clothes away and left her naked before this beautiful, desperate creature. And as Christina gathered up these clothes, Samantha entered the room.

The two she-males immediately curtsied very deeply. A strange wave of shame washed over Denise and she covered her very stiff, nyloned sex, her eyes fighting to avert the incredible sexual spectacle that was Mistress Samantha.

The short black leather skirt was indeed very short, displaying her superb legs in the finest of black silk stockings and gorgeous black patent-leather, high-heeled court shoes. She tossed her startling mane of jet-black hair back over her shoulders and smiled teasingly at Denise.

'I see Christina is preparing you for a night of fun.'

Denise could only curtsy an embarrassed affirmative as Christina visibly shook before her mistress.

'Strip,' she whispered to Christina.

The lovely young she-male obeyed, placing Denise's clothes at her feet and beginning to undress.

'I'd be very amused to know what Helen would make of all this,' Samantha whispered, her eyes burning into Denise.

These words, cruel, sudden, struck deep into Denise's own aroused state. The image of Helen returned. Beautiful, regal Helen. Helen laughing, smirking, mocking her pansy she-husband, her homosexualised transvestite pet. A bomb exploded in the middle of her desire and destroyed it. Her erection slipped away, her heart sank, a much darker, bitter shame engulfed her.

'Yes, you still want Helen so badly, Denise,' Samantha said. 'And that want is the root of your resistance. And while it is so easy to provoke, you will never be a true she-male slave. But Christina will help you. And so will I. Tonight and every night until you accept your true sissy fate.'

As she battered Denise with these cruel words, and as Christina carefully removed her layers of delicate, erotic underwear to eventually reveal her heavenly sex-bomb figure with its strange but still very beautiful and tightly restrained male sex, large tears of despair and humiliation began to trickle down the older she-male's rose-red cheeks. It was through tear-stained eyes that Denise watched Christina stand proudly and hungrily before Samantha to allow her mistress to release the delicate lengths of pink satin that kept the wicked restrained sex tied so teasingly in place. And as Christina released a loud gasp of relief and pleasure, Samantha laughed encouragingly.

'You know what to do, Chrissie. If she resists, you have my permission to restrain her in any way necessary.' With this, Samantha left the room.

Christina turned to face Denise, her eyes filled with the lightning of unstoppable need, her large, perfectly shaped breasts bouncing before her like two gorgeous warrior-woman weapons of desire. Denise was doomed, and she knew it. Yet she also knew she was Helen's property, Helen's slave, and that here, in this weird adult nursery, her true she-male identity was being destroyed. She shook her head, she squealed like a trapped little girl into the gag. Then her eyes fell on Christina's long-restrained, very large sex and she *screamed* into the gag. But even as she tried to back away, Christina's hands, elegant, very powerful, were upon her, pulling her into the soft, smothering embrace of the younger she-male's impressive bosom.

'Don't struggle, babikins. Think of the pleasure I've given you. Now it's your turn to reciprocate.'

And as she pulled tighter, her fiercely erect sex pushed against Denise's own stockinged and treacherously tumescent counterpart.

'You know what I want,' Christina continued. 'What I've given you. Your first true lesson, my sweet: how to be a good cock sucker.'

Denise struggled and squealed, but Christina was so much stronger. And within a few minutes, the older she-male found herself forced to her knees, her wrists and ankles tightly secured with discarded nylon stockings, her face directly level with Christina's furious sex.

'Now, there are two ways we can do this, my pretty. One is we show each other true love and respect. The other is I get a bottle of castor oil and a funnel and force-feed you until you're prepared to co-operate.'

Sobbing pathetically now, poor Denise could only stare at the violent erection and squeal for mercy.

How quickly things had changed: from desire to suffering, from hunger to horror. But how could she resist?

Then the dummy gag was being untied.

'Don't worry, babikins. The first time I did this, they had me in a straightjacket!'

The gag popped out and immediately Denise tried to beg for mercy, but somehow nothing happened. Her voice had gone! And Christina was laughing!

'Now open wide!'

Suddenly Christina grabbed Denise violently by the back of her head and rammed her sex deep into the older she-male's mouth. Denise tried to struggle, but Christina was possessed of a truly savage strength. Poor Denise coughed and spluttered. The hot, stiff, salty-flavoured flesh filled her mouth. She fought for breath and wriggled angrily in her bonds. The only noises she could make were the moans and squeals of a baby.

'Calm down, petal. Just relax and become part of the motion.'

Christina's bizarre words of instruction were delivered with a voice increasingly undermined by an intense sexual excitement. Poor Denise could feel the vein in her captor's sizeable sex throb angrily in her mouth and knew a very violent eruption was only seconds away. And then, amazingly, she did relax. The struggling stopped, the crying slowed, and, to her utter astonishment, the sucking began. Maybe she just got sick of fighting this beautiful, powerful she-male and was now looking for the quickest way to bring this ordeal to an end; or maybe the deeper she-male, the strange inner force that had first been brought to the surface by Samantha, was again exerting its fundamental will. Either way, she suddenly found herself easing her body up toward Christina and beginning to rock with the motion of the younger she-male's desperate desire. Suddenly her tongue was tentatively exploring the rigid, boiling shaft of Christina's penis and allowing it to push repeatedly against the roof of her mouth. Bound, gagged, her own nylon-sealed sex betraying her, she was quite deliberately teasing Christina to orgasm. And Christina was crying out pleasure-ridden 'thank yous', her hands caressing Denise's gorgeous face and hair, tears of pleasure trickling down her face. And then she was coming. Then there was the explosion. Accompanied by a scream of sheer animal ecstasy, a torrential hot jet of semen erupted into Denise's mouth, an eruption that threatened to drown her unless it was swallowed in long, desperate gulps. Denise drunk deep of Christina's sex essence as the younger she-male tightly gripped her. Then, after what seemed like minutes, the flow of sex lava stopped. Christina fell back, taking her rapidly shrinking sex with her. She collapsed on to the floor and poor Denise rolled over on to her side, semen trickling over her lips and down her chin, gasping for breath, both horrified and, to her astonishment, highly aroused.

As she tried to pull herself upright, Christina crawled to her side and planted a huge and very passionate kiss on her damp lips, a kiss Denise returned. Then Christina was turning her bound charge on to her back, a huge, satisfied, yet also conspiratorial smile on the younger she-male beauty's dazzling, flushed face. Denise was now facing directly into Christina's truly spectacular breasts. The younger she-male then proceeded to lower these wondrous orbs down on to Denise's face and Denise responded by covering them in hungry kisses. And as she enjoyed these sweet melons, gentle hands began working the stocking free of her sex, gentle hands that then began to delicately, lovingly caress this well-proportioned shaft to full, fierce erection.

'I want you so much, babikins. And you've been so good to me. So now it's your turn.'

Words delivered over a sudden meeting of eyes – Christina's beautiful brown pools, holding so much need and energy; and Denise's pale blue pearls, twinkling with a natural sissy intensity in the light of this baby girl's nursery.

Then Christina's mouth engulfed Denise's enlivened sex. And as she came, as she was teased to yet another giant orgasm, it was Christina's name she cried out, a name she would cry out many times that evening, a name almost blasting out the darker thoughts of Helen, of her wife-mistress, of the woman she loved and worshipped – a name which would not disappear easily.

Part Three
Fate and Femininity

Chapter Twelve

The next four weeks passed in a whirlpool of desire, submission and fear. Slowly, but surely, Denise became the model image of the sissified she-male slave. Not only in her movement and mannerisms, not only in her dress and make-up, but also physically. Gradually, under the powerful influence of the regular hormone injections and laced milk, her hips began to broaden, her skin soften, her lips thicken into a natural, helplessly sexy and very voluptuous pout, her neck become more slender, and her lovely blonde hair grew beyond her shoulders in a torrent of sweet and apparently natural curls.

And, of course, there were her breasts. Each day they seemed to be a little larger, a little firmer: two petite pale rose orbs topped off by almost permanently erect and surprisingly long nipples. Soon her bra was no longer a humiliation, a psychological tool – soon it was a necessity. And, to Denise's amazement and joy, these lovely, modest breasts were sources of an almost constant physical pleasure. Every touch and brush sent shivers of pleasure through her body. The ultra-sensitive mounds were teased and tormented by the layers of soft, delicate undergarments she was constantly imprisoned within, adding a new intensity to the multitude of excitements that filled each long, hard day of absolute servitude. Days in which, despite the relentless round of domestic slavery and the regular addition of ever stranger and more painful punishments at the hands of her many mistresses, the burning sex heat was a constant companion. Her tightly restrained erection was constant, her need more so. As she minced prettily through each day, she was accompanied by an unending, utterly unforgiving sexual hunger. The world of the Last Straw Society and the mansion house that was its headquarters was constant sex, and Denise was the constant sex slave.

Each night was now spent with Christina. Each night was now a night of ravishment. Driven mad by desire and by the teasing beauty of her mistresses, she found herself unable to resist Christina's expert ministrations. Once she had so easily returned the younger she-male's affections, she found herself a willing participant in the subsequent nightly sex sessions, an eager explorer in the land of she-male love. All that is except for the most profound exploration. For at no point was anal intercourse ever placed on the menu. Denise remained tightly plugged at all times, except when she was forced to endure the humiliating 'toilet sessions' at the hands of a relentlessly wicked and deeply perverse Mary. The she males' love-making thus never strayed beyond fellatio and a variety of other mainly oral explorations. But this was certainly enough to bring Denise a brief, nightly relief from her burning physical need, a genuine pleasure and, no doubt as a consequence, a dreadful sense of guilt.

The guilt, like the sex heat, remained constant. The image of Helen tormented poor Denise during every second of her passionate encounters with Christina. A torment made worse by the relentless teasing Denise suffered at the hands of her gorgeous, cruel mistresses. They lost no opportunity to mock the relationship between the two sissies, especially Mary. The afternoon dance and movement sessions, which became increasingly intense physical exercise classes, were punctuated by a relentless stream of teasing remarks regarding the two she-males physical relationship. Yet despite this endless mockery, there was never ever any question that Denise could turn away from the lovely, tempting Christina.

Sexed up to the point of explosion by the sight of the gorgeous brunette she-male in one of her many ultra-sexy

French maid's dresses, her legs wrapped in the sheerest of black nylon and resting on the highest heeled of black patent-leather court shoes, her wide, full, blood-red mouth curving into a teasing smile of bottomless promise, Denise could only fall before her and eagerly accept all she wished to give. And so the terrible dialectic that beat the rhythm of each day was quickly established: guilt and desire; unyielding; cancelling each other out in the animal screams of the coming.

Yet Denise was not the only one to suffer. Christina's own torments were obvious and depressingly constant. Their physical manifestation was Mistress Mary. The sister, the daughter, the eighteen-year-old dominatrix whose passion for the humiliation and utter degradation of her she-brother seemed unending. At first Denise thought that Mary's mistreatment of Christina was in some way part of her own punishment: she was to endure the mental torture consequent upon knowing that any wrongdoing or failure on her part resulted not only in her own punishment, but in Christina's punishment as well. Yet it quickly became apparent that the perils of Christina were not the result of Denise's failings: they were the result of a long-established pattern of cruelty routed in the very birth of Christina. The story of Christina was one told in the cut of the crop across her shapely, tightly pantied and hosed buttocks, a crop wielded with absolute authority and determination by her sister.

And it was in the minutes before Christina put her charge to bed each evening, the minutes following their increasingly delicate and tender love-making, that Christina told the story of her birth. Naked, sweat-coated, locked in each other's arms on the floor of the nursery, a very strange and secret history was revealed.

Christina had, of course, been Christopher. She had once, like Denise, been he. And, just over two years ago, he had been sixteen. The son and heir to Katherine Shelly, one of the richest women in the country. A famous clothes designer and businesswoman. A multi-millionairess whom Denise, as Denis, had once known reasonably well. Christopher, Chris. Chris Shelly and his sister, Mary. Mary had been eighteen, and Mary's best friend, Liz, had said she was seventeen. Liz: beautiful, energetic and very flirtatious. A striking redhead who looked a good five years older than her actual age. A girl who had enjoyed teasing Chris and who had enjoyed the teasing power her beauty brought. A power that she had eventually abused, allowing Chris to go perhaps a little too far one evening, turning a heavy petting session into an angry struggle, a violent ravishment – a rape. But a rape interrupted by his sister and, worst of all, by his mother. Summoned to the library by Liz's screams, they had discovered Chris standing over her, her clothes ripped, her eyes filled with tears and a genuine, confused fear.

They had bathed her, calmed her, talked her out of taking the matter further. Convinced of her own role in teasing him to rape, of the terrible embarrassment and humiliation public exposure might bring, and of the definite financial advantages silence would produce, Liz agreed to take the matter no further. But Katherine Shelly could never forget.

'I was raped when I was barely eighteen,' she had told Christopher that evening, tears in her eyes, tears of anger and disbelief. 'Raped by a much older man. And to see you do this – I can't believe it. And I can't forgive it. You have the illness of your sex, Chris, and I intend to cure you of it – for your own good.'

The cure, the drastic solution to her son's virgin desire, began immediately, that very evening. Liz was sent home in a taxi and Christopher began his journey on the road that led to Christina and a life of intricately feminised slavery.

'I had no choice, really,' Christina whispered to Denise. 'They threatened me with the police, with psychiatrists. Mummy was – is – a very powerful woman. She can do pretty much what she likes. So they, she and Mary, concocted the story that I was ill, that I'd been packed off to a sanatorium in Switzerland, when in fact, I was living with them, as Christina, as their maidservant.

'At first, I was like you: they kept me as a baby. Mummy had a huge wardrobe of baby-girl costumes designed and my bedroom was refurbished as a huge nursery. I was kept dummy-gagged and nappied and placed completely under Mistress Mary's control. At first I fought them terribly. But every act of resistance just increased the intensity of my feminisation. Mary was given carte blanche to punish me as she saw fit, and although I had the physical power to resist her, I knew that, at the first sign of a raised hand, Mummy would cart me off to the police. I was beaten and humiliated in every way imaginable. Mary's imagination was endless and so was my suffering. And if I wanted to stop suffering, I had to accept my lot. And I suppose I did – at first. I pretended this was a short-term measure, that eventually they would forgive me and return me to my true male self. But then Mistress Bridget arrived on the scene, and then there was no turning back.

'They started the hormone injections after about two weeks. I couldn't sleep, I couldn't think, I couldn't work. Mummy became worried. I was kept tied up in my cot each night and given no relief at all. But Mistress Bridget refused to relent. And then there was Mistress Mary. She made it so much worse. You've seen how she treats me. Well, this is nothing compared with what she made me do when the hormones were first administered. Even now –'

Even in the relative privacy of the room, Christina had been unable to go on. Whatever had happened in those early days had been so terrible, so perverse, that the younger she-male was unable to describe it to Denise. But she did describe the operation that followed the injections, the transformation that Mistress Bridget brought about: her superb breasts, her helplessly sexy voice, her classically feminine features.

'She turned me into a living doll. Completely transformed me. I awoke from the operation as you see me now and was immediately dragged before a mirror by Mistress Mary. When I saw my reflection, I cried and cried. I knew there was no going back. From then on I was kept dressed in an endless variety of maid's costumes and made to work.

I was trained in the domestic arts, I was taught to dance. I gradually became a totally convincing lady's maid, serving Mummy and Mistress Mary in any way they saw fit. Like you, I was plugged and restrained. Unlike you, I was denied any form of sexual release for over two months. If there was anything that broke my will completely and utterly it was that terrible torment. That and Daphne.'

It was perhaps two or three nights later that Christina found the courage to tell the strange, ultra-kinky tale of Daphne.

At the peak of her sexual torment, having undergone two months of intensive feminisation training, Christina was presented to Mistress Yolanda, a professional dominatrix, and her slave, Daphne. Yolanda was a beautiful, six-foot black woman, who stood a good two inches higher than Christina. Attired in a skin-tight rubber body suit, five-inch stilettos and riding crop, her large breasts stretched tight against jet-black rubber, her straightened hair worn in a strict bun, her black eyes shining with a particularly contemptuous amusement, she was the ideal image of dominant womanhood. And Daphne? Daphne was surely the ideal sissy maid, a petite and extremely delicate creature who Christina initially took to be a real girl. A lovely china doll dressed in a splendid white silk maid's costume, consisting of a striking white dress covered in satin roses, a forest of lace petticoating, sheer, white nylon tights and incredible seven-inch stilettos that ensured every charming step was a tiny declaration of absolute servitude. On top of this, was the slimmest waist imaginable and breasts which, while the result of much more conventional and prolonged hormone treatment, were still large and very well proportioned.

Of course, poor Christina had been violently attracted to Daphne, much to the amusement of the women present. Then Christina had been sent up to bed with her after an evening of constant mockery and humiliation. In her room, she had allowed herself to be kissed and fondled, allowed herself to be slowly undressed with teasing words of love, had even allowed her restrainer to be untied and slipped from her sex while moaning her extraordinary pleasure into a long French kiss. Then Daphne had fellated her, quickly bringing the amazed girl-boy to a massive, screaming climax, and leaving her sprawled naked and exhausted on the bed. Then, before Christina's amazed eyes, Daphne had begun to undress, an elegantly performed striptease that quickly reinvigorated Christina's sex. Surely this was the prelude to a session of intense love-making, the reward for her long weeks of feminised torment! And then only Daphne's pretty white silk panties were left, and Christina's eyes were drinking up her gorgeous, perfect breasts. But there was, of course, something wrong, an odd bulge beneath Daphne's delicate panties, a bulge quickly revealed to be the truth of Daphne: her sex, very much like Christina's – long, hard and rampant.

Christina had cried out in horror, but Daphne had been upon her in an instant. A brief fight had ensued. Christina had screamed and struggled before allowing herself to be subdued. Daphne had been trained well: using a form of martial art, she forced the younger she-male's arms behind her back and dragged her on to the bed. Within seconds, Christina's hands had been bound behind her back and Daphne's panties were filling her mouth. Bound and gagged, forced face down on the bed, she had only been able to squeal as Daphne took a jar of vaseline from the dressing table opposite and covered her left index finger in a thick layer of the slimy golden substance. Then the terrible trial had begun and Christina had truly confronted her she-male destiny.

First Daphne had pulled the long anal plug from her captive's squirming backside. To her horror, Christina had found the sensations produced by this removal highly arousing and her struggles had lessened considerably. The guilt that gripped Denise had been sadly articulated by Christina: she saw her own doubts, her own resistance in Christina's description of the torment that came with the obvious pleasure brought by Daphne's gentle ministrations, ministrations that progressed to a full-scale lubrication of her stretched anal passage and then the final act of ravishment. As Daphne had climbed on to the bed and spread Christina's legs, the younger she-male had squealed desperately for mercy, tossing her head from side to side, crying angrily, tears of outrage pouring over her crimson cheeks and on to silk sheets. But no amount of struggling or squealing would stop Daphne and in a few terrible moments, she had slipped her rock-hard sex deep into Christina's helpless and expertly prepared back passage. And then the cries of pain and suffering, of appalling humiliation and degradation, had faded to an ambiguous silence. Then, out of this confused quiet, there had come the slightest moan of pleasure, a moan that grew into a cry and a cry into a scream. Then Christina had responded to the careful rhythm of Daphne's penetration, and as the older she-male had brought herself to a violent orgasm punctuated by a cry of animal joy, Christina had screamed her own excitement into the fat pantie gag.

'She left me tied up on the bed,' Christina said, her eyes filled with exciting memories of that first taking. 'She kissed me on the forehead, took up her clothes and left. A few minutes later Mary came to the room, untied me and prepared me for bed, a smile of triumph lighting up her face like a beacon. Yet she said nothing, merely made me bathe, refitted the restrainer and plug, put me in my nightwear and tucked me in. But the next morning, I was pulled from bed before dawn, by both Mary and Mummy, and stripped naked. Then they dressed me in a white nylon body stocking and cocooned me in thick ribbons of pink silk. Mummified, from my hosed toes to my neck. A fat pink ball gag was tied in place and a parcel label tied around my neck, a label reading 'To Daphne, Love Kathy and Mary. Enjoy!' Then a pink silk hood was pulled over my head and tied in place. An eyeless silk hood that plunged me into darkness. Then there was a jab, a sudden, sharp jab, and I passed out.

'They must have drugged me, for I woke up hours later in Daphne's bedroom, in the home she shared with Mistress Yolanda. Naked. Spread-eagled to the bed, still fitted with the ball gag. And there I stayed, in that large, strange house, for six months, trained by Daphne in the art of absolute servitude. And by the time I was returned to Mummy and Mistress Mary, I was completely transformed, both physically and, most importantly, mentally. Daphne had shown me the joys of complete submission and the endless pleasures of she-male-love. By the time I was given back to Mummy, I was addicted to femininity – and cock.'

This last, hard, shocking word was delivered without contempt. It had been a simple statement of the reality of Christina's sexual life, a reality she had so expertly demonstrated to Denise. And it was a reality she would continue to demonstrate both during that first surreal month and the rest of Denise's stay at the bizarre home of Samantha.

Thirteen

They came for her early in the morning. Christina had only just finished fitting Denise into a new baby maid's costume of striking yellow silk when the door to the nursery opened and Mistresses Bridget and Samantha marched into the room, Bridget in her usual softly coloured, feminine dress suit and Samantha in a typically striking skin-tight red sweater, matching leather miniskirt and white hose.

'Congratulations, Denise,' Samantha said, only the slightest trace of sarcasm in her deep, sensual voice. 'You've passed phase one of your training. Now all we need to do is complete your physical transformation and you'll be ready for your role as my personal maidservant.'

As she spoke, Mistress Bridget took a large, evil-looking syringe from her white leather handbag and approached a wide-eyed, terrified Denise.

'There'll be no pain,' the tall, ice-cool blonde whispered, rolling up one of the frilled sleeves of the dress. 'You will sleep and then wake. It is as simple as that.'

A slight sting was all she felt as the needle punctured her silky she-male skin. Then she was being helped to the dressing-table stool as the room became a blur. Then it was fading out. Then there was a flat, black silence, a pit of nothing into which she fell head first, only to emerge what seemed like seconds later. Yet when she awoke, she was in a different room, possibly in a different house. Her vision was shaky and she fought to remain still as the room slowly spun to a halt around her.

She was beneath a single white silk sheet. The bed was the only item of furniture in the room besides a mirror on the far wall. The walls were a bare, clinical white; the floor was plain wooden tiling. As she looked over the edge of the bed at the floor, she felt an odd weight around her chest and looked down at the large, oval bulge rising through the sheets just below her chin. She knew before she pulled back the sheets that she had undergone plastic surgery and that the bulge was her new, expanded bosom. But when it was finally revealed to her eyes, she still could not restrain a cry of amazement, of surprise, of genuine, soul-shattering shock. For before her was a truly magnificent pair of very large and perfectly shaped breasts, easily over forty inches in size, yet still exactly matched to her dainty, she-male form. And, of course, her first instinct was to reach out and touch them, to confirm through the simple act of feeling, their fundamental reality. And as her hands, her long, delicate, feminine hands, gently stroked these amazing pale rose orbs, intense waves of pleasure coursed through her body: they were even more sensitive than before – deliberately designed to emit signals of incredible sexual pleasure at the slightest caress!

Denise found herself taking the breasts in her hands, judging their significant weight, coming to terms with the effect this weight had on the rest of her body. Seeking to judge the effect they would have on her balance, she climbed off the bed. As she did so, she noticed more changes. Her waist seemed even tinier, her hips much broader and, to her amazement, her sex, her inescapable penis, seemed much bigger! It stood before her, tightly wrapped in a pink satin restrainer, violently erect, fighting the soft but unyielding and very arousing material, a good three inches longer than she ever remembered seeing it. And as she stepped on to the floor, she was sure her feet seemed smaller and her ankles much thinner, changes that made her long, slender legs seem even more feminine.

As she walked carefully up and down the bed, taking her now quite natural tiny, dainty steps, she noticed her hips swing with a helplessly erotic rhythm and her bottom wiggle with a teasing feminine naughtiness. And her breasts, her splendid, impressive breasts, swung gently from side to side, distorting her sense of balance at first, but then establishing their own easy rhythm, a rhythm that helped to counteract the effect of their weight on her general posture. Indeed, as she minced around the room, she realised the key to this new ultra-feminine body was rhythm – the balance and counterbalance of physical forces created by her breasts, her hips and her ankles.

Then, with her heart in her mouth, she approached the mirror, apprehension gripping her like a tight, cruel fist. But there was nothing to fear. Before her was a new Denise, without doubt, a Denise perfected perhaps, but also the same essential Denise that had been created over the last five weeks by Helen, Samantha, Mary, Katherine and, of course, Christina. But this was also Denise plus ten, Denise remixed by Mistress Bridget in the private operating theatre of some top-secret hospital. Her hair was the same long, flowing blonde curls, but her lovely baby-blue eyes seemed larger, now with a naturally doe-like stare of shy fascination, and her cheeks seemed softer, less angular. Then there were her lips. Now naturally cherry red and very full, bows of teasing perfection. And her neck, now seemingly longer, more slender, a delicate swan's neck leading down to softer, thinner shoulders and the splendid breasts with their large, permanently erect nipples jutting out like perversely phallic confessions of her true biological sex.

As Denise stared, as she consumed herself, lost in a mirror image collision of narcissism and voyeurism, Samantha entered the room. Samantha followed by Katherine, Bridget and finally, Christina. Samantha dressed in a black sweater, black leather jacket, black leather miniskirt, black hose and high heels. Samantha with her thick, black hair bound in a tight bun, her eyes filled with her own fascination. With Katherine at her side, dressed in another simple, but still sexy trouser suit and high heels, her short, brown hair shining under the powerful electric light illuminating the room. And then there was Bridget, in a white doctor's coat, beneath which was no doubt another of her almost ironically feminine costumes. And beside Bridget, the lovely Christina, in a typically erotic French maid's costume, every inch of her expertly feminised form quite deliberately designed to portray submission and complete sissy obedience. Christina, whose gorgeous brown eyes ate up this transformed Denise, this new improved and desperately sexy Denise.

It was Mistress Bridget who spoke first, stepping forward, walking around Denise, examining every change, every inch of this magnificent transformation.

'Yes. Very good. Proof positive that the process works completely, in every respect. She is nearly perfect, I think.'

Samantha laughed. 'You have a gift for understatement, Bridget. She is perfection. You should be very proud. And you, Denise, you should be very grateful.'

Denise curtsied sweetly before Mistress Bridget, her breasts swaying elegantly before her.

'You may thank her,' Katherine said, a wicked fire in her eyes. 'Verbally.'

Denise had not spoken for four weeks – since the fitting of the dummy gag.

'Thank you, Mistress Bridget.'

The words felt like hers, yet they were spoken in another's voice, in the voice of a little girl, a soft, high-pitched, teasingly erotic baby doll's voice. A voice designed to represent the most extreme form of ultra-femininity and complete submission. Christina's voice exaggerated ten times. Poor Denise blushed violently, embarrassed by the nitrogen comic-book tone that had been forced upon her. And as she blushed, the women laughed cruel, contemptuous laughter.

'Very good!' Samantha boomed. 'Perfect! Every time she speaks she will be reminded of her true sissy status. Every spoken word a lash of the whip of female domination.'

Katherine, amused but less entertained than Samantha, stepped forward. 'Who would have thought that a pathetic PR man could turn into the perfect sissy. You certainly have come a very long way, Denise. And you've proved to us beyond doubt that our little feminisation treatment can be repeated, can be used to benefit all womankind. You and Christina have provided vital evidence and inspiration. And now you must complete your mental conditioning. So you will spend the next five months as Mistress Samantha's personal maid. You will be moved into a new room and begin your new role immediately. But you will also continue to assist Christina in her duties. She will also remain responsible for your sexual reorientation, but your main task will be to serve Samantha. Under her instruction, you will learn the essence of service to a woman.

'Christina will prepare you. Report to Samantha in one hour.'

As the three beautiful, supremely dominant women left the room, Samantha turned to face Denise, a far from enigmatic smile of cruel promise lighting up her gorgeous face.

Once the door was closed, Christina stepped forward and placed her hands on Denise's breasts. Denise gasped with pleasure and moved into the younger she-male's hungry caress, gasps turning to cries as Christina began to twiddle her charge's splendid, erect nipples like two control knobs.

'Mistress Bridget has made you a pure pleasure machine, my love. Your breasts have been ultra-sensitised, as has your skin. And your sex – well, wait until we get it out of the restrainer. It's inches longer and stays permanently erect. Mistress Bridget has altered your hormonal balance to ensure you stay constantly aroused. And that means much more fun for me, for both of us!'

As she spoke, her hands moved over Denise's breasts, explored her tiny waist, her broad, shapely hips, her petite, perfectly feminine bottom, and then slipped over her restrained sex. Denise moaned and wiggled under her caresses, her big blue eyes never leaving Christina's.

'The restrainer is a terrible tease. I've worn one for over a year. It lets you get hard, but never hard enough, and it's so soft that it makes you want to get hard and to come *so* desperately. The perfect torture device for silly sissy she-males like you and me. But don't worry: if you please Mistress Samantha, she'll take it off, and then we can play again. And now there's so much more to play with!'

'I can't believe how sexy I feel,' Denise moaned in the sissy voice, her first she-male sentence.

'You sound so delightful, petal! Mistress Samantha was so right: the perfect voice! And do you know how jealous I am? So very, terribly jealous! You'll spend each day in a state of virtual ecstasy, experience pleasure I can only dream about. But, of course, there are advantages for me as well – you'll never know when to stop!'.

Denise, despite her terrible excitement, found Christina's enthusiasm a little disturbing. A vague sense of depression suddenly cut through the waves of sex hunger as she realised she was still gripped by the fundamental guilt that seemed to accompany her every sexual thought. It was clear that Christina would now attempt to stretch the limits of their sexual relationship, that this, in combination with her enslavement by Samantha, would form the final, prolonged chapter of her feminisation. And, although Denise knew she could do nothing to stop the inevitable, she still felt a helpless longing for her wife and a sense of deep shame at the way she had been forced to betray her love.

These dark thoughts were forgotten when Christina suddenly grabbed Denise's hand and led her out of the room. To her surprise they minced out into the long first-floor corridor of Samantha's house. They had never left the house! They then proceeded to walk quickly towards the stairs, each step a desperate wiggle-mince accompanied by the sexy, rhythmic swaying of her new, spectacular breasts and her perfectly rounded hips.

'I never left the house,' Denise whispered.

'No. Mistress Bridget operated on you here.'

'How long have I been –'

'Be quiet, Denise. I love your sexy voice, but you must only talk when given permission.'

Denise fell silent and let herself be led to a door next to the anteroom area where she had originally been presented to Samantha and Katherine, all the while fighting to keep her eyes from the perfectly straight seams of Christina's elegant silk stockings and her daintily wiggling backside.

The door led to a room, *her room*: a medium-sized bedroom decorated in sweet pinks and creams, a young lady's room, with a lovely oak dressing table, a large walk-in closet, a pink leather sofa and a beautiful oval double bed. On the walls, there were pictures of beautiful women, from elegant drawings to full scale portraits, all historical, all erotic, all with an unavoidable lesbian theme.

'Your room, Denny,' Christina announced.

A new name for Denise, a name recognising her new status but still rooted in her essential sissy femininity.

Denise smiled, nodded.

'Do you like it?' Christina asked.

'Yes. It's lovely.'

'Mummy had it decorated especially. And it's got everything you'll ever need. Now just stand there, hands behind your back, and I'll go get your uniform.'

Denise obeyed, standing as much to attention as her lovely bosom would allow, her hands glasped behind her back, her long, sexy legs tightly together, her erect, restrained sex also stiffly to attention. Perhaps an absurd sight, she found herself thinking, but also a helplessly erotic one. She listened to Christina singing a sissy tune to herself as she sorted Denise's new clothes. She listened and she studied this beautiful, yet simple room, her eyes drawn to the pictures, excited by the tender, yet intense acts of love they portrayed, only noticing after some careful analysis that these were not in fact lesbian images: each picture depicted an act of she-male love, each woman was a beautiful she-male; the pictures were reflections of her destiny!

Christina returned with a vast collection of underwear and a stunning black satin dress, a dress that perfectly matched her own elaborate, erotic costume.

The dressing was a repeat of the formal ceremony that was followed every morning. But now Denise was dressing as a lady's maid, as an *adult* she-male. Now, finally, she would be allowed to experience the joys of a true femininity. And what joys they were! Firstly, a pair of the most delightfully detailed white silk panties, with each leg trimmed with the most delicate French lace. Panties especially designed to cover easily her considerable, satin-restrained sex, but through which this physical symbol of her she-male essence remained clearly visible. And as she drew the panties up her legs, she began to realise just how sensitised her skin had become. As the panties brushed against her perfectly smooth legs, it was as if her legs were being covered in a thousand soft, teasing kisses. And if this was pleasure, what followed was heaven. For up each of her long, sexy legs she then guided a self-supporting, ultra-sheer, delicately seamed silk stocking.

'Oh, it's wonderful, they feel so divine!' she gasped.

These helpless sissy exclamations brought a smile form Christina, but also a scolding.

'Yes, Denny. But you must be quiet. If you don't keep quiet I'll have to gag and spank you. But I'm sure you'd love me to do that!'

There was no denying this. 'Yes,' she confessed. 'Please spank me, Christina. Gag me and spank me!'

Christina grabbed Denise and led her to the bed, pushing her down on to the soft, pink silk covers with a single teasing shove. She used a balled-up stocking nylon to gag the naughty older she-male, and tied it in place with yet another stocking. Yet more stockings were used to bind her arms and legs. Denise squirmed in ecstasy, her breasts tormented by the silk sheets, her sex fighting the satin restrainer, squeals of pleasure pouring from the gag.

'You really are a very naughty girl,' Christina said, taking up a flat-handled hairbrush from the dressing table and pulling the bound Denise across the bed and over her silk-sheathed knees. The petite, older she-male was easily manipulated, and it was only a matter of seconds before her pretty panties were around her ankles and hard, sharp blows were raining down on her delightfully exposed and very girlish bottom.

'You're loving every second of this, you horny little slut,' Christina teased, her voice filled with a savage arousal.

'And so am I. And there's going to be lots more of this, my pet. You and me. *Forever*. You're going to be my sex slave, doing whatever I want. Yes, anything, my darling. And you'll do it willingly, because you won't be able to help yourself. Because Mistress Bridget has programmed you to desire without limit.'

These passionate words were punctuated by repeated blows of the hairbrush, blows which turned Denise's lovely behind a dark red within a few painful minutes. Blows which brought tears to Denise's eyes, yet which also drove her mad with pleasure. Her deepest masochistic self would now be exposed twenty-four hours a day. She was revelling in this punishment, she was begging through the gag for more. Despite the guilt, the sense of shame, she wished for nothing else than to be Christina's slave, to be punished, to be dominated, to be utterly suppressed and redesigned in any way this beautiful, cruel she-male saw fit.

But then the spanking was over. Denise was untied and returned to the centre of the room, her bottom on fire. Then the gag was pulled from her mouth and the tears that Christina gently wiped from her flushed cheeks were tears of joy.

Then the dressing continued. The panties were replaced. A spectacular black and red satin corset was wrapped tightly around her tiny waist and laced firmly into place. An exquisite white silk, lace-trimmed brassiere was pulled carefully over her large breasts and clipped delicately into place. The bra felt truly amazing, holding her substantial chest firmly and yet seeming to cover it in gentle silk caresses at the same time. Denise moaned helplessly as it was secured and Christina slipped a warning hand against her pantied behind, slipping it between her buttocks as she did so and pressing hard against the gusset. Denise responded by pushing her bottom firmly against her lover's hand.

At this point, the dressing was suspended, as it always was, for Denise to apply her make-up. Christina left her charge to prepare her own face, Denise having become very proficient in this most feminine art.

Denise stared at her reflection in true astonishment. It was almost as if her face had been permanently made up: her lips were a natural cherry-red, her suddenly much larger eyes seemed to radiate an intense sky blue that needed no eyeshadow, and her rounded cheeks appeared to be permanently rouged a dark pink. Yet she still found use for a light powder foundation, some eyeliner and just a touch of lip gloss. She then combed her hair into the sculpture of waves that Helen had originally encouraged and which was now her favourite look. Then there was a subtle mixture of scents and perfumes selected with a genuine expertise from the array of exotically coloured bottles set out on the dressing table.

By the time Christina returned to the dressing table, Denise had completed what little preparation was now necessary. Christina's reflection once again filled Denise with a violent sexual need. Christina appeared more beautiful each time Denise set eyes on her – desire was inescapable and total. Yet deep in the heart of desire, there remained an undoubted shame.

'It's time to complete the dressing, precious.'

Christina then helped her pretty, busty charge into the glorious French maid's dress, the formal uniform of a servant of the Last Straw society. It fell over her body in ornate waves of soft, black satin, as light as the air itself. Fitted to the wide, pleated skirt were thick layers of familiar frou-frou petticoating, and as Christina buttoned the dress up, Denise carefully straightened the skirt over her stockinged thighs, feeling a marvellous rush of pure fetishistic pleasure and a strange, but very real pride in this she-male graduation. White silk gloves followed the dress, and after these gorgeously soft items came a white silk pinafore which Christina tied in place with the almost statutory wide and very fat bow at the base of her spine.

Next, there was a pair of beautiful, black patent-leather court shoes, classical in design, and with relatively modest five-inch heels. Despite her new breasts, Denise stepped into the heels with ease and quickly found the wiggle rhythm that would allow her to walk with comfort. Indeed, it was almost as if the broader hips, thinner ankles and large breasts helped her to balance more effectively in the heels, as if the shoes were an intricate part of the set of forces that kept her luscious she-male form mobile.

Then, finally, the dainty, white lace and silk maid's cap, the final symbol of her utter servitude as Samantha's domestic slave, was tied sweetly in place.

As Christina led Denise from the room, the older she-male found new, addictive pleasure in her feminisation. Her ultra-sensitive skin turned every movement into multiple sexy caresses of soft, sensual fabrics – just to walk was to be ravished.

They stopped almost immediately by the door next to Denise's new room. Christina knocked softly and Samantha's clear command to enter followed. Christina opened the door, but did not enter. Instead, she indicated that her sexy she-male lover was to enter alone. A look of apprehension filled Denise's lovely face, but Christina smiled reassuringly.

'It's your dream come true, my love. It's your destiny.'

Denise smiled nervously and entered the room.

Fourteen

Mistress Samantha stood in the centre of the bedroom. Denise minced towards her, gripped by a terror filled with sexual hunger, a craving for this image of the superior female that towered before her: Mistress Samantha, the woman who had forced her into panties and hose so many weeks before, the cruel, contemptuous dominatrix who had entered her home and transformed a dowdy, defeated and neurotic half-man into a stunning, totally obedient sissy she-male, who had seen inside her heart and pulled from it the beautiful creature who was now Denise.

'Kneel before me,' Samantha ordered.

These irresistible words wrapped around Denise's sissy soul and proclaimed every inch of it Samantha's personal property.

Denise obeyed, as she always obeyed, unable to pull her large, baby-blue eyes from this goddess. For Samantha had prepared herself carefully. She was dressed in a tight black basque, a second skin of shining black leather, long black rubber gloves, sheer nylon black stockings and stunning stiletto-heeled ankle boots of gleaming black patent leather. An ivory-handled riding crop was grasped menacingly between her rubber gloved hands. She was a dream made reality.

Samantha's eyes, her gorgeous brown eyes, were filled with scorn and cruel humour, her wide, perfect mouth was curved into a blood-red smile of triumph, and her long, thick black hair flooded over her tanned, muscular shoulders. She accepted her slave's timid curtsy of obedience and watched as Denise carefully, daintily, positioned herself on her silk-sheathed knees before her ultimate mistress.

'You've come a long way, Denise. I've always said you were a natural she-male, a born sissy. And I was right – there's absolutely no escaping that. And in time, you'll be the perfect maidservant, and, more importantly, the perfect servant of the Last Straw Society. Your destiny is to be our brightest creation. Yes, I doubt very much we'll ever find a subject as perfect as you. But your perfection is only a potential, something that still has to be drawn out of you. And that means something has to be removed – the obstacle between you and the realisation of your potential. That something, which we still see, which is in every secret humiliation and petty anger we can so easily inspire, is your residue masculinity. And it's that which we must now eradicate.'

Denise listened to these words and saw her future. There was no escape from the truth now. Things had gone too far. But she still hoped, even here, even before this startling symbol of inescapable transformation, for a compromise, a compromise whose name was Helen. And this, she knew, was the residue that Samantha would surely, finally destroy.

'During the next five months you will continue to serve all your mistresses in this house. However, you will spend the majority of your time serving me personally. There will be no more formal lessons, no more structured learning. Now your apprenticeship truly begins, your vocational training, as it were. You'll be responsible for keeping this room and my bathroom spotlessly clean; you will wash and iron all my clothes and ensure that my wardrobe is kept neat and orderly at all times. You will wash and dress me. You will be present at my side at all times, except when you are specifically not required. When not needed, you will either be used to help Christina or serve your other mistresses, or you will be kept bound and gagged in this room. At nights, unless I require you, you will sleep in the room next door. Christina will have access to your room and your body at any time when you are not required for the amusement of myself or the other mistresses. Do you understand?'

'Yes, Mistress,' Denise replied in her still unnerving little-girl voice.

'Good. You may kiss my feet and rise.'

Denise leaned forward and placed a long, heartfelt kiss on each glistening toe of the gorgeous ankle boots and rose gracefully to her feet, her eyes now firmly pinned to her own high-heeled feet.

'Oh, and by the way, you will also be required to service me sexually in any way I see fit.'

These last words, unleashed so casually, took the lovely she-male completely by surprise. She suddenly looked up into Samantha's fiery, almost satanic eyes, a look of genuine amazement on her face. Samantha burst out laughing.

'Don't worry, Denise, you won't get to fuck me. But you will learn how to give sexual pleasure to a woman without receiving or expecting to receive any form of return. You will give unconditionally. Restrained at all times, you will learn exactly how and where I like to be pleasured. Your tongue will become my personal pleasure tool. You will also learn that I take particular pleasure in the restraint of the she-male form. You will become my personal bondage doll. You will finally understand what it is like to be truly and utterly helpless.'

Then, to Denise's astonishment, Samantha began to undress! Within a few incredible minutes, the gorgeous dominatrix was totally naked before an amazed Denise. Staring in utter awe, she barely noticed as her hands were lashed between her back with rubber cording and she was forced up on to large four-poster bed that dominated the room. She was then made to kneel before her mistress as Samantha lay down on her back and spread her long, perfectly shaped legs out before the startled sissy. Denise faced Samantha's beautiful, soaking sex in a state of utter awe. Helen had made sure Denise was well trained in the oral sex art and had clearly informed her mother of her she-husband's natural ability to give a woman pleasure with her sissy tongue.

'You know what to do, Denise,' Samantha purred.

Denise wiggled forward and carefully lowered her pretty head between her mistress's thighs. Within seconds, she was covered in a virtual torrent of sex juice, her head held firmly in place by Mistress Samantha's powerful thighs. She practised her oral art with a patience and skill that left Samantha screaming into a pillow and bucking like an untamed mustang. For two whole hours, Denise teased Samantha to orgasm after orgasm. And although there was no release for Denise, there was pleasure, a terrible, unyielding pleasure created by her restrained, rocking, rubbing body, created by her ultra-sensitive breasts pressing hard into the soft embrace of the brassiere and the silk sheets covering the bed, of the satin restrainer tormenting her sex as she struggled in her tight, teasing underwear to keep her balance and continue to please her gorgeous mistress. Yes, poor Denise was driven mad as she drove Samantha mad. But for Samantha there was release, the cruelly boasted cries of orgasm, the filthy language that accompanied this spectacular coming. For Denise, there was only absolute submission.

And then, after this marathon oral session, as Samantha hauled herself upright from the bed, there was Denise's reward. Sweating, panting, smiling, Samantha quickly unbuttoned her slave's stained, crumpled dress, threw it to the floor and set about tightly binding and gagging her.

Firstly the gag: a pair of her sexiest, softest silk panties, cream-coloured, lace-trimmed, bundled into a fat ball and pushed deep into Denise's come-lined mouth.

'They're dirty from yesterday, my little honeypot,' she said, cruel laughter in her eyes as she took up a thick roll of silver masking tape from the bedside table.

Denise moaned into the fat, pungent gag, recalling the other times that this stunning woman had revealed her taste for bondage, and knowing that she was about to experience a new, highly exciting and truly perverse level of restraint.

A thick strip of the tape was spread over her soft, voluptuous lips, sealing the damp panties firmly in place. Then more rubber cording was used to bind her elbows, then her thighs, knees and slender, silk-sheathed ankles. As her huge breasts jutted out before her, she moaned desperately into the gag. A stunning damsel in distress, totally helpless before her glorious mistress.

'You look fabulous, Denise.'

These words were whispered in a voice of sheer sexual excitement. It was obvious Samantha took a powerful, kinky pleasure in bondage, in turning Denise into her bondage doll. And it was equally obvious that Denise enjoyed this intricate, unyielding restraint, for she squealed with pleasure into her gag, shook her impressive breasts desperately, and wiggled her bottom in the sweetest, sexiest way imaginable; all, of course, for Samantha's very real entertainment.

But this wasn't the end of the little game. As Denise performed her bondage ballet, Samantha knelt down by the front of the bed and pulled from it a very long, black rubber-lined drawer, a strange coffin-like space built into its ornate heart.

'Your nest for the rest of the afternoon, my sweet,' Samantha announced, helping a now fearful Denise hop to the edge of the long, narrow drawer. Then, to Denise's amazement, Samantha lifted the sissy beauty by her waist over the edge of the drawer and gently assisted her to lie face down inside it.

'This will be your bondage home, my little petal. We've found that sensory deprivation has a particularly therapeutic effect on sissies with guilt complexes about their true natures. I think you'll find it reasonably comfortable, especially once you have the company of an anal vibrator.'

As she teased the now terrified she-male, she took up another, longer length of rubberised cording and used it to tie Denise's shapely ankles to her crossed, tightly bound wrists, thus creating an incredibly strict hog-tie that left the metal tips of her high heels pressing into the palms of her hands.

As Samantha tightened this final, painful knot, poor Denise squealed fearfully into her fat, tasty gag, a squeal that turned into a wail of terror as Samantha begun to push the drawer back into the belly of the huge bed.

'Don't worry, babikins: I'll be back in about two hours.'

Then darkness, total, absolute darkness. And a grim silence relieved only by the desperate, tightly gagged pants that fought to escape the unyielding strip of masking tape covering her sweet, she-male lips.

At first poor Denise wiggled desperately in her bizarre bedroom coffin, yet it soon became apparent that Mistress Samantha had tied a set of particularly fiendish knots – the more she struggled, the tighter they seemed to become! So she lay still, the sound of her sissy heart pounding in her ears, a deep bass percussion accompanying the dissonant melody of her laboured breathing. Immobilised and utterly alone, the first thing she noticed was her own body. This carefully transformed she-male frame, which now held so many inescapable pleasures. Her skin seemed to be tingling with intense physical excitement and she soon found that she was rubbing her more than ample breasts hungrily against the rubberised covering of the box, inspiring a gentle, teasing friction communicated by the soft, gentle fabric of the brassiere. So tightly bound, so expertly gagged, so completely helpless, she became, once again, deeply aroused. An arousal without end here, with the restrainer teasing and tormenting, but ultimately denying any chance of relief. Yes, even here, in this perfect black silence, there was no time to think, no stable moment to contemplate what was happening to her. Despite her confusion and the hundreds of questions, sex heat made a coherent, rational examination of her lot utterly impossible.

Soon, even the slightest form of self-reflection was impossible. Soon, she was only sexual need, the electrical torment of an unforgiving desire, a charge of cosmic fire burning in an external nothingness. Her bondage became the most precise, all encompassing pleasure. She had been sucked into the atavistic whirlpool of fundamental animal passion and there seemed no possible route of return. Her body consumed her mind. The hormonal rage that Bridget had set off in her body flowered into a cannibalistic monster and swallowed the dainty, terrified she-male-in-distress whole.

There was no time, no space, no Denise. Only the sex heat. And by the time Samantha pulled open the drawer, as the blinding, ice-white light of a forgotten world flooded into her premature tomb, poor Denise was lost even to herself.

She awoke in her own room, on the large oval bed, dressed only in her bra and panties (and, of course, the restrainer). She had no idea of how much time had passed, or how she had been returned to this room. But she did know she was still rock hard and desperate.

She pulled herself up and confronted Christina. Christina, in a basque, black stockings and nothing else. Christina with her lovely jet hair spilling over her shoulders and the tops of her splendid breasts. Christina staring at her with a simple, one-dimensional sexual need.

Denise licked her blood-red lips, the taste of Samantha still all over her face. She ran a hand through her hair. She had been stripped, but not washed or scented. Her bonds were gone. She was confused and exhausted.

'What time is it?' she asked, her sissy voice shocking, alien.

'Late, Denny. After midnight,' came Christina's whispered, distracted reply.

'I need to sleep. I need a drink. I need –'

'You need me.'

Then Christina was upon her, pulling the bra from her body, smothering her large, exposed breasts in tender kisses, her free hand pulling Denise's panties over her thighs.

'Mummy says I can go all the way tonight, my love. She says you're ready for a true deflowering.'

Weak, yet still riddled with the perpetual horniness, she allowed Christina to ravish her with her mouth and desperately caress her restrained sex. Then the younger she-male was turning her over, placing her face down on the soft silk sheets of the bed and pulling her legs part. Denise turned her tired head and saw Christina working on a hidden pouch at the base of the basque, then saw her huge, swollen sex emerge from it, a sex aimed directly between Denise's legs.

'I've waited so long for this, darling. And I know you have, too.'

But despite her own sexual torment, Denise knew she had only waited for this moment as a condemned man awaits the gallows. This was the final barrier, the last true vestige of her resistance. After this, she was lost to everyone and everything, most importantly to Helen. And perhaps this is why she cried out a horrified 'No!' and, with one surprisingly firm push, shoved Christina off the bed.

The younger she-male was caught off guard and fell badly, banging her head on the floor and bursting into sissy tears. Denise pulled herself up once again and tried to lean over, to help Christina up, but the lovely younger sissy was outraged and pushed Denise back angrily.

'You awful bitch!' she screamed, grasping a cut on her forehead. 'Mummy will make you pay for this!'

Then she climbed to her feet and wiggle-minced angrily from the room. Denise, shocked, yet also angry herself, her sense of time and space, even her sense of identity distorted by the rapid pace of events over the last hours, collapsed back on the bed and feel into a deep, dreamless sleep.

When she awoke, she was still naked and Katherine and Mary were standing over her, both looking angry and upset.

Instinctively, Denise tried to pull herself up, uttering a hoarse 'Yes, Mistresses, how can I serve you?' But Mary stepped forward and pushed her violently backwards.

'You can shut your foul sissy mouth,' Mary snapped, her voice riddled with a genuine anger.

Katherine stepped forward and pulled Mary back.

'Thank you, Mary. That's quite enough.'

Mary nodded and let her mother sit down on the bed at Denise's side. Dressed in a black leather jacket, a short checked skirt and black hose, she appeared uncharacteristically feminine.

'I'm very disappointed in you, Denise. You were doing so well. We actually thought you were progressing marvellously. And now this terrible incident. An assault, of all things. A brutal manifestation of male anger. Here, in this of all places. Well, of course it can't go unpunished. And it will not. But we feel the punishment should fit the crime. And as the crime is your desire, or rather its lack of correct focus, the source of your desire shall be punished. Show her the restrainer, Mary.'

Mary stepped forward again, holding what seemed to be another restraining device. This one was made of black rubber, but as Mary carefully turned it inside out, Denise saw that it was lined with a hundred very tiny pins!

'You will wear this until you accept your role as Christina's lover. It will cause you considerable discomfort, but it will also teach you a lesson. When you have learned that lesson, when you come to me or Mistress Samantha and beg to be allowed to become Christina's lover, and not only her lover, but her complete and absolute slave, a slave who will do *anything* she tells you, then, and only then, will this apt tool be removed.'

With a typically cruel smile lighting up her lovely face, Mary, who was dressed in a lovely white silk blouse and a pair of very tight black cotton slacks, quickly untied the satin restrainer and pulled it from Denise's sex with one angry tug. The she-male's erect penis automatically sprung to full, desperate life and poor Denise could only gasp in amazement at how good it felt to be fully engorged. Yet this feeling was very short-lived: within seconds Mary had pulled the rubber restrainer tightly over her permanently aroused sex and forced it back into a state of carefully frustrated imprisonment. Normally even the angry ministrations of the beautiful Mary, whose splendid teenage breasts brushed against Denise's stomach as she leaned forward to pull the restrainer down over her slave's scrotum and then secure it with a tiny silver padlock, would have driven the gorgeous she-male insane with excitement. But the pain that came almost immediately forced any sense of genuine arousal from even her hormonally distorted mind. It was as if a hundred tiny teeth were nibbling at her sex!

As Mary stepped back, leaving Denise's erect sex a tower of slick black rubber rising about her tiny waist, the she-male's sex was enveloped in a severe irritation. But as she moved on the bed, as she tried to pull herself up from the bed, the teeth suddenly became sharper and she winced in genuine pain.

'Yes,' Katherine said, a smile of revenge burning into Denise's fearful eyes. 'It's movement that really inspires the pain. And as you'll be wearing this all day, while serving Mistress Samantha and the rest of us, you'll be moving quite a lot. But this is only the beginning, I'm afraid.'

At her mother's command, Mary then disappeared into the closet. As she did so, the bedroom door opened and Christina minced into the room, a small plaster covering a cut on her forehead, her lovely eyes filled with hurt. Denise noticed immediately that she was wearing rubber gloves and carrying a slick pink rubber phallus in her hands.

'Turn on to your chest, Denise,' Katherine ordered.

Denise, finding it difficult to keep her eyes off the long, glistening phallus, obeyed, wincing as what felt like a mass of bee stings tormented her sex.

'Now spread your legs as wide as you can.'

Denise again obeyed Katherine, her heart sinking as she realised what the second stage of this dreadful punishment entailed.

Hands, most probably Christina's, then pushed the phallus between Denise's parted buttocks, finding an easy, forgiving home for nine inches of hard, sticky rubber. Poor Denise gasped with an instinctive pleasure as the phallus was driven home with some enthusiasm.

'Now get up off the bed and stand to attention before me.'

The urgency in Katherine's voice brought an immediate and painful response. More sharp shocks bit into her sex as she quickly rose to her feet and stood before Katherine and Christina, the lovely she-male now clad in her stunning red maid's uniform, an image of feminine perfection bringing only more torment as Denise's sex fought that little bit harder against its fiendish imprisonment.

Then a new pain began – a pain deep in her backside. A slow, burning pain that quickly transformed itself into an intense itching. Suddenly she was fighting the urge to wiggle violently and pull the phallus from her backside.

'Stand still, Denise!' Katherine snapped, her cruel smile broadening.

But Denise couldn't stand still: her anus was filled with what felt like thousands of scratching ants.

'The phallus is lined with a very powerful skin irritant,' Katherine explained, her smile now a grim, knowing smirk. 'It's effective for twenty-four hours and can cause substantial discomfort, as you're discovering. But this really is no excuse for your sissy gyrations. It's a good job we have a means of stopping them.'

This means was almost immediately produced, carried by Mary from the closet and placed on the bed before the extremely agitated she-male. Initially, it appeared to be another pile of fetish clothing, but closer examination revealed a black rubber body stocking, complete with fitted glove and feet sections. Next to this was a matching black rubber dress. As Mary returned to the closet, Christina stepped forward and took the body stocking from the bed.

'Legs apart, Denny. This is a rather difficult one.'

Her eyes now full of pained pleading, poor Denise obeyed Christina and watched in horror as the younger she-male took the body stocking by the neck and began to roll it down to the two long, black legs and then roll the legs down to the two feet, an amazing act of reduction that immediately demonstrated the flexibility of this sinister material.

Christina then helped Denise step into the stocking and began to unroll it up her legs. Within a few minutes her legs were encased up to the thighs and the material was being carefully rolled over her painfully restrained sex. Then the stocking was climbing her tiny waist. Then it was being pulled carefully over her huge breasts and at the same time over her now outstretched arms. Then, finally, the stocking seemed to come together around her neck, enveloping her body in a tight, latex second skin. But not just tight. As the material settled, it became painfully clear that it was actually contracting, shrinking to make a perfect fit against every sheathed inch of her feminised form. Suddenly her breasts were almost perfectly outlined against the material, her erect nipples clearly visible through a film of black rubber, as was her tightly bound and tormented sex. And as the material tightened, it sought out the dark valley between her buttocks and pushed the wicked phallus even deeper into her infuriated anus.

Now Denise was truly still, held in place by the tightening fabric, unable to do anything but stand rigid and upright before Mistress Katherine and Christina. However, Christina then proceeded to demonstrate that there was actually some movement in the material by taking up the heavy black rubber dress and drawing it over Denise's cocooned form, pulling her arms up to draw the dress down over her body and guide it firmly into place. And by the time the dress was in place, Mary had returned with more bizarre items of clothing and a small black box.

At Mary's instruction, Christina took up the first of the new items, a lovely white silk pinafore and fixed it around Denise's rubberised form with the now standard fat bow. The pinafore was quickly followed by gleaming white-glacé gloves which were stretched tightly over the black rubber-glove attachments fitted on to each arm of the body stocking. A white lace maid's cap was then fitted on to her lovely blonde hair.

As this dressing progressed, the burning, itching sensation travelling through Denise's anus and up into her tormented sex increased. Soon tears were trickling down the she-male's silky smooth, make-up-free face and little moans of helpless discomfort were trickling from her full, strawberry lips.

'She's making far too much noise, Chrissie,' Mary snapped. 'Gag her.'

With a cruel, vengeful smile, Christina removed the lid from the shoebox and pulled from it a large, black rubber penis gag, attached to which appeared to be a rubber hand pump. She quickly forced the long, thick gag into Denise's mouth and strapped it tightly into place, leaving the pump tangling by the poor sissy's chin. Denise's eyes widened in horror as Mary then stepped forward and began to work the pump with her right hand, forcing air into the body of the penis gag and causing it to expand to the point where every inch of her mouth was filled by the gag, leaving Denise to breathe heavily and desperately through her nose.

Once satisfied that the gag had been expanded to its maximum size, Mary unscrewed the pump from the front piece of the gag and left poor Denise standing before her amused captors with her cheeks stretched grotesquely. And this was not the end of the cruel humiliation; for no sooner was the gag secured, than Christina produced a pair of the sadistic seven inch high-heeled court shoes used for the movement classes and forced her charge to climb into them, a painful and very difficult act thanks to the twin restrictions of her physical torment and the rubber body stocking. And as she tottered desperately in the towering heels, unable even to release a moan of despair, Christina began to fit heavy silver shackles to her rubberised wrists, below her knees and around her perfect feminine ankles. Each set of shackles was linked by a horizontal silver chain, which was in turn linked to a vertical master chain that ran down from her wrists via her knees to her ankles. The horizontal chains were only a few inches in length and reduced any forward movement to a tiny sissy totter. Even worse, the central chain tended to pull her body forward, which made her already precarious, pain-undermined balance, incredibly shaky.

'Perfect,' Katherine said, a broad smile lighting up her face. 'You'll remain like this for the rest of the day and be supervised by Christina. You will treat Christina as you would treat a true mistress. At the end of the day, you'll be taken to Mistress Samantha and given the opportunity to apologise. Do you understand?'

Rubberised, tightly gagged and hobbled, Denise could only nod slightly, tears of pain now flooding over her big, baby-blue eyes and down her bulging, bright red cheeks. Katherine and Mary, highly amused by the bizarre spectacle they had created, then left the room.

Denise faced Christina, the younger she-male standing tall and indignant before her charge, her eyes ablaze with hurt and anger.

'I hope you're satisfied, Denny. You deserve every inch of your bondage.'

Denise tried to protest into the appallingly fat gag, but not even a squeak escaped her perfectly stopped mouth. Instead, she managed only a vague, desperate shake of her lovely head. She tried to mince forward on the impossibly high heels to relieve the maddening itching torturing her back passage, but this only managed to inspire more fiendish caresses from the wicked restrainer. There was nowhere to totter – every avenue led to the same place: the house of pain.

And even now her suffering had not reached its zenith: no sooner had Denise tried to move forward, than Christina produced the familiar collar and silver chain leash. Despite Denise's widening, angry eyes and tossing head, Christina managed to secure the collar around her neck and then fix the chain to the collar.

'Mummy wants the hallway and adjacent corridors polished this morning, Denny. Then, after lunch, there's a ton of undies to sort and iron. A normal day's work for a sissy maid, but for you, in your condition – well, it should be perfect hell. And if you do the jobs badly, you'll suffer even more.'

Tossing her head frantically and screaming into a void of tight, black rubber, poor Denise was led from the room by a smiling, happily mincing Christina. Despite her terrible bondage, the torment of the phallus filling her backside and the constantly nibbling, scratching restrainer, Denise wiggle-minced forward in a series of tiny, desperate steps. The tight, restricting rubber made her feel as if she had suddenly travelled to a low gravity alternative reality.

Each tiny step was a genuine physical effort, and even before they had reached the end of the long, seemingly endless corridor, she was covered in sweat. And as the sweat mingled with the tears staining her lovely face, she suddenly realised why no make-up had been applied and her sissy heart sunk into a bottomless pit of horror and self-pity.

Never had Denise or the being once known as Denis endured such relentless, unforgiving and apparently limitless torment. First she was made to polish the main entrance floor on her shackled, rubberised knees. The body stocking tightened around her delicate, feminine form as she did so, forcing the cruel phallus deeper into her anus and pressing the savage restrainer more tightly and uncomfortably against her slender, girlish and now tightly compressed waist. Through a series of tiny, painful movements, the only kind of movements allowed by the chains and rubber costume, she managed, somehow, to take-up a large duster and, inch by agonising inch, clean the already spotless marble surface. Huge droplets of sweat splashed on to the floor before her, mingling with desperate, hopeless tears to create a strange, sad lubricant for the duster.

To make things even worse, the rubber dress began to ride up her backside and reveal her rubber-sheathed behind, thus leaving her helplessly exposed to regular, vicious blows from an ivory-handled riding crop Christina produced once her charge was down on her restrained hands and knees.

It took perhaps three hours to complete the entrance area. Another two hours were spent on the adjacent corridors. Each second of each minute tolled in Denise's tortured she-male mind like a bell of ultimate doom. This was a punishment that would never end. And by the time it did end, by the time each inch of the floor was even more ridiculously clean, Denise was ready to accept any humiliation, any advance, any sexual position. As she was pulled to her heeled, tired feet, her face crimson with fatigue and bathed in a sheet of sweat, her sex and anus aflame with the various appalling and fiendishly complementary pains, she desperately wanted to beg forgiveness. Her eyes were forced wide with a terrible eagerness to communicate, she tossed her head from side to side frantically and fought to gesticulate in her bondage. But Christina just laughed and tapped her slave's backside with the crop, forcing her into the laundry room with a series of cruel gibes.

To her surprise Mary was in the laundry room, seated, her lovely, black-hosed legs crossed. As Denise was forced into the room, she stood, took up a small black handbag and walked over to the terrified, tormented she-male.

'I see you've been keeping her entertained,' she said to Christina.

'Yes, Mistress,' the younger she-male replied, curtsying sweetly.

'Good. I like to see a sissy happy in her work.'

Then Mary smiled sweetly at Denise and left the room, her shapely bottom wiggling teasingly through the fabric of her surprisingly long black skirt. Denise was then led over to two huge piles of undergarments.

'The one on the left is dirty stuff. That needs shorting and washing. The one on the right is clean. That needs ironing.'

Denise stared at the two piles in despair. There was at least another two hours work here and that meant another two hours of pain.

'I'll leave you to it, then,' Christina added. 'If you haven't sorted this lot by the time I get back, you'll spend the night and all of tomorrow in this outfit.'

Giving no indication of when she would return, Christina left the large room, locking the door behind her. Poor Denise burst into silent, tortured tears as the key sounded in the lock and shuffled forward to the dirty pile.

There followed a dreadful afternoon lost in a sea of physical pain and underwear. She struggled with every imaginable variety: knickers, bras, tights, stockings, petticoats, slips, girdles, G-strings. Then there were the various items of fetish wear that the mistresses and the she-males wore as part of their respective sadomasochistic uniforms.

She worked hard and without a break, her fear of another twenty-four hours in this appalling outfit all the inspiration she needed to reach Christina's ill-defined target.

Drenched in sweat, raked by the torments of the phallus and the restrainer, each movement a terrible test of fading strength in the rubber body stocking, constantly fighting to keep her balance in the highest of heels, weighed down by the shackles and chains, and forced to breathe in desperate short bursts through her nose by the massive, all pervasive penis gag, poor Denise was indeed a sorry and most pathetic sight, a beautiful she-male caught in a bondage trap set by her uniformly beautiful and wicked captors. And yet, as she sorted clumsily through the intimate garments, as familiar, teasing and very private aromas tickled her desperately flaring nostrils, she could still feel the addictive, unending sexual excitement that was now part of her fundamental biological make-up. And, to her amazement, her sex still fought its evil restrainer, sending new waves of pain through her brutalised body and the most bizarre waves of masochistic pleasure through her so-feminine, sissy mind.

It was well over two hours by the time Christina returned and Denise had only just finished ironing and sorting the last undergarment, an unmistakable pair of Mary's red silk panties.

Denise performed a ragged, exhausted curtsy before her new mistress. Christina smiled, the crop still held threateningly in her hands, her eyes pinned to Denise's heaving, tightly rubberised chest.

'You look all worked up, Denny. I hope you haven't been trying to play with yourself while I've been out.'

Denise shook her head wearily and awaited the next, inevitable humiliation.

But it didn't come. Instead Christina minced within a few inches of Denise and laid a gentle hand on her shoulder.

'Have you seen the error of your ways, babikins?'

Denise nodded desperately, now ready to accept any humiliation or subjugation to escape this terrible torture.

'So you're ready to be a good little girl and play with me tonight?'

Again, Denise nodded violently, her eyes wide with pleading, with absolute defeat.

'Good. Then we'll take you up to see Mistress Samantha.'

And so Christina led the devastated, pain-possessed Denise from the washroom and down the corridor, into the hall and up the winding stairs. An oppressively slow journey that was also a final, dreadful torment for the unfortunate she-male.

But, eventually, soaked in sweat, panting desperately, more tears of woe flooding from her beautiful blue eyes, Denise, flanked by Christina, found herself performing another messy curtsy before the gorgeous Mistress Samantha. Dressed in only the skimpiest of see-through silk nighties, her naked body shockingly apparent beneath, Samantha stood before the two she-males, hands on hips, a look of pure contempt in her eyes.

'Remove the gag, Chrissie,' she said.

Christina screwed a rubber tube into the front of the gag and then pushed it hard against the rubber plate covering Denise's mouth. A hiss of escaping air followed and, to Denise's infinite relief, the penis gag began to deflate. Christina then unstrapped the gag and removed it from her charge's tormented mouth. Denise gasped her thanks, yet also found herself tempted to sob loudly.

'Are you sorry, Denise?' Samantha asked.

'Please, Mistress, I'm so sorry! I don't know what came over me. I'll do whatever you want. I'll do whatever Christina wants. I was so very naughty. Punish me in any other way, but please, *please*, remove this terrible restrainer!'

Then she burst into agonised, desperate tears.

'I'm disappointed in you, Denise,' Mistress Samantha replied. 'I expected you to suffer with a bit more dignity. But this – well, you really are just the biggest sissy imaginable. And anyway, I have to be convinced that you'll do what you say. Katherine and Mary want to keep the restrainer on you for at least a week – you'll really have to convince them that you genuinely want to atone for your sins.'

The thought of being trapped in this dreadful device for a week brought a moan of horror to her freed lips. 'Please, Mistress, anything – anything you or the other mistresses require. I've learned my lesson!'

Her little-girl voice, pleading so pathetically, filled her with shame. Yet shame was irrelevant now.

'Well, tonight you can prove it. We'll release you from your bonds and return you to your room. There you will find suitable night attire and a nice romantic meal. You will bathe and change. Christina will come to you in an hour. Then you will serve her in any way she wishes. Do you understand?'

Denise performed another shaky curtsy and whispered a tired 'Yes, Mistress'.

'Good. Christina will take you back to your room and undress you.'

Once back in Denise's room, Christina set to work removing the shackles and various items of restrictive clothing that the unfortunate older she-male had been imprisoned within for so many painful hours. Now Christina's manner was more forgiving, her hands gentle, her breathing heavy with a renewed desire for her charge.

As each item of clothing was peeled from her body, Denise felt a little more human. But it wasn't until the brutal restrainer was carefully unlocked and slid from her helplessly erect, tormented sex, and the long, irritant-greased phallus was pulled from her inflamed backside, that a true sense of relief began to wash over her, that she felt truly free from the grim punishments that had made the day such an appalling misery.

'You should wash your sex and anus thoroughly, Denny,' Christina whispered hoarsely. 'Both for your benefit and mine.'

Christina nodded warily and stepped back from the younger she-male, naked and covered in a film of sweat, her beautiful, glistening body filling Christina's lovely eyes with a powerful sexual hunger.

'As you wish, Mistress,' she replied, her words almost helplessly teasing.

Christina smiled and stepped forward, running a long, blood-red nailed index finger along the bruised, rock-hard shaft of Denise's sex and inspiring a gasp of shocked delight in the older she-male.

'Yes, as *I* wish, Denny. Now go and clean yourself up. When I come back, you'll be suitably prepared. You must wear the clothes on the bed – I picked them especially.'

Denise curtsied cutely and smiled an obedient, willing smile.

Christina left the room and Denise burst into tears. She could see there was absolutely no escape: she was doomed to become Christina's sex slave, her purpose to provide every kind of sexual pleasure for the younger she-male and an endless source of amusement for the other mistresses.

But, despite her despair, she realised there was no point in trying to rebel. With a defeated heart and a very sore sex, she minced into the bathroom, barely glancing at the clothes laid out on the bed. She showered every inch of her tired, tormented body, taking some kind of pleasure in its great beauty and fighting the powerful urge to masturbate that her sudden freedom from restraint made possible. Then she dried and powdered herself, returning to the bedroom and to the ornate dressing table opposite the massive oval bed. Here she sat and faced her now strikingly feminine reflection, proud of her large, perfect breasts, of the baby-girl good looks that needed virtually no make-up, of her thick, golden hair. She perfumed her body carefully, then added the slightest hint of make-up in those places where it would have most impact: touching up lips, adding a hint of eye shadow, a little rouge. Then she carefully combed her hair into the thick, Monroe waves that Christina seemed so impressed by. Satisfied with her work, she rose stiffly from the chair and turned towards the bed.

Here she found a beautiful pink silk baby-doll nightie, matching bra and panties and a pair of sheer white nylons. At the foot of the bed were a pair of stunning pink leather, stiletto-heeled court shoes. Denise dressed in the sexy lingerie with a helpless arousal. Her ultra-sensitive, silky smooth she-male body delighting in the caress of the layers of silk, in the soft kiss of the self-supporting stockings, in the sense of perfect counterbalance the shoes brought to her striking, busty form.

She carefully adjusted the stockings in the dressing-table mirror, noticing that their beautifully patterned tops were clearly visible through the skimpy, short hem of the baby doll. Then she returned to the bed, sat carefully on the edge, crossed her long, sheathed legs and pushed out her lovely bosom, feeling every inch the she-male seductress awaiting her lover, her sex almost burning through the straining material of the sexy panties.

Then the door was opening and Christina entered the room. She was dressed in a black satin panelled basque, black silk, seamed stockings, open-toed stiletto-heeled mules, a slender black velvet choker around her neck, her hair untied and pouring over her broad, golden shoulders, her arms sheathed in elbow-length, black glacé ball gloves She was a vision of a paradoxically feminine power. And Denise could not help but rise up from the bed and curtsy her utter submissiveness to this great beauty.

Christina stepped forward and took Denise's perfect face in her gloved hands. A quiver of ecstasy sped through Denise's ultra-feminised body as her eyes met Christina's. Her sex strained desperately against her silk panties and her breasts pushed forward towards those of the younger she-male.

'You look delicious, Denny, my perfect love.'

Denise smiled modestly, blushing a sweet crimson and performing a suitably servile curtsy. 'Thank you, Mistress.'

Her baby girl's voice climbed to a squeal of aroused surprise as Christina slid a gloved hand beneath the baby doll and grasped Denise's silk-encased sex.

Then they were upon one another, their mouths forced passionately together, Denise's hands gripping Christina's heavy bosom, Christina pulling Denise's panties down around her stockinged thighs and taking a firm, determined grip on her exposed sex. Denise cried into

Christina's mouth and forced her sex in and out of Christina's hand. Christina pushed her charge back on to the bed and used her superior physical strength to pin Denise beneath her. Then, in a frenzy of sexual madness, she literally ripped the clothes from Denise's gorgeous, trapped body.

As the sound of tearing silk echoed around the room, Denise found herself nearly swooning with the pleasure of this ravishment. Now, in the heat of this most intense sexual battle, all guilt and shame were lost as profound masochistic desire took complete control. Soon Christina was sitting astride the prone figure of Denise, unzipping the basque with a wicked smile and letting her spectacular breasts pop out for the sexual entertainment of the wildly aroused older she-male. Then Denise's own flimsy brassiere was ripped away. Christina's eyes widened and her hands fell upon these wondrous, ultra-sensitive orbs. Denise squealed with an intense physical delight as her nipples were caressed to an even fiercer stiffness. She watched in amazement as Christina wriggled out of the basque and towered over her, naked except for the choker and her stockings. Her huge, rampant sex pressed into the older she-male's stomach as she leaned forward and began to cover Denise's breasts in soft, teasing kisses. As she pulled her body down over Denise, Christina forced her buttocks apart and then lowered her backside on to Denise's desperate sex. Before Denise could protest, her sex had slid inside Christina and the younger she-male began to ride her charge.

It was that quick, that sudden. No struggle, no fight, no debate. Just a clever movement and Denise was locked in the most intimate and terrifying moment of she-male sexual communication. Christina's back passage had been expertly stretched and was well used to this kind of penetration. Denise found herself pushing deeper into a welcoming, warm cavern of she-male desire and became even more aroused. Christina, her eyes wide with animal pleasure, her mouth shaped in an 'O' of ecstasy, cried out as Denise pushed harder. Then Denise came, helplessly, violently, an explosion of she-male lava that flooded Christina's back passage and inspired screams of wild pleasure in both of them. This was the supreme moment, the blinding light of a profound ecstasy filled their lovely, sissy eyes. They were bound together in an epiphany, at the heart of which was overwhelming sexual love.

Then Christina was hauling herself off her charge and turning Denise over. Denise, spent, exhausted, ecstatic, hardly able to focus on the room and Christina, could only moan with delight as she fell on to her large breasts. She felt Christina's hands on her thighs, her legs being spread apart. She knew what was about to happen and did not resist. As Christina slipped into her, she squealed with pleasure, her high-pitched, baby-girl cries bringing a warm, life-affirming laugh from Christina, a laugh turning to a scream as she filled Denise with her own thick sex lava.

It happened so fast, so suddenly, this final and most intimate act of she-male love, this act that Denise had known would be a true point of no return. Yet now, in the moments after she had been so willingly taken, there was no shame or guilt, no terrible images of Helen haunting her ravished mind. Now there was only a tremendous sense of relief and inner peace. The awful sufferings of the day, the ultra-perverse humiliations she had been made to endure, were now, in a blink of a tired eye, forgotten, or if not quite forgotten, then remembered by a deeply masochistic Denise as the strangely pleasurable prelude to this act of ultimate she-male passion.

It was after midnight when they fell asleep in each other's arms. Both had followed the first bout of love-making with tender oral pleasuring and then a less dramatic repetition of the first heated taking. Two beautiful, glorious she-males, perfectly feminised, created to serve and obey without question, experiencing the deepest delights of their sissy natures.

Fifteen

The months passed with surprising speed, yet to say that Denise was truly aware of the passage of time would be to exaggerate. For the beautiful she-male, each day was very much like any other in the sense that each day was a routine of continual sexual arousal, absolute servitude and relentless, highly erotic punishment. As Mistress Samantha's maidservant and bondage doll, the lovely sissy experienced the bliss of a profound submission, devoting herself with an absolute selflessness to the needs to the startling amazon beauty whose own sadomasochistic tastes ensured an endless array of highly imaginative 'therapies'. A day didn't pass without at least three sound spankings and an equal number of kinky bondage scenarios. Often the punishments were more severe, certainly more painful, but Denise accepted them all with a devotion that bordered on worship. And then there were the daily pleasurings, the wonderful private moments when Samantha required Denise to use her tongue and hands to provide her mistress with sexual relief. It was in these moments that Denise truly came to love her role as the most personal of maidservants.

Yes, during these timeless days, weeks and months, a time that was not time, this dreamlike descent into the deepest, most perfect servitude, Denise didn't just become Mistress Samantha's slave, she became her devotee, an utterly committed follower of the goddess Samantha, a sissified priestess of a cult of the supreme female. So tightly bound and wickedly gagged (virtually always with Samantha's soiled panties), so securely locked in the isolation drawer beneath her mistress's enormous bed, her sex so tightly restrained, a large anal vibrator buzzing in her more than accommodating backside, she experienced not only the most intense sexual pleasure imaginable, but a form of revelation, a profound insight not only into her true role as a sissy slave, but into her destiny as Samantha's creation.

And then there was Christina. Beautiful, flawless, unending in her desire for the lovely Denise. Now they became true lovers. The younger she-male moved into Denise's room. They shared not only a bed, not only each other's gorgeous bodies, but every intimate moment of their daily lives when not required to serve their mistresses. They became true girlfriends, helping each other with make-up and dress, delicately bathing each other every morning. Clothes became their obsession: the vast variety of fetishistic costumes became a source of pleasure and pride, and they became experts on the details of fabrics, sizes, types, styles. Their femininity and their superb she-male bodies became their life interest as well as the core of their desire. Sex and being were welded together in the heat of a beloved slavery.

Throughout this period, the she-males' sexes remained restrained at all times other than when Samantha allowed them to have sex. Although they were freed most nights, it was not unusual for them to be put to bed still restrained as a punishment for some minor inefficiency. During these restrained nights, the two lovers were driven mad with unquenchable lust and, eventually, kneeling before Samantha, Denise begged that they be bound and gagged when forced to sleep restrained, a request that the lovely mistress was more than willing to meet, ensuring that each sweet she-male mouth was filled with tangy, soiled panties and that the lovers were strictly hog-tied beneath a tent of soft, scented silk sheets, their moans of masochistic pleasure evidence of the success of their sissy feminisation.

Then, one typical day, as Denise slaved happily over her morning cleaning duties in the washroom, Mistress

Samantha suddenly appeared. Denise, clad in her beautiful maid's attire, immediately stopped what she was doing and performed a deep curtsy before her mistress, pulling her thick petticoating high enough to expose her dark nylon stocking tops and a glimmer of befrilled, black silk panties.

'I have some good news for you, Denise,' the gorgeous mistress announced. 'Phase two of your training is now complete. This means you may regard yourself as a fully sissified servant of the Last Straw Society.'

Denise performed another spectacular curtsy and thanked her mistress.

'To celebrate this event, we've decided to throw a special party. Invite all our members. Including Helen. It's been such a long time since you've seen Helen.'

Helen. Her wife-mistress. A woman almost forgotten during the last few months, a woman she thought she would never see again. The mention of her name created a sudden flood of tormenting memories, memories that left an aftertaste of shame. Suddenly, she was painfully aware of her utter subjugation, of her strange homosexual enslavement to Christina, of the ease with which she had accepted every humiliation and the speed with which Helen had disappeared from her conscious mind.

'I can see that you remember Helen. She's very keen to see you, Denise. Very keen to see how her little she-husband has turned out. I've also invited Wendy and Adele Parsons. This will be their formal induction meeting. They are to be treated as full mistresses. And, for a special treat, Katherine has invited Yolanda and Daphne. I'm sure you'll love meeting Daphne. She's certainly wants to meet you – and to see Christina again.

'The party will be on Saturday. Mary will be in charge of the overall event and Grace will organise the catering. You and Christina will act as the formal serving maids for the evening. And by the way, Saturday is tomorrow – in case you can't remember.'

Denise curtsied her understanding and watched in a state of shocked numbness as Samantha left the room. Almost immediately she returned to her chores, but now dark thoughts were seeping into her mind, thoughts that had been repressed for nearly five months, a repression which had allowed her to embrace her role as a sissy maidservant and she-male sex object without hesitation. But now there *was* hesitation, and there was also fear. How would Helen react to the creature that Denise had been transformed into? Would she be taken back home, as had been originally promised? Did she want to be taken back home? This last thought startled her. Could she really want to stay here, under the complete control of Samantha, the love slave of the lovely Christina? Yet even as she thought this, she thought of the previous night of wild love-making, of the perfect compatibility of the two gorgeous she-males, of their exciting lives of utter servitude and submission. She thought of her beautiful mistress and the spectacular pleasure that her complete captivation before this divine woman brought her. Yes, to her not so great amazement, she knew she could quite easily stay as a slave in this house.

Throughout that night and most of the next morning, Christina appeared nervous, unsure, short-tempered. At one point on Saturday morning she had pulled Denise over her silk-stockinged knees and spanked her until she cried with a flat-handled hairbrush merely for 'the pleasure of it'.

And by mid-afternoon, there was real fear in Christina's eyes.

They had spent most of the day preparing the various guest rooms, the large dinning room and the ballroom. By 3 p.m., they were both exhausted, and while Denise was greatly relieved when Mary ordered the sissy maidservants to their room to bathe and change, Christina seemed even more upset.

As Denise helped Christina out of her gorgeous black satin maid's dress, her body pressing close to her dazzling lover's, she could not help but seek the cause of her obvious discomfort.

'Why are you so upset, my love? I would have thought the prospect of seeing Daphne again would excite you?'

Christina tensed, turned suddenly and glared at Denise. Then the anger in her splendid, dark brown eyes faded and a weak, defeated smile finally lit up her beautiful face.

'Yes. But it doesn't. Actually, the thought of seeing Daphne again terrifies me.'

'Why?'

'Because she's my test, Denny. Just like Mistress Helen is your test.'

Denise understood immediately and cursed herself for being so naive.

'She's the past for you. The previous you.'

'Yes. When Daphne took me under her control, I was still very much Christopher. In many ways she created Christina. And when she comes here this afternoon, she will view her creation. And she will know me in a way that only Mummy and Mistress Mary know me, and in many ways much more intimately. When she sees me, she'll see through me to the sissy slave lover she taught. And then there's you –'

'Me?'

'She'll see you, see our relationship. And she'll want to –'

'To what?'

'To become involved. She'll want me to share you with her.'

Now Denise could see the real cause of Christina's despair. Not only was Daphne the threat of the past – she was also a threat to the future, *their* future.

Denise tried to calm her gorgeous, tearful lover. 'But she'll only be here a few days. Then –'

'Then what? Then you go back to Mistress Helen. Then I don't even get to share you with Daphne.'

There was no further discussion. Despite her fears, Christina insisted they bathe and change into the special costumes that had been laid out on the bed.

They bathed together, luxuriating in their ample bodies, stroking, caressing, kissing and soaping every intimate, flawless inch of silken she-male skin. This was the most gentle love-making, and also the most exciting. Their proud sexes stood stiff, hungry and tightly imprisoned in the teasing pink silk restrainers, their long, sensitive nipples erect, and they gasped with pleasure into each other's full, sexy mouths and fought the terrible, continual urge to fulfil the wondrous potential of this aquatic sex ballet, an urge made so much worse by the fact that the restrainers made its aim quite impossible.

Afterwards, with an equal care and arousal, they dried each other. Then they helped each other with their make-up and dressed, delighted by the beautiful, sexy costumes that Mary had insisted they wear to greet the guests.

Rather than the standard yet exotic maid's dresses, the two she-males were now required to wear very tight leather and satin panelled basques, a pink one for Denise and a white one for Christina. Yet before the basques came a pair of silk panties, again pink and white respectively, a pair of very sheer, seamed nylon tights (pink and white) and matching, five-inch-heeled, open-toed mules. There were no brassieres: as they pulled the incredibly figure-hugging basques over their bodies, it quickly became apparent that these very sexy items of fetish wear were deliberately designed to restrict and exaggerate their substantial chests.

The basques were laced up the back with silk ribbons and each lovely she-male made sure that the other was tightly imprisoned, thus ensuring both a tiny waist and a very apparent, bouncy chest. And once secured, small, white silk pinafores were tied over the basques, secured at the back of their tiny waists in the traditional ultra-feminine and very fat bow.

They were both delighted by the basques, especially the way they rode up between their buttocks and exposed their nylon-sheathed backsides to full view. The front panel also slipped tightly between their legs and made it strikingly apparent that they were two very well endowed and very excited sissies.

They blushed and giggled as they examined each other, two incredibly sexy maidservants designed to pleasure their mistresses in any way, at any time.

Once suitably prepared, they minced from the room, their hosed buttocks swinging with a helplessly sluttish rhythm created by the heels and their tightly restrained, counterbalancing breasts, breasts which threatened to explode out of the front of the basques at any moment.

They reported to Mary's room a few minutes later, Christina knocking at her door with a fearful gentleness. Mary snapped a brief, curt 'Enter!' and the two sissies minced into the room. Over the last twenty-four hours Mary had been a particularly tough mistress, as their sore bottoms still testified. But now, despite her tone, she appeared much more relaxed. She lay on her bed, clad in highly erotic black underwear, reading what seemed to be a pornographic magazine.

The two sissy maidservants curtsied deeply before their mistress, their tightly restrained breasts bouncing angrily as their gorgeous bodies tipped forward. Mary placed the magazine at her side and sat up.

'Oh dear, don't you two look lovely. Won't Daphne be impressed. And let's not forget Helen, Denise.'

Crimson blushes washed over the two she-males, Mary's cruel words scoring painful direct hits on already damaged sissy egos.

'And Liz. Yes, let's not forget Liz.'

Christina released an audible moan of despair and Mary burst out laughing.

'What? You didn't know? Oh yes, Chrissie, your old flame will most certainly be coming along. And I so want Wendy to meet her. Wendy! Wendy, come and see the sissies!'

The two she-males turned in surprise as the door to the private bathroom opened and the lovely Wendy Parsons stepped into the room, her eyes wide with excitement. Clad in only a tiny black silk night-gown and heeled slippers, she was a vision of teenage sexual beauty. Poor Denise's pretty blue eyes nearly popped out of her sissy head at the site of this long-forgotten nubile. Suddenly memories of the terrible and delightful humiliation on the garden lawn came flooding back.

Wendy tottered over to the two sissy beauties. 'Is this really lovely little Denise! How you've changed! You're absolutely perfect. And these titties! Good grief! Just as Samantha promised. And I hope you like them!'

Denise performed another delicate curtsy and whispered a subdued 'Yes, Mistress. Very much so.'

Wendy's vicious laughter echoed throughout the room. 'Just like a little girl! She sounds just like a little baby girl. Excellent!'

It was as Wendy bounced around the two intricately feminised sissies, that Denise began to understand. At first she was shocked to see Wendy again, still as beautiful, still as playfully bright and cheerful. But her state of dress, together with Mary's scanty attire, could lead to only one conclusion in this house where the joys of Lesbos were so intensely celebrated: at some point during the last six months, Mary and Wendy had become lovers. As Denise had been so surely transformed into the perfect she-male slave, Mary had pursued, outside of this house, the sexy, shapely teenage beauty, no doubt on the recommendation of Samantha, and now she was truly ready for induction into the Last Straw Society.

'She is absolutely smashing, Mary. But I still prefer her as a little baby girl. Can't we put her back in nappies?'

Wendy's teasing words filled Denise with a fierce excitement. A sweet memory of Wendy feeding her the bottle of warm, sugared milk brought new tingles of pleasure to her sex.

'I'll see if Samantha will let us have her tomorrow afternoon for a few hours,' Mary replied, her eyes burning into Denise. 'I'm sure something can be arranged.'

Denise found herself nearly smiling and tried to fight this wayward expression of emotion before Mistress Mary. Mary climbed down from the bed and came over to Wendy, pecking her lovingly on the cheek and letting her hands rest tenderly on her lover's large, heaving breasts.

'I have to get dressed and take these two down to welcome the guests. Keep an eye on them while I'm in the bathroom.'

And so Denise and Christina were left under the control of the lovely, sunny-eyed Wendy.

'Mary tells me you're lovers,' she said, moving closer to Denise, her eyes now fixed on the she-male's large breasts.

'Yes, Mistress,' Denise replied.

'Do you enjoy being together, intimately?'

'Yes, Mistress.'

'And you, Christina?'

Christina performed a slight curtsy and also replied in the affirmative.

'Mary says you get the best of both worlds. And I can see you're both very well endowed. It must be a lot of fun. You certainly look good in these outfits.

And Mary tells me that you're hard all the time, Denise. That they have to keep you permanently restrained to stop you wanking yourself to death. It must be terribly frustrating being around all these gorgeous women all day, and being dressed up in all these lovely, sexy clothes.'

As she spoke, she moved even closer to Denise and placed a hand on her hosed left buttock.

'You've got a great arse and fantastic legs. These tights really show them off. I doubt I could keep my seams that straight.'

Then her hand moved around Denise's hip to the tight front panel of the basque, and then directly over the rigid bulge that was her rock-hard sex.

'Dear me, this is big one. Specially enhanced, I'm told. A real arse filler, I bet. What a shame you can't use it on a real woman – I'm sure you'd give some lucky girl a lot of pleasure. But then again, you do –'

Her lovely blue eyes fell on Christina, but her hand remained firmly on Denise's imprisoned sex, a hand now gently caressing, wickedly teasing, and inspiring tiny moans of helpless pleasure.

'What's it like, having this in you every night?'

Christina, blushing furiously, mumbled a hoarse 'Wonderful, Mistress.'

'I'll have to come and watch you sometime, when you make love. Maybe we can make-up a threesome. Although tongues only as far as getting inside me is concerned.'

Poor Denise couldn't believe her pretty girlish ears and gasped with a desperate arousal.

At this bizarre moment the bathroom door opened and Mary walked back into the room. Wendy quickly removed her hand and stood back from Denise. Mary, dressed in a tight black sweater, black leather miniskirt, matching hose and heels, her face made up, her hair swept into a tight bun, looked her usual beautiful, fierce self. And after a quick kiss goodbye for Wendy, she led the two she-males out into the corridor and down the winding staircase to the entrance foyer.

'It is four o'clock,' Mary announced as they drew to a halt in the foyer. 'The first guests are expected at 4.15 p.m. You will stand here and take their coats and bags. Mistress Samantha and Mummy will be down soon to provide a formal welcome. You will take the bags to the guest rooms once all the guests have arrived.'

The sissy maids curtsied their understanding and stood to beautiful, high-heeled attention.

It was only now that Denise began to feel nervous. At some point in the next few hours, Mistress Helen would walk into the foyer. At some point, she would be facing her beautiful wife-mistress for the first time in six months. And what would she think? Surely Samantha had told her that she and Christina had become lovers, had been forced to become lovers. Would she reject Denise? Would she refuse to take her back? And then there was the deeper question: did Denise actually want to go back home?

A few minutes later Mistress Samantha and Mistress Katherine entered the foyer and the two she-males curtsied deeply before them. Samantha was dressed in a long black dress, a figure-hugging gown which accentuated every superb inch of her form and brought a frustrated wiggle to Denise's pert backside. Her mistress was truly the most beautiful woman in the world, with her striking, shoulder-length black hair, passion-filled dark eyes and sensual, full mouth. Thanks to high-heeled court shoes, she stood well over six feet and Denise fought the desire to fall at her feet and worship her as the goddess she had surely become in the ultra sissy she-male's sky-blue doe eyes.

Katherine, by contrast, was in a cream trouser suit, a matching silk blouse and what appeared to be high-heeled cowboy boots, a large ruby-red brooch securing the high-necked blouse around her neck. As usual she appeared both feminine and masculine at the same time, the perfect paradox of dominant womanhood.

Samantha's lovely eyes passed slowly over the two she-males and she smiled slightly. In that smile Denise saw the strange history of her transformation and her future as a sissy slave.

The doorbell rang seconds later and Christina minced forward to greet the first guest.

It took over two hours to welcome the array of female guests who had been invited to attend the party. In that two hours, Denise began to learn the true scope of the Last Straw Society and the power of its membership. For before her were many famous faces: politicians, television personalities and sportswomen. And to Denise's surprise, they all treated Katherine and Samantha with the respect reserved for a great guru or religious leader, shaking hands, kissing hands, kissing cheeks, all with a deference that seemed incredible under the circumstances.

Then there were the women Denise knew. Most embarrassing were the friends of Helen, colleagues from the hospital, close personal friends who had seemingly disappeared during the terrible days of Denis's pathetic illness. But now here they were, all with teasing smiles and cruel, humiliating words for the sweet sissy who curtsied so sexily before them, revealing huge, bouncy breasts and an obvious, fully aroused, utterly contradictory manhood. Many of these women took great delight in pinching Denise's delicately hosed buttocks or tickling her or planting giant kisses on her crimson cheeks.

After an hour or so, Christina minced forward yet again to answer the door and visibly tottered backwards on her high heels as a stunningly beautiful and very tall black woman strode into the hall, tugging firmly on a leash that led to collared neck of a smaller, very petite and very attractive woman attired in the very obvious costume of a slave. This, Denise realised, was Yolanda, and the pretty creature mincing desperately behind her was Daphne.

Yolanda was considerably over six feet tall, dressed in a striking red leather trouser suit and high stiletto heels. The leather clung to her superb Amazonian form like a primitive second skin and with her thick, fuzzy red hair spilling over her shoulders like an exploding fountain of blood and her black shark eyes, she appeared the perfect and most fundamental vision of female dominance.

As Yolanda marched up to Katherine and Samantha, Denise's amazed gaze fell upon the sissy slave being dragged along behind her. Daphne was dressed in a skin-tight, pink rubber body stocking that revealed every inch of her impressive figure to perfection. Indeed, it was quite clear that she was quite naked beneath the rubber costume: her large breasts with their long, erect nipples were perfectly outlined, as was her fully erect and impressively proportioned sex. The stocking also exposed the curves of her small, shapely buttocks and their helpless wiggles as she was pulled forward. These wiggles were made more pronounced by the fact that her feet were impressed in at least five-inch high, pink patent-leather court shoes and by her arms being tightly lashed behind her back at the elbows and wrists with what appeared to be white silk ribbons. On top of all this, her small, pink-lipped mouth was filled to bursting point by a huge pink rubber ball gag.

Like Yolanda, Daphne had striking red hair. It was very long and bound into a ponytail which was swinging violently from side to side as she tottered forward. Her eyes, wide with concentration and discomfort, but also with arousal, were a striking emerald green, and when they met Denise's, there was an instant of undoubted and very mutual attraction. Much to Denise's unease, she found Daphne quite beautiful.

As the three women exchanged greetings, Denise noticed that Christina was watching Daphne with very confused eyes. It was clear she too was attracted to this new sissy, yet Denise also sensed that Christina saw Daphne as a genuine threat to their relationship.

Then Samantha called Denise over and the lovely she-male minced up to the three women and performed a suitably submissive curtsy.

'She's a stunner,' Yolanda whispered in a thick American accent. 'Just like you said. Chrissie's a very lucky little sissy.'

'Daphne certainly seems to like her,' Samantha teased, drawing the women's collective gaze to the tethered slave, whose own eyes were pinned hungrily on an embarrassed, but also very excited Denise.

'Daphne can share Denise and Christina's room while she's here,' Samantha continued, a cruel smile lighting up her beautiful face. 'I'm sure we can fit three in that huge bed.'

Denise looked towards Christina. Tears had begun to well up in the older she-male's lovely eyes. Her worst nightmare was turning into terrible reality.

Yolanda and Katherine strolled off towards the ballroom and Daphne was dragged along behind them. Denise caught a look of dark amusement from Samantha and then returned to her duties.

As the female guests continued to arrive, Denise fought to calm her sissy heart. She was overwhelmed by a terrible anticipation that the next woman might be Mistress Helen; yet, even after two hours, there remained no sign of her.

Adele Parsons, however, did arrive. She was accompanied by a young woman Denise had never seen before, a woman who was carefully pushing before her a large, black leather trunk perched on a porter's cart.

As Denise curtsied before Mistress Adele, she couldn't help staring at the strange trunk. Adele embraced Samantha then came over to Denise.

'Incredible,' she whispered, her blue eyes wide with genuine fascination. 'This is what you can achieve. And after only a few months. She's absolutely gorgeous.'

Denise curtsied her appreciation of the compliment and purred a happy 'Thank you, Mistress.'

Adele stood back and laughed loudly. 'Good grief! What a charming little voice! I really do hope you can do the same for Sally.'

Samantha stepped forward. 'I'm sure we can. She seems another ideal subject. And I'm sure Denise will be more than willing to assist with her transformation.'

Denise curtsied again, despite having no idea what the two beautiful women were talking about. Then, as the trunk was pushed down the corridor towards the ballroom, Denise found herself facing Helen.

Stunned by this sudden manifestation, she was pinned to the spot. There was no curtsy, no swooning, no sign even of recognition. Just an immediate and absolute freezing. Helen, dressed in a black silk blouse, black leather trousers and stiletto-heeled ankle boots, her hair worn very short now, almost like Katherine's, appeared not to be aware of Denise, to look straight through her. Indeed, in a gesture of startling indifference, she proceeded to walk straight past Denise and embrace Samantha. And even then there was no talk of Denise, just pleasant greetings before she walked off towards the ballroom, leaving her bag on the floor before Denise.

Then there was a hard slap to the sissy's exposed, hosed buttocks.

'Denise!' Samantha snapped. 'Wake up! That was the last guest. Christina will show you where the bags should go. When you have sorted them, you should both return to your room and await Mistress Mary.'

The two she-male maidservants spent the next hour mincing up and down the stairs, Denise following Christina, both weighed down with bags and cases. They placed the cases in the twenty guest rooms that made up the majority of the accommodation on the first floor, Denise amazed at how Christina seemed to know where each bag should go.

Christina remained sad and silent throughout this hard, monotonous labour and did not speak until they had returned to their own bedroom. Then her words were full of anger and fear.

'I saw the way she looked at you, Denny. And you heard what Mummy said. They're putting us all together. Tonight.'

Tears welled up in her lovely eyes and Denise stepped forward to embrace her lover.

'It doesn't mean anything, Chrissie. You know I love you. We have to do what the mistresses want. But it's you I really want. Not Daphne.'

Christina smiled bravely and then kissed Denise passionately on the mouth. Denise pressed her gorgeous, tightly restrained body into the younger she-male and returned the desperate passion of the kiss.

'But you don't know Daphne,' Christina mumbled between kisses. 'She's very gifted. She can give you pleasure in a way I can't.'

Denise smiled patiently and released Christina. 'Don't be silly. It's not just about sex. It's about feelings, the special feelings I have for you.'

'But what about Mistress Helen?'

The smile quickly faded from Denise's sweet lips. 'I don't know any more. I thought she'd want me to return with her. But you saw her – she ignored me completely. She looked like a completely different person. I don't understand what's happening.'

A silence fell over them then, a silence broken only by the sudden entrance of Mary.

'You are to undress and bathe,' she snapped, slamming the door behind her. 'You will find special soaps and perfumes set out in the bathroom. Once you've bathed, return here immediately. Your costumes will be laid out, but do not attempt to put them on. I'll return in thirty minutes. I expect you to be bathed, perfumed and naked, and standing to attention by the bed.'

Mary left and the two she-males began to undress each other. Soon they were under the powerful jets of hot water that exploded out of the shower, carefully soaping each other's beautiful, flawless bodies with an intense, helpless desire, their sexes rigid as metal poles in their tight satin restrainers and nearly flat against their tiny, trim waists. All doubt and anxiety had faded. Now there was only tenderness, devotion and love. Denise marvelled in the perfection of her own body and the sensual brilliance of Christina's. Her soapy hands kneaded her lover's large, pale-rose breasts, bringing moans of pleasure from the younger she-male's full, soft lips. Their satin sheathed sexes rubbed together as they moved closer, as washing became caressing, then long, gentle kissing and final hungry fondling. They squealed with a genuine, life-affirming joy. But, as Denise slipped a hand between Christina's buttocks, the younger she-male pulled it away.

'We must get back to the bedroom, Denny. Now.'

After an equally teasing drying, the two gorgeous sissies minced back to the bedroom. What they found there amazed even their kinky eyes. For on the bed were two exquisite, incredibly intricate maid's dresses. As with the basques, one was pink and one white. Both were made from a delicate satin and covered in silk flowers. Both had very high, lace-lined necks, and long, lace-lined sleeves. At the chest area, however, the satin material gave way to a matching sheer nylon. Yet this was not the most unusual part of their design. The truly bizarre element of the dresses appeared around the skirt. Initially, it appeared that both had full skirts beneath which was the standard explosion of lace frou-frou petticoating. Yet closer examination revealed that the skirts abruptly ended at a strange rubber front piece which stretched beneath the dress and seemed to connect to a hidden rear section, thus creating a kind of fitted rubber pantie, complete with two lace-lined leg holes. Yet even this was not the most bizarre part; for in middle of the rubber front piece was what appeared to a fitted nylon sheath, each one coloured to match the overall colour scheme of the particular dress.

Beside these two startling dresses, there were two rubber mini corsets, each again of an appropriate colour, matching seamed nylon stockings, two pairs of glacé gloves (again appropriately coloured) and, at the foot of the bed, two pairs of matching patent-leather stiletto-heeled court shoes, both with the terrible seven-inch heels that the she-males had come to associate with punishment.

Then there were the gags: two large rubber penis gags, both coloured to match the dresses. And by the gags, two appropriately coloured, very long and deeply ribbed vibrators.

The she-males stared at this array of fetish wear in amazement. Then the door opened and they immediately stood to attention, their large breasts bouncing frantically before them. Mary matched in, followed, to Christina's obvious horror, by another young woman, a very pretty blonde, significantly taller than Mary, yet nowhere near as physically imposing.

The blonde's eyes widened in astonishment and a gasp of genuine surprise escaped her wide, thin mouth. This gasp quickly turned into titters of embarrassed amusement and she turned a very bright red.

'Yes, they really are quite something,' Mary said. 'And I suppose Christina has changed quite a lot since the first time you saw her, Liz.'

Now Denise understood – this was Liz, Christina's first girlfriend, the original cause of her feminisation!

The two she-males curtsied deeply before the two women, despite their nakedness, although large tears of humiliation were now welling up in Christina's eyes.

'Yes,' Liz mumbled. 'She certainly has. And this one? This is Denise?'

Mary nodded, her cold eyes appraising the older she-male contemptuously.

'And they are actually lovers?'

'Oh yes, they're mad for each other.'

Liz then moved closer to Christina. 'She's very beautiful. And, well, very big. Is it kept wrapped up all the time?'

'Mummy takes the restrainer off most evenings, so she can fuck Denise.'

Liz was wearing a simple, very short black dress, black hose, and relatively low-healed court shoes. Her long blonde hair fell freely over her shoulders. She was very well built and seemed to possess a strangely friendly, relaxed manner that was totally at odds with this strange ritual of humiliation and revenge.

Liz moved closer to Christina, her friendly smile fading into a contemptuous grin.

'You really are a sex bomb, Chrissie. And isn't that just poetic justice, considering the way you treated me. Now you're the busty sex object. How does it feel? Do you like it? Do your big tits and pretty girly clothes turn you on? I hope they do, because this is as close as you'll ever get to a real woman.'

As the tears poured from her lovely face, Christina curtsied again before Liz and confessed her helpless pleasure. 'Yes, Mistress, I do like it. I love it.'

Liz laughed bitterly and turned back towards Mary. 'The perfect sissies.'

Mary smiled coldly. 'Indeed. And it's about time we dressed them for the role.'

The next thirty minutes were a true revelation of the wickedness that informed the imagination of the women who had transformed Christina and Denise into such glorious sissy she-males. It quickly became clear that Mary would dress Denise and Liz would have the sadistic pleasure of dressing Christina. As the two lovely young women stepped forward to begin this strange task, the two she-males stood to a rigid, fearful attention. Yet attention quickly dissolved into helpless wiggles of pleasure as the women began by untying the ribbon that held the satin restrainers tightly in place. Mary slapped Denise's buttocks repeatedly as she teased the restrainer off the older she-male's sex, angrily telling her to stand still. Liz just laughed loudly, her cool eyes feasting on Christina's helplessly bouncing breasts.

Once the restrainers were removed and cast aside, the women sealed the two lovely she-males into the rubber corsets, lacing the sissies painfully tight and bringing gasps of discomfort from their girlish mouths. The corsets were followed by the stockings, which the she-males were made to put on while still standing up, the cruel corsets turning this delicate act into a ballet of pained struggling. Yet despite this, Liz was very impressed with the feminine grace exhibited by Christina.

'You really know how to tease those stockings up your legs,' she said.

Christina muttered a pained 'thank you, Mistress', her exposed, engorged sex rising up before her like a confession of kinky pleasure.

After the stockings, the two she-males were made to face the bed, bend forward and then touch their toes. Mary then ordered them to spread their legs wide apart. Both sissies knew what was coming and moaned with an almost co-ordinated pleasure as their captors began to ease the long, hard vibrators into their arses. Liz took particular pleasure in making sure the insertion of the vibrator was as soft and gentle as possible, eventually managing to tease squeals of helpless pleasure from Christina.

'Don't let her get too excited,' Mary scolded Liz. 'If she comes, there'll be mess and a delay. Then you'll have to explain what happened to Mummy.'

Once the vibrator was firmly locked in place, the two gorgeous sissies were pulled to their delicately stockinged feet. The caress of the vibrators was instantaneous and both she-males found it very difficult to resist gasps and wiggles of pleasure.

Then came the dresses, the weird and wonderful dresses. They were unbuttoned and then Denise and Christina were made to step into them. Their eyes widened in astonishment as the dresses were pulled up their expertly feminised forms and carefully manipulated into position. As the buttons were secured and the dresses closed perfectly around their gorgeous bodies, the she-males were even more surprised. The sheer nylon front piece above the bodice area clung tightly to their large breasts as the dresses were secured, providing the missing support and a sheer, fetishistic second skin through which every lovely detail of these impressive orbs, including their long, erect nipples, was clearly visible. Yet the strange nylon sheath and rubber panel fitted below the waist remained loose and appeared very odd. But then Mary and Liz took the panels firmly in their hands and positioned them so that the stocking sheaths were placed directly over the sissies exposed, furious sexes.

'A variation on the sex stocking, babikins,' Mary teased. 'But this time open to public inspection.'

The sensual pleasure provided by having the stocking slowly pulled over her sex was almost unbearable. Poor Denise squealed loudly and almost angrily, fighting the terrible teasing and the awful urge to explode into the stocking. But she knew Mary and she knew that any orgasm not sanctioned by a mistress would result in the severest punishment. And as Christina's squeals of pleasure mixed with her own, she bravely resisted ejaculation.

When the sheaths were in place, the young mistresses pulled the rubber panels between the she-males legs, stretching them tightly against the space between their shapely buttocks and locking them in place using attachments fastened to the rear of the dress. The pressure this created pushed their stockinged sexes bolt upright and ensured that they would stay that way.

As the two sissies beheld the strange and intensely arousing spectacular of their exposed, nylon-sheathed breasts and sexes, Mary and Liz took the long, fat penis gags and dangled them before their captives' eyes, bringing the two she-males back to reality with a sadistic jolt.

'Open up, ladies,' Mary sneered, pushing the gag firmly between Denise's soft, red lips and then buckling it tightly in place at the back of her slender neck.

The mouth-filling gag flattened poor Denise's tongue against the floor of her mouth and forced her to suck on its smooth, rubber surface in a helplessly obscene manner. As Liz silenced Christina in a similar manner, she teased the lovely sissy relentlessly.

'I bet you wish this was a real cock, Chrissie. Pretty Denise's rather substantial meat, perhaps?'

Christina moaned pathetically, her tear-filled eyes wide with a masochistic arousal made worse by the fact that, once the gag was secured, Liz began to delicately stroke her white nylon-sheathed sex.

'You really have grown, Chrissie. And it's so pretty in its tight little stocking. I bet it feels terribly sexy. And don't you just want to come? Wouldn't you like me to tease you to a big, sticky explosion?'

Poor Christina looked only seconds away from orgasm when Mary intervened.

'Stop it, Liz. If they come, it'll ruin the party. The trick is to leave them dangling for as long as possible.'

And so the teasing stopped and the dressing drew to a conclusion. The sissies were quickly forced into the ultra-high heels and then their elegant, feminine hands were sealed in the soft, gleaming glacé gloves. The two mistresses then spent a few minutes adding a touch of make-up to each pretty she-male face and combing their hair into sculptures of suitable ultra-femininity.

Standing back to admire their work, they beheld two perfect visions of she-male transformation. First there was Denise, the petite, shapely blonde, her very large breasts straining against the strange pink nylon prison affixed to the top of the stunning pink dress, her long, shapely legs set alight by the seamed pink nylon stockings and matching, ultra-high stiletto heels. And, at the centre of this creation, her proudly erect, stockinged sex, exposed in all its extended glory, forced into a perfectly upright position by the pressure of the pink rubber panel stretching tightly beneath her legs. Her eyes wide with arousal, her mouth so firmly and expertly filled by the fat penis gag, she was a stunning masterpiece. And then there was Christina. Beside Denise, taller, fuller figured, her attire a white mirror of Denise's pink perfection. Her tears dried, her eyes streaked with desire and fear, presenting her she-male secrets to the world with a helpless pride.

'It's time to take them downstairs,' Mary said, clearly impressed by the spectacle she and Liz had created. 'I think Mummy will be very pleased.'

As the she-males tottered forward, Mary produced a small black box from a pocket in her skirt.

'I nearly forgot,' she said, laughing to herself. 'The vibrators are remote controlled.'

In the centre of the box was a large red button. With a typically cruel giggle, she then pushed the button and activated the vibrators. Christina and Denise became immediately aware of teasing tremors seeping into the delicate walls of their well-filled backsides, tremors that quickly became extremely pleasurable vibrations.

Moans of pleasure began to trickle from their fat gags, and as they were led from the room they found themselves mincing forward in a helplessly sluttish manner, their barely covered buttocks wiggling with an extra provocation, their stockinged sexes swaying violently from side to side, their large breasts bouncing excitedly in their tight nylon prisons.

In this state of intense arousal they were led along the corridor, down the stairs and into the large ballroom, Mary and Liz teasing their moaning charges all the way.

The ballroom was filled with the female guests, all of who seemed to turn as one and behold the two sissies with an almost common gaze of fascinated amusement. Denise and Christina were utterly humiliated by this dreadfully public entrance. Suddenly, they were tottering on the highest of heels before a crowd of cruelly smiling women, their fiercely erect sexes swaying before them, their large breasts bouncing madly, their own helpless arousal painfully obvious. Yet at the heart of this arousal was a masochistic joy in the very fact of this wicked exposure. As the women crowded forward to view the mincing sissies close up, a kind of twisted ecstasy washed over the two she-males.

A barrage of teasing, spiteful comments filled their pretty ears; to their horror and delight, hands swept over their ultra-feminine forms, brushing against nylon-sheathed and ultra-sensitive breasts and quite deliberately stroking their enraged, straining, stockinged sexes. They squealed helplessly into their tight gags, struggling against the constant urge to explode into the stocking sheaths.

Then the crowd parted to reveal Katherine and Samantha.

'Please, ladies, leave the poor things alone,' Katherine joked. 'You're driving them mad. There'll be plenty of time to get to know them as the evening progresses. But for now, just let them do their jobs.'

Denise and Christina were guided by Mary and Liz through the crowd of lovely, fascinated females to a long table. On the table was a vast selection of buffet foods and alcohol. Behind the table were two young women, one of whom had helped Mistress Adele with the strange leather trunk. Both were dressed in simple white blouses and long black skirts; both stared at the two she-males in absolute amazement.

'Your job is to serve the wine,' Mary said, her eyes already wandering towards a small crowd of women gathered in a strange huddle a few feet away, their loud, cruel laughter echoing above the general din of chatter and party revelry. 'You get the trays from Beth and Sandie here and mingle, offering the drinks to the mistresses. Do you understand?'

The two sissies curtsied their understanding and watched as Mary, taking Liz by the arm, rushed over to the small crowd of excited women.

Two trays loaded with glasses of golden white wine were handed to them by the two amazed girls and the sissies, riddled with the tormenting pleasure of the vibrators, the teasing caress of the sex stocking and the dreadfully ambivalent pleasure of this extreme humiliation, minced fearfully into the mass of beautiful, powerful and highly amused women.

As they tottered about, the two gorgeous, exposed she-males quickly became separated. Denise minced up to each woman and offered drinks with a mute look of aroused fear and a pleasing curtsy. Inevitably the woman or group of women would begin to gently mock and tease the lovely she-male. Unfortunately, this teasing inevitably involved caresses of her nylon-sheathed breasts and sex, inducing helpless moans of pleasure and a desperate struggle to resist an immediate, savage orgasm. Yet this torment was also ecstasy. Each woman was dressed in her finest party wear, and Denise underwent her humiliation in a whirlpool of tight, revealing frocks, shapely, hosed legs, very high heels and a vast, swirling mist of expense perfumes.

By the time she reached the edge of the group of women who appeared huddled around something or somebody, Denise was in a state of unbearable excitement. Her rigid sex rose before her like a pet begging for caresses and her breasts bounced to the whorish vibrations flowing through her body from the pink phallus rammed deep into her arse.

The first woman to notice her was Mistress Mary.

'Look!' she exclaimed, dragging the attention of the women away from the secret spectacle. 'It's another sissy!'

The group of women turned as one, yet Denise's aroused, baby-blue eyes saw only Helen, beautiful, once-beloved Mistress Helen. And, again, her wife-mistress beheld her with a terrible indifference, a heartbreaking scorn which suddenly plunged Denise back to her previous male self, to a belittled and useless male who found his only pleasure in hiding from the world.

'Are these drinks for us?'

The voice of Wendy. Wendy Parsons, looking quite dazzling in a very short red rubber dress, white hose and red high heels, her gorgeous blonde hair bound into a deceptively girlish ponytail, her lovely eyes filled with an alcohol-fuelled happiness.

Wendy was at the centre of this odd circle, standing by the source of the rowdy amusement. Mary ushered Denise into the centre to join Wendy. The poor she-male tottered forward, the women closing the circle behind her. Suddenly the tray was whisked out of her gloved hands and she was facing another victim of the Last Straw Society.

Sitting on a leather-backed stool was a very pretty blonde dressed in a lovely pink baby girl's dress. Her long, feminine legs were sheathed in very sheer, white nylon tights decorated with hundreds of tiny pink flowers. On her hosed feet she wore five-inch-heeled, pink court shoes. The thick layers of petticoating beneath the dress rose up to reveal matching pink plastic panties covering a very thick nappy. A perfectly sissified she-male, another servant of the Last Straw Society at the beginning of her long, hard training.

Her arms were forced tightly behind her back and tied together with pink rubber cording at the wrists and elbows, and her lovely legs were secured in a similar manner at her ankles and knees. Then there was the thick strip of white masking tape that covered her lips and the bulging gag that filled her mouth beneath it.

'Meet Sally,' Wendy announced. 'My cousin. Recently a happy male fool. Now well on the way to being a she-male.'

As she spoke, her eyes flashing with cruel satisfaction, her mother, Mistress Adele, entered the circle.

'Sally is with us as a going-away present,' she said. 'Her mother has gone to live in America and left this pretty bundle in our care. Sally, when previously known as Steven, was a terror. But I'm sure our little band of female friends can cure her of her wayward tendencies.'

'And you will train her,' Wendy said, turning to Denise. 'Just as Christina trained you.'

Denise tottered backwards, looking at Sally in horror. The circle of women burst into laughter. Sally, Denise realised, had been locked in the strange trunk: Sally had been brought here to be feminised.

Sally was now looking directly at Denise, as if seeing the stunning she-male for the first time. Her eyes wandered fearfully over her splendid, nylon-sheathed breasts and then down to her tightly stockinged sex. Then her eyes widened even further and began to shine.

'If her mouth wasn't stuffed full of my soiled panties, I'm sure she'd be singing your obvious praises, Denny,' Wendy joked. 'But don't get too anxious. You won't have to see her all the way through the process. In fact, what we want you and your clever mistresses to do is create something quite different from you and Chrissie. A proper physical she-male, of course, with lovely big tits and a well-trained cock, plus a love of other sissies. All those things. But we don't want a big grown-up girl like you. We want a baby girl. We want you to create a big baby girl, permanently nappied and dummy gagged.'

As the women continued to laugh and tease Sally, a hand rested on Denise's shoulder. The lovely sissy turned and beheld Mistress Samantha. She curtsied deeply and allowed herself to be led from the circle to a quiet corner of the room.

'I hope you like Sally,' she whispered, her eyes filled with teasing sarcasm.

Denise could only curtsy her wary agreement.

'Good, because you'll spend the next six months training her – a very important first test of your abilities.'

Again Denise curtsied, perversely proud to be offered such responsibility.

'Yes, you've come a very long way, Denise. And as a reward for your progress, I think it's time you learned a few truths about yourself.'

Denise stared in confusion at her beautiful mistress.

'Things probably haven't turned out the way we said they would, and you're probably not that surprised. I think you're quite happy here with Christina, and, as you've no doubt noticed, Helen is really not interested in having you back. But there is a reason for that, Denise. You see, she was never really interested in having you in the first place.'

Denise listened as Samantha, an ironic smile never far from her lovely cherry lips, revealed an amazing plot, a terrible conspiracy to turn a grown man into a mincing sissy she-male; a plot that began in the offices of Shelly Cosmetics two years previously, about the time that Christina was first being forced into panties and hose, and ended here, in this elegant room filled with beautiful, cruel women.

It had been Katherine's idea, concocted with her lover Samantha and the gorgeous Helen. As work progressed on Christina, the women had sought a test subject from outside the family, a subject who could be lured into a web of deceit that would span two years and undermine the very nature of the subject's sense of reality.

'I'm afraid you lived a lie, Denny. Katherine identified you as the ideal test subject while you were working for her company. It was then just a question of creating the right environment for a person like you, a person with all the weaknesses and inadequacies that we knew would make feminisation an inevitability.'

At one of Katherine's parties, Denis had been introduced to Helen. Strangely, they had hit it off. To Denis's surprise, Helen, beautiful, intelligent Helen, had seemed to like him. For the first time in his life, he had felt fate smile on him. But fate wasn't smiling – it was laughing.

'Helen, with my help, set about undermining your self-esteem from the day you were married. It was simple for us to make a little bit of stress into a nightmare, to push you into a permanent state of fear and anxiety. And you know the rest. And the one you should thank, the one we should *all* thank, is Helen. She sacrificed two years of her life to help create you, Denise. You should go to her now and demonstrate your gratitude.'

Denise listened in amazement, then despair and horror. Her whole marriage had been a sham, a carefully conceived trick to encourage her eventual transformation! What love she had felt had been a terrible illusion, a brutal deception. And as she realised this, she saw that her whole male personality had been a grotesque lie.

Tears flooded from her eyes, tears of terrible inner pain. In this moment of truth, she felt something wrench away from her, something break off and disappear for ever. This was the last, wrinkled, battered remnants of her male self disintegrating into oblivion.

She turned to face Helen, but Helen was with Mistress Bridget, their heads close together, seconds from a passionate kiss. She began to mince towards them. Helen's eyes, her beautiful, brown eyes, fell upon Denise, eyes filled with contempt and utter rejection. Yet still Denise wiggle minced prettily towards her, the she-male's nylon imprisoned breasts and sex bouncing furiously, the humming vibrator making each step a terrible, but ecstatic sexual torment.

But she never reached her wife-mistress. Suddenly a voice filled the room – the amplified voice of Katherine.

'Ladies, please. Your attention.'

Denise turned towards the voice. Katherine was standing on a stage at the other end of the room, standing before a microphone, the large French windows behind her.

The room fell silent. Samantha stepped in front of Denise.

'You can thank Helen another time. Follow me.'

As Katherine spoke, Samantha led Denise through the crowd.

'We're gathered here tonight to celebrate the arrival of two new members,' Katherine said, a spotlight suddenly engulfing the stage. 'To welcome Adele and Wendy. We're also here to celebrate a new chapter in our Society's history.'

The women clapped and cheered. Denise fought to stop her tears.

'Tonight we can truly begin to define the destiny of the Last Straw Society.'

There was more clapping and cheering.

'Over the last six months we have proved it is possible to feminise the male completely. That it is possible to turn a carefully chosen test subject into a beautiful, obedient sissy. Now we must apply the lessons we have learned to a larger number of subjects. We must begin to create an army of she-male slaves. And tonight, we begin this process with the opening of the Last Straw Academy.'

As Katherine spoke, light flooded the grounds beyond the windows and revealed a large, brand new building in the distance. This was the Last Straw Academy. This was the building that Denise had seen in various stages of construction over the last six months.

The crowd cheered wildly now. Denise was pushed to the front of the stage and forced up on to it. As she staggered on to the stage, Christina was suddenly elevated out of a group of women on the opposite side. Suddenly the two sissies were mincing towards the centre of the stage and surrounded by a sea of teasing laughter, both now bathed in powerful spotlights.

'Yes, applaud,' Katherine laughed. 'Applaud Christina and Denise: our prototypes. The foundation stones of our feminisation therapy!'

Katherine beckoned the two she-males to her side. Now they were finally and fully exposed, their huge breasts bouncing in their nylon prisons uncontrollably, their sexes wobbling prettily and desperately before so many fascinated and amused female eyes.

'It is Christina and Denise who will help us turn the Academy into a sissy production line. They will entice suitable male subjects to the Academy and then oversee their transformation. We will send them out into the city dressed as the loveliest sex objects imaginable, our own sissy agents. They will lure the subjects to safe houses, relax them with their oral skills. Once they are amenable, the subjects will be transported here.'

Denise listened in amazement. So this was the final humiliation, the final degradation: she was to be turned into a sissy whore whose function was to trap men and bring them to the Last Straw Academy. Here she was to act as a trainer of sissies, in very much the same way as Christina had trained her. This was her strange she-male destiny.

As the crowd continued to applaud and cheer, Denise noticed that poor Sally was being led from the room by Wendy and Mary, still bound and gagged, but now hobbled and with a leash and chain attached to her befrilled neck. Denise knew that Sally was being taken to the nursery and that tomorrow the new she-male would begin her training in earnest.

As Denise watched Sally disappear squealing and struggling from the room, Samantha walked on to the stage, accompanied by the gorgeous Daphne. The crowd cheered even louder at the appearance of yet another stunning she-male.

Samantha walked up to Denise and smiled. Daphne, still in the striking rubber costume, but now ungagged, also smiled, a teasing, coy, promising smile.

'I've decided that Daphne should spend the night with you exclusively, Denise,' Samantha said. 'Liz is very keen to get to know Christina, so you'll have the room to yourselves.'

Denise looked over to Christina. Large tears of despair were already beginning to well up in her lovely brown eyes and a moan of terrible sadness trickled from her fat penis gag. It seemed all her fears were about to become terribly true.

As they were led from the stage, Denise noticed Christina mince apprehensively over to a gesticulating Liz and then disappear into the mass of women.

The cheering and applauding continued as Samantha led Daphne and Denise from the room. Daphne's eyes were filled with a very obvious attraction towards Denise, an attraction Denise knew to be mutual.

The last eager, curious hands brushed against her sex and breasts, then they were in the corridor. And within a few minutes they were back in the large bedroom Denise and Christina had shared for the last five months.

Samantha made Denise sit on the bed, turned to smile briefly and triumphantly at Denise and then left the two she-males alone.

The buzzing ministrations of the vibrator suddenly seemed to become much stronger and poor Denise moaned angrily into her gag. Daphne smiled and moved closer to her prey.

'You're really very pretty, Denise,' she whispered, her voice silky smooth and filled with erotic longing. 'Mistress Samantha wants us to become very good friends in the next few months. I'm to be seconded here on a part-time basis, to fill in for Christina. Mistress Mary has arranged for Christina to become Mistress Elizabeth's maid, so you're going to need some help, as well as some company.'

Denise listened to these teasing words with surprise and sadness. It was clear that Mary was determined to continue her campaign of cruelty against Christina, that the humiliation and punishment would never end. Not only would Christina have to endure the torment of being placed in the care of her first and last real girlfriend, the original source of her elaborate and permanent feminisation, but she would also be tortured by the knowledge that Denise, her only true love, would be in the arms of this beautiful, knowing she-male. Yet these thoughts did not depress Denise for too long. Indeed, since the true story of her own entrapment and feminisation had been revealed by Mistress Samantha, Denise felt no real regret. If anything, she was relieved: there was no longer a reason to fight, no longer a reason to feel even the slightest shame or guilt. Her transformation into the perfect sissy she-male was now complete. She was beautiful and desired. Her future was laid out like the straight seam of a silk stocking. She could even pretend to be a real girl – a thought that thrilled her intensely.

As Daphne knelt down before Denise, her gorgeous emerald eyes sparkling with desire, as she began to stroke the stocking covering her lovely captive's rampant sex, Denise could only moan with a savage pleasure and wiggle sexily. Daphne then took the head of the stocking sheath and ripped it with one surprisingly strong tug from the rubber panel of the dress, exposing Denise's large, rigid, crimson sex. The stocking was thrown aside and Daphne, after smiling lovingly at her charge, slipped her warm mouth over the head of Denise's engorged penis. Denise squealed with a terrible, fundamental pleasure into her fat, phallic gag. Seconds away from a very powerful orgasm, she was, perhaps for the first time in her life, truly happy.

Nexus

NEXUS NEW BOOKS

To be published in September

DISPLAYS OF PENITENTS
Lucy Golden
£5.99

In this, the third volume of tales from Lucy Golden, the lives of ordinary people are turned upside down as they submit to the allure of a totally new experience. It may be a medical examination. It may be a drinking game with very wet forfeits. It may be a bet. It may be an encounter with friends, family, neighbours or colleagues that takes a turn for the bizarre. Whatever the circumstances, whatever aspects of pain, pleasure, domination and submission are encountered, these tales explore every facet of the wide world of perverse eroticism with a haunting power and intensity.

ISBN 0 352 33646 3

TEMPER TANTRUMS
Penny Birch
£5.99

Natasha Linnet has a weakness for dirty old men – hence her relationship with wine buff and accomplished spanker Percy Ottershaw. When Percy visits a former colleague, the louche Dr Blondeau, in France, Natasha tags along. Blondeau, figuring correctly that any girlfriend of his perverted old friend must be a willing submissive, has extreme ideas of his own, for which he considers Natasha fair game. Natasha sees right through his wiles, of course. But how can she give in, and still have the last laugh?

ISBN 0 352 33647 1

DARK DESIRES
Maria del Rey
£5.99

Sexual diversity is the hallmark of Maria del Rey's work. Here, for the first time in one volume, is a collection of her kinkiest stories – each one striking in its originality – with settings to suit all tastes. Fetishists, submissives and errant tax inspectors mingle with bitch goddesses, naughty girls and French maids in this eclectic anthology of forbidden games. A Nexus Classic.

ISBN 0 352 33648 X

To be published in October

CAGED!
Yolanda Celbridge
£5.99

Tucked away in the Yorkshire Dales is a women's corrective institution where uniforms and catspats are the order of the day, the first often shredded by the second! But are the bars and fences to keep the women confined, or the locals out?

ISBN 0 352 33650 1

BEAST
Wendy Swanscombe
£5.99

Without time to draw breath from the indignities already heaped on them, the three sisters of *Disciplined Skin* – blonde Anna, redhead Beth, reven Gwen – are plunged into the new tortures and humiliations gleefully devised for them by their mysterious leather-clad captor Herr Abraham Bärengelt. Putting its heroines through ordeals that range from mild to perversely bizarre, *Beast* is sure to confirm the reputation its author has already established for surreal erotic depravity that entertains as much as it arouses.

ISBN 0 352 33649 8

PENNY IN HARNESS
Penny Birch
£5.99

When naughty Penny is walking in the woods one day, she is surprised to find a couple pony-carting. Penny is so excited by watching this new form of adult fun that she has to pleasure herself on the spot. Realising how keen she is to discover for herself what it is all about, she begins to investigate this bizarre world of whips and harnesses. Will she ever be able to win the highest accolade in their world of kinky games – the honour of being a pony-girl? A Nexus Classic.

ISBN 0 352 33651 X

If you would like more information about Nexus titles, please visit our website at www.nexus-books.co.uk, or send a stamped addressed envelope to:
  Nexus, Thames Wharf Studios,
  Rainville Road, London W6 9HA

BLACK lace

BLACK LACE NEW BOOKS

To be published in September

CHEAP TRICK
Astrid Fox
£5.99

Super-8 filmmaker Tesser Roget is a girl who takes no prisoners. An American slacker, living in London, she dresses in funky charity-shop clothes and wears blue fishnets. She looks hot and she knows it. She likes to have sex, and she frequently does. Life on the fringe is very good indeed, but when she meets artist Jamie Desmond things take a sudden swerve into the weird. Her outsider lifestyle is threatened by disgruntled ex-lovers, big-business corruption and, worst of all, cinematic sabotage of her precious film. With all this on the go, and a libido that craves regular attention, Tesser is a very busy girl.

ISBN 0 352 33640 4

GAME FOR ANYTHING
Lyn Wood
£5.99

Fiona – Fee to her friends – finds herself on a word-games holiday with her best pal. At first it seems like a boring way to spend a week away. Then she realises it's a treasure hunt with a difference. Solving the riddles embroils her in a series of erotic situations as the clues get ever more outrageous. It's a race to the finish with people cheating, partnerships changing and lots of the competitors shagging. Fiona needs an analytical mind and an encyclopaedic knowledge of sex to be in with a chance of winning. And she can't do it all on her own.

ISBN 0 352 33639 0

FORBIDDEN FRUIT
Susie Raymond
£5.99

When thirty-something divorcee Beth realises someone is spying on her in the work changing room, she is both shocked and excited. When she finds out it's a sixteen-year-old shop assistant Jonathan she cannot believe her eyes. Try as she might, she cannot get the thought of his fit young body out of her mind. Although she knows she shouldn't encourage him, the temptation is irresistible. To Jonathan, Beth is a real woman: sexy, sophisticated and experienced. But once Beth and Jonathan have tasted the forbidden fruit, what will happen? A Black Lace special reprint.

ISBN 0 352 33306 5

To be published in October

ALL THE TRIMMINGS
Tesni Morgan
£5.99

Cheryl and Laura, two fast friends, find themselves single. When the women find out that each secretly harbours a desire to be a whorehouse madam, there's nothing to stop them. On the surface their establishment is a five-star hotel, but to a select clientele it's a bawdy fun hose for both sexes, where fantasies – from the mild to the increasingly perverse – are indulged. But when attractive, sinister John Dempsey comes on the scene, Cheryl is smitten and Laura less so, convinced he's out to con them, bust them or both. Which of the women is right?

ISBN 0 352 33641 2

WICKED WORDS 5
ed. Kerri Sharp
£5.99

Hugely popular and deliciously daring, *Wicked Words* short story collections are a showcase of the best in women's erotic writing from the Uk and USA. Hot, upbeat, fresh and cheeky, this is fun erotica at the cutting edge.

ISBN 0 352 33642 0

PLEASURE'S DAUGHTER
Sedalia Johnson
£5.99

It's 1750. Orphaned Amelia, headstrong and voluptuous, goes to live with wealthy relatives. During the journey she meets the exciting, untrustworthy Marquis of Beechwood. She manages to escape his clutches only to find he is a good friend of her aunt and uncle. Although aroused by him, she flees his relentless pursuit, taking up residence in a Convent Garden establishment dedicated to pleasure. When the marquis catches up with her, Amelia is only too happy to demonstrate her new-found disciplinary skills. A Black Lace Special Reprint.

ISBN 0 352 33237 9

Nexus

NEXUS BACKLIST

This information is correct at time of printing. For up-to-date information, please visit our website at www.nexus-books.co.uk

All books are priced at £5.99 unless another price is given.

Nexus books with a contemporary setting

ACCIDENTS WILL HAPPEN	Lucy Golden ISBN 0 352 33596 3	☐
ANGEL	Lindsay Gordon ISBN 0 352 33590 4	☐
THE BLACK MASQUE	Lisette Ashton ISBN 0 352 33372 3	☐
THE BLACK WIDOW	Lisette Ashton ISBN 0 352 33338 3	☐
THE BOND	Lindsay Gordon ISBN 0 352 33480 0	☐
BROUGHT TO HEEL	Arabella Knight ISBN 0 352 33508 4	☐
CANDY IN CAPTIVITY	Arabella Knight ISBN 0 352 33495 9	☐
CAPTIVES OF THE PRIVATE HOUSE	Esme Ombreux ISBN 0 352 33619 6	☐
DANCE OF SUBMISSION	Lisette Ashton ISBN 0 352 33450 9	☐
DARK DELIGHTS	Maria del Rey ISBN 0 352 33276 X	☐
DARK DESIRES	Maria del Rey ISBN 0 352 33072 4	☐
DISCIPLES OF SHAME	Stephanie Calvin ISBN 0 352 33343 X	☐
DISCIPLINE OF THE PRIVATE HOUSE	Esme Ombreux ISBN 0 352 33459 2	☐

DISCIPLINED SKIN	Wendy Swanscombe ISBN 0 352 33541 6	☐
DISPLAYS OF EXPERIENCE	Lucy Golden ISBN 0 352 33505 X	☐
AN EDUCATION IN THE PRIVATE HOUSE	Esme Ombreux ISBN 0 352 33525 4	☐
EMMA'S SECRET DOMINATION	Hilary James ISBN 0 352 33226 3	☐
GISELLE	Jean Aveline ISBN 0 352 33440 1	☐
GROOMING LUCY	Yvonne Marshall ISBN 0 352 33529 7	☐
HEART OF DESIRE	Maria del Rey ISBN 0 352 32900 9	☐
HIS MISTRESS'S VOICE	G. C. Scott ISBN 0 352 33425 8	☐
HOUSE RULES	G. C. Scott ISBN 0 352 33441 X	☐
IN FOR A PENNY	Penny Birch ISBN 0 352 33449 5	☐
LESSONS IN OBEDIENCE	Lucy Golden ISBN 0 352 33550 5	☐
NURSES ENSLAVED	Yolanda Celbridge ISBN 0 352 33601 3	☐
ONE WEEK IN THE PRIVATE HOUSE	Esme Ombreux ISBN 0 352 32788 X	☐
THE ORDER	Nadine Somers ISBN 0 352 33460 6	☐
THE PALACE OF EROS	Delver Maddingley ISBN 0 352 32921 1	☐
PEEPING AT PAMELA	Yolanda Celbridge ISBN 0 352 33538 6	☐
PLAYTHING	Penny Birch ISBN 0 352 33493 2	☐
THE PLEASURE CHAMBER	Brigitte Markham ISBN 0 352 33371 5	☐
POLICE LADIES	Yolanda Celbridge ISBN 0 352 33489 4	☐
SANDRA'S NEW SCHOOL	Yolanda Celbridge ISBN 0 352 33454 1	☐

SKIN SLAVE	Yolanda Celbridge ISBN 0 352 33507 6	☐
THE SLAVE AUCTION	Lisette Ashton ISBN 0 352 34481 9	☐
SLAVE EXODUS	Jennifer Jane Pope ISBN 0 352 33551 3	☐
SLAVE GENESIS	Jennifer Jane Pope ISBN 0 352 33503 3	☐
SLAVE SENTENCE	Lisette Ashton ISBN 0 352 33494 0	☐
SOLDIER GIRLS	Yolanda Celbridge ISBN 0 352 33586 6	☐
THE SUBMISSION GALLERY	Lindsay Gordon ISBN 0 352 33370 7	☐
SURRENDER	Laura Bowen ISBN 0 352 33524 6	☐
TAKING PAINS TO PLEASE	Arabella Knight ISBN 0 352 33369 3	☐
TIE AND TEASE	Penny Birch ISBN 0 352 33591 2	☐
TIGHT WHITE COTTON	Penny Birch ISBN 0 352 33537 8	☐
THE TORTURE CHAMBER	Lisette Ashton ISBN 0 352 33530 0	☐
THE TRAINING OF FALLEN ANGELS	Kendal Grahame ISBN 0 352 33224 7	☐
THE YOUNG WIFE	Stephanie Calvin ISBN 0 352 33502 5	☐
WHIPPING BOY	G. C. Scott ISBN 0 352 33595 5	☐

Nexus books with Ancient and Fantasy settings

CAPTIVE	Aishling Morgan ISBN 0 352 33585 8	☐
THE CASTLE OF MALDONA	Yolanda Celbridge ISBN 0 352 33149 6	☐
DEEP BLUE	Aishling Morgan ISBN 0 352 33600 5	☐
THE FOREST OF BONDAGE	Aran Ashe ISBN 0 352 32803 7	☐

MAIDEN	Aishling Morgan ISBN 0 352 33466 5	☐
NYMPHS OF DIONYSUS £4.99	Susan Tinoff ISBN 0 352 33150 X	☐
THE SLAVE OF LIDIR	Aran Ashe ISBN 0 352 33504 1	☐
TIGER, TIGER	Aishling Morgan ISBN 0 352 33455 X	☐
THE WARRIOR QUEEN	Kendal Grahame ISBN 0 352 33294 8	☐

Edwardian, Victorian and older erotica

BEATRICE	Anonymous ISBN 0 352 31326 9	☐
CONFESSION OF AN ENGLISH SLAVE	Yolanda Celbridge ISBN 0 352 33433 9	☐
DEVON CREAM	Aishling Morgan ISBN 0 352 33488 6	☐
THE GOVERNESS AT ST AGATHA'S	Yolanda Celbridge ISBN 0 352 32986 6	☐
PURITY	Aishling Morgan ISBN 0 352 33510 6	☐
THE TRAINING OF AN ENGLISH GENTLEMAN	Yolanda Celbridge ISBN 0 352 33348 0	☐

Samplers and collections

NEW EROTICA 4	Various ISBN 0 352 33290 5	☐
NEW EROTICA 5	Various ISBN 0 352 33540 8	☐
EROTICON 1	Various ISBN 0 352 33593 9	☐
EROTICON 2	Various ISBN 0 352 33594 7	☐
EROTICON 3	Various ISBN 0 352 33597 1	☐
EROTICON 4	Various ISBN 0 352 33602 1	☐

Nexus Classics
A new imprint dedicated to putting the finest works of erotic fiction back in print.

AGONY AUNT	G.C. Scott	☐
	ISBN 0 352 33353 7	
BOUND TO SERVE	Amanda Ware	☐
	ISBN 0 352 33457 6	
BOUND TO SUBMIT	Amanda Ware	☐
	ISBN 0 352 33451 7	
CHOOSING LOVERS FOR JUSTINE	Aran Ashe	☐
	ISBN 0 352 33351 0	
DIFFERENT STROKES	Sarah Veitch	☐
	ISBN 0 352 33531 9	
EDEN UNVEILED	Maria del Rey	☐
	ISBN 0 352 33542 4	
THE HANDMAIDENS	Aran Ashe	☐
	ISBN 0 352 33282 4	
HIS MISTRESS'S VOICE	G. C. Scott	☐
	ISBN 0 352 33425 8	
THE IMAGE	Jean de Berg	☐
	ISBN 0 352 33350 2	
THE INSTITUTE	Maria del Rey	☐
	ISBN 0 352 33352 9	
LINGERING LESSONS	Sarah Veitch	☐
	ISBN 0 352 33539 4	
A MATTER OF POSSESSION	G. C. Scott	☐
	ISBN 0 352 33468 1	
OBSESSION	Maria del Rey	☐
	ISBN 0 352 33375 8	
THE PLEASURE PRINCIPLE	Maria del Rey	☐
	ISBN 0 352 33482 7	
SERVING TIME	Sarah Veitch	☐
	ISBN 0 352 33509 2	
SISTERHOOD OF THE INSTITUTE	Maria del Rey	☐
	ISBN 0 352 33456 8	
THE TRAINING GROUNDS	Sarah Veitch	☐
	ISBN 0 352 33526 2	
UNDERWORLD	Maria del Rey	☐
	ISBN 0 352 33552 1	

------ ✂ ------------------------

Please send me the books I have ticked above.

Name ....

Address ....

....

....

.... Post code ....

Send to: **Cash Sales, Nexus Books, Thames Wharf Studios, Rainville Road, London W6 9HA**

US customers: for prices and details of how to order books for delivery by mail, call 1-800-805-1083.

Please enclose a cheque or postal order, made payable to **Nexus Books Ltd**, to the value of the books you have ordered plus postage and packing costs as follows:
 UK and BFPO – £1.00 for the first book, 50p for each subsequent book.
 Overseas (including Republic of Ireland) – £2.00 for the first book, £1.00 for each subsequent book.

If you would prefer to pay by VISA, ACCESS/MASTERCARD, AMEX, DINERS CLUB, AMEX or SWITCH, please write your card number and expiry date here:

....

Please allow up to 28 days for delivery.

Signature ....

------ ✂ ------------------------